MEN AND ANGELS

MARY GORDON

MEN AND ANGELS

RANDOM HOUSE

NEW YORK

All rights reserved under International and Pan-American
Copyright Conventions. Published in the United States
by Random House, Inc., New York, and simultaneously
in Canada by Random House of Canada Limited,
Toronto.

Grateful acknowledgment is made to Random House,
Inc., for permission to reprint an excerpt from *W. H.
Auden: Collected Poems,* edited by Edward Mendelson.
Copyright 1945 by W. H. Auden. Reprinted by
permission of Random House, Inc.

Library of Congress Cataloging in Publication Data
Gordon, Mary, 1949–
Men and angels.
I. Title.
PS3557.O669M4   1985   813'.54   84-45761
ISBN 0-394-52403-9

Manufactured in the United States of America
Typography and binding design by J. K. Lambert
98765432
First Edition

for Arthur

That we, though lovers, may love soberly,
O Fate, O *Felix Osculum,* to us
Remain nocturnal and mysterious:
Preserve us from presumption and delay;
O hold us to the voluntary way.

W.H. AUDEN

Though I speak with the tongues of men and
of angels, and have not charity, I am become as
sounding brass, or a tinkling cymbal.

I CORINTHIANS 13:1

ACKNOWLEDGMENTS

Caroline Watson is a fictional character, but
in creating her I have drawn upon details of
the lives of actual painters, particularly
Cecilia Beaux, Mary Cassatt, and Suzanne
Valadon. Of great help to me were Cecilia
Beaux's autobiography, *Background with
Figures,* and the letters of Mary Cassatt and
Paula Modersohn-Becker.

In addition, my deepest thanks go to
Linda Nochlin for her advice on art history
and art historians, and to Alexander Martin
for helping me to understand how a painter
paints.

MEN AND ANGELS

She had nothing to fear. She was flying from London to New York; when she landed, she would have no place to go. But why should she be frightened? She opened her Bible and turned to the words of the Lord: "Can a woman forget her sucking child, that she should have no compassion on the child of her womb? Even these may forget, yet I will not forget you. Behold, I have graven you on the palms of my hands; your walls are continually before me."

Isaiah the prophet. She had made a collection of the words of Scripture which showed that family love was not important. Which proved that it was weak and unreliable and should be left. I have graven you on the palms of my hands. What human parent would do that? She laughed to think of her mother doing that. Once she had tried it herself, tried to make herself carve her mother's name on the palms of her hands. She couldn't do it. She feared the knife, the blood, the skin that flapped, the shock. She did not have the courage for her mother's name.

Jesus had said a man should leave father and mother. She had done this, had been misunderstood, unwelcomed, asked to leave places, but Jesus had said this would happen to the chosen. Leave your parents, He had said. Take no gold, nor silver, He had said, nor copper in your belts, no bag for your journey, nor two tunics, nor sandals, nor a staff; for the laborer deserves his food. And whatever town or village you enter, find out who is worthy in it and stay with him until you depart. As you enter the house, salute it. And if the house is worthy, let your peace come upon it; but if it is not worthy, let your peace return to you. And if any one will not receive you or listen to your words, shake off the dust from your feet as you leave that house or town. Truly, I say to you, it shall be more tolerable on the day of judgment for the land of Sodom and Gomorrah than for that town.

Behold, He had said, I send you out as sheep in the midst of wolves; so be wise as serpents and innocent as doves.

She had made her mistake by not heeding this counsel of Jesus. Wise as serpents. She had been too trusting, been too open with her stories of the Spirit coming to her.

The Chamberlains had hired her in Syracuse to go with them to London. For six months while they worked there, to take care of the children. He was a scientist; he studied the brains of fish. Then, after a month, "As it turns out, there's not as much work for Joan as we originally thought. So she can take care of the kids. So we won't be needing you. Guess our eyes turned out to be bigger than our stomachs. Ha ha. But we won't leave you stranded. I want you to know that, Laura," Jack Chamberlain had said. "We found out from a friend of ours, a guy I work with, about a woman over in Chalk Farm who rents rooms to students. People your own age. You'll have a ball, believe me. And then you'll have your ticket home in August. It'll be a great time for you, believe me."

Shake the dust from your feet as you leave that house or town. She knew what they thought, that she was bad for the children. But the children liked her. Jennifer, the youngest child, cried when Laura said good-bye to her. Their parents didn't understand them. But she understood. She always understood children. Their great unhappiness she always saw. They were victims of injustice from the moment of their birth. Believing human love to be important, they must suffer. This was how she could help them. She could teach them human love was not important, and their suffering would end, as hers had ended.

How she had suffered every day before she knew. She had been a good child, and her mother had not loved her. She was slow, her mother said. And her mother was full of quickness; her movements danced, all the gestures of her hands, her words (her mother would make people laugh with her quickness) ended in points of silver. Laura was slow, slow in her movements like her father's family. Yet the teachers said she showed great promise in some subjects. And Miss Gildersleeve, the home economics teacher, said Laura sewed like a dream. That's good, said her mother, it's a good hobby for an old maid.

Yet she had loved her mother, wanted to be near her, loved the feel of her bones through her light flesh, loved the quick movements of her skirt. She had loved her mother's body as a child.

If only her father had loved her. But her father loved her mother. Daughters frightened him. He would have liked a son.

But she no longer said, "If only they had loved me." Now she knew that it was not important. She had suffered thinking that a parent's love had meaning. Now she knew a parent's love was nothing. She was the favorite, the chosen, and her parents had not known it. So she had suffered as all children must suffer till they know the truth.

It was in a garden that the Spirit first had come to her. Four years ago, when she was seventeen. She had been so unhappy then. Had always been, before she knew the truth. Before it had been shown to her. The way of the Lord was beauty, was the Spirit in the garden. It was also fire. And it also was the sword.

The Spirit now would lead her. She would find work somewhere taking care of children. She loved them; she knew what they were thinking. She knew what they needed for their lives. The knowledge of the Spirit, the knowledge that human love meant nothing. It was only the Love of God that could protect and lead and cover. If they didn't know that, they would not feel safe. She would teach that to the next children she cared for.

Now she was flying; she could see the clouds thick, blunted, distant, solid as the earth. And that morning she had been in London in the house of Mrs. Bates, who had no top teeth and on the bottom only two. Whose hair seemed made of what she found in the bottom of the filthy bucket where she stored her mop. Whose son never got out of his dirty bathrobe. Where the radio sent words like bent pins through the ceiling to her. Here the Spirit had come to her most clearly. Here she was reminded that she was the chosen of the Lord. That she must be anxious about nothing. That she was greatly favored of her Father.

How could she be unhappy, when she had been chosen, had been singled out, and had been called the favorite? Because she knew she must be open to the plans the Lord had for her, she left her room each morning after breakfast, having eaten her bread and margarine and jelly, having drunk, out of a bottle, the pint of rich milk she bought each evening at the Pakistani grocer's. All morning she walked the streets smiling, ready to meet the next person who, believing he was helping her, would be buying for himself a treasure that thieves could not steal. Yet no one talked to her. She passed the small dark shops that had odd things in their cluttered windows: shoes and teapots next to one another, old women's clothing. She walked beneath the railroad bridge with its billboard advertising Cadbury's chocolate, showing a child devouring a candy bar. Each day she walked till it was time for lunch. A smell of slowly burning wires hung above the street all day. A close unhealthy smoke was always near.

Each day she had lunch at the Wimpy bar on Camden High Street. It seemed a good place for her to be; the food would not surprise her. The tops of the tables were always sticky. Always on the surface of the ketchup bottles and the vinegar bottles she found a sticky film. She thought that since there were always so many people eating there, she would meet the next person who would help her on her journey. Or who believed he was helping her. For she needed no one. Other people needed her.

But six weeks passed, and no one talked to her. Except the Indian boy who changed the sugar bowls, and she believed he was interested in having sex. On the first of August she arrived at the airport holding only her small canvas bag. She left the rest of her things at Mrs. Bates's. For Jesus had said to the disciples: nor take two tunics, nor sandals, nor a staff.

She had got on the plane unworried. Her Father had something in store for her. She needed merely to live her life, bathed in the Light of the Spirit. Sheltered in her Father's arms.

She must smile now at the woman sitting next to her. For she must always be ready. Anyone could be the person, the person showing her the next part of the journey. Not knowing that she needed nothing. That she was the chosen of the Lord.

She smiled now; she put down her Bible. The woman's skin was mottled, red and white; she'd tried to hide it, but the powder made it worse. She turned around and smiled at everyone as she took her jacket off, trying to have her smile returned. So Laura saw it; she could always see it, the hunger. Talk to me, it said, that smile, looking around to be met. Her eye fell upon Laura. "Let me put that up above for you," said Laura. "I'm a lot taller."

"How kind," the woman said with a slight accent. "But then Americans are always kind to me. Where are you going, what do you do?"

Laura said, "New York. I'm not quite sure what I'll do when I get there."

She knew what the woman wanted. Let me talk, the eyes said, the plain eyes. Men did not love her. Yes, I will let you talk. I will make you feel that I am listening. I will not be listening. But you may want to help me.

So the woman talked and talked. She was from Paris. She was going to Massachusetts, quite near New York, to a town called Selby. Selby College, of course you've heard of it, of course.

"Of course," Laura said. Though she had not.

The woman was going to teach there a year. She'd traded places with a friend of hers. He was taking her place at Toulouse, where he would teach English a year; she would teach French at Selby. But not until September. Until then she would visit her beloved American friends. All over they are scattered, she said, fluttering her hands. New Jersey, Georgia,

Illinois. And one in California. So this summer I will visit all over your fascinating country, keeping my friendships in repair as the great Dr. Johnson said.

Laura had to pretend she knew who the great Dr. Johnson was. And smile. And make the woman glad she was near her. For perhaps then she would help Laura.

She asked Laura about her parents. "They are dead," she told the woman. It was not true, but they were dead to her. And if people heard that, they wanted to help you. "I'm on my own," she said. "That's why I don't know quite what to do next."

The woman, Hélène her name was, looked at Laura's lap, down at her Bible.

"Do you have a religious life? Or are you reading for the poetry?"

Laura did not know what she meant. But she thought if the woman asked her, she must be religious. People who weren't looked away when they saw the Bible, as if it were a sore that she unwrapped before their eyes.

"I have a religious life," she said. It was a way of putting it. She would not say, "I am the chosen of the Lord." The woman had given her a way of putting it. "I have a religious life," she would say from now on. She would be wise as serpents. Now that the Lord had shown her.

So then the woman said she, too, had a religious life. She talked about the love of God. Laura stopped listening but looked as if she was listening with love. She knew the woman was a fool. But perhaps the woman could help her. She knew what the woman wanted. She was always talking about her friends, her darling English friends she wept to leave at the airport. "Five of them came to see me off!" she said. Her wonderful American friends, some of whom she had not seen for years. And she told Laura—you will understand, she said, having a religious life—about her friends the worker priests, her friend the missionary nun in Guatemala. Laura smiled. She let her mind think of the Chamberlains. It would be more terrible for them than for Sodom and Gomorrah. The Lord had said it.

"You must be a wonderful friend to have so many friends," said Laura, knowing that was what Hélène wanted. Pride and loneliness. They ate the woman up. It would be easy to make her think that she was helping Laura; it would be easy, she could see it now; this was the person who would help her next. Not that she needed help. Not really. Only in the things that perished, that the moths ate, that rusted, that ended in the drain. If only she had no need of clothes and food and shelter. As it was, she needed very little. But she did need that. So she would smile at the woman and listen to the stories of her friends, listen with half her mind while with the other she remembered who she was. The chosen of the Lord.

She told the woman that although she had faith the Lord would provide, she was worried for her immediate future. "I have nowhere to go," she said. She told her about the Chamberlains. But did not tell her they had made her leave. I have nowhere to go, she said, hoping the woman would remember she had said both her parents were dead.

"I have it," said Hélène. "Why don't you live in my house in Selby? The college has got it for me. It's a nice town, a lot of young people. Two hours from New York and two from Boston. You'd like it, you could probably find a job. Unfortunately, my darling friend will not be there. But probably I could find some names of people who need help caring for their children. In America the women do not want to take care of their children. They say they want to find themselves. I did not know that they were lost."

She laughed, and Laura laughed, pretending that she understood. She thanked Hélène. She said the Lord had sent her. Why should we be afraid, she said, when we are in the hands of the Lord?

"How beautiful it is, your faith," Hélène said. "That is why, of course, I trust you, although I do not know you. What is our faith for if we suspect the stranger, if we close the open hand out of fear?"

She listened to Hélène tell about her dear friend Michael. What a tragedy that he would not be in Selby for Laura to meet. A great man. A kind man, and so intelligent and handsome. His wife, Anne, was sweet, but nothing up to him. Pretty and sweet, but essentially rather empty. A person of no ideas. Her looks have served her badly, they have hindered her development. She has that kind of prettiness that people like. So she has never had to stretch herself, or grow. It is a pity. She will never understand her husband. She can never be a true companion to him.

Laura saw that Hélène loved the husband, hated the pretty wife. And that the man would never love her. And the wife would have the husband and the children and the house, and Hélène's bitter heart would say the woman was a fool. But Hélène would never have what she wanted. So she would always be talking to people on planes. She would always be giving the keys of her house to strangers.

Laura kissed her. Took the keys. Said she would see the house was spotless when Hélène arrived in a week. "I'm good at that. I like that sort of thing," she said.

"Thank God. I am quite hopeless. I'm afraid my mother spoiled me in this way."

Laura said good-bye to Hélène, taking her keys, the numbers of her friends in Georgia. In Detroit. In Illinois. In California. I will see you in a week, she said, leaving her at the gate of her next flight.

She had only ten dollars. She would eat bread and margarine and jelly as she had in London for these months. She would go to Selby, Massachusetts. To the house she had the key to. She would find work taking care of children. Then she would teach them. She would teach them the word of the Lord. That the love they longed for was as nothing. That the way of the Lord was light. And that she was the favored one, the chosen of the Lord. And they would see it. But at first she would not speak of these things. Until she saw they loved her. She would be wise as serpents. Wise as serpents and innocent as doves.

Anne had always worried that so many people thought her good. That morning as she stood by the window waiting for Hélène and the girl she had met on the plane, she wondered once again if it could be her looks that so took people in. She reminded people, she'd often feared, of their dream of the perfect first-grade teacher: it was her white skin and blue eyes that did it, her light, straight reddish hair, her figure—a small bosom and no waist—her comical size-eleven feet. Once a perfect stranger at a party, very drunk, had said to her, "You've no idea what a comfort a forehead like yours is to a certain kind of person." She hadn't known exactly what he'd meant, but the implications hadn't pleased her.

Like most young girls, she hadn't liked her looks, but she'd come to understand, at thirty-eight, that she was lucky in them because they didn't excite envy or threat. Threat. People were using that word so much now. But what sort of person *threatened* people? Homicidal teenagers, loan sharks, blackmailers? Yet people used the word now for law-abiding citizens. Was it because people felt in danger now? It was a dangerous world, and they were right to feel it. Only, they didn't feel it about her. And so, she suspected, looking at her face, taking in her quietness, her slight stoop, and frequent failure at quick comment, they had no other category in their imaginations into which they could fit her but the good. She knew, though, that that was wrong; she knew that goodness shouldn't be confused with safety.

No one would imagine her good, she thought, if they knew what she was feeling at that moment about Hélène. Hélène was one of the people in the world she most disliked, and she could only feel mean-hearted in disliking her. She was one of Anne's husband's best friends. She'd done extraordinary things to help him with his work, allowed him access to areas of French academic life most Americans would be barred from. She was generous to everyone; she had money of her own and traveled frequently, and she was always smuggling in things that her friends in other countries couldn't live without. She was full of stories about having concealed English sausages in her bra, French cigarettes in the tops of her stockings, packets of seeds in her sanitary napkins—always for her friends. It was said that after her sabbatical in Tübingen, she had so many people to say good-bye to that she had to rent a beer hall for her farewell party.

But even knowing all this, Anne couldn't like her, for Hélène's presence in her life hardened her own position and made it false. In Hélène's presence she became a figure in a drama of Hélène's invention. She had to become Michael Foster's pretty wife, imaginatively raising Darling Peter, Darling Sarah. She had to give up her intellectual and conversational place beside her husband. Hélène pushed her off, past the horizon, a rowboat nosed away by a tanker. In willfully inventing her awry—but only just—Hélène cut off her life. For it was a struggle for a woman in Selby to feel she had a genuine existence. Maleness shaped the town; it had for two hundred years. Since the eighteenth century, young men had come to Selby to be educated into their fathers. Women had only recently been admitted into the college; there were, as yet, the president kept saying with uneasiness, no female full professors. And if the college didn't quite know what to do with women students and faculty, it knew even less what to do with faculty wives. They were like the people who worked in the dark basement offices handling money or records behind doors marked COMPTROLLER or PERSONNEL—words that had nothing to do with the rest of college life. Their function was acknowledged to be necessary, but it was much better if they lived unseen.

Anne knew she had been luckier than most. Four years after they'd arrived at Selby, she'd been made assistant director of the college gallery, a job her Harvard Ph.D. had shamed the college into giving her. But it was the director's job she'd applied for, and that was given to a stranger, someone whom no one in the administration would ever have to imagine making the bed for one of the male faculty, washing his underwear, wiping the noses of his children, mopping the floor he walked upon on his way out *her* door to *their* real life. When the president told her she hadn't got the director's job she'd applied for, and offered her the assistant's job, he said he knew she'd be happy that they'd offered the job to a woman, as if he believed she were applying for the job only as a gesture, as a member of a class, interchangeable with any other member, and so it didn't matter that she didn't get the job herself, since it existed for her only symbolically.

If Hélène had done merely what so many others in Selby had done, if Anne could simply say that Hélène needed, for her own self-love, to make Anne insignificant and dull, the inferior wife of a superior husband, she would have been able to pass it off. But Hélène did more than that. She upset Anne's moral balance. To dislike someone so publicly acknowledged as embodying everyone's ideal of goodness made her doubt herself. For when she wasn't around Hélène, she could think that goodness was of great importance to her; and she could believe in its force. But with Hélène before her she had to acknowledge the limits of goodness, and its weakness, to recognize that in itself it could do nothing to win love. Without the grease of accident—looks, wit, a deft hand or a quick eye—the machinery of affection never started. You could try to like someone you merely admired for his goodness—she had tried with Hélène—but you rarely succeeded. Whatever examples of changed lives and fortunes resulting from Hélène's acts she'd brought to her mind, she hadn't been able to stop herself from flinching when Hélène had embraced her once and said, "I think you do the most important work in the world. Making a man and children happy. This I could never do. I am too greedy, too impatient. You are so good."

The minutes she waited for Hélène loomed and thickened, a small corridor of solitude she could inhabit but could not enjoy or use. She was a mother, and she had a job; time was a precious object: it had mass, extension, force that formed themselves in relation to her work and to her children's lives. Always she'd treasured solitude, and now, in its rarity, her time alone in her house shimmered with instinct value. Alone, she could collect herself; she could smooth herself until she felt her spirit gather and fall in, till she could feel herself once more entire, sheathed. She could watch her life, see how it lapped like a wave against a lakeshore, slow and noiseless, coming from a place that couldn't be determined, not even landing, finally, but starting out again, back to its source. But this morning, her time alone did not shimmer; it was broken up and muddied by the image of Hélène.

And every minute that she waited was filled with anxiety: each might be her last alone. At any moment her hoard of silence would be broken into; all she had gathered in would be spilled out; she would be with someone she disliked. And then it happened: she could see Hélène and the girl walking up the sidewalk. Something closed down with a sharp, excluding sound. It was over; they were at the door.

The sight of them made Anne suddenly feel the weather. It was September, but it was still summer. A moist and downcast heat hung close above the ground. It was a heat that no one could take joy in; summer had gone on too long, and limbs grew heavy yearning for a hint of cold. Yet Hélène wore wool, and Anne felt she did it to make some sort of point. And the girl who was with her—Hélène introduced her as Laura Post—was dressed too warmly as well, in brown corduroy pants and a green pullover sweater that had been carefully, expertly darned. The sweater marked her instantly as not a Selby student; no Selby students mended their clothes. They wore them with holes, or they threw them away. And her sandals weren't the kind that students had; they looked as if they might belong to a Presbyterian missionary or an English nurse on holiday in the tropics. But Laura Post had not crossed that mysterious bridge into the world of finally assumed adulthood. She was young, and wanted to be seen so: tentative, experimental, ready to take on whatever might come up. That, though, was why she was there: to see about working for Anne as a live-in baby-sitter. If her life were fully settled, she wouldn't be free to do, at a moment's notice, the kind of work Anne needed done. Thinking of her in this way, Anne tried to study her face. She had the light blue watery eyes of many redheads, which her thick glasses clouded and enlarged. There was something opulent about her skin: it was white, translucent, like an Ingres nude's. But as if she'd guessed that, and wanted to offset those implications, she'd clipped her thick red hair to the back of her head in a way that unnecessarily, puritanically, revealed her large, protruding ears.

Anne felt herself move away from Laura Post because she found it difficult to place her. But that was the problem with living in Selby, she thought; everyone was so easy to place. She'd often felt that it was like living in a mill town or a sanitarium. Everyone was recognizable, by caste or type. Everyone took an identity from his relation to the college: childish, resentful, rebellious, cringing, proud, servile, workmanlike, enraged. It affected even their postures and the set of their mouths.

Laura and Hélène sat on the couch. Hélène took out of her bag the presents she had brought the children: Swiss chocolates beautifully wrapped in colored foil, an Elizabeth I cutout book for Sarah, and for Peter a model of Nelson's ship.

"How are you surviving Selby?" Anne asked Hélène.

"Oh, if there were only twelve more hours in the day!" Hélène said, fluttering her hands. "So many students wanting to talk, so hungry for conversation. Always in my office! Always I am there in the office till seven o'clock in the evening, hearing about their so terrible lives. I make them speak to me in French; I tell them it is educational."

Immediately, Anne felt for every member of the faculty who left his office before dark, the blow of unspoken reproach.

"And how do *you* like Selby?" she asked Laura.

"I'm very happy," said the girl.

"The children are not here," Hélène said. "But they are in school, of course. How silly of me. And you, you were doing your lovely work with them out of the house."

The way Hélène said "lovely work" made Anne feel she put it in the category of needlepoint or macramé. She answered noncommittally; she didn't want to talk about her work to Hélène. It was too fragile, too newborn; she felt unwilling to expose it to any but the most friendly gaze. She explained to Laura that she had a new job writing the catalogue notes to accompany an exhibit of the work of Caroline Watson, an American painter of the early twentieth century whose work had been neglected for years.

"I need to be in New York now a few days a week, which is why child care has become a problem."

As she looked at Laura she thought again what a problem it was. Her present arrangements were as bad as they could be and still be considered functional. The girl whom she'd hired in the spring to live in, beginning in September, had decided, over the course of the summer, not to return to school, and as a last resort, Anne had turned to Mrs. Davenport, a woman in her sixties whom people employed only when no one else was available. Peter hated her. He said her bad breath made him sick. He said she wouldn't let him keep his night light on and she told Sarah that if she looked in the mirror too long the Devil would appear. Peter and Sarah hadn't been told anything about the Devil, so Sarah was riveted; she sat at Mrs. Davenport's knee, asking questions about the Devil every night. Peter said those are the nights she has nightmares. Every night that you're home late, he added, looking at his mother as Cotton Mather might have looked at a Salem woman in the stocks. Besides her personal shortcomings Mrs. Davenport refused to stay after nine o'clock; she wanted to be home to feed her husband his dinner, which he'd had, she told Anne—suggesting Anne's instability, her own permanence—at five-thirty every night of his life.

"I've just come back from England," Laura said. "I was working for two professors, from Syracuse, taking care of their two children. They were on sabbatical. I could give you their name and address."

Anne wrote down the information. "I was in London for a summer, when I was about your age," she said. "I still think of all those wonderful places: the Tate, the British Museum, Kew Gardens. I was enormously happy there."

Laura smiled blankly at Anne, as if Anne were talking about a place she'd never been. Her patient smile, her silence, made Anne feel foolish, inexpert and young. She talked about her children.

"Sarah is six," she said, "and Peter is nine." She spoke about her children to Hélène and Laura in a way that made her feel that she was betraying them at every word. She presented the image that the outside world saw: Sarah is independent; Peter is intellectual. She heard herself reduce them, flatten them out. But that was all she wanted to give these women, a reduced image, not the intimate full figures, breathing, vulnerable, that she saw. So she stopped talking about them; she did the other thing she did when she was nervous, she offered them food.

"No, no," said Hélène, fluttering her hands. "It is Thursday, you see. Each Thursday Laura and I participate in a program run by the Student Christian Center. We fast, then contribute what we would have spent on food to a fund for world hunger. It is a way of feeling the problem in your gut."

Hélène pronounced the word "gut" as if it were the German for good. Anne felt herself encased entirely in flesh.

"It's a wonderful idea," Anne said. "Really admirable. But you must come back when the children are here, someday that's not a Thursday. A weekend, perhaps. One Saturday you could come for lunch."

At the door, Hélène kissed Anne on both cheeks. "*A bientôt,*" she said. "I must see these terrible children of yours soon, before they are off for college."

"I'll see to it," Anne said, realizing she'd decided not to hire Laura. She knew her own unfairness. The girl had done nothing, said almost nothing. But something about her—her too heavy, too carefully darned sweater, her large feet and disproportionately delicate hands, and probably, in fact, her friendship with Hélène had made Anne feel that Laura wasn't a person she wanted to share her house with. She wondered what excuse she'd give to Laura and to Hélène for not hiring her when, after all, she really needed help.

She went to the refrigerator to choose what she would have for lunch. Before Hélène and Laura's visit, she'd thought she'd have an orange, half an avocado, and a wedge of *chevrotin* left over from a piece she'd treated herself to the day before. Had her family been with her, she would have had to eat things that were more substantial, more communal, less expensive: she'd looked forward to her imagined lunch. But now she'd just been with people who were fasting the whole day. How could she eat such an enjoyable, such a constructed meal? She fixed herself a peanut butter sandwich, and, while she ate, read a book she'd just got from the Selby College library, a biography of Inigo Jones. After lunch she mopped the floor, thinking how strange it was that every summer everyone in Jacobean London but the poor left the city, as a matter of course, to preserve their lives.

She looked at the clock. It was two-thirty; soon the children would be home. She waited for the sound of their arrival as if she were dressed for a party, listening for a taxi. No one had told her what it would be like, the way she loved her children. What a thing of the body it was, as physically rooted as sexual desire, but without its edge of danger. The urge to touch one's child, she often thought, was like, and wasn't like, the hunger that one felt to touch a lover: it lacked suspense and greed and the component parts of insecurity and vanity that made so trying the beloved's near approach. Once the children were in the house, the air became more vivid and more heated: every object in the house grew more alive. How I love you, she always wanted to say, and you can never know it. I would die for you without a thought. You have given to my life its sheerest, its profoundest pleasure. But she could never say that. Instead, she would say, "How was school?" "Was lunch all right?" "Did you have your math test?"

They ran into the kitchen, opened the refrigerator. Peter began telling her about his science project. He and Daniel Greenspan were going to build a solar clock. It had begun already, that queer thing: her son knew more about some things than she did. He was trying to explain something about a pendulum; she didn't understand. Impatiently he shoved the cookie he was eating into his mouth and fiddled in his school things for a pen and paper. He began to sketch: here is the sun, here is the clock, this is the force of gravity. For years, she felt, males had been impatiently making sketches of the world for uncomprehending females. But his sketch was good; he made her see something, and he was proud of her pride in him, she could see it: his teaching had given him a courtliness so he could drop favor over his mother's shoulders like the mantle of a king. He was impatient to get on with things, to leave her. He ran when he heard Daniel knocking at the door.

It shocked her when she'd learned how much she could like or dislike other children, depending on their treatment of her own. She'd always adored Daniel, she'd known him all his life. He shared with Peter a precocious, dry intellectuality, a pointed energy, and an unpopularity with other children, but he added to it an irony that Peter could never approach.

"I'm going to get dressed for ballet class," said Sarah. Then she was gone, they were both gone. Anne was alone again, but this time she felt lonely. No one would ever know the passion she felt for her children. It was savage, lively, volatile. It would smash, in one minute, the image people had of her of someone who lived life serenely, steering always the same sure, slow course. As it was, as they would never know, she was rocked back and forth, she was lifted up and down by waves of passion: of fear, of longing, and delight.

It was such an odd thing, motherhood. She didn't understand how people could say, "She's a good mother," in the same way they said, "She's a good neurosurgeon," or "She sings well." It wasn't a skill: there was no past practice to be consulted and perfected by strict application and attention to detail; there was no wisdom you could turn to; every history was inadequate, for each new case was fresh—each new case was a person born, she was sure of it, with a nature more fixed than modern thought led people to believe. She loved that, that her children were not *tabulae rasae,* but had been born themselves. She loved the intransigence of their natures, all that could never be molded and so was free from her. She liked to stand back a little from her children—it was why some people thought her, as a mother, vague. But she respected the fixity of her children's souls, what they were born with, what she had, from the first months, seen. She admired, for example, Peter's fastidiousness—it wasn't only physical, although it had its roots in the physical—she admired it even when it exhausted her and made her feel quite futile. Since he could talk he had come to her in positions of outraged justice with questions that had no answers, although she agreed with him they should have had: "Why did Jessica's father go away and never see her?" "Why does Amanda like to play with Oliver better than me when I share all my toys and he hogs his?" He was always ardent; he took things to heart, and she was proud of his seriousness, his suffering, his fine, inflexible standards, but she wished she could protect him from himself. He would not be easily beloved, she could see that, but perhaps he would be honored. Perhaps, she had often thought, with a thrill of atavistic pride, an ancient, probably ignoble pride open only to the mothers of sons, he would one day be feared.

Sarah was nothing like him. She stood back from life, found it amusing, looked on it with a slant, ironic gaze that judged, particularly the actions of adults, *de haut en bas,* with kindness, but with condescension. She had more hidden life than Peter, her dramas were inward, sometimes only to be guessed at or eavesdropped upon.

Anne worried that Sarah's evenness excluded her from too much maternal concern. Perhaps in apportioning her worries toward her son, she was depriving her daughter. But when she thought of Sarah's future she could only imagine the two of them—she and her daughter—sitting across from each other, drinking coffee, having wonderful conversations, full and calm and rich. She could only imagine a good life for her daughter; it was for her son alone she feared. But it was absurd, these fears and these imaginings. There was no way of knowing what would happen to them, and, she often felt, not much that you could do to influence the course of things determined so much by their natures and their fates. All you could do was, while they were still children, keep them safe.

With the children gone, she sat down at the kitchen table and tried to pay bills. But Laura Post's face kept swimming up, past numbers and receipts and postpaid envelopes, to the top of her mind. She hadn't liked her, although she tended to like most young women. They interested her; their position was so unreal. It was assumed by everyone but them that they were easily desired, that they held some power in their skins, that they had merely to walk down a street, to turn a shoulder, to have laid down before them whatever they wanted. But it wasn't like that for them at all. They were nearly always unhappy. Young men were timid or voracious; they were afraid to talk. And young women had been made to feel that they must engage in the most intimate of physical acts with whoever was their current lover but must never ask, "Do you like me?" "Does this make you happy?" or even "Will we see each other again?" And what of the ones outside the circle of desirability, by choice or nature, the ones who weren't beautiful or who felt for the young men beside them only coldness or contempt? Suppose they were ambitious; suppose their greatest passion went toward some clear, consuming work? Suppose they were naturally ironic or depressed?

She wanted to tell them, Michael's students who came to the house, who talked to her as if they were looking for clues to a crime or buried treasure, that it would be much better for them in ten years. That they could get married if they wanted to (for it was marriage, still, that worried them, though they weren't allowed to say so now) and that the marriages would probably be happy. She wanted to say that, though she knew it was not at all likely: young men didn't seem much interested in marriage, and most marriages were bad.

But Laura was unlike any of the young women she knew. It was her fault
for not liking Laura, she told herself. If she felt reproached by someone
wearing a darned sweater and fasting one day a week, it was something in
her that was amiss. Yet she really couldn't hire her. She'd have to make
do with Mrs. Davenport. And Sally Devereux, who worked in the college
employment office, had told her that if she would just hang on, something
would turn up. People were always deciding they hated their roommates,
or they went broke or their fathers lost their jobs. It was just a matter of
time, Sally had assured her. Meanwhile, she could hold off going to the
city more than one day a week; there was still a lot she could do at home.

She wondered what she would have done about Laura if Michael had
been home. The decisions about the course their lives would take had
always been made jointly, so their individual positions had been concealed,
as the parts of a machine are concealed when it works. Married at twenty-
two, they'd had no experience in dealing with the outside world separately
as adults.

You'd done nothing yet at twenty-two, she thought, knew nothing. And
yet, she thought, they'd been right to marry. What else could they have
done? Gone off somewhere, each separately? Taken up with others?
They'd thought of it, of course, for it was unfashionable, highly unfashionable, what they'd done: one simply didn't get married at twenty-two in
1968. But anything else would have been false. They were in love; they
were going to be in the same graduate school; it would have caused some
unease to her family if they'd lived together. And so why not marry?

For, ashamedly, she'd recognized that what she wanted went with
marriage. She'd wanted a home not her parents' and yet not quite a
student's either. She wanted to be an adult. And since she had no money,
no profession, only a student's status, which she was weary of, marriage
was a way that she could feel she had closed a chapter of her life—
childhood, you could have called it—that she was eager to be rid of and
that otherwise she might feel she had indecorously prolonged.

Michael, too, had wanted to close a chapter of the past, which had
wounded him, though he was gallant about it. You never would have
known what he'd come from. He'd waited a year before he'd brought her
home, to the shambles of a house, the nearly ruined mother tipsy every
night by eight, so he never felt safe inviting people for dinner. He'd got
a motel room for Anne that first visit, and kept her there as much as
possible, bringing her to his house for breakfast and lunch only, bringing
hamburgers to her room in the motel, in Akron, near the airport so he
wouldn't run into anyone he knew, making love to her over and over,

hungrily, gratefully, for he was grateful to her for still wanting him after she'd seen his home, and she was grateful that he'd shown her, grateful for the trust. Grateful for allowing her to understand him, for there was no knowing him without his mother. Poor Lucy, whom she'd genuinely loved but whose death, she must be honest, had been a relief.

Lucy, too, had been gallant, in her way, but her way wasn't sufficient, not for the mother of a son. Abandoned by her husband at thirty, left with a four-year-old boy, she'd simply turned her back on domestic life, or turned over in the face of it, like a wounded animal, declaring itself helpless, out of the running, everything in its posture expressing its desire to be left alone, simply to be allowed not to take part. Anne often wondered how Michael had physically survived his early childhood. As early as possible, Lucy had abdicated; at eight, Michael had told her, he'd done all the shopping, the cooking such as it was, the little cleaning that got done. She'd thought of him so often, that bookish little boy, going down to the corner store, buying bologna, white bread, iceberg lettuce, Kraft French dressing. Having the sandwiches and salad ready for his mother when she walked in the door, home from work, from the beauty parlor where she was astonishingly successful (her house was a hovel but she was always perfectly manicured, impeccably coiffed). She was greatly charming, and her specialty was brief encounters. To the women whose hair she fixed she was a bolster, a beacon, a tower of strength. And to her son she gave much that was important in a mother's love: a steamy, rich affection, redolent of the cave. Always he knew she loved him; always he knew himself first in her heart. And for that Anne loved her, was able to see her charm, her virtues. It was lucky that she did; Michael would never have been able to marry someone who didn't like his mother, who didn't appreciate her, who was shocked at her domestic chaos or interpreted it as a lack of regard. It was all right for him to lament her failures, to call himself an orphan, but had Anne joined him in condemning his mother, he would have drawn away. What he needed was someone who could be different from his mother yet assure him that his mother had not, as a woman, failed.

It wasn't difficult for Anne to ignore or see through Lucy's domestic chaos. She, too, had been brought up in a home bereft of ordinary graces, though its tone was vastly different from the cluttered, sexy, female mess of Lucy's den. Her mother hadn't liked home life, so she had not been good at it. Only recently Anne had realized that her mother must have been depressed for years. Only depression could account for her thorough failure, the spiritless performance of a woman of spirit, the gross blundering of a woman whose whole talent was for fineness, for distinction. She thought of the elaborate meals her mother had planned and burned, the dresses she had made and then ruined with her iron, the wallpapers that cried out horribly against the brocade chairs. Then it had changed: she had gone back to school, had got her degree. It was too late for Anne; she was in college by then.

Anne thought of her mother's wedding picture. Susan Holliwell, Mount Holyoke, class of '41, looking more the honor student than the bride, holding her bouquet over her head like a basketball or a torch. She was laughing, and one could see the joke: this dashing girl was going to pretend to settle down. How had that girl turned into the mother Anne remembered, covering her ears and begging her children not to fight, crying when her younger daughter refused, for the fiftieth time, to drink her milk? Seeing her mother like this, it had early become clear to Anne that she had to be the mother in the house.

That was the secret of her bond with Michael: they had both been, as children, mothers, both involved in the conspiracy at the center of the lives of children of deficient parents, the conspiracy to keep from the world this shame, this failure, above all to make it appear that the life inside the sorrowing house was the same as any other.

They had married early because they wanted to reinvent domestic life. It was a romance dear to both of them. They never could understand, really, their friends who wanted to live in purposefully ugly places: bare mattresses on the floor, empty tuna cans for ashtrays, posters stuck to the wall with thumbtacks, half falling down. For them a vase of living flowers was a miracle, a loaf of bread they'd made together was a precious vessel holding all they wanted for their lives.

It was only after they'd done it all, bought the house, had the babies, that they realized that others who'd done what they had done thought they were reinventing domestic life. But by that time it was no longer an invention, it was simply their life.

Now all that was interrupted. Michael was four thousand miles away. He'd been gone three weeks, and she felt it still, that hesitancy, that waiting, almost as if she heard him, as if, any minute, she might see him in another room. All her ordinary actions seemed unreal and incomplete, as if she were doing them for the camera.

Three weeks he'd been gone and she still slept badly each night. For sixteen years she had held him every night, and now the bed was vacant, a lot abandoned with a half-finished house. Her relation to the children was different too; the rhythm she and Michael heard that told them when the other had become inadequate, impatient, unreasonable, tyrannical or lax was silent. She was alone with the children now; she was alone.

She could hardly believe that they had done it. She tried to remember exactly how it had all started. It had been in a New York City restaurant. Benedict Hardy, whom she'd known since she was twenty and in London with a grant to study the Elgin Marbles, had taken them out to dinner as he did once a year, when he came to New York. He was an eminent British art historian, self-consciously aristocratic and fantastical, whose specialty was nineteenth-century French painting. Each year their night with him stood out from the rest of the year like a secret national holiday in a community of illegal immigrants. This year, when they'd finished their meal, Benedict leaned back and luxuriously lit a cigarette, without a hint of apology, as if it were another course. "I don't suppose you'd like a job writing a catalogue for me," he said to Anne, assuming the laconic expression he felt it his duty to adopt whenever he said anything of importance.

He was arranging an exhibit at a gallery in New York of the works of Caroline Watson, a woman whose paintings had been neglected since her death in 1938. She was one of those painters, he explained, who had painted the wrong things at the wrong time. In the late twenties, when Cubism was the rage and Surrealism was following hard on it, she was doing dark Fauve studies of women and children. And landscapes, he said, which no one in fashionable circles considered anything but a genre to induce a blush. "Her misfortune was to be a merely first-rate painter in an age of geniuses," he finished, leaning back, proud of his aphorism, which he could not just then have invented. He had known her in Paris and London in the twenties. Her daughter-in-law, the heir of the estate, was someone, he said, "to whom I am very much in the nature of being devoted.

"Caroline left America for Paris in the 1880's, never really to return. At thirty-six, to everyone's astonishment, particularly her father's—he was very Philadelphia, a banker, right clubs and all that sort of thing—she produced an illegitimate child. A son. Stephen Watson. Poor soul, one of those born miserable. Caroline's father said he'd cut her off if she brought the boy up anywhere but in Philadelphia. She tried to stick it, but she couldn't and left the child behind. She said she had to live in France. Stephen drank himself to death at twenty-eight. Everyone said it was pneumonia, but one knew, really. He'd married Jane, and Jane and Caroline were inseparable. They lived together, greatly devoted, until Caroline died. You see, one of the reasons I thought of you, darling Anne, is that

Jane, much as I adore her, can be difficult. Would not be everyone's dish of tea. But you, of course, will be able to see her greatness and to get round the difficult bits. And then there's your lovely thesis on Mary Cassatt and Eakins. So you're a natural. It's a marriage made in heaven."

He brought them to the gallery to look at some of Caroline's paintings. It was exciting, in a charged, theatrical way, to enter the building at night, to be cleared by a guard, to watch Ben press a series of numbers on a keyboard at the gallery door, and, magically, to have the door open before them onto the pitch-dark room. Conscious of the potency of his gesture, Ben turned on the lights. He quickly showed them to a back room, not giving them a moment to look at the pictures currently on exhibit, and unlocked the large closet where Caroline's paintings were stored.

The first two he brought out meant nothing much to Anne; she made polite, graduate-student comments on the landscapes and still lifes. Then he brought out one called *Flowers*. The background was a brownish red; the flowers, on a dark green table, still wrapped in blue paper, seemed hastily laid down. They were full of the energy bestowed on objects by a just completed motion: they had been put down almost carelessly, angrily. And the colors of the flowers, purposely almost unnatural—magenta, cobalt, scarlet—effaced the notion of flowers as things that were in the world to decorate, or to domesticate. They thrummed with an almost animal life; they might be dangerous.

Ben showed her another one, called *Jane*. A woman in a black suit sat in a restaurant. Before her on the table were a cup of coffee and a book. Reading, she leaned her head on her hand—she was wearing an emerald ring. Her hair was the center of the composition; wound around her head, a dense curve, definite and tender, its line shaped the foreground. Around the woman sat the other diners, sketched in lightly, as if they were figures in a dream.

Seeing those paintings, something grew in Anne, something she'd lived with since but hadn't known before, a push or a desire, like the hunger for a definite but hard-to-come-by food. The paintings made her greedy to be with them, to speak of them: they belonged to her. She saw in her mind a catalogue with the early and late paintings next to one another on the page. She imagined all that she could say, all that could be said by simply comparing them slowly, painstakingly, using everything she knew now, and all that she would learn.

Then she heard Michael and Ben talking behind her. Michael walked toward her, took her hand. "We're going to be in France next year," he said.

Michael had a Strafford grant. He was going to change places with Hélène.

Anne looked at Ben. "I'd forgotten," she said. "We'll be in France next year."

"Think about it for a while," he said. "You could see each other at Christmas. The whole separation would be only eight or nine months."

"No," she said. "You'll have to find someone else."

"Take this to look at, just for fun," said Ben, handing a morocco-bound book with the word *Diary* stamped on the front in gold.

That night, while Michael, exhausted by the drive from New York, slept, she read the journal for the first time.

"I must leave, and I will," Caroline had written at twenty in her journal:

> I know what I want to paint, the miracle of atmosphere, invisible, and
> pure, yet full of conduct, action. And the clarity of water, now the color
> of pebbles, then suffused entirely with the mood of blue summer. This
> cannot be seen, only revealed by a film of reflected sky. And the long
> line of grassy pasture, great trees without undergrowth, snowy geese,
> bending necks here and there, spreading wings or lowering yellow bills.
> All this I must set down—but how? Now I paint like an ignorant
> farmer's wife, or worse, a lady. But what have I to look at? Pictures of
> gravy-colored skies with leaves the shade and textures of Brussels sprouts,
> birds like mashed potatoes, utterly unanimated, without the slightest
> sense of creatures drawing breath. I will prevail over Papa; I will not
> relent.

In the back of the diary, Ben had taped an envelope of photographs. The first picture was formal: at sixteen, Caroline stood over her father's left shoulder, a daunting, judging girl, taller than her brothers, her foot ready to tap impatience on the carpet, or to walk away. The father, in the center, dominated the scene with his serious, formal whiskers and his broad manufactured chest. Next to the father was the mother, looking as if every other word her family spoke might do her injury. On either side of the father and the mother sat small brothers, ready to take the father at his word. Over the mother's left shoulder stood the other sister, holding her body still, making her shoulders an apologetic curve to keep the family from fighting till the photographer, probably no gentleman, had done his work.

The second photograph showed Caroline on the deck of a ship, laughing with her sister, who looked cold. You could see Caroline thought it a joke, her sister's coldness, she would make her walk the deck a hundred times. The third picture was Caroline beside a car, clearly her treasure. A stout leg peeked uncomfortably beneath a modern skirt. In the last photograph Caroline stood with her son, looking reluctant and about to walk away. And Stephen's eyes looked off, with the attitude of someone always ready to accept reproach.

"I will prevail over Papa; I will not relent," Caroline had written at twenty. And she had done it: had not relented, had prevailed. What was that hard shining thing in the center of Caroline Watson that had never lodged in Anne? All her life she'd been a good girl; all her life she had been pleasing. At the center of her was not something hard and brilliant, but something soft and flat. But as she thought of Caroline, read the diary, looked at the photographs, above all when she thought about the paintings, something embedded itself, dug in, and sharpened. Caroline entered her life. Intrusive, overwhelming, siphoning attention, like a new lover, she entered and took over. She cast her light on everything and colored it, or revealed it as bleak. And, like a lover, she was the vehicle of infidelity, for as Anne felt her longing turn toward Caroline she felt herself more and more distant from Michael. And she felt his perception of her distance, as if he were on a ship anchored at shore, watching her sail out to sea, small, fading out, away from him. It had happened before; it happened, she imagined, in all good marriages, this sailing in and out of intimacy, this removal to a private realm. For privacy, she felt, was one of the important benefits of marriage. It was much easier to have privacy in a marriage than as a single woman; there was time for it, and time to come back out of it, a place to come back to. It didn't rip the curtain through; it didn't bring the house down.

But something new had happened. She wasn't sailing now; she was rowing away. She felt the strain against her heart as she pushed harder to be farther and more certainly away. And one night, as she lay awake while Michael slept, she knew that whether she took the job or not, the way she felt about her family had changed. If she didn't take it, she would continue rowing away from them. If she did, she would become different in her relation to them. She would have done something daring, something perhaps shocking. It would be the first time in her life that she had shocked.

How had she become the woman she was? At thirty-eight, never to have performed a daring action. She was tired of it, tired of the weakness that had marked her life. She thought of Caroline at twenty, defying her father to study abroad, leaving her child ten months of the year. Unwomanly, they would have called her, but was that what people meant, had always meant, by womanliness—mere submission?

So the talks began, first tentative, then daily changing tone: tearful, unfriendly, lacerating, hurt, apologetic, pleading, blandishing, rational, cold. Pictures were created: think of the sunsets, the olive trees, the children in the square. Think of them among French children, speaking French. Think of us walking among the cypresses. But in the end, it was Michael who said to her that they must do it, that it was mostly fear that kept them back. And Caroline, this work, was too important to lose because they lacked courage. Of course they would do it, they both said, as if their indecision had been merely good form, a gesture proffered to a hostile universe so as not to appear, before its punitive gaze, too confident. People did it all the time, they said; now they would try it. It will only be a few months, they said, and we'll have years.

But even as they said it she was worried. Suppose they didn't have years together. Suppose he left her—he would be without her for months. No one could relax about a marriage now; one in two failed, the corpses lay out everywhere. No one of her generation could imagine with any confidence a separation that would leave chastity—to say nothing of the marriage itself—intact. She knew her husband was attractive. He was one of those men who grow into their bodies only in their thirties. She'd married a gangly boy but the man she lived with was lean and princely, a young nobleman Piero della Francesca would have liked to paint in profile.

"Would you like me to take the children, so you can really do it right?" he'd asked. "That way, they wouldn't lose the advantages of being in France for a year."

She'd felt ill with fear when he suggested it. She could barely explain to him what the prospect of living without her children made her feel: derelict, unfranchised, as if she were sleeping on the street. No, no, she said; they're better off here. Leave them with me.

And so the summer passed, amorous, familial. Her work was pleasant and absorbing. Everyone behaved unnaturally well because they knew Michael would be leaving soon; they could see it rolling at them like a stone down a mountain. She didn't allow it, till the last few days, to take over: the grief, the small fears, the apprehension that she couldn't, even for a few months, run a house alone and rear two children. Michael had left detailed instructions about the things he usually took care of: the oil burner, the electrical system, the storm windows. But it wasn't those she was most afraid of; she was afraid that she wouldn't be anyone she recognized without Michael; she was afraid of discovering a fathomless weakness that the darkness of marriage, its dense, tough material, had covered up.

The week before Michael's departure she woke regularly at five in the morning. I can't do it; I've made a terrible mistake, she would tell herself. But she would think of Caroline; the daunting girl, the challenging matron, her foot on the running board of the car she drove herself. She thought of Caroline's paintings. So there was a woman, forty-five years dead, whom she would know as she knew her own family. But to do it she had to let her husband go away from her. For a while, she kept telling herself. Not long. We'll be together in four months, she kept saying. It isn't much.

But when the day came and she saw Michael zip his suitcase shut, it was unbearable. All morning the children cried, on and off; they argued about ridiculous things; Michael mislaid his passport.

They arrived at JFK two hours before the flight. Anne kept squeezing Michael's hand; he kept giving her the name of the plumber. When the flight was announced, all of them cried except Sarah, who sat in her chair not looking up and reading *Goodnight Moon,* an atavistic gesture she performed when she was frightened. Peter made Michael sign an agreement that they would see each other on December 15. And then, Michael was simply gone. There was nothing more to wave to: the door of the plane closed up, and they couldn't see where he was sitting.

The children slept in the car on the way up to Selby. When they got home, the children were cross and sleepy, and she felt she had used up all her strength on the drive. She didn't even make the children bathe or brush their teeth. She said they could sleep in their underwear. When Peter asked if they couldn't all sleep in the parents' bed, just for one night, she agreed. She could have fallen down on her knees in gratitude before her son. Never, she thought, had anyone had such a good idea.

Now she was doing it all, all they had talked about and thought about and planned for. She was researching Caroline; she was living alone. The only problem was to find someone wonderful to take care of the children. But Laura Post wasn't that person. It was too bad, really, but she simply wasn't right.

———

By the third week of September Anne hadn't found a live-in baby-sitter. But she had to go down to New York again. One day she talked Mrs. Davenport into staying until eleven so she could have supper with Ben. He had something to give her, he said, and handed her a packet of

Caroline's letters to Derain. She touched them, trembling with excitement. By the time they were ready to leave the restaurant, she'd looked
at them all. But she'd missed the last bus. She called Mrs. Davenport, who
sniffed when she answered the phone and said, "It's the first time for you,
but it won't be the last. It's always the way. Luckily, I don't have to be
no place tonight."

Anne said that she hadn't dreamed of asking Mrs. Davenport to stay;
she could simply bring the children next door to the Greenspans. But Mrs.
Davenport said *she* happened to care too much about the children to risk
their health getting them up out of a warm bed to go out on a cold night.
Anne said she would phone the children in the morning before they left
for school.

"I won't tell them nothing," Mrs. Davenport said. "In case you don't
get around to it."

She went back to the table where Ben was sitting and began to cry.

"The children are perfectly fine," he said. "Ghastly woman. You must
get rid of her, darling."

"There's no one else around."

"Something will turn up. It's bound to. Meanwhile, have another
brandy. It'll help you sleep."

The waiter brought them a brandy, and Anne asked Ben if he had
minded, as a child, being left so much to servants and then being sent off
to school so early.

"I minded awfully at the time. But in retrospect, I think it was good.
It taught one early not to expect too much from human attachments."

She looked at Ben, his long spatulate fingers around the brandy glass,
and thought, I am abandoning my children. I am teaching them not to
believe in human attachments. Mrs. Davenport is making my younger
child a superstitious nervous wreck. She wanted to tell Ben it was no good;
she couldn't do the job, she was boarding, with the children, the next plane
to France.

She thought of Caroline Watson's son, who died at twenty-eight, an
alcoholic. Peter would probably not become an alcoholic. Sarah would
probably not jump out a window trying to flee the Devil. If only she could
find the right person to stay with them.

———

When she got home the next morning at eleven, she surprised Mrs.
Davenport asleep in front of a TV game show. The woman was befuddled
and distraught, and Anne felt sorry for her, waking up in front of so many
strange televisions, in so many strange houses. For the first time, she saw

Mrs. Davenport as old and vulnerable and unfortunate rather than aggressive and unpleasant and ill-bred. She lied and said she didn't have the right change and gave Mrs. Davenport an extra five dollars.

"We'll straighten it out next time," said Mrs. Davenport, quickly folding the money and pushing it into her purse, as if she expected Anne to change her mind.

Anne went into the kitchen to make herself a cup of coffee. She saw a pad of lined notepaper that Mrs. Davenport had left and thought that she should put it in a drawer so the children wouldn't use it. A slip of paper fell out of the pad onto the floor. She picked it up. It was written on, and she didn't want to read it, but she saw her own name. Her name riveted her; she couldn't keep her eyes away.

"This one's such a slob," the letter said. "Just to test her last week, I left a cookie behind the door of the playroom. Well, it's still there. I'm leaving it there to see how long it takes her to get around to it."

Anne ran up the stairs as if she had been shot out of a cannon. She opened the door of the playroom. The room was a mess: pieces of puzzles, crayons, blocks, naked dolls were sprawled around the floor. She looked behind the door. There it was, a chocolate chip cookie, covered with dust and hair. She remembered that she had just given Mrs. Davenport an extra five dollars. How had she allowed that woman in her house, with her children, even for a moment? She picked up the cookie, and crushing it in the palm of her hand she walked to the telephone.

Trembling, she dialed the number of the people in Syracuse that Laura had worked for.

"Oh, she's a model of patience," said Joan Chamberlain. "And, you know, she's always ready to do extra housework. She's quiet, though, she keeps to herself. And I think she's very religious. Not that that makes any difference, I mean, if you know it ahead of time."

"But you feel you can recommend her?" Anne said.

"Oh yes, sure, there's nothing wrong with Laura. Really, I'm sure you'll be happy with her. I'm sure she'll be just fine in your house."

The cookie was beginning to melt in her hand. She flushed it down the toilet, walked back to the telephone and dialed Hélène's number. Laura answered the phone.

"I was wondering if you could start working for me," Anne said.

"What about tomorrow?" Laura said.

"Splendid," said Anne. "I'll be here all day. Just come whenever you're ready."

"I'm ready," said Laura.

She knew she had been sent to Anne to save her. Once she might have worried. She might have been afraid Anne wouldn't like her. Anne was the sort of person who used to be able to make her feel bad about herself. Now she never felt bad about herself. Anne was very pretty. People liked Anne. She had one of those houses people wanted to be in. Once she would have wanted Anne to be her friend, to invite her to her house. She would have wanted Anne to tell Laura's mother that Laura was a wonderful person. Anne was the sort of person her mother would listen to. If Anne told Laura's mother that Laura was the best thing that had happened in the children's lives, her mother would have to change her mind. Not like what happened with the other people. The Rutherfords at home. They told her mother she wasn't good for the children. But that was the parents, not the children. The children liked her, she knew they did. They wanted her to stay. They said so when she asked them.

Her mother said she wasn't any good with children. Her mother said she didn't know why Laura got it in her head to work with children, because she wasn't any good. She said Laura had never been good with children, she hadn't been any good with her own sister, why did she think she'd be good with anybody else's children. If she couldn't be good with her own sister. If she couldn't get along in her own family. If she never had been able to. What did she think the world was all about?

When she was twelve, her mother told her she would never be beautiful. She enrolled her in a typing course that summer, because she would have to work to support herself. Her mother said men married beauty: it gave them pleasure. It gave pleasure to the world, her mother said. If you were not beautiful, you did not give pleasure. If you were not good-natured. If you were not lively, were not smart. "She's a pleasure." "It's a pleasure to be near her." "The pleasure of her company." What was this pleasure that she could not give? Pleasure, the word sounded to her heavy and fat, like sheep. They ate grass and then were shorn and then were eaten.

Her mother was beautiful. That was why her father loved her. "Try and please your mother," her father would tell her when her mother sent her away, sent her to her room. "I can't stand the sight of you," her mother said. "Try and please your mother." Tears. "Don't cry or I'll give you something to cry for." Tears. "Out of my sight." "Try and please your mother." "Your mother doesn't mean it. What she says." Do you, my father, mean it, what you say? No, never. Because her mother was beautiful. "I can still fit my hands around your waist," her father said to her mother. Her mother was small. At eleven, Laura weighed more than her mother. At twelve, she was taller.

Anne was tall. Laura saw that she was more like Anne than she was like her mother. Her mother would think Anne was pretty. Was good-natured. Was lively and smart. Her mother would like Anne. When Anne told her mother that Laura was the best thing that had happened to the children, her mother would change her mind. She would say, "Why don't you come home and live for a while. Come and live with me. Here is your room."

But Laura would say no. Because none of it was important. There was nothing that she needed now. She would say no to her mother. After she had saved Anne, saved the children. After they loved her. But it didn't matter if they loved her. It only mattered that she saved them.

She was so happy now. Before she found the Lord, she would have worried about all these things. Anne. Her mother. Now that she no longer needed anyone, now that her strength was in the Lord, she could feel sorry for Anne. Before, she would have been afraid Anne wouldn't like her. Now she just felt sorry for her.

Hélène said Anne had never known trouble. Hélène had been kind to Laura. But people like Hélène were always kind to her. Hélène liked her. But people like Hélène always liked her. Her mother wouldn't like Hélène. She wouldn't like her clothes. Hélène wouldn't make her mother change her mind, think that she had been wrong about her daughter. Hélène's house wouldn't make her change her mind. It was a college house, but she did nothing to it. It had no pictures on the walls. The dishes were from the dime store. Laura knew that Hélène's house was like that because Hélène knew that beauty didn't mean anything. Often it was a lure. Hélène said that Anne had gotten through the world too easily because of beauty. Anne's husband had been deceived by it. Hélène said she knew Michael was not happy in his marriage. "He has sold his birthright for a mess of pottage," Hélène said. He chose a companion with a pretty face, an alluring body, instead of a partner for his mind and his spirit. Michael was a very spiritual person, Hélène said, although it wasn't evident until one knew him well. But Anne had nothing in her of the spirit. She was a complete materialist. Even what she called her intellectual life was sensual. Pictures of fat mothers with fat babies, that was what she studied. Anne had no ideas, Hélène said. She had no life above the flesh. Putting her hand on Laura's hand (the palms of her hands were damp) Hélène told her that she would be very good for Anne and for the children.

When she saw Anne sitting by the window in her living room, looking at the asters in her garden, when she ate the food Anne offered her, when she wore the clothes Anne lent her, she knew she would save Anne and the children. Anne was not a bad person. But she was sinking in the flesh. The flesh of her hands was cool and dry; her forehead was cool. There were pink spots on her cheeks that gave her white skin color. For a while, that first day in the living room, Laura was afraid Anne didn't like her, didn't want her to take care of the children. But Anne did like her; she had called her back. She probably had to check on something. Money, maybe. Laura would have worked without money, for her food, her bed.

One day Anne, if Laura helped her, would be saved. But now she was drowning. Laura could see her; drowning as the damned souls drowned in flames of eternal fire. She could see Anne as no one else could see her. She was drowning in flesh. Her own cool flesh. The soft flesh of her children.

From the bedroom Anne had fixed for her, Laura could look out the window to the garden. Now there were chrysanthemums, and later, Anne had said, the crocuses would come, and then there would be daffodils. Anne asked Laura if she was interested in gardening. She lied and said she was. She would learn to be. Her mother had not been. She would know more than her mother. Of course she already knew more of the Spirit. But Anne would teach her something (the flowers in the garden, the herbs in their clay pots) that her mother wanted to know but did not. Wanted to do but could not.

It was in a garden that the Spirit had first come to her.

The first coming of the Spirit had been beautiful. She was at her grandmother's. Her grandmother was good at gardens. Laura was in her grandmother's garden. Her mother had just been unkind to her. What was it she had said, "Go outside and blow the stink off you"? It was because her sister Deborah had taken the blouse she had wanted to wear that morning. Laura had planned the clothes that she would wear each day on their visit to their grandmother. Debbie had taken her blouse. It was pink with embroidered flowers on it. Laura had embroidered them. She washed the blouse by hand and ironed it. She particularly wanted to show it to her grandmother. Then her sister came down wearing it. Debbie looked just like their mother. She was beautiful, just like their mother. And their mother loved her best, loved her only.

Her sister Debbie walked into their grandmother's kitchen wearing Laura's blouse. Even now, even though she no longer felt anger because the Spirit lived in her, Laura could remember how she felt that day. Behind her eyes were dark things, sea creatures, the roots of trees uprooted, buildings falling on buildings. She ran toward her sister and hit her hard across the back.

"It's mine," she said. "You can't wear it."

Her mother came toward them. She pulled Laura away from Debbie. With the back of her hand she struck Laura. The large ring that their father had bought her for their fifteenth anniversary hit Laura in the eye. Her mother kept on hitting her. Four times she hit her in the face.

"How dare you touch that child," their mother said. Debbie was fourteen, three years younger than Laura. She was not a child.

Laura remembered how her teeth felt on the inside of her lips. She had bitten her lips until they bled. The blood was salt and thick, her teeth were dry against the sore flesh she had bitten. She stood before her mother. She was bigger than her mother. She could feel her eyes were wild.

"It's my blouse, and she can't have it."

She was standing above her mother. Then she realized that she could kill her. It was possible; it might be easy. In a minute it could happen, and it would be done. And she knew her mother knew. With small steps, frightened, Laura's mother moved toward her own mother, Laura's grandmother.

"You don't deserve this family," her mother said. "I don't know where you came from. You can't be my child."

"Cecilia," said the grandmother.

Her mother was not afraid any longer. She knew that Laura was not going to kill her. The skin around her eyes looked bruised; her dark eyes, swelling with her anger, were a monster's eyes. They reached out, as if they were hands, as if they could choke her daughter. She walked close to her.

"You great big ugly clod. You might as well let your sister have all your clothes. You'll never be anything. You're not my child, you never were. Get out of here. I can't stand the sight of you. Get out and blow the stink off you. Don't come back till you're fit to be a member of this family."

Even now, even now that she no longer felt anger, she remembered. She had run to the end of the garden. Her tears were splitting her body, as if lightning had split her, as if her veins were fire, as if the nerves that spread out from her spine were wires, cutting her hot flesh. She lay down on the grass. She pressed her eyes into the flesh of her arms. She was thinking that she wanted her mother to die. She was thinking that she could have killed her.

Then it came. It was not anything she saw or heard. She knew only that it was with her. She knew she had been chosen. In her heart she knew the words, "You are the chosen one, the favored of the Lord."

She was not frightened, for she knew it was the Spirit of the Lord inside her, coming with power and with love. She walked back into her grandmother's kitchen. That was the beginning of her power. No one was there but her father.

"I'm sorry," said her father. "I guess your mother got a little carried away."

She smiled at him with her new smile, the smile that she always had now, the smile that had the wisdom of the Spirit, and the Spirit's peace. "It doesn't matter," she said to her father.

And it didn't. Before the Spirit came, she would have been grateful to her father. Angry that he had not spoken sooner, but grateful that he was on her side. But she knew then that she would never need him anymore. Her poor father. She prayed that he, too, would one day find the Spirit. Her mother's flesh was choking him. But with her mother dead, he would find the Spirit. She prayed for him to find it, but no more than for anyone else. He meant nothing special to her. Once she had needed him to love her. But now she was loved in the Spirit. She was the chosen of the Lord. Now people needed *her*.

She was good with children; she understood them, and they liked her, she was sure they did. Even that time with the Chamberlains, the children had liked her. Only the parents hadn't understood. They said the things she told the children gave them nightmares. But it wasn't true. It was the presence of the Spirit that made the parents uneasy. She showed them their uncleanness by her life among them, by the presence of the Spirit. It was the darkness in the parents that gave the children nightmares. Her power was not great enough, the evil in the Chamberlains had beaten her. Now she knew, from Jesus' words to the apostles, how she must proceed with Anne and with her children. She had not been wise with the Chamberlains, she had spoken the name of the Spirit too early, and the darkness had overcome them. Now she would not speak the name of God, not speak of the Spirit, until the time was right. They would not know the Spirit was among them until the power of the Spirit had subdued their darkness. Then she would conquer. Then they would all be saved.

The Chamberlains had asked her to leave. But they had said they would recommend her to another family. Their children had learned a great deal, the Chamberlains said, from Laura. She had taught the little girl to cross-stitch, the boy to make flowers, birds and animals from clay. Perhaps another family, the Chamberlains had said, with a more religious background. . . . As it is, we are not believers.

Not believers. Of course not, you are choked with wickedness. She had not said this to them. She wanted them to recommend her.

It would be different with Anne Foster. Now she knew more; now the power of the Spirit was much greater. It would not be difficult to save them all. She would begin with the children.

As a little child, she had wanted the heat that jetted round her mother's body. But her mother said, "Don't hang on me." Once, when Laura was a child, her mother had pushed her off the arm of the couch and she had cut her lip and bled and bled so that everyone was frightened. "Well, I told her not to hang on me," her mother said, cleaning Laura's face with quick, sharp hands that did not linger, did not treasure. "Why can't you be more like your sister? Do you see her hanging on me all the time?"

Debbie was quick and dark and like the mother dancing. She sang and snapped her fingers. She told stories with mistakes in them just to make people laugh. She hung upside down from the trapeze on the swing set. The children in the swimming pool were her friends, dove and rose up from the water holding hands with her, played treasure hunt and went for shining pennies with her at the bottom of the pool. Laura wore a bathing cap because she didn't like to get her thick hair wet, swam by herself in straight rows that she counted up like gold, feared hanging from the trapeze and swung alone in silence, kicking the sand with the toe of her shoe. Then her mother shouted at her for her dirty shoes. "Make friends, be more independent."

She had one friend named Warren. He came to the house. He went into the pool with her. But then he had an accident. He moved his bowels in the pool. He spoiled the clearness of the water (so clear you could see pennies on the bottom that her father threw for children to go after). The pool had to be completely emptied, her mother said, screaming at her, hitting her, saying it was just like her to bring filth home with her. Warren was not allowed to come again.

But she wasn't filthy. She was careful, she was tidy. Debbie was the one whose book covers were ripped, whose clothes were on the floor after she tried on outfit after outfit to see which ones would make her girlfriends love her. Debbie never helped. Laura helped her mother in the kitchen. She tried to help her mother keep the house clean, but her mother wasn't interested and thought Laura cleaned house to make her feel bad. "You love it, don't you, putting me in a bad light."

Debbie taught their mother the new dances. Married at seventeen, a mother six months later (Laura had been conceived in sin), her mother said she had never had the time to be young. She liked to stand next to Debbie at the mirror. She liked to say, "We could be sisters, couldn't we," putting her hands around her waist, then around Debbie's. Laura would hang back, heavy, her braids a weight on her shoulders, pushing her down to the earth while they danced high above it, light, like stars that burnt and dazzled.

She would teach Anne's children that the flesh was nothing; a mother and her children, all that famous love, was nothing more than flesh to flesh, would drown them all, would keep them from the Spirit.

But she must be careful. She must not make the mistake she had made with the Chamberlains. She would teach the girl to make clay animals. She would build models with the little boy. She would let them cook with her in the kitchen, make whatever mess they wanted and then clean it up without a word. They would look through field glasses at birds. They would pick wildflowers. They would dip leaves in glycerine and paste them into books. The children would love her. They would have fun. She would not talk to them about the Spirit until she knew that they loved her.

D arling, it's Ianthe," said the voice on the telephone. "You've got to come over quick, right now, immediately. I'm dying, I'm in absolutely desperate straits. You've no idea."

"What is it, Ianthe?" Anne said distantly. Ianthe had interrupted her while she was working, and she'd known her long enough to be wary of her reports of disaster. Ianthe was the woman to whom she'd lost the job of director of the college gallery. Tall, knife-thin, with a shock of Veronica Lake blond hair and lips colored in red and outlined in a darker reddish purple, she had become, improbably, one of Anne's best friends. For one thing, they worked well together.

"You can keep track of the fucking old masters in the basement," Ianthe had said to Anne when they began working together, "and deal with the alums who want to give us their uncles' watercolors for a tax writeoff. Whereas I can suck off the entire Board of Trustees for a Stella when the time comes. We'll make a splendid team."

And, in fact, they did. Ianthe's vision of their division of labor was not far off. Anne organized the gallery's holdings, kept records, varied the displays and wrote exhibit notes that were generally admired. Ianthe expanded the collection so that the gallery was lauded as unusually representative of current trends. Anne knew that she could never have done what Ianthe did. She could never, for example, have accomplished Ianthe's latest feat, the purchase, for a hundred and twenty-five thousand dollars, of a painting by an Italian Neo-Expressionist. In tabloid colors, it presented a dog biting the thigh of a child who sprawled among his schoolbooks, screaming.

"Darling, it's this brain-damaged child they've hired to replace you," Ianthe was saying. "I don't know where they found him, the state hospital, no doubt. He's probably the latest experiment in community care. I know they dope him up and let him out in the morning and send him to me to help me run the gallery."

"Jack is really very good, Ianthe. If you'll calm down and explain things to him, I'm sure he can handle everything."

"There's no use explaining things to him, my love. He doesn't have a brain. Simply, physiologically, he doesn't have one. So there's no use wasting each other's time. You speak to him; you're used to your adorable children. Speak to him as you would to Peter. Or to Sarah, perhaps. Draw him pictures."

"I'll speak to him, Ianthe. Only not right now."

"He's right here, darling. At my elbow, as usual; he's free to talk."

"But I'm not. I'm working. I'll come over in the afternoon."

"Oh, excuse me. I forgot that you'd suddenly joined the ranks of the illustrious. Forgive this poor day laborer for daring to interrupt."

"I'll come to the gallery this afternoon. I'll see you at three."

Ianthe's insults disturbed Anne not at all. It was part of the texture of their friendship. Ianthe felt free to say perfectly dreadful things to Anne, but, unlike the things that Hélène said to her, they were never really disturbing because either they were so far off the mark as to have no wounding power, or they were clearly true, something she'd known about herself forever. And with Ianthe, she had access to a life that had nothing to do with Selby. Ianthe left town on the first bus she could on Thursday afternoons to spend the weekends in New York, where she had an apartment. She was the only person in the town, Anne reckoned, not to own a down coat; in the winter she pushed through the snow in her mink, ruining pair after pair of Charles Jourdan shoes while the rest of the community made its wholesome unbeautiful way, every inch puffed out, protected and concealed. And in Selby, where everyone behaved well, where even homosexuals kept up a premise of solid and undangerous monogamy, Ianthe had flamboyant, public love affairs. Each of her affairs was like a brilliant, terrible child she brooded over—now Medea, now the Angel of the house. It was one of the things Anne admired her for; it took real courage, she felt, at forty-eight to give oneself over so wholeheartedly —the quick rush of initial faith, the brief *luxe* of the heyday of a love affair, the bitter unraveling, and with Ianthe, the long period of diamond vengeance. Her vengeances were splendid. She ended her affair with Adrian Rosen—who was, of all the people in Selby, Anne's closest friend—by throwing all his clothes into the wood stove and falling asleep in his bed while they burned.

Anne would always be grateful to Ianthe for returning to her her faith in her own abilities. After she'd lost her job at the Gardner Museum in Boston, she'd been convinced she had no talents and no right to the world of work.

It was 1974 when she'd lost the job. The Arabs had raised the price of oil. Of course people would take their money from museums. Nothing to do with you, they reassured her, those silvery administrators telling her that they must let her go. Your work is excellent. It's just our funding's been cut way back. And we have to get rid of a few of the younger people.

But how could it not reflect on her, that great exposing beam they cast upon her? Nine other people had been let go, people she respected, whose work she knew had been praised. But three had been kept on, and she hadn't been one of them. For months, she'd reviewed her performance and her work: what had she failed to do or done too much of? In the end, she felt she simply lacked distinction, that she was the sort of person no one would be afraid to let go: there would be no need to feel uncomfortable, to feel afraid.

She had felt shame then, as she had never in her life felt it before. Always, she had been the one who got the prizes, was accepted into the right schools, earned the high honors. For the first time then, she understood the pain of all the children sent down after missing a word in the spelling bee while she had stood on the stage, triumphant; she understood the desire to hide that friends of hers who hadn't been let into the right schools had felt. She knew, for the first time then, that failure made you feel like a criminal; that it became a part of your physical life, like the convict's shaved head. For years she'd felt marked by it, and only Ianthe had allowed her to enter the world again, almost naturally. In praising her —particularly since she praised so rarely—it was as though Ianthe had bought her new clothes and allowed her to leave behind her convict's suit; it was as if she'd built her a house in which she could grow her hair so that she could, once more, walk out into the street unmarked and common.

Besides all that, Ianthe made her laugh, and she loved to laugh; that was the common thread among her three best friends in town, Ianthe, Adrian and Barbara Greenspan. They made her laugh. She had always known herself to be the perfect straight man; she was like her father in that. It was fine; she enjoyed her friends enormously. And now she could endure Ianthe's insult, for, after all, she had got her way. She would *not* go to the gallery until afternoon. She could go back to work.

She'd taken over Michael's study. For days she'd hesitated. The room was his; it was the one room in the house set apart, exclusively owned. Even the air seemed of a different quality: cooler, lighter, as if the children's flesh, the smells of cooking, the fog of argument, the quick dense breath of sex had not come near it. The books were Michael's, and the furniture; he had chosen the color of the walls—Williamsburg blue—and the Turkish carpet, light blue and red, the best in the house. On the walls were his pictures, the photograph of Colette, a page from an eighteenth-century edition of *Candide,* the Daumier print she had saved for six months to buy him. She fingered the raised letters on the spine of the bound copy of his dissertation: *The Image of the City in Balzac, Zola, and Proust.*

She had been working at the dining room table. That was all right as long as the children were in school or asleep in the evenings. But Laura was around now, and she didn't feel it was right to limit her free access through the dining room. With Laura around she never felt that she was unobserved.

Yet she had to admire the job Laura was doing; she was wonderful with the children, marvelous around the house. On one of Anne's days in the city, the refrigerator stopped running. Laura took care of the melting ice cream, running to the floor like a sticky cartoon rainbow; she saved the stews and casseroles and vegetables Anne had spent days cooking and freezing. She scrubbed the floors and moved the refrigerator, stowed the perishables next door at the Greenspans', kept the milk safe for the children by filling the sink with bags of ice. When Anne got home, there was only the report of a crisis averted, not the desperate physical evidence. Laura had even called the electrician Barbara had recommended, for she saw that the lights were dimming and there had to be a problem with the wiring. The electrician had come and had concurred; he could fix the problem temporarily, but the house would need complete rewiring. Laura had made an appointment with him for Saturday, when Anne would be around to talk to him at length.

Everything was working out extremely well. It was simply that Anne didn't want a stranger in her house. She was ashamed at her own unreasonableness. She needed help, and certainly Laura did not intrude. She was quiet; she spent a great deal of time reading. Anne knew she had no right to ask her to read in her bedroom instead of the living room.

She sat on the couch and read the Bible. In Anne's inner life there were no grounds that could allow her to accept her unease about this. Nevertheless it made her uneasy, and she was afraid that Laura sensed it. Laura was sensitive, Anne knew, for she was homeless, and she had the sharp or, rather, limpid understanding of the thoroughly displaced who earn their place by knowing what will be the next thing to occur. What had happened to her parents? Anne knew there must have been something, some clear damaging event, for Laura didn't speak of her family.

It was hard to say what interested Laura. She was devoted to the children. No one, Anne felt, had ever before satisfied Peter's enormous craving for attention, had given him so much that there was enough for Sarah's more modest appetite without making him feel starved. And Laura was fond of doing needlework. She was making a pillow cover; she was duplicating, on her own, the pattern of the pillow on the couch, a Shaker tree of life, which Anne loved and whose ragged dull condition she had, in Laura's presence, mourned. Yet she was also working a large and simple pattern of Minnie Mouse on a shirt of Sarah's. And she gave no indication that one piece of work pleased her more than the other. She'd seemed surprised when Anne suggested it was only out of kindness that she did Sarah's shirt, that the Shaker pattern must be a particular pleasure, a particular satisfaction. Work, beauty, those abstractions one can apply to tasks only after reading many books—what did they mean to a girl like Laura? And what was in her mind as she sat reading the Bible?

Anne knew that it was like no reading she had ever done; what Laura was doing wasn't really reading. She was doing what she did not to get information, or for pleasure, or to get ahead. She was reading, Anne could see, to keep her place. Or perhaps there was something more to it. Anne had never understood the religious life. She could be moved by it when it led to some large public generosity—the worker priests, the nuns in El Salvador. But there was another side to it she couldn't comprehend. People had religious lives in the way that people wrote poetry, heard music. She had read, in the course of her education, since she had been interested in medieval art, the writings of the mystics. She understood that they lived in the desire for something like beauty, and that they had experienced something like creative inspiration. But it was something like and something like. What it was, finally, she could come in no way close to.

That was what disturbed her, watching Laura read the Bible with the same expression on her face as she had when she embroidered the tail of Minnie Mouse. Was she experiencing something great, something profound? What made Anne uneasy was that she didn't know *what* Laura was doing, sitting there appearing to read. Some other life was going on, and Anne had no access to it. So it disturbed her. Yet she couldn't ask Laura to read in her room. Finally she wrote to Michael. He answered the moment he got the letter, teasing her for her hesitation, telling her of course she must use the study, it was foolish for the best room in the house to go to waste.

How unsatisfactory both those letters had been, like all the letters between them. How much had been left out! The feel of the room, its air and weather, the physical truth of her sense of usurpation—it was in her shoulders that she felt it; if she had been with Michael and moved her shoulder half an inch, he would immediately have understood. And there was no way of writing about sexual desire, no proper words for body parts that felt drawn up, stretched, emptied out. There was no such thing, she thought, as an honest letter for a modern. We no longer need wait months, years, for the sound of the actual voice, the glimpse of the actual body. Therefore we cannot sit without self-consciousness and write a letter.

It was very different for Caroline's age, she thought, turning to a packet of her letters. At twenty-four, Caroline was writing to her father from Paris. Dissatisfied with her instruction at the Pennsylvania Academy, she had battled for two years to go abroad, to work at the Académie Julian.

You can save your fears about my debauched life for your friends at the Atheneum. I arrive at the Academy at eight, where I work all day beside a Miss Oglethorpe of Bangor, Maine, with the demeanor precisely of a boiled owl, and a character to match. On the other side is Mlle. Dubuffet, of a good Norman family, whose complexion is, I assure you, the shade and grain of a raw beefsteak. I work till the light fails, what there is of it, and dine in a heatless *pension* with the inestimable Aunt Addie, on a soup and meat. For which you ought to envy and commend me, for reasons at once gustatory and economic.

At night it is so cold that we retire early to our beds, unless we are invited out by one of the ubiquitous Americans, tipped off, one supposes, by you or your minions, to keep an eye out for the health and safety of two American ladies from the right sort of family. I assure you, our family tree takes on a stature here it can in no way aspire to in Philadelphia. But then the soil is poorer here, the forests thinner, the branches less leafy and the leaves less lush. This, of course, applies only to American species. Of the native nothing can be said yet, since this correspondent has dined out only with Americans!

That I have discovered Rembrandt in the Louvre, that his *Christ at Emmaus* made me reach for the excellent linen of my pocket handkerchief, so awash was I on the flood tide of feminine artistic feelings, cannot, I know, interest you in the least. Yet since I have crossed the ocean on the magic carpet of your banknotes, I feel you've a right to know of my doings. I am one of the best in my class.

Did she love her father? Did she hate him? Such a letter made it impossible to know: the tone made the question seem irrelevant. The weak concerns of a weakly spirit. On the same day she had written to her sister:

Dearest Magpie,
I have only now begun to live. I am excited as a baby. From the
moment I got off the boat at Antwerp, everything entranced me:
impressions cling to my skin like sea spray. Just off the boat at Antwerp
I saw the Rubens on the ceiling of the Cathedral. Maggie, there was
never painting like it—blues and reds of richness indescribable. All the
canvases in America have been painted with mud. Everything inspires
me here: the rooves, tawny, alive as sleeping animals, the faces, the girl
who does my laundry with the arms of a goddess. That I can see my
breath in my bedroom, that we have had no sun in a fortnight, means
nothing. I work all day and sleep like a farmer, unless I have spent the
night being dined by some odious Yankee. I speak less French here than
I did at Miss Thwaite's. I long to meet the natives. Come join me,
dearest mouse, there is nothing to look at in America. I miss you all,
though I haven't much room in me for that sort of thing right now, so
stuffed am I with the joy of this new life. Yet I wish to know that you
all cannot do without me, including our Reverend Father.

To her father, she was baiting, forced, bullying of him and of herself. Her passions were "feminine artistic feelings," in which he would not be interested. She was right, no doubt; he never wrote a word to her about her work. Yet she could say to him what she could not say to her sister, "I am one of the best in my class." The proud daughter of a proud father. Was there any residue, Anne wondered, of what was siphoned off by pride, by dull, domestic tyranny, hurt feelings, spirits quenched? Some durable tough skin that kept love safe and fresh and lively? As a young woman, Caroline had been proud of her father, with a pride only remoteness could inspire. Something in her drew up straighter in her love for him, this successful lawyer, club member, community face. He was a Philistine, a despot, yet he gave her the money to go abroad and study. From him she learned her love of sailing, of the sea itself; it was he who taught her to ride. She wrote him, after a bad fall from a horse in the Bois de Boulogne: "For this I have you to thank. The one skill you saw fit to impart to a daughter has not left me with a broken neck only through God's grace and the stubborn stuff I'm made of, for which, I suppose, I am also in your debt." Did Caroline know her father? He was the only member of the immediate family whom she never painted. The lovely early Impressionist canvases recorded a universe exclusively female. *The Breakfast Party* implied a summer world of women left in the country with their children, while the men sat, hot in their wool suits, unable even to strip to their shirt sleeves, traveling on the weekend to the husband's and the father's role.

Anne thought of her own father, that loving and yet vague man whom she felt she knew, even now, as a figure of romance. What was his place in the mess of the family life? She could never cast him as a villain. Even to call his face into her mind made her smile. His face had something goofy about it: his cheeks were round; his chin disappeared into his neck; he was six feet four, two hundred and fifty pounds. He'd been bald as long as she had memory of him. She was sure that his success as a lawyer was due to his goofy look: he appeared too simple to be planning something underhanded. Yet in court he could be eloquent. She had heard him plead, had watched him, overcome with pride. He believed in justice and reason; he lived justly, reasonably. He had defended blacks in the segregation years, demonstrators, draft evaders at the time of Vietnam. She'd always been proud of him in a way she couldn't ever have been proud of her mother. There was distance between them; he left the family in the morning, bringing them at night, as if they were in quarantine, news of the world.

That romance of the distant father, which in their different ways both she and Caroline had shared, would be utterly foreign to her children. Would they have lost anything, never having lived beside a stranger in the family? Michael had tended his children in illness, changed their diapers, fed them, come home, when they were little, every day for lunch. She could have wept, sometimes, at his tenderness toward the children when he performed for them what to her were ordinary tasks. He had no memory of a father's tenderness; his father was a cipher, less than that, a hole, a wound. Impossible to know if he was even living. Michael had no memory of him, and his mother kept no pictures. Her descriptions of him Anne always believed untrustworthy, rendered as they were in the language of fan magazines or romance novels. Could he really have been so perfectly the stage villain? Was "tall, dark and handsome" really the way to describe him? Did he really twirl a black mustache? She would never know, and more important, neither would Michael. But his success as a father was a product of his history; whether he was successful because he had no model for paternity, or because he was trying to overshadow one, she never knew.

She put Caroline's letters away. Now she would go down to her family. She could explain to no one that opening the door of her study (Michael's study, really), she reentered the temperate climate, walked again on land. She felt as if, opening the door, walking into the hallway, she should shed some clothing or equipment, like an astronaut. Walking into the hallway, she put on weight; one foot went in front of the other. Only when she was out of it could she realize her different life behind the door. She was with Caroline there, a woman dead for forty-five years. She knew, she felt, a tremendous amount about her. Yet she knew nothing, or it could all be wrong. She didn't know, for instance, how her voice had sounded. Had Caroline Watson walked into the house and, standing at the bottom of the landing, called her name, she would not have known who was calling. She would have come out fearfully, expecting a stranger.

And yet I know her, Anne thought; I know her almost as I know my own children. I know her eighteen-year-old drawings, her watercolors of her dogs, her sisters, her charcoal sketches from antique casts, her first dark oils. I feel, although I cannot say it, what would have pleased her in this room, what on the street would have caught her eye. I understand what happened, how her blood raced, when, seeing the canvases of Manet, she felt the nature of light had been revealed. How, later, looking at Japanese prints like everybody else in Paris, she believed she had been wrong to crowd her canvases, learned something of the airiness of simple space. I know what she felt seeing the colors of Kandinsky, of Matisse. I know why she envied her friend Bonnard: his calm exuberance, his simple joy. I know all this, and looking at a painting, at the curve of a girl's neck, I am drawn to this woman. I am connected. Because alone, like someone on the moon, I have looked again and again in silence. I have read her handwriting, learned the names of her friends. Because alone in silence slowly I have thought about her many hours, putting from my mind all other things I love. And now we are connected. In the bone. This woman, whom I know and do not know at all, is part of my life like my own children.

Yet, she thought, walking down the stairs of her house, hearing her heels on the wooden floor as if they were somebody else's, it is nothing like life with the children. In the room with Caroline she was weightless. Sometimes it frightened her, the speed of her blood, the giddy sense of being somewhere else, in some high territory, inaccessible. With the children, there was never any flying off, flying up. A mother was encumbered and held down. Anne felt that she was fortunate in that she loved the weighing down, the vivid body life the children lived and gave her. Yet it was always a shock—walking into her kitchen, seeing her stove, her pots, real fruit in a real bowl, not one of Caroline's still lifes. There was a moment always, when she saw the children, when her body gave a start as if she had missed a step. Then there was a click, and her mind slipped into a smooth familiar track. She thought about meals, about laundry; the names of her children's teachers appeared, replacing the names of Caroline's friends in Paris. The children came to her, and in a still, heavy heat she entered once more the life of their bodies, her body. She put back on her skins; she embraced, was embraced. She put on, once again, that other life, beautiful and heavy-scented as a dark fruit that grew up in shadow, the life of the family.

But that day when she came downstairs, no one was in the kitchen. Laura had left a note saying she had taken the children for a walk to look for leaves. It was November now. She worried that the children weren't warm enough. But Laura was entirely dependable. She knew she ought to be glad that the children were with her, doing something enjoyable, something interesting. Yet she felt let down. She wanted the presence of her children, their voices, the feel of their skin, their clothes. The house seemed too large, and chill and damp. She made herself a cup of coffee she did not want.

Suddenly she felt a failure. She ought not to want the children now. If she were really gifted, really meant to do distinguished work, she wouldn't be missing her children. She'd feel freed to go back to work. But for her it was impossible. Having thought of the children, having desired them, she couldn't now go back into the room to Caroline. She sat at her kitchen table watching the sky turn vivid, turn colder. She walked over to the window, listening for voices.

The children came in with Laura, already beginning, as they saw their mother in the kitchen, to fight over the leaves they had collected, over who saw what first and who owned which specimen. Laura hung back as they strove toward Anne: grievance flickered round their heads like haloes.

"The thing is," Peter said, "I saw this copper beech leaf in the book, and we don't even have any in the neighborhood. It's a *miracle*. She doesn't need it. She doesn't have a real collection like I do. I'm the one that needs it."

"I saw it first," said Sarah.

"Tell her I'm the one that needs it."

Need. Would he always be saying that to women? *"I'm the one that needs it."* And would Sarah, stuck in the track of a useless justice, always be saying no through pride of claim? And now they turned to her.

"Peter," she said, "part of having a collection is the difficulty of completing it. It's the satisfaction of getting something after you've waited for it."

"But I need it, and she doesn't."

"But I saw it first."

"Couldn't you trade her something for it, Peter?"

"I don't want anything else," said Sarah.

"Well, then, Peter, if you've found *one,* surely there must be others."

"No. There are no copper beeches around here. It's a *miracle* that it was there. I'll never find another one."

"It's awfully important to Peter, Sarah. Couldn't you give it to him this once?"

"No, because I found it. And you're always on his side."

Was it true? Did she favor one over the other? For her, each incident was discrete. But for them, the decisions were a Persian carpet, the Bayeux tapestry, mercilessly telling some complicated sibylline tale.

"There are no sides, Sarah," she said.

"Yes there are. There's his and mine."

Exasperated, Anne took the leaf and put it in the high cabinet where she hid things from them.

"You're both being awful. Neither of you can have it."

"You stink," said Peter to his mother.

Sarah began to cry. Anne took Peter by the shoulders and shook him. "You may not speak to me like that. Go upstairs until I call you."

Sarah sat on the floor, rubbing her eyes with her fists; Laura was still holding back, holding the children's coats, watching their mother. Ashamed, aware that she was being watched, as if she had been caught in some indecent petty crime, Anne smiled at Laura, granting her the complicitous look she hated: adults locking eyes in knowing, close agreement over the deficiencies of children, their injustices, their wrong proportions. She hated it because she understood how children thought, what it was that cut their issues out for them, a diamond knife on glass. Justice. Property. What they fought for was not trivial. Yet it could not be allowed. They couldn't keep their knife-hard edges or all life would be impossible. And it had an astonishing power to ruin life for her, when her children fought. It broke up everything, destroyed all hope. Alone with the children, she could understand all this, her part in it, their part. But it was a business like an adulterous love affair that should never be made public; opening it to outsiders could only coarsen the grain. She smiled at Laura, and Laura smiled back at her, that odd smile with its mixture of amusement and unamusement, with its cool, withholding certainty, and, just possibly, with its contempt.

Anne bent over and took Sarah in her arms. She must stop attributing these complicated things to Laura, finding messages in her looks like a soothsayer examining birds' entrails. To make up to Laura for her crabbed surveillance, she offered her a glass of wine.

"I never drink, Anne, thank you," Laura said.

Anne felt herself blush, as if the girl had accused her of being both a drunkard and a boor. "Of course you don't. How stupid of me. Would you like cocoa?"

"Wonderful."

"Cocoa?" Sarah said. "Can I get Peter?"

"Yes," said Anne. "We'll all make it together."

Peter came down the stairs with his sister, both of them chastened, loving, guilt drawing them together like a weak magnetic field. Sarah got down the measuring cup. Peter took out the cocoa. They took turns measuring the cocoa, the sugar, the milk, the pinch of salt. They took turns stirring the mixture. There are my children, Anne said to herself, these are the ones I missed. She could smell their thin high sweat; they should have taken off their sweaters. But it was autumn and she understood their feelings: woolen clothes on such a day were a pleasure in themselves.

She brought the cocoa to the table on a tray. The children sat next to her, showing her their leaves. The thickish light fell on their hair. She touched the heads of her children, feeling the texture of their hair. Then she looked up at Laura. She was standing back and smiling. They had excluded her; she sat outside the frame, outside the circle of the light. Guiltily, Anne said, "You must thank Laura for the wonderful expedition."

"Oh, yes," Peter said.

"Why don't you give her a thank-you kiss?" Anne said to Sarah.

The children got up and walked out of the circle of the lamplight. How sweet they were; how hungrily the poor girl took their kisses. She was a girl who had not, it was clear, been held enough, been treasured. So it was a fine thing: she was good for the children, the children were good for her. Things were really working wonderfully. Anne knew she was very lucky. She was sure that when she got more used to living with a stranger, her unpleasant feelings would just disappear. She brought the cups to the sink, ashamed of herself for wishing Laura were not there.

———————

It was a clear day early in November. That morning as she'd come down on the bus, the mist had risen. Gradually it revealed the road. A little at a time it burned away and left behind it hills and mountains. Trees appeared where seconds earlier a white fog seemed a permanence, like earth or stone. But it was lunchtime now; she walked the forty-five blocks from the Columbia library to the restaurant that Ben had chosen. The streets she walked on were struck by sun. She watched it glance off buildings, fall in solid bars upon the sidewalks and the streets.

She'd worked all morning in the library. All the time she worked, she felt like an impostor. She had no business being there, she thought. It was possible that she looked like the others, but it was a lie. She was nothing like them. They were twenty, they were twenty-five or they had written fifteen books and thirty articles, they could sit for hours turning pages, writing things on cards. They never wanted to get up. Their minds—she could almost see their minds hovering above their pages, lively, angular— could settle on the things before them. They weren't always thinking of their children—they didn't have children, none of them had children, she was sure of it—they were thinking of the words, the print. They were saying words in their minds like "iconography" and "plastic form." Of course she said them too, but she was also thinking words of one syllable, home words, the names of foods, toys, children's games. She was looking at Eakins' *The Clinic of Dr. Agnew* and worrying that she hadn't taken Sarah to the dentist. She thought she'd have to tell Ben it was impossible. She couldn't do the job. He had misjudged her, imagining she still was what she once had been.

How could she possibly do it? What she had to do was build a house for a woman she loved. Like a pioneer husband claiming the forest, she must clear through the wilderness. She must create the house entire. She must make sure the structure was sound; but she must also make the details beautiful: the walls must be the right color, the sheets must be perfectly embroidered. Without the house that she would build, the woman she loved, dead forty-five years, unknown to almost everyone, could not be made to live.

Her feelings of insecurity, always high when she worked in a room with other people, were stronger today because she was about to meet Caroline's daughter-in-law, Jane Watson. Anne's first encounter with her, by letter, hadn't been promising. Anne had written, at Ben's suggestion, to ask if she could have access to Caroline's letters that were in Jane's possession. "I hope," she'd written, "these will help me understand the progress of Caroline Watson's work."

"You would do well," Jane had replied, "to look for the explanation of Caroline Watson's progress in the history of art rather than her own personal history. Far too much is made of the biographical today, particularly in the case of women. Marriage, childbirth, menstrual cycles, hysterectomies: they have nothing to do with the work. Give no more attention to them in the career of Caroline Watson than you would in the career of Matisse."

She'd resented Jane's tone. What was she afraid of? People were hungry for details of the lives of women, and there was an industry that provided them. But she would be writing about the work. Menstrual cycles, hys-terectomies—she hadn't dreamed of including anything like that. Of course she was interested in Caroline's life, because she loved the painting. Without it, Caroline would have been simply another unhappy woman of a certain period who had made more mistakes than most.

But that wasn't quite right, she knew; that wasn't quite all of it. There was that hunger that she felt, that women felt, to know details: where women stood in relation to their families, as daughters, sisters, mothers. It wasn't just; it wasn't creditable. Yet one wanted to know, when the women had accomplished something. Whom did they love in relation to their bodies? Whom were they connected to by blood? Like dogs, she thought, like horses. But it wasn't the fact of the connection that was interesting; it was how they got around it. The truth of the matter was that for a woman to have accomplished something, she had to get out of the way of her own body. This was the trick people wanted to know about. Did she pull it off? As if a life were a trick, making doves fly out of a hat, turning an egg into a flower. Stupidly, like the watchers of soap operas, people who were interested in the achievements of women wanted the grossest facts: Whom did they sleep with? Did they have any babies? Were their fathers kind to them, cruel to them? Did they obey or go against their mothers? Infantile questions, yet one felt one had to know. It gave courage, somehow. One wanted to believe that the price was not impossible for these accomplished women, that there were fathers, husbands, babies, beautifully flourishing beside the beautiful work. For there so rarely were.

As she walked she tried to remember everything that Ben had said about Jane Watson. Like most men trying to describe a woman, he began with her looks. His description—beginning with this saying that she had been, in her day, incomparable—made Anne imagine a beauty that was no longer in vogue. It was more than that, a beauty that had somehow ceased appearing in young women. Was it that they were thinner, wore fewer clothes, cut their hair short or left it hanging? Yet Ben had talked about Jane's hair as if it had been deliberately and carefully acquired, an original possession, rare, *trouvé*. Chestnut, he had said, and one must think of the silky shell of a chestnut, smooth and polished and resistant to the lips.

She was a large woman, Ben had said, she had a quite exhausting energy. Knowing herself to be beautiful, understanding that she was from the simple fact of her physical existence craved by people, she didn't worry if people liked her. She was terrifically intelligent, a medievalist. The four-teenth century, you know. Made her career at Bryn Mawr. She didn't care what she said, so she hurt people's feelings. But she didn't notice. She walked through crowds of people, Ben had said, like an admiral walking a deck. People hadn't interested her much when she was young. Except her mother-in-law. They would come to parties and speak only to each other. Cut from the same cloth you might say, Ben had said.

"And what about Stephen?" Anne had asked.

"Poor old Steve. He was one of those disappearing types. On your own with him he could become invisible. And with his mother and then Jane, he was entirely blotted out."

"And yet you're fond of Jane."

"Immensely."

"She sounds so daunting."

"Yes, well, naturally. She's like a swim in a rough ocean. Nothing more exhilarating. Nothing has ever given me the sense of human possibility like an afternoon with Jane."

"All the same I'm frightened. I identify with Stephen in this story. I'm afraid I'll disappear or be blotted out."

"Nonsense. Jane will love you. You're devoted to the same dead woman. What could be a stronger bond?"

"What if Caroline were alive?"

Ben smiled. "She wouldn't let you near her."

Jane was standing in front of the restaurant when Anne approached her, introducing herself. "I've been looking forward to meeting you," Jane said, smiling formally.

There was nothing of the personal about that smile. It was the well-used instrument of a woman who for years has known her power. And Jane Watson stopped the smile, shut it down really, at the first moment it was imaginably civil to do so. Then she used her hand to shield her eyes so that she needn't squint as she looked up the street.

"It's unlike Ben to be late," Jane said. It was unfortunate, Anne thought, how obvious she made her wish, both their wish, for Ben to come to their rescue.

"Yes, but the traffic's bad," Anne said.

"Ben would have walked."

"Of course," Anne said, feeling the point Jane meant to make: she knew Ben better, longer. Anne needn't imagine an equality that wasn't there.

"Ben has known you a long time, I gather. How clever of him to have pulled you out of the hat for this," said Jane.

The comparison made Anne uneasy; it was too apt. A rabbit in a hat. She had felt like that: foolish, white, vulnerable, blinking her eyes at the light. And then there was the audience, the strangers, who would applaud or hiss or not notice. What would happen to her? Would she have to go back into the hat? What did the rabbits do between performances? She didn't have a chance with Jane; she could see it. Jane had decided she was a fool.

"Sorry I'm late," Ben said, insincerely, walking up to them.

"It's bad enough you're making me have a large meal in the middle of the day, and wasting my time in restaurants, which, on the whole, you know I detest. You make it worse by being late," Jane said crossly.

"Yes, darling, I know, you've better things to do with your time. I, on the other hand, can't imagine anything more perfect than a good meal with my two favorite women in the world."

"Nonsense," Jane said, walking into the restaurant before them.

Jane said that they must order lobster. Ben was rolling in money, and besides, it was a tradition for them: they always ordered lobster for their first meal together in America. She ordered for the three of them; she chose the wine. When the waiter approached with their lobsters, she set to with an enthusiasm which, had she not had those light eyes, that straight back, that thick white hair, that perfectly formed head, might almost have shocked. She sucked the legs to get the smallest scraps of meat; she cracked the claws with one swift movement; she ruthlessly bent the back, then poked the tail meat through with a cheerful and expert energy. She accused Ben and Anne of leaving half the good untouched; she took off their plates all they had thought inedible.

The food made her kinder. Pleasantly, she turned to Anne and said, "Now, what do you want to know about Caroline," dismissing as impossible the waiter's offer of dessert.

The question came too suddenly: there was no lead-up. There had been the first near-rudeness, then the food, then Jane had gone straight to the matter: it was, after all, why they were there. She had leapt up to the high place that they all, really, had their eye on. But for herself, Anne knew she had wanted a slow, gradual climb. Now there was Jane, at the top of the precipice, challenging, her hands on her hips, planting her flag. Anne felt she didn't know what to ask, because sitting across from her, still wearing a paper bib with a picture of a lobster printed on it, was a woman whose identity was so complex that it could only baffle her. Jane had known Caroline; she had loved her; she was her daughter-in-law. She and Caroline had built devotion on the usual ground of discord, on the ancient territory of blood feud. It was always odd to reconstruct the relations of the living and the dead; there was something brutal and unreal about it, but with Jane and Caroline the strangeness was more pronounced, for Anne's own relation to Caroline was singular. It ought to have been the same relation she had to Cassatt and Eakins when she was doing her thesis; she was a kind of servant to the work, she was supposed to reveal things, restore things. But now, like a servant whose value might be inestimable, or whose obsession might render her useless, she had fallen in love with her charge.

What would she have felt if, sitting across from her, had been Mary Cassatt's niece, Thomas Eakins' son? What would she have felt if she had just lunched with Vermeer's daughter? It was hard to understand that, outside of the work one was the servant to, the people who had done the work had ordinary lives, ate meals, carried raincoats. One wanted and did not want to believe it; it was a comfort, of course, to think that beautiful things were created by people like oneself, but it was also a disappointment. And what did the world have the right to know about the eater of the meal, the carrier of the raincoat? She remembered Jane's letter; she was, clearly, not of the school that felt the world had the right to full revelation. How far could one go with a woman like Jane? What was the intrusion that made the barely open gate shut down on the forward criminal's impertinent neck? Anne had to meet the challenge. She had planned for this moment; she had prepared what she would do: she would ask a question that had nothing to do with the life.

"I was wondering if Caroline had ever said anything to you about Grünewald. If she, perhaps, had been to Colmar, to see the *Isenheim Altarpiece.*"

Jane looked at Anne as if she held a smoking gun. "What makes you ask about Grünewald?"

Anne met Jane's eye. She felt she had to meet it, or everything would be lost. And she felt that she had a right to say what she had said; it might be wrong, but it was not ridiculous. It wasn't a whim, or a feeling. It was an idea. It had solidity even if it was wrong; it needn't be instantly dissolved by the beam of Jane Watson's extraordinary personal force.

"I got the idea," she said, "from looking at a series of paintings Caroline did of the crippled woman selling flowers. They made me think of the altarpiece—I saw it ten years or more ago, but it kept coming to mind. With those paintings she came to a new use of color, a new willingness to distort the figure, a new attention to detail. And I suspected that she was moved by his genius of the depiction of the posture of grief—I felt that perhaps she had drawn on it a great deal, beginning in about 1906, but continuing, really, throughout her career."

For a moment, Anne thought Jane was about to be angry with her. Her eyes seemed to harden, the high, almost masculine forehead constricted, the beautifully cut nostrils flared and closed, her hand went to her fore-head. Anne stiffened, as if she expected a blow.

"That's right," Jane said. "What you say is exactly right. And tremen-dously good of you to see. No one would think of Grünewald as an influence, but yes, it's exactly right. She made a trip to Germany in 1905, and she never forgot what she saw in Colmar. We went again in 1930, she and I. For years she'd wanted me to see the Grünewalds, she said seeing them was one of the most important events of her life."

She looked up at Anne; for the first time, she met Anne's eye.

"We went to Germany in 1930. Disaster about to be was everywhere, an evil breath. Nazi boys were on the street corners. At the same time, our friends were flourishing, in some doomed way that made one fear. There was a dreadful hectic sickish feeling in the air—one simply couldn't rest. And then we went up to Colmar, to the Grünewalds. We entered the church. Caroline sat down quickly, very heavily. It was the first time I had to see she was an old woman."

Jane took Anne's hand. "I believe we are lucky to have you." She took both Anne's hands and shook them. It was a strange gesture, an awkward gesture, something one of the children would have done to get attention.

"I suppose you want to know why I'm selling the paintings now, after all this time," she went on.

"Of course she does, darling, being rational, unlike yourself," said Ben.

Jane's color rose. "Rational. Send her to that nasty German at the Metropolitan. He was the height of rationality."

"My darling, that was 1954."

"You see, Mrs. Foster," Jane said, "as you know, of course, Caroline died in 1938. Then the war came, and I was in rather a mess about things. I only wanted to do my own work; I lived in the fourteenth century. I tried not to think about Caroline's death. The loss was too great. She was like my mother."

"What about your own mother?" asked Anne boldly.

"She played golf," said Jane.

As a mother, Anne heard the sentence as terrible. Would Sarah or Peter one day tie her up, dispose of her with one dismissive sentence?

"I didn't try to sell any of Caroline's paintings until 1948, when the war was well over. By then she had gone out of date. It was all Abstract Expressionism. Caroline was considered an anachronism, an embarrassing one at that. Embarrassing because she was a woman who painted women, children, landscapes. People reacted as if I were offering them dogs painted on china plates. I got so angry that after a while I stopped trying. I gave several oils to Bryn Mawr; I gave one to the Metropolitan. That was disgusting."

"Disgusting?" asked Anne.

"The man who was in charge nearly sneered when he took it. I'll never forget his look when he unrolled the canvas. He said, 'Spare me lady painters with three names.' He never hung the painting. Do you know about it?"

"It's in their archives. I haven't seen it yet. But I expect it will be different now."

"Perhaps," Jane said. "But, you see, my dear, I resent almost as much people who want to look at Caroline's work *only* because she was a woman. She was the greatest painter of the century. She had nothing to learn from anyone."

No, you are wrong in that, Anne wanted to say, but looked at her coffee cup. Jane would be bound to be disappointed with what she wrote about Caroline. She would not say: "She was greater than all the Fauves, she had nothing to learn from Matisse, Kandinsky." That wasn't the truth. In range, in breaking through new ground, she wasn't the equal of those large men who walked across the twentieth century as if it were Russia. And Anne couldn't go along with Jane's fantasies of her mother-in-law: that she was alone, uninfluenced, unaided. She had had warm and friendly correspondences with Derain and Vlaminck. They were helpful in getting collectors to look at her work. To say what Jane believed would be dishonest, and in doing service to the work of this woman whom she honored, she must keep her honor. Perhaps that would mean she and Jane wouldn't be friends. She had gained Jane's favor through a judgment Jane thought right; she knew that she could lose it just as easily.

"Enough of this," said Jane. "This talk about women makes me bad-tempered. Do you cook, Mrs. Foster?"

"Well, of course, I cook a lot, I have a family. But I don't know how well."

"This cooking can be a dangerous thing for a woman. I used to tell the people at the college I couldn't cook; I always took people out to dinner when I wanted to entertain them. It worked very well; it made people think I had resources. You must never cook a meal for your colleagues, my dear; it makes them imagine a chink in your armor. It makes them think you have too much free time."

"This is all perfect nonsense," said Ben. "I've had meals from Jane for fifty-five years."

"Yes, but we trusted you. Caroline more than I."

"Thank you very much."

"Well, of course, I had reasons she didn't."

"You've never had a reason to mistrust me."

"Only in the least interesting, least important ways. But we believed you liked women; we never felt you were trying to prove we were sports of nature for your own comfort. Anyway, Mrs. Foster, will you call me Jane now?"

"And I'm Anne."

"Anyway, Caroline and I made each other heavenly meals. Then we'd lie to everyone and say we lived on boiled eggs. Which brings me to my point. Will you come to my house on Long Island for Thanksgiving dinner? Bring your children. It will free you from the burden of that burdensome meal, and you can look at the paintings I haven't been able to part with, even for the exhibit. Ben will be there too, so you needn't be terrified."

Anne was so pleased with the invitation that she began to blush. "We'd love to come," she said.

"And now, Benedict, what time is it?"

"Two-thirty-five."

"I really must go. I haven't told you all of why I've decided to sell the paintings. The climate is receptive now, of course. But, you see, we're quite old, Ben and I. We'll probably be dead rather soon. And at least if this exhibit happens while we're alive and nondecrepit, we'll have some hand in it. Now I've told you that, I really will leave you. You see what I mean, Ben, this meal's taken far too long."

She stood up. "Listen, my dear, this is marvelous. We'll have a wonderful time. I'll send the letters and the diaries to you as soon as I get back."

She kissed both Anne's cheeks, kissed the top of Ben's head, and walked out of the restaurant. For a moment, Anne was surprised that all the seated people didn't rise and follow her.

"We'll have a wonderful time," she had said. Anne felt her blood lighten; her skin tingled; she wanted to break into a run. Yes, they would have a wonderful time. Jane had said it. She took Ben's hand and kissed it.

"Let's have dessert," she said.

The waiter brought the pastry cart. Anne took a piece of Black Forest cake, ate it, and called the waiter back for a slice of walnut pie. Licking her fork, she laughed at Ben, abstemious over espresso.

"We're going to have a wonderful time," she said, as if the words were new to her, a foreigner, learning her first English sentence.

She walked to the Frick, not opening the high, formal doors, not entering the cool rooms with their greenish light, inhabited by people with mere leisure. Like a servant, she rang at the side library entrance, a small door cut in the wall, the door to a children's garden. Having only three hours, she quickly requested the sales catalogues of exhibitions where Caroline's work had hung, made notes, and checked her information. It was, as an activity, cool, fast and businesslike, but she had wanted that. Her head was hot from wine in the afternoon, which she rarely had, from meeting Jane, who to anyone, she imagined, was like a series of big waves washing over, sometimes overturning, coating the skin with a cool salt. Yet it was different for Anne: Jane was not only herself, she was Anne's connection to Caroline. And she was the model, the subject, she was the woman in *The Striped Dress*, in *Woman Reading a Letter*. In loving those paintings, one somehow was loving her. And she had sat across the table, eating lobster, talking about Chaucer, Nazis, her mother-in-law, boiled eggs. It was a relief to sit in this overcrowded room, so bottom-heavy with activity. The earnest, worried, or delighted scholars sat in a horizontal line while above them two-thirds of the room was empty air. And Anne belonged there. She was one of them.

The children's room of the Selby library was small and square and overheated; the temperature made the children's complexions look hectic, but they moved in a trance of peace. It was a privilege to be nearly silent there, to look and comment upon books in whispers, to sit at the oak tables turning pages and to smell the smell of paste and crumbling paper. She couldn't bear to hurry the children, so she knew she would be late for the appointment Laura had made with the electrician. She would have to apologize, and that would start things off on the wrong foot. But nothing was worth introducing any element that jarred; she watched their heads bent over their books and saw her children had found sanctuary and must not be disturbed.

When she arrived home the electrician's truck was parked in front of the house. EDWARD CORCORAN, ELECTRICIAN, it said formally, black paint on white metal. She liked the looks of the man who got out. He was a large, heavy man, almost a caricature of a workman—only, he was dressed exactly like Peter, in jeans, a red hooded sweatshirt and sneakers that had once been white. The contrast between the two figures heightened, comically, each of their natures, Peter so thin, edgy, and electrified, Edward Corcoran so slow-moving and massive. He had thin, uncontrollable hair that sprang out in patches and wanted to clump. There were wood chips in his hair. Perhaps he had been walking in the woods. Imagining this, Anne was pleased; she hated to think that the people she did business with had less enjoyable lives than she did.

A small boy got out of the truck and walked seriously beside the man toward the driveway.

"I hope you don't mind me bringing my son with me. My wife's sick," he said.

"Of course. I mean, of course not. Come in. I'll make some coffee. The children can have juice and cookies."

Edward Corcoran's son stood slightly behind him, peeping out at people to the right of his father's thigh. She remembered Peter at that age; each time she saw a younger child, she felt a sharp joy, then a loss, as if she had seen a beloved place—no longer open to her kind—in a geographic film.

Anne said to the little boy, "These are my children, Peter and Sarah. They can show you the house and their rooms. Or you could stay with your father if you like."

The boy disappeared behind his father.

Peter and Sarah went in first. Peter held the door for everyone, as if the occasion called for his best manners. Behind them, Laura walked into the kitchen, smiling.

Anne knew she had to be businesslike and efficient. She wondered if she had made a mistake. Perhaps she shouldn't have offered this man coffee until he had looked around the house. The point was, she knew, not to entertain the man, but to get him to give a fair price, do a good job. Michael always did this sort of thing; she felt on shaky ground; she felt she could be easily cheated. She saw once more that it was nearly impossible as a woman without a man to act on impulse and feel safe.

She decided to speak to Barbara Greenspan. Barbara had recommended him, and Barbara was impossible to cheat. She put the coffee cups in the sink and, showing the man to the basement, walked next door.

"I'm a bit miffed with you," Barbara said, after agreeing to come over. "It's been two weeks since I've had a minute with you. Just the occasional communication from Rebecca of Sunnybrook Farm on the state of your wiring."

Anne felt her shoulders give once more into the stoop of apology. She loved Barbara, but it wasn't always easy, for Barbara was perennially frustrated and ready to see each of Anne's victories as an offense. Their friendship had started in the first years she and Michael had lived in this house; Anne's children and Barbara's were close in age, and neither she nor Barbara was working. Both could think, lingeringly, resentfully, about their Ph.D.'s—Barbara's in comparative literature from Stanford was even more useless, they'd both agreed, than Anne's. Languorously, inefficiently they'd lived their mornings, letting the children stay in pajamas while they drank coffee and cleaned, bundling them up for errands or excursions in the afternoon, trading baby-sitting in the evening or hiring one baby-sitter while the four parents went out. Then Anne had got the job at the gallery, and the balance shifted. Resentment took the place of mutual complicity, apology stepped in where partnership had been. But they still had that rare, valuable thing: they knew each other's children intimately; they could talk to each other about them, respecting each other first as women with good minds. So they got through difficult patches; they were friends. Anne loved Barbara for her dependable generosity, for her mocking wit, which, she felt, could cut through the haze she often slipped into. It was worth the hostility, because with Barbara she always felt at the edge of something.

Barbara hummed with unused power like a machine left to run. She wore her hair long; it was prematurely gray, and you could see she meant her hair to be defiant, as if her mother had always told her that past a certain age women cut their hair or pinned it up. She applied for every job that came up in the town or at the college and got none of them; she bristled with hostility at every interview, and even before she got there, the fame of her rough tongue had preceded her. She was always thinking up plans for herself and her retraining. She would go to dental school; she would become a CPA. She kept saying that she had to do it soon because the median age at which academics left their wives was forty-five and she had only seven years to go with Howard.

But no one was more impossible to imagine leaving his wife than Howard Greenspan. Small, four inches shorter than his wife, looking as if he'd been born in glasses, brought up the only Jew in an Oklahoma town, and a most brilliant mathematician, he thanked fortune every day that a woman like Barbara had seen fit to marry him. He adored his wife, his children. He'd move in a minute, he said, if she could find a job she liked. But nothing ever seemed worth it to her, and so they simply went on, living in Selby next door to the Fosters.

When Anne apologized for her neglect, Barbara said quickly, "Okay, cut the Hester Prynne look. I can't stand it. You shouldn't listen to me, I'm jealous."

"No, you're perfectly right. I just need a little rope."

"To hang yourself? Watch it, you've been talking to children and idiots too much today. Speaking of whom, why don't you get Laura to sit for all the kids tonight, and Howard and you and Adrian and I will go to a movie. Adrian feels quite abandoned since you've taken up a productive life. He's shifted his allegiance to me, and you can imagine what cold comfort that is."

Anne hesitated a moment. She had wanted to use the night to read some of Caroline's letters. But there was Barbara standing in front of her, Barbara whom she had neglected, who was just now doing her a favor, whom she had shared all her time with when time was open, vacant, threatening to swallow them in. She couldn't say no to Barbara. She would try to have them all make it an early night and read the letters when she got home. She could sleep late in the morning; Laura would get the children breakfast. It was the kind of luxury, she knew, that Laura's presence in the house allowed her.

"That would be great," Anne said. "And think of the wonderful gossip it will create: me out with the beautiful Adrian and my husband thousands of miles away."

"Oh, it won't excite gossip. Everyone in town knows Adrian's type. You're about fifteen years too old."

She laughed at Barbara as they walked back to the Foster house, but felt unsettled. Did people think of her as no longer young? Certainly when she was a teenager, people of thirty-eight seemed distant, formidable, immune from romance or real change. But when she was a teenager, thirty-eight-year-old women *were* different. They wore girdles, hats; the children of their friends called them Mrs., they didn't own jeans or sit on the floor at parties. In relation to Laura, for example, she felt terribly young. She felt painfully the absence of authority behind all her domestic requests. But perhaps Laura thought of her as old. Perhaps young men did. Perhaps even Adrian did. She wondered. She would never dare to ask him. Barbara would, about herself, and he would tell her. But between Anne and Adrian there was a formality, a tenderness protected by restraint. So he would sense her fear and calm her with a compliment. She wouldn't know the truth.

Ed Corcoran came up from the basement, writing figures on a clipboard. He smiled when he saw Barbara.

Barbara lowered her eyes, stepped backwards, shifted her weight. Anne had never seen Barbara so off center. Then she understood: Barbara found Ed Corcoran attractive. Anne looked over at him. He was nice-looking; he had nice eyes, nice hands, his air of amused puzzlement was likable, and the way he spoke to his son. But his shirt strained over his belly, he had

had a lot of dental work, his hair was quite peculiar. If he were a woman, he would never be found attractive. She thought that was unfair.

He passed Anne the sheet of paper he had been writing on as if it were bad news.

"Everything's so expensive, it's just terrible. But I think I'm giving you a good price."

Barbara snatched the paper out of Anne's hand before she was able to make sense of the numbers.

"A very good price," she said, smiling over the top of the paper like the younger, clever daughter in a movie about Victorian England.

Anne looked at the paper. It was a terrible amount of money. She had no way of knowing whether it was fair. But she would hire Ed Corcoran. He was such a nice man; he brought his son with him, and Barbara would be furious if she asked for an estimate from anybody else.

========

After the movies, Anne sat next to Adrian in the booth across from Barbara and Howard at the Captree Tavern.

"How's life?" he asked. "I never get to see you."

"You never *come* to see me anymore."

"I do, but you're never available. Your baby-sitter says I mustn't disturb you when you're working. Maybe she thinks I'm a dangerous influence. She always invites me in for coffee, you know."

"Do you come in, Adrian? Have you been in my house while I've been there without my knowing it? How awful. I suppose I've made such a point of telling her I'm not to be interrupted that she's taken me too literally. I must tell her always to interrupt me for you."

"No, love, you mustn't. She's right. You've got more important things to do than talk to me because I'm too neurotic to work in the afternoons."

She leaned against his arm with pleasure. Adrian's regard was a soft pillow that made her feel secure and bolstered. His friendship was a great joy to her. As a lover, she knew, he could only bring a woman grief. She knew more about his love life than she wished she did, for he never confided in her, and he tried to be discreet, but Selby was a small town, and he should never have lived in a small town. He was always having to step over his own sexual history like a defeated general pacing the field. He'd explained his sexual theories to her. What, he'd asked her, is of all human relations the most volatile, the least dependable? The sexual, of course. And what do people put the greatest hope for lasting happiness into? What a foolish investment. One should never be sexually involved with anyone one genuinely cares for. A sexual relationship almost guarantees a loss.

She'd never known if he was being merely courtly, explaining, without saying it, his failure to seduce her. She knew he found her attractive, and that was part of his great value to her as a friend—his obvious, public desirability only heightened the effect. His appreciation of her was, of course, partly sexual—with Adrian it couldn't be otherwise. But it contained no hunger to possess or to diminish: she could bask in the rather florid light in which he bathed all women whom he thought attractive, but on her the light fell muted, cooled. And she could allow herself a minor and entirely benign stirring of sexual feeling without worry. They would never be lovers, but she could lean against his arm, she could take his hand or playfully embrace him as she could not have done had she not been sexually attracted to him in just this right way. Tonight, she was surprised, though; the stirring was the slightest degree stronger. Sexual hunger had added an edge to her pleasure so that she could not, as she customarily did with Adrian, quite relax. She was distracted, but having felt this slight disturbance, she was determined not to betray the beat that she felt had been missed.

"Only you would have this kind of luck," said Barbara, not kindly. "The rest of us, when we're twenty, get picked up by wholesale rug dealers. Anne gets picked up by a famous art historian."

"Barbara, it was hardly a pickup," Anne said. She rarely defended herself from Barbara's attacks, but her friendship with Ben was precious to her in a way that heightened its fragility. She'd known Ben longer than anyone in her life she still kept up with, except her family.

She thought of the time that she had met Ben, eighteen years before, in London. The English summer had seemed strange to her. Strange for it to be July and not to feel the sun at noon with the American insistence that suggests that some appropriate new action, seasonable, transitory, must at that one moment be performed. At home she had never felt totally relaxed in summer. She was incapable of those long sustained torpors that American teenagers who like their summers are born to inhabit. So she was happy walking the London streets, a sweater over her shoulders, wearing stockings, as she had never been entirely happy in the summers at her parents' home.

She had been to college for two years, but in London she felt that she was really alone for the first time. The other Radcliffe girl who had got the same grant she had, but whose course was on Constable and Turner, had moved out of the room she had next to Anne's in the Bloomsbury student hostel. She had met a Lebanese student at the Tate who had invited her to share his flat in Kensington. So she didn't see the other girl again until they sat together on the plane ride home, and the girl, guilty at having deserted Anne for greater luxury, sat silently reading *The Fountainhead* (the Lebanese had been studying architecture) throughout the seven-hour flight.

For two weeks Anne spoke to almost no one. The people in her class, also foreigners, were as reticent as she. And she knew after a week that she hated the Elgin Marbles, all that cool perfection, that imperial restraint, and she was afraid that if she talked too much to her colleagues this would be discovered, and her feeling that she was fraudulently taking money—studying something that she had no interest in, that she would never pursue—would be exposed.

The days were very long, and she often felt that if someone, even a shopkeeper, said a kind word to her, she would burst into tears and beg the person to take her home for supper. Her room at the hostel was bare and anonymous. She bought postcards of the museums she went to and propped them up against the deal-framed mirror, but they didn't help. Her bed was too narrow, the chenille spread had been mended too often, the knobs on her dresser looked menacing if her eyes fell on them in the middle of the night.

The evenings were the worst. She didn't have much money, and her meals were paid for at the YWCA on Great Russell Street. But sometimes she went out anyway—she would go to one of the trattorie run by Sicilians for spaghetti and a glass of wine. That summer, she read Faulkner—it was *Absalom, Absalom!* the first two weeks, and she would bring her book with her to the dark restaurant, thinking how grateful she should be for this opportunity. Once a week she went to a movie, often an American film she would never have dreamed of seeing if she were home. But it was comforting to hear the accents, to see New York or Chicago backgrounds. Often she cried at the movies, wondering how she could endure six more weeks of this life, the life her friends were, perhaps at just that moment, envying her for leading.

Her only real pleasure was the reading room at the British Museum. She had been issued a reader's card because of the course, and every day, after eating her sandwich on a bench in Tavistock Square, she would come back to the museum. Sitting under the high blue dome, she felt happy. The air was light, the atmosphere of concentrated attention made her feel attached once more to things; the smell of the books, the look of the eccentrics—the woman who ordered twelve books a day on Scottish farming and spent her time sleeping on the pile of them, the tiny Indian whose books were all on Jewish history—made her feel less marginal. They were young, handsome men and serious-looking women, mostly American, who seemed obsessed with some terribly important work. They wrote things fiercely on index cards and walked with small, frantic steps to the catalogue. They never looked at Anne, and she wouldn't have thought of trying to catch their eyes; they were engaged in something essential, and she was merely sitting there, only just legitimately, taking dilatory notes on Roman history and reading a biography of George Eliot.

One afternoon, instead of going to the reading room, she went to a gallery that was having a small exhibit of the watercolors of Raoul Dufy. In the large, rectangular room the paintings glowed on the walls, the blue skies, the silvery green olive trees. She stood in front of one of them and imagined herself in that landscape, imagined the fragrant air, the smell of lemon, of basil, the bright pink streaks of sun in the evening sky. She was interrupted by a voice, shockingly loud, behind her.

"Are you at all interested in pictures?"

It was the first personal question that had been addressed to her since she had left America. She turned around to see who had spoken to her. It was a tall man in his late fifties with a large head, light blue eyes and a long thin nose, the kind of nose she had, in her imagination, granted only to Europeans. He told her he had organized the show and walked her around the room, stopping not at every painting, only at the ones he gave her to believe merited her singular attention. He knew everything about the pictures, and about Dufy's life. For the first time she had the sense of what it was to be intimate with a painter, and a painter's work, as intimate as one was with one's family. There was no formality in the way this man spoke about the paintings; he didn't change his voice, as so many of her professors did, he didn't get the glazed look they adopted to indicate reverence. Everything he said was spoken in that same rather embarrassing boom with which he had first addressed her. She thought how unfair it was that people accused Americans of being loud when no tourist could have come near the volume of this man's voice. But she knew, although she couldn't say why, that his loudness was proprietary, rather than unconscious, the loudness born of giving orders, not of shouting over the noise of machinery. She wanted him to go on and on. But they came to the last of the paintings, and he turned to her and said, "Quite enough of that, don't you think?"

"Oh, no," she said, "it's been such a long time since I've been so happy." And she began to cry.

He took her into his office and had his secretary make her a cup of tea. She told him about the girl who had taken up with the Lebanese, about her bedspread, her hatred for the Elgin Marbles, and the greengrocer who wouldn't speak to her.

"What a perfectly wretched little life," he said. "We must do something about that."

He invited her to dinner. But first, he said, he would show her London.

He was always making large insupportable statements like, "London was nothing after the eighteenth century," and "There's no sense ordering anything to eat in the West End but an omelette." He took her to the Wallace Collection, to George Eliot's house in Cheyne Walk, to Regent's Park to look at the Nash buildings. Every day they had their sandwiches together. He seemed interested in every part of her life; he learned her sister's name, the name of her street, the names of her professors and her dog. Early on he had explained about his wife. "We've no end of respect for each other, but we lead quite separate lives."

Four weeks after she met him, it was time for her to go home. She spent hours wondering how she would do it, how she would declare her love on their final evening. Or perhaps she would wait till she got home and then write him, passionately but with measure. On that last night, he was more than usually talkative. He suggested that she turn in early so she wouldn't be tired for her flight. He gave her an ivory miniature, a likeness of a fair woman in a low-cut blue dress; he said it had been in his family since the 1780's. He kissed her cheek, as he always did; he told her she must write to him faithfully, must work on her French, must have a wonderful year and have ten smashing boys fall in love with her before Christmas.

She said she would work on her French, she would write him, she would miss him very much. She gave him her farewell gift: a collection of Emily Dickinson. It was the only American thing she could think of that seemed good enough for Benedict. Then she embraced him, kissing him shyly just above the collar.

"I must say you do make the world warmer and brighter," he said.

She wanted to say, "I am dying with love for you," but said instead, "Do you really think you'll have the time to write me back?" He was going to Paris in September to research his next project, an exhibit of Vuillard.

"Of course. Now, you really must turn in," he said, and headed toward a rank of taxis.

Because of Ben, she signed up that fall for a course on nineteenth-century French literature, where she met Michael. As soon as she knew she was in love with Michael, she began mentioning him in her letters to

Ben. Two years later, when she married him, Ben sent them a Georgian silver teapot. It was by far the most valuable gift anyone had given them: she wanted to protect it from the toasters, the irons, the electric knives that sat on her mother's dining room table, waiting for the ceremony, waiting to be of use.

She often wondered if Ben had been in love with her that summer. She understood now, though it had taken her many years to get over feeling grateful to him for his friendship, that she must have been a pleasing companion: she was pretty; she knew enough about painting that he didn't always have to be explaining himself; she was cheerful, she laughed at his jokes. But they had seen each other every day; it was possible to say he was devoted. But had he been in love? Had he wanted to go to bed with her? Perhaps he was waiting for a sign from her, a sign, being the kind of twenty-year-old she had been, she could in no way have given. If she had been another kind, she would have been able to express her desire: she might have put her hand on his thigh under the dinner table, she might have closed the door to his office and taken off her blouse, she might have sent him—as a student of Michael's had once done—a pair of her underpants in the mail. At the very least, she might have written him an explicit letter. Now, because she had been the kind of twenty-year-old she had been, she would never know.

She thought of Laura, who was not much more than twenty now.

"What do you and Laura talk about when you have coffee?" she asked Adrian. "I can hardly imagine a more unlikely combination."

"There's no such thing as Adrian being an unlikely combination with anything in a skirt," Barbara said.

"There's nothing like the bitchiness of approaching middle age," Adrian said. "I think it's got to do with a loss of estrogen."

Anne looked around the table at her friends. She felt she hadn't missed them. In a few weeks' time, she had changed. Her generosity was less now, and her patience. She felt she barely had time now for these friends; she felt it was only as a favor to them that she sat there. Was she going to become one of those women who made impossible demands on everyone because they had too much to do? Perhaps what she had thought of in herself as good nature was only youth, leisure, the need to take and give affection because she lacked the work that could engage her heart.

———

She tried the front door of the house and found it locked. She had told Laura to lock the door if she was alone with the children, although she herself never did. She felt that she was safe in the house but Laura wasn't. Was it because Laura was younger, a stranger, not connected to the house life by necessity or blood? Was it because Laura seemed to lack discrimination, that she might let in a killer disguised as a Bible salesman? Or, Anne wondered, was she making a point: this is my house; it is not yours.

As she sat in the living room, turning the pages of a magazine under a light too low for actual reading, she felt the luxury of Laura's absence. She could not enjoy any of the rooms in her house if Laura was in them, and for the hundredth time she asked herself why. The girl had done nothing to earn dislike. She had been careful, punctual, dutiful. She had gone out of her way to make the children happy. Anne knew that it was her fault.

She sat back and looked at her living room in the insufficient light. Only rarely had she been alone in this room so late. The dark, uncut silence pleased her. The clock that had belonged to her grandmother said twelve-thirty. She was not tired. She touched the chairs, the lamps as she turned off the lights. Thank you, thank you, she said to her things, her furniture. They had soothed her, smoothed the scratches that the day had made, allowed her, in the silent hall, to think of walking into her study comforted, quieted, to turn the light above her desk on fearlessly, knowing the house would close around her and the children, sleeping.

In the packet of letters Ben had given her, there were three to Jane and Stephen from Caroline's apartment in the Rue Jacob, where she had lived from 1920 to 1924. Anne read the first:

Dear Children:
    I am worried you are not spending enough money, not eating well, that Jane, with her perverse Yankee pride, is spending her days stewing horsemeat on a gas ring when she ought to be in the library. Here is a cheque; buy yourselves some fruit, some flowers; pretend you are here in a civilized country, where one expects to eat well as one's due as a human being. I wish Stephen had your health, Jane, which is mine. Of course the two of us could pull a wagon over the prairies after the horses gave out, but we can't expect that of the rest of mortals.
    This reminds me of a story that will amuse you, Jane. A very rich American whose husband's fortune, I believe, was made in the rendering of lard (which explains his taste in wives) stopped by the studio with the view to adding one of mine to her collection. She saw nothing to suit her fastidious tastes; my mothers and children, she said, looked as if they didn't like one another, and my fruit looked not quite fresh. She kept coming back to the picture of you in your black Worth suit. "Your

model," she said, "is unworthy of her clothes." "Go on," I said, "tell me
what you mean. What do you make of the model?" "A peasant," said
Mrs. M———. "Now, I know, Miss Watson, you go in for health and
strength and all that, but it's ridiculous to imagine a girl like that in
such an elegant getup." I was interested in letting her hang herself.
"Not everyone," I ventured, "has the same criterion of beauty." "Yes,
but this girl's beauty is of the coarsest type," said my guest. Only then
did I tell her that the model was my daughter-in-law, that while she was
posing she was reading Thucydides in the original, that she was Radcliffe
College's most brilliant student, that the only reason my son was able to
win her from the hordes of young men of America's first families who
would have died for her hand was that he stole her from the cradle
while the rest of them waited to make their move.

The months are slow until I see you. How do you bear it in that
barbarous country, and especially the odious Boston which sits on its
haunches like a great stuffed bear? But I have been told I do not
understand the young. Jane, do not overwork. Perhaps you could pass
some of your ambition to your husband. Stephen, are you still trying to
paint? Give it up, it's a mug's game.

Anne put the letter down and thought of Stephen, of Caroline's letters
to Stephen in comparison to this one. Her letters to her son had been
perfunctory and short. None of the pride, the private jokes, the motherly
concern, she showered on Jane had come through when she wrote to her
son.

Whenever Anne thought of Caroline's treatment of Stephen she came
upon a barrier between them that was as profound as one of language. She
could speak of her feelings about her children in sentences they themselves
might have formulated: they are the most important things in all the
world, she could say; there is no one I care more for. Some deep encoded
pattern drew her to her children and made her circle them: her body itself
was a divide between them and the rest of the human world. She couldn't
imagine Peter or Sarah marrying anyone she would prefer to them, as
Caroline had preferred Jane to Stephen.

You have done wrong, she always wanted to tell Caroline. Caroline, the
ghost who had taken over her life, hovering, accepting worship. She had
made Anne feel that veil after veil had been removed; seeing what Caroline had seen had made her feel she lived on the underside of a wave that
furled and revealed treasures. But then she came upon a letter such as this
one, which the woman she worshipped had written, in perfect cruelty, to
her son. And she drew back, and the drawing back made her doubt

everything she did. Only if she lived with Caroline as a beloved presence could she come close to her in understanding. To do justice to the dead required an intimacy in which justice had no part. So far away they were, and so removed: you needed to embrace them with the unquestioning love with which you embraced an infant. You needed to be always on their side.

And even as she wanted to tell Caroline, "You have done wrong," an anger rose up in her as if the accusation had come from someone else. No one would have pored through a male artist's letters to his children as she had through Caroline's to Stephen. It was that Caroline was a woman and had a child and had created art; because the three could be connected in some grammar, it was as though the pressure to do so were one of logic. Then she wanted to defend Caroline from the accusation she herself had laid against her. What did it matter, she wanted to say to the shivering ghost whom she had left unsheltered. You were a great painter. You did what you had to do. Yet even as she shielded the ghost, she could not still the accusation: "You should not have let your child die young." For as a mother, she felt it was the most important thing in the world. You did not hurt your children. You kept your children safe.

Stephen had died at twenty-eight, miserable, a failure. Yet Jane at seventy-eight was magnificent. The heat of Caroline Watson had come close to both of them, warming one of them, leaving the other ashes. Dead at twenty-eight, Stephen had left nothing. No, she thought, that wasn't true. He'd left his wife and mother to themselves.

========

She had promised the children a walk in the woods. The morning flared, quick, solid, there was no gradualness to the sun's progress. The sky was flame-blue after dawn, the light, hard-edged at seven, was at nine a sheet of pure and potent color. It was not possible to linger over breakfast, although it was Saturday and that was an established family luxury. Only action could satisfy; Anne no less than the children yearned to move through the exciting air.

Everyone but Laura had a knapsack. The children packed sandwiches and fruit in theirs, convinced of the seriousness of their charge as if they were bringing serum to a plague-infested town. Anne worried about Laura's shoes. She had only sandals, and even with thick socks, they would not be protection enough for the walk with its muddy spots, jumping from stone to stone if the brook was high, tracking through the undergrowth. All through breakfast, Anne worried about Laura's feet. She could see her sandals, her wool socks caked with mud, twigs and cockleburs sticking to them, poking through the cloth into the flesh. By the time she backed the car into the driveway she was convinced that they would have to stop and buy Laura a pair of hiking boots—she would need them for the winter anyway. And since the boots were a need that Anne perceived, a concern that Laura would not share (she was curiously impervious to her own physical comfort), Anne saw that she would have to pay for them.

She knew it would be frustrating to the children to delay, however briefly, beginning their walk, and so she told them they could have a dollar each to buy nuts at the health food store three doors down from the shoe shop. She, too, resented the delay, and she knew she would have to work particularly hard not to convey her resentment, not to rush Laura, or to make her feel in any way deficient. It was, after all, admirable to be as unencumbered as Laura was. Hadn't Anne often lamented in herself her terrible attachment to things, her almost superstitious need to place herself in the world with heavy objects as if, without them, she might fly off into some unknown, identityless sky? Every year in the springtime, she tried to make herself give things away. Michael laughed at her agonies, her pitiful show of goods, culled after enormous labor, to give to the Salvation Army. She should admire this girl who was, after all, quite brave in the way she lived her life.

But Anne felt herself grow irritated as Laura tried on pair after pair of boots, unable to make a decision, not out of fastidiousness but because she was incapable of finding a basis upon which to choose one over the other. The children had fallen to fighting: they had spilled a bag of sunflower seeds on the floor amid the empty boxes and sheets of tissue paper that lay at Laura's feet; the harassed clerk shot Anne a look of pure hatred, which Anne could only accept as just. Laura simply sat there smiling, taking shoes off, putting them on, as if someone had ordered her to kill as much time as possible so as not to arrive too early at a party. Anne felt she had to do something or they would be there all day.

"Don't you think these are the best?" she said to Laura, pointing to a pair of boots that Laura had tried on more than some of the others.

"If that's what you want, Anne," said Laura, smiling a smile that Anne found, in the circumstances, incomprehensible.

Anger was an emotion Anne had rarely; when it came, she felt it in the way she felt a headache, a sensation unusual but not entirely unfamiliar, reported on enough by others so as not to be a shock. She picked the boots up quickly and walked with the clerk to the checkout counter. She had to get away from Laura quickly, so that she wouldn't say what she wanted to say, "This is a favor to *you*. I am doing *you* a kindness. I get nothing out of this. I'm giving you my time, my money, for your comfort. How dare you suggest that you're accommodating *me.*" She rubbed her forehead, as if she could rid herself of these thoughts by massage. Blindly, she signed the charge slip, not taking in the amount on the bottom line.

The children tumbled out of the car like colorful birds. They had forgotten their bad temper; they ran ahead of Anne and Laura, looking for a spot where they could have their lunch. Seeing them ahead of her, Peter slowing himself down so Sarah could keep up, she felt love rise in her like mercury. What nice children she had! She could take no credit; they were born with their natures, and their natures were fortunate. That Peter might find life arduous, that Sarah might grow stubborn or vague with age, did nothing to disturb a truth that was lovely: her children were people that she liked. She thought of Stephen Watson, whose existence was a reminder to his mother of the cheat of her sex.

Walking beside Laura, she watched her looking up at the sky as if she had been told she ought to see something there. Perhaps it was part of her religious life; perhaps she thought of the sky as the home of God. Clearly, the girl had no home. She carried her homelessness about with her, an almost ignorable congenital disease, a slight deformation of the spine. That was why she had so much trouble buying the shoes: no one had asked her preference, given her the leisure of her own taste, her own choice. Guiltily, Anne put her hand on Laura's shoulder.

"It's a beautiful day for a walk," she said.

"Here come the children," Laura said, as if Anne had just been foolish and she wanted to change the subject to protect her.

Peter and Sarah hopped with excitement. A tree had fallen down by the creek; it made a natural bench for the four of them. Peter started a fantasy about all of them taking a camping trip to the Grand Canyon. They would get a trailer, he said—some kids in his class lived in a trailer, and it was terrific. It had everything—a television, a bathtub—and you could just drive anywhere you wanted with your whole house with you.

Sarah began to cry. "I miss Daddy," she said. "If we go on a camping trip to the Grand Canyon and move out of our house into a trailer, will we ever see Daddy again?"

Peter jumped off the log and sat beside his sister, putting his arm around her as if they were the only living people on a ruined ship. Frightened that the vividness of his storytelling had so disturbed her, he offered her one of his cupcakes. She took it without humility or gratitude, as if it were her due. Anne watched the two of them, who seemed not to need her.

"Daddy will be home before your birthday," Peter said. "Why don't you think about your birthday. What kind of cake do you want Mommy to make this year?"

"I want a cake in the shape of a ballerina with pink icing on the skirt."

"I want a cake in the shape of a crocodile. With green icing, and white for the teeth."

"I want a geranium," Anne said. "Orange icing for the flowers, green for the leaves, and chocolate for the pot."

"What do you want for yours, Laura?" Peter asked, turning suddenly.

"I don't know," Laura said, smiling.

"You see," Anne said quickly, wanting to temper their exclusion of Laura, "I make cakes in the shape of things for their birthdays. Very crudely, of course."

"I see," said Laura.

"When's your birthday, Laura?" Sarah asked.

Laura hesitated a moment. "In ten days," she said.

"That's November twenty-sixth," Peter said. "The Monday after Thanksgiving. We'll have a party. Our mom will make you a cake. What kind do you want?"

"Oh, it doesn't matter. Maybe some kind of flower."

"How about a daisy?" Peter said. "Our mother can do that, can't you?"

"Sure I can," said Anne. "I'm glad this came up. We wouldn't have known if you hadn't told us."

"Oh, it doesn't matter," Laura said.

"Of course it does," said Anne. "It's terrible not to have your birthday celebrated."

Anne wondered how long it had been since anyone had celebrated Laura's birthday. November thirtieth. That would be the day after they got back from Jane's. She would have an enormous amount to do; she would want to write her first impressions of the paintings. She saw her workday lost to making a cake in the shape of a daisy. The children were asking Laura what she wanted for her birthday.

"Oh, it doesn't matter," she said. "Anything you want."

"We'll surprise you," said Peter, pulling Sarah ahead to whisper something to her.

Laura sat on the bench, her eyes straight ahead of her, fixed on nothing. Anne wondered if she was trying to keep from crying. She felt terrible about her own resentment. She could give up a day's work, of course she could. It would mean so much to this girl who had so little. Once more, Anne felt the clear sensation of her own good luck.

"I'll tell you what," she said. "I'll take you to lunch on your birthday. Just the two of us."

Laura looked up at her. "The two of us? Alone?"

"No kiddos," Anne said, laughing.

"Oh, Anne, that would be wonderful."

She looked up at Anne with a smile that Anne could find no fault with. For the first time since she'd known her, Laura seemed genuinely happy.

S he had made that up about the birthday, but it was all right. Because she had been wise as serpents. Had said nothing of the Spirit humming in her like a radio. She was powerful; her body vibrated like a radio with the sound turned off. The lie was as wise as a serpent. And she was happy.

That day in the woods with the children after Anne was angry with her, it had come to her that she must lie. She had been afraid of what to do about the hiking boots. Anne wanted something from her, but she did not know what. Did not know what to choose or do or say. The heavy shoes lay in their paper, in their boxes, all the same. Which should she choose, and why should she want them? Anne knew, but it was a test. Anne knew things like that, like Laura's mother: the right shoes, the right dresses. With her mother there were always tests. Choose. Now you have chosen, you are wrong. You have chosen that dress, those shoes, and now I do not love you. How could she choose? So much depended on it. Then Anne chose for her. And Anne was angry, angry just like Laura's mother.

The water covered her. She walked through water, falling. She could hear the children talking, see the bright colors of their clothes. Send help, she had prayed, for everything I have is going from me. She was walking in the woods behind Anne. Anne was tall, taller than she, but beautiful. Her hair shone in the sun like the bright colors of the children. Her back was straight. She was a beautiful tree. Laura wanted to touch her, to lean her head on her like a tree, to say, "Please tell me what you want, and I will do it."

The danger of Anne was that she made Laura forget the truth. The truth that it was Laura who was powerful and Anne who needed her. That day she had forgotten she was powerful. Dropped down in the dark water, she had lost herself. Then she had prayed. And had been rescued. Because the lie came from the Spirit and brought forth a sign.

Her birthday was not in November. It was in July. But the children were talking about birthdays. She could hear them through her miserable dark water. First they were saying that their mother made them beautiful cakes, pink, green, and white. She could see the colors clearly. She could see the table, the white paper tablecloth, the candles, the children, the colorful boxes piled in front of the child of honor. So when Sarah, her favorite, asked, "When's your birthday?" she could see herself at the table, which, even behind the dark water, shone with beauty. She said, "In ten days."

At first she was frightened. She had not lied much in her life. Even her mother said, "Laura tells the truth because she isn't quick enough to lie." But it had come to her then that she should lie. And Anne said, "We'll go out to lunch."

Which was her sign. Which parted the dark waters, lifted her out shining. Anne loved her. Anne wanted her company. Anne wanted them to be together, by themselves, to talk.

Anne was her friend. Who wanted to do things to make her happy. Who wanted to take her to restaurants, to bake a cake. She had not had a friend like that. When girls sat in the booths of diners, eating hamburgers together, giggling behind their hands, when girls walked into stores and said to one another, "Oh, buy that, buy that, it's perfect for you," she had been the one who looked, who was not with another, who walked up and down the aisles of stores, pressed down, made stupid, made slow with unhappiness. But now Anne was her friend. The kind of friend that she had wanted. Whose looks said, Be with me. You are the one I want to be with. Although she did not need it now. Now that she had the Spirit. Still, she knew Anne loved her.

She had won Anne's love through wisdom. The mistake that she had made with the people in the churches was that she had not been wise.

First it was the Reverend Carr, the minister of the church she had always gone to, the First Methodist, at home in Meridian. She had thought he was a nice man. She was sure he had liked her, or pretty sure, for that was the time, the terrible time before the Spirit was revealed to her, when she thought no one liked her. But he had praised her for her work for the youth group, praised the embroidered dresser scarves she made for the bazaar, the cakes she made for the bake sale. He had even told her mother how lucky she was to have a daughter who was so helpful.

(Her mother snorted, "At that age I was too interested in boys to be cooking and sewing. Which is why I'm in the mess I'm in right now.") She had flicked her head at Reverend Carr, and he smiled. She had charmed him. He was no longer thinking about Laura, but about her mother and her small, tanned arms. Laura had gone to him to tell him of the coming of the Spirit, thinking he was a kind man, knowing the Spirit was of God.

He frowned. He put the white tips of his fingers together. He looked at her sadly. "Laura, dear," he said. He had never called her dear before. She thought for a minute that he was about to praise the Spirit in her, that he knew. But he knew nothing. He looked at her, concern in his stupid eyes. "I've been wanting to talk to you for a long time. I've thought for some time that you perhaps were lonely. That you've kept to yourself too much. And that your mother, wonderful as she is"—he was thinking of her small, tanned arms, she knew, her dark hair, thick and shining— "doesn't understand you. Sometimes parents, even meaning well . . ."

She looked at him, smiling. It was a smile she felt come on her when she could see blindness, when she could see people stumbling against truth, when they refused to light the candle that she held for them.

"I see that you don't understand," she said. "It has nothing to do with my mother."

She got up to leave.

"Laura, dear," said Reverend Mr. Carr, now standing, "stay and talk awhile."

"No, thank you," she said. She was proud that she was always polite, in the face of misunderstanding. It was wonderful how, since the Spirit had revealed itself to her, she was never angry. Before, she had been angry so often, at her mother, her sister, her father, the teachers who had been impatient with her thoroughness, her carefulness, who called it slowness, who said she was falling behind. But since the Spirit, she was never angry. When people misunderstood her and she once would have been angry, she could feel herself begin to smile. For the Spirit of Darkness had no strength; evil had no power over her. She was the chosen of the Lord. Nothing could harm her. "And these signs shall follow them that believe," the Lord had said. "They shall take up serpents; and if they drink any deadly thing, it shall not hurt them."

Still, for a while, she thought she needed someone else. Not knowing that the Spirit was sufficient for all things, not knowing that she needed no one, that people needed her. She went from church to church, talking to strangers of the Spirit. They suggested she was overwrought, that she needed a psychiatrist, a rest, a change of diet. She had gone to six churches before she ran into Father Delaney.

At first she had been happy, thinking that he understood her. But even he, believing he was shot through with the Spirit, that the power of the Spirit rushed through his veins like his own blood, reached to the tips of his fingers for healing, for the blind to see, the lame to walk (he had made some rise from their wheelchairs), even he was choking on his own flesh, drowning in it.

At first he had been kind to her. At first, not knowing, she was pleased with his indiscriminate embraces. He was a large man, a handsome man, and she had been deceived into finding the warmth of his body a comfort, a solace. Forgetting that all solace was the Spirit's. Cool and without body.

She had seen him at his Healing Masses (it had upset her mother to see her going to a Catholic church), had seen him lift his strong arms, lay his large hands with the reddish-gold hairs (he called her Red; he said she was like him) on the heads of the sick. They raised their arms, they prayed; some fell down with exhaustion; some rose up, walked, knelt before him. ("Not before *me*," he would say. "It's Jesus.") A woman she had known from the post office declared she had been cured of cancer. She pitied these people now. The Spirit of Darkness, too, could cure, to lead the righteous man astray.

She began spending all her evenings at Saint Bartholomew's rectory. She asked Father Delaney if she could have a moment with him. He took her into his office. She admired that room. There was nothing in it but a metal desk, a metal filing cabinet, a crucifix, a telephone, six metal chairs, boxes of index cards of written testimonies of the people who believed they had been helped. He kept them, he said, as proof, for many doubted him. He would not say that he had enemies, but many were against his work. In the next room, she could hear people who were his friends tallying the collection from the Healing Mass, putting coins into wrappers, separating bills. He insisted that the tally from his Mass be kept separately from the other Masses. It was one way, he said, of making friends with the Mammon of Wickedness. Then he threw his head back and laughed, and all his friends laughed with him.

That day she sat across the metal desk from him. She told him of the Spirit. He smiled. He put his hands on her head. "Let's pray about it, that's the best." For a while she had been happy with those people. Father Joe told her every week she was a very special person. He embraced her every week and put his warm hand on her head when she was leaving. Soon he asked if she would help with the collection tally.

She had been pleased. Every week she baked things to share with the other people who did the collection, baked special things for Father Joe. When a large check appeared, everyone took it to Father Joe and everyone said, "Praise the Lord." They ate the cake Laura had baked and praised her, said the Lord had given her special gifts. One old man, who claimed he had been cured by Father Joe of rheumatism, said that if more young girls spent their time like Laura instead of gallivanting with boys, the Blessed Mother would spend more time smiling and less time crying. The younger people asked if she would like to join in their guitar group. Singing ministry, they called it. She was grateful, but she said she preferred helping Father Joe count the money.

She was very good at it. She was careful; she was exact. There were never any errors in her tally, as there were with the others. Soon Father Joe put her in charge of the final tally. Some of the women were resentful; they reminded Father Joe that Laura wasn't Catholic. But Father Joe embraced the women and told them that the ways of the Spirit were broad, that there were varieties of gifts, but the One Giver.

Soon Laura was tired of the financial ministry. She wanted to help with the Healing Masses. She had seen Father Joe laying his hands on the heads of the sick. She had felt his power. She knew she, too, had that power. She knew that one day she would be beside him, sharing in his work, healing even as he healed, healing those whose sickness was beyond him.

Father Joe asked if she would have time to do both: to help with the Healing Masses and to work on the tally afterwards. She told him she thought she would. She didn't want him to know that this was all she had, him, the church, the work she did for him. In the daytime, or weekdays, she worked in the knitting store, selling yarns and threads and needles, giving instructions in knitting and needlepoint. But the weekends were empty; she had nothing to do but stay home, where her parents wished she was not. So she told Father Joe that she was sure she would have time for both the healing and financial ministries.

He assigned her to helping the sick to the altar, to making sure they had seats if they couldn't stand on the long lines, to getting them drinks of water, taking them to the bathroom.

She liked this less than she liked counting the money, putting the dull-green heavy paper tubes of coins in perfect rows, writing the numbers down in black ink on the clean white ledger. The sick people were querulous and talkative. Sometimes they had trouble with their underclothes and didn't get to the bathroom in time. But she knew she could cure them. She was only waiting. For now, she would walk slowly beside them, her hand under their elbows, taking one step when she would have taken four, wiping the floor from them, rubbing dry the spots on the backs of their dresses with the church's paper towels.

She developed a friendship with one of the sick women she helped. Mrs. Prendergast was crippled with arthritis. Her spine was bent, so she could not walk straight ahead. She listed like a heavy ship. Her hands, gripping her cane, were knobbed. Mrs. Prendergast had been coming to Father Joe for thirteen months now. He had been able to do nothing for her. This winter had been her worst. Her children refused to take her to the Healing Masses any longer. They lived twenty miles away and said they would no longer give up their Sundays for some smart aleck's mumbo jumbo.

Father Joe asked Laura if she could get Mrs. Prendergast in a taxi (Mrs. Prendergast would pay, of course) and bring her to the church on Sundays. He put his arm on her shoulder and told her she was terrific, she was incredible, she was one in a million. She smiled up at him. She thought then that he knew, that the Spirit had spoken to him.

Every Sunday for three months she took the bus to Mrs. Prendergast's, helped her out the door into the taxi. After church, someone else drove her home, since Laura had the collection. But during the week, Laura visited Mrs. Prendergast in the evenings.

Mrs. Prendergast said God had sent Laura to her. She showed Laura pictures of herself as a young girl, pictures of her wedding, her babies, her children's graduations, their weddings, and their children sitting under Christmas trees, in swimming pools. Laura was not interested in any of this. She wasn't really interested in Mrs. Prendergast. Except she knew that she could cure her.

One day in the winter when Laura arrived, Mrs. Prendergast was crying. The pain, she said, was terrible, as if her fingers had grown roots, like tree roots in her fingers. She couldn't button her clothes; the top of her dress was open. Laura could see the old skin at the top of her breast, the yellowish slip, the loose pink straps of her bra. Laura buttoned Mrs. Prendergast's dress for her, and Mrs. Prendergast thanked her. She said just being with Laura made her feel better.

When she said that, a jet of flame lit up Laura's spine, as if a match had been lit at the base. It sent light through her veins, and fire. She felt herself newly powerful. She looked at Mrs. Prendergast. Pain had swollen her features, drained the color from her eyes, turned her skin a brownish yellow.

Laura brought Mrs. Prendergast to the couch. She said they weren't going to church today.

Mrs. Prendergast looked up at her with fear. "I must," she said. "I need to see Father Joe."

"Father Joe can't help you," said Laura, looking in the woman's eyes, grown smaller now with pain, with fear. "We'll pray here. I can help you."

But the Spirit of Darkness entered. When Laura put her hands on the old woman's head, felt the thin, limp hair under her fingers, she knew she had no power.

"You must pray with me," Laura said firmly.

"But you're not a priest," the old woman said and began to whimper. The Spirit of Darkness had made her fear. "You have to leave," said the old woman. "What you're doing isn't right."

Laura smiled. The Spirit of Darkness had conquered. She was not ready yet; she had tried too soon. Now the old woman would sit in pain, go on walking like a twisted animal. She deserved it for her lack of faith. Laura knew she could have cured her. But the woman's blindness had stopped her hand.

It was late afternoon when she got home. Her mother was playing cards with Debbie; her father was watching the television. She went to sleep. She could imagine the garish colors her father was watching, green false grass, red uniforms. Half asleep, she heard the doorbell, then the voice of Father Joe. She got up, expecting to be called. But no one called her. From the end of the hall, she saw the priest walk into the den with her parents. She saw her father close the door.

She heard the priest's voice, then her parents': grave and troubled, the sounds had weight, they thickened in the air, some heavy liquid metal that would harden in a moment like a dense coiled spring. She heard her mother's voice, thin needles stitching gold and some bright color. She heard the priest laugh.

It was then she knew. It was then the Spirit revealed that that man was not of the Spirit. She heard her father making coffee in the kitchen, and in the den her mother's words, and laughing. She heard her parents close the door behind the priest.

She left home the next morning. What she could fit in her Girl Scout knapsack she took. An extra pair of shoes, a pair of jeans, a shirt, some underwear. Already she was taking more than Jesus said to take.

In the clear light of that fall morning, she walked to the bus station and took a bus west to Syracuse. She left no word for her parents, for the Scripture said, "A man shall leave father and mother."

It had been a year since she had left her father and mother. Her parents had not found her. Had they looked for her? She knew they couldn't send the police after her. She was of age; her life was her own.

She had been traveling a year; it would be good to settle someplace now. At Anne's house. She would live with Anne. That was the Spirit, looking out for her, caring for her with a love more tender than any human parent could begin to try for.

At first in Syracuse she thought it would be easy. She had found a room two blocks from the university on the top floor of an old yellow house. From her window she could see an aspen. Although she had never noticed what people referred to as nature, she liked the tree outside her window. Or perhaps it was simply having a window that was her own, a window she could sit at for hours without fearing the voices of her mother and her sister, high, sharp, shattering the texture, the clear pane, of things (her life, her thoughts), springing against her life like shot against a window. Or her father's voice, heavy as a wounded bird, flapping, flying blind against the glass with his defeats and his apologies. Here she could sit for the first time in front of a window, looking at the aspen with its flat gold leaves, embroidering them into a dresser scarf that she was making to cover the gray plastic surface people had burned with cigarettes, ringed with the glasses holding what they drank there at the window. She could read her Bible, close her eyes, pray for guidance, open anywhere and know the Spirit was directing her.

One day as she got off the bus coming back from her job at Nettie's Needles—the same job she had had at home—a young man walked up to her as if he knew her. He smiled at her and said, "Excuse me, miss, but have you accepted Jesus Christ as your personal Lord and Savior?"

She felt her heart light up, grow solid against the bones of her breast. It was the messenger of the Lord. How kind his voice was (she had spoken little since she had arrived, except to Nettie Rosa, whom she worked with, and they spoke about her work). How clear, how open his eyes seemed. He looked straight into her eyes, took both her hands and held them. "Praise the Lord," he said. "Welcome, my sister."

Wise as serpents, innocent as doves. She had not been wise. She had followed the young man—Don Kingston was his name—to the house where he lived with what he told her was his family. He belonged to a community that called itself the Children of the Light.

They lived in a house five blocks from where her room had been, six of them, and their leader, whom they called Father but whose name was Fletcher Voss. They embraced her—all seven of them—when they saw her; they embraced her when she left the house and when she came back into it. They sang as they did the tasks they'd been assigned—the girls cooked, the boys did yard work and repairs. They told her to give up her room. No need to be alone, they said, you are one of us, the family, we love you as our own. She moved in with them; she slept in a room with Shelley and Susan. They called each other sister and embraced each night after the evening prayers were said. And each day before they left for their "outside jobs," they prayed together and embraced each other. For the world was wicked and dangerous, they were sent out among wolves, they were safe only in the walls of the house.

She had told them of the Spirit coming to her and they had said, "Praise the Lord," and taken her hands and thanked God that she was among them. She had friends around her, more than friends, brothers and sisters who loved her, who appreciated her gifts. She was never lonely. There were chores for her to do when she came home from work, and since her outside job was a day job (as were Shelley's and Susan's; Scott worked at night in the donut shop and Robert at the post office so they could be free for the daytime ministry), at night she went out onto the streets to speak to people, to warn them of the Coming of the Lord, the Blood of the Lamb, the corruption of their flesh, the wickedness in which they walked, the separation of the sheep and goats that was coming, coming, for the Lord was on His way, and many would not be saved.

She did not know that she was prophesying falsely, that they were all false prophets, that they walked not in the Spirit but in Darkness led by the Devil in the guise of Fletcher Voss.

Many came and went while Laura lived there. Some off buses stayed only for the meals, the beds, left when they had saved up money, when they had bathed and washed their clothes and eaten regularly for a week. These, Fletcher said, were minions of the Devil. But devils themselves were those who left because they disagreed with Fletcher, because they wouldn't give up their money, or wouldn't go out on the streets at night, every night, to preach the Word. She, too, had had contempt for them, had prayed with joy and with thanksgiving when they left that the house (where they were safe, the only place they could be safe) was cleansed of their presence.

Fletcher Voss was older than the rest of them and handsome with his dark hair and dark blue eyes. He had been to Vietnam. He had fought and suffered, he said, seen those he loved die, seen immorality, committed sin himself. And then he had had his vision.

His vision was not like the coming of the Spirit to Laura, the Spirit who came in love. At the time she believed it was because he had seen war and she had not, had suffered as she had not. But now she knew it was because his vision—if he ever had a vision—was the work of Darkness. The vision of Fletcher Voss had come in fire and thunder; it was a man with flaming hair whose voice boomed like thunder, whose swords glittered in the sun, their golden handles burning. He had told Fletcher that Fletcher had been sent by the Lord to save a chosen remnant from the vengeance of the Lord. The remnant would be called the Children of Light; they would be recognized on the last day by the oil of anointing placed upon their foreheads by the hand of Fletcher Voss.

At first she thought that he was greater than she; that the coming of the Lord to him was greater, since the Lord spoke to him of the people he was to save, while the Spirit spoke to her only of her personal condition, to say she was the chosen one, the favored of the Lord. So for three months she was pleased to be subordinate to him, glad to follow his instructions, to ask his permission to keep some of her money for toilet articles, for thread and patterns, for stamps. (She had written to her parents at Fletcher's suggestion; he said it was better not to antagonize the natural family, since the Devil working through them and through the law could do the Children of Light harm. Her father had written to say he was glad she was well, they were worried about her, the door was always open to her. From her mother she heard nothing.)

She could see that Voss was fond of her. He complimented her on her work in the kitchen, on never complaining about money, on her zeal in bringing converts in. She had brought two African boys, students at the university, to the weekly prayer meetings. They came for two months, then stopped coming. She saw them later, dancing with other students in a bar.

By March she had been in the house longer than anyone except Don. She told Voss that she had helped the healing priest (Voss said he was the Devil in priest's robes; established churches were the Devil's favorite seat), that she was good at bookkeeping, that Mrs. Rosa, whose only real interest was knitting, left all the books to her. She said she would help him keep track of the household money so that he would be more free to preach, to bring in converts from the street.

Voss smiled at her. He took her hand. "Thank you," he said. "I realize that you believe you're trying to help me. But money is evil, not only is it the root of evil, it is evil in itself. I believe that anyone who touches it is in danger; I will run the risk myself rather than expose one who has been less tried, whose spirit is more delicate, more fine and beautiful."

Then he began to invite her into his room, to pray alone with him. "You are so beautiful," he would say when they had prayed. White skin and shining hair, he would say, touching her so that something stirred in her. He knew how to touch her to make these things happen. He said the Lord wanted them to be joined flesh to flesh and not just in the spirit. He took her, he took her innocence, and she gave it, believing she was doing the work of the Lord. But then she saw. Saw that he was full of lies and was a thief. She saw, in his room at night, that he kept some of the money people brought in for himself. She let him know she saw.

"No one will believe you," he said, turning away from her. "I'll tell them you're insane, that you have visions. You've talked to the others about your visions, it's me they'll believe. I'll call the police and tell them you've stolen money from me. They'll lock you up and throw away the key. I'll get the others to testify against you."

She had not been wise. Had had too much faith in the friendship of others.

"Tell them, the Spirit will determine which is the greater spirit. They will discover yours is the Spirit of Lies, of Thieving, of the Flesh that steals the flesh of others."

In a family meeting, he denounced her. And the others stood behind him, circled around her like wolves. She was a dove in the midst of wolves. "Leave us," they chanted. "Leave, Spirit of Darkness. Leave us," they kept shouting, all of them together, again, and then again. Who had said they were her brothers and her sisters. Who had said they knew she was the chosen of the Lord.

She ran out of the house, leaving her bag behind. She walked through the dark streets, past the bars where college students laughed and danced and shouted from their cars. The car lights hurt her eyes, the sounds of the loud music hurt her skin, as she ran, ran past them, past their laughter and their shouted messages, ran past the government project, past the bars where men sat silent, solitary, ran across the highway, letting cars swerve to miss her. She ran till she got to the bus station, where she sat all night. She sat erect and terrified, afraid to sleep, afraid to see the eyes of Fletcher Voss that had grown into hands to choke her. Then she reached into her pocketbook and found her Bible. She prayed for comfort and for succor. The Spirit of Darkness had almost overcome her. She needed the shelter of the Lord.

Then she remembered Matthew 10. She had written it out in her notebook: "If the house is worthy, let your peace come upon it; but if it is not worthy, let your peace return to you. And if any one will not receive you or listen to your words, shake off the dust from your feet as you leave that house or town. Truly, I say to you, it shall be more tolerable on the day of judgment for the land of Sodom and Gomorrah than for that town."

She felt the smile rising within her. The smile of triumph. Her enemies had vanquished her now, but they would be repaid in kind a hundredfold.

Her fear vanished. She knew she would be cared for. For it said, in the same chapter of Matthew: "So have no fear of them; for nothing is covered that will not be revealed, or hidden that will not be known. Are not two sparrows sold for a penny? And not one of them will fall to the ground without your Father's will. But even the hairs of your head are all numbered. Fear not, therefore; you are of more value than many sparrows."

And she knew that she was of great value. For that reason she had been persecuted. Beware of men, Jesus had said, for they will deliver you up to councils, and flog you in their synagogues, and you will be dragged before governors and kings.

This had almost happened to her. He said if he told people about what the Spirit had told her, she would be locked up. He said he would get the people in the house to testify against her. Yet she would triumph, and her enemies go down to ruin. She imagined the house of the Children of Light in flames. But she would not be able to help them, for the flames would be the judgment of the Lord.

She slept sitting up in the bus station. In the morning she went back to Mrs. Rosa's store. She knew she would not stay there long. If they will not receive you, Jesus said, or listen to your words, shake off the dust from your feet as you leave the house or town. When they persecute you in one town, flee to the next.

She knew she would be going somewhere soon, so she didn't want to get a room. She slept in the bus station and got to Nettie's early in the morning, where she washed her body and her clothes, hiding them in the basement of the store to dry.

In less than a week the Spirit had shown her what to do.

She was working at Nettie's Needles patiently explaining how to work a simple pattern to Mrs. Chamberlain, explaining the same thing for the fiftieth time. She wanted to tell Joan Chamberlain that she had no talent for needlework; her fingers were slow and thick, she had no concentration, she would never finish the pillow cover for her little girl, the one with the squirrel and the nuts, in time for her birthday. But she knew she couldn't say that, and Joan Chamberlain had been nice to her, asked her about her family, praised Laura's skill, her clear teaching. So, after ripping out the red threads that were supposed to be green, green of course for the leaves of the tree in the background, and knowing that something was being arranged for her by her Father, who cared for her more than for many sparrows, she was not surprised to hear Joan Chamberlain say, "You wouldn't be interested in going to London for six months, would you? In January as a mother's helper for my family. Of course, you'd be one of the family yourself. But paid, of course. We could talk about that later. That is, if you'd like to. But you're probably happy here, and I wouldn't want to take you away from Nettie."

That was the way Joan Chamberlain was. She was a small, light woman with colorless eyelashes; she never finished anything. She twitched; she twittered; she was a nervous little rodent in a cage, first sipping water, then pushing a wheel, then scattering its food, then running from one corner to another, appearing to look for something it could never actually possess.

Shake off the dust from your feet. She knew she was meant to leave the city. London. She didn't care that it was London; it could have been Buffalo, Detroit. A place had been found for her; her Father had provided.

She told Joan that the lease had just run out on her apartment, and asked if she could move into their house early. Joan said terrific, terrific, she would have to ask her husband first, but he would probably be ecstatic, because maybe she could help out with the housework, only if she wanted to, but that would be terrific because she, Joan, was such a slob.

She said she'd be glad to, that she liked housework, that she found it soothing. Joan said that was just incredible, and just terrific. Laura told Joan to call her at Nettie's Needles. She did not want the woman she was working for to know that she was sleeping in the bus station.

———

Laura didn't like Jack Chamberlain. He was a tall, lean, fair-haired man, joking with his children, exasperated with his wife. Laura never understood how he could have married Joan. Perhaps she had once been pretty. Laura did not understand marriage; the idea of it disgusted her: choosing a partner for the urges of the flesh, in filth creating children to be hurt and caused to suffer.

Certainly the Chamberlains were unhappy. Jack raged; Joan cried; the children were disobedient and worried. She knew that she was good for the children. She taught them many things. It wasn't her fault they weren't happy.

She had overheard them talking to their mother. "She's no fun," they said. "She's boring."

"Listen, you," said Joan, "thank your lucky stars we've got her. She's got the patience of a saint. You could have a real monster. And when we get to London, you'll have so much to do you won't even notice her."

She felt, always, the Chamberlains congratulating themselves for including her in their wonderful lives. She felt them doing it with each museum they took her to, each historic building they pointed out to her, each meal in each restaurant they offered. Food did not interest her; she despised the Chamberlains for their sense that each new food they found was a treasure. They smacked their lips like animals over the desserts at an Indian restaurant. They could talk for a week about English cream. They did not think, they never understood, that the things that entered their mouths ended up in the drain. "I believe that food is so much more than something to fill the belly," said Jack Chamberlain, congratulating himself on educating Laura. "It's an art in itself, not only in its preparation but in its consumption."

And ends up in the drain, Laura wanted to tell him, but did not. Instead she smiled, appeared to take an interest. She wished that she didn't want to eat, but in fact she was often hungry. She would have preferred to eat the same foods every day. In food she savored what was sweet, white, soft, familiar. She kept in her room in the London flat a loaf of white bread, a tub of soft margarine, a jar of strawberry jam.

When Joan found these things, she tried to make a joke of them. "You don't need to eat *this* stuff. Just help yourself to anything in the refrigerator. Anytime, for heaven's sakes. Margarine, ugh. Laura, you poor darling."

She could not say to Joan that she preferred her margarine to Danish butter, her soft white sliced bread to the hard brown loaf they kept, her strawberry jam to their plum preserves. That she liked eating in her room, in her bed in silence, preferred it to the Chamberlain family table, where the children were forbidden to fight and where it was demanded that the conversation be intelligent.

She knew she was not pleasing to the Chamberlains. The children were not interested in the things she thought of for them to do. She was nearly silent on the excursions the Chamberlains planned for her and the children: the Tower of London, Madame Tussaud's. These were the wrong things to be teaching the children. She began reading to them from the Bible. Jessica, the oldest child, said, "Our family doesn't believe in religion. Our father says it's superstition."

Then she knew for certain that the Devil was in the house, had taken root, been fed and nourished, welcomed and revered. So it was no surprise to her when Jack Chamberlain told her they would not be needing her, no surprise that things worked out as they had with Hélène. She knew that Hélène hated Anne. Because Anne was beautiful, and Hélène was not. Because Anne had only to walk into a room to make people love her. Things came easily to her; people wanted to be near Anne for the things she did that were not difficult for her. She did not have to do favors, write letters, have people to live in her house.

Hélène hated Anne because she did not understand that the things that drew people to Anne, that gave her her house, her husband and her children were of no importance. Hélène was angry, as Laura had once been angry. Now she knew she needed no one; so she need never be angry. People needed her. Anne Foster needed her particularly. She would teach Anne that the things that made up her life were of no importance. And she would teach the children.

Anne wanted to get an early start to beat, as far as possible, the rush of the Thanksgiving weekend, so she picked the children up at school and drove from there to Jane's house on Long Island. Driving in the light that at three-thirty was already beginning to fade, she watched Laura pouring drinks for the children, giving them cookies. I would be doing that, she thought, and Michael would be driving. She began to feel teary at the thought of a holiday without him, her first in sixteen years.

Michael. Her husband. All the days together, nights. Food cooked and eaten, children waited for and born, held, nursed in sickness. "I'll go. . . . No, you sleep, I will this time." All the hours shared in sleep, the folded dreams. The sex, two bodies, knowing, known. The arguments, estrangements, lonelinesses: "The person I most love knows not a thing about me, is a stranger, wants to do me harm." Afterwards, the coming together, exciting, tender after the hard butts of willed misunderstanding, innocent uncomprehending tiredness, resentment, fear. She missed her husband terribly. There were things she wanted to tell him, ask him, every day, that she could say to no one else. And his body, yes, she had the dull ache of desire, constant now. It made her feel ashamed. No one had made love to her in ten weeks. If she weren't married, that would be the ordinary thing. Single people, widows, divorcées: that was their life. She was a coward. She could only just get by without her husband.

That was the sort of thing she was afraid Jane would find out about her, and despise her for. Marriage, that little dovecote for weak hearts, fearful spirits. The great did not need marriage, entered into it for some convenience: money, sex, domestic comforts, the need for some general fealty formally contracted and arranged. But all the meals at home, the small conversations, the pleasure in familiar furniture, the late-night reading, all those dreams so badly realized in most houses were not the dreams of the great. Caroline had recoiled from those dreams as if they were dangerous. Yet her work was all about them. Was it dishonest of her? Feeling as she did, ought she to have painted flowers like Georgia O'Keeffe, forbidding rocks that would push the children from the room, skyscrapers jutting into skies of industry or carnival but not of birds? When Caroline's work was dismissed as irrelevant, it was on the ground of excessive domesticity. But she was estranged from her family, kept her child from her, lived in hotels until she was sixty.

Anne wondered what Jane's house would be like. Women who lived alone revealed themselves in their houses in some clear way that men who lived alone could not. A man who lived alone comfortably was an invention of the will; a woman who lived without comfort, without order, was defying some curse of domestic servitude. It was hard to predict how Jane would live. She had worked hard, yet she had been a beauty; she had lived alone most of her life, yet she had been beloved. Anne hoped the children would be all right in her house. Perhaps she should not have brought them on her first visit, before she knew what the house was like, before she knew Jane better. It was good that Ben would be there. The children adored him, and he was wonderful at taking them off the scene for small trips they considered fabulous.

As they drove up the long pebbled driveway a light above the door of the house switched on. Jane appeared in the light, shielding her eyes; Ben stood behind her. She was wearing a bright blue rough-woven shirt, black corduroy trousers, white socks and black Chinese cloth shoes with straps across the instep. Anne had thought of buying a pair for Sarah, but never for herself. It was partly silly for Jane to wear them: her thick white socks made her feet in those shoes look puffy, like a doll's or a Japanese painting of a baby. Yet, standing in the harsh light, she struck Anne once again as astonishingly beautiful, powerful in her beauty, single in it, like a navigable river.

"I ought to have put the light on for you earlier, but it's terrifyingly bright so I can see thieves or marauders coming through the night. I can't bear to keep it on a second longer than I have to. It costs a fortune. Welcome. How was the drive? And you are Peter and Sarah."

The children shook hands with Jane and said How do you do.

"It's a great pleasure to meet you," Jane said. "Mr. Hardy has said how very nice you are, and your mother of course, though everybody's mother says they're nice, you can't believe *that.*"

The children laughed and looked at Ben. "Actually," said Peter, "not everybody's mother says they're nice. I mean, I have this one friend, his mother always says to my mother when he comes to my house, 'If Oliver is terrible, I don't want to know about it.' "

He was imitating Cheryl Jackson. He was showing off. In one minute, Jane had made a conquest; her son was in love.

"Sarah," said Jane. "I have a room with a beautiful bed in it. It used to be my bed. Do you want to see it?"

"Yes, please," said Sarah. If only, Anne thought, they would act like this for the rest of the weekend. They all walked into the house. Laura hung back, a few feet behind them. Anne had forgotten to introduce her. She put her arm on Laura's shoulder.

"This is my friend, Laura, who helps me with the children," Anne said.

Jane looked at her perfunctorily. "How do you do," she said, and turned away.

"Just fine," said Laura, smiling, to Jane's back.

Peter was jabbering to Jane about his friend Oliver, about how terrible he really was. The children disappeared upstairs with Jane and Ben; Anne put her bags down in the kitchen. It was a wide, high room, painted white, with blue-and-white plates hung on the wall and copper pots on hooks. There was a step down to the eating area, dominated by a refectory table. Places were set for seven, and in the center, yellow chrysanthemums stood in a blue vase. There were skylights in the ceiling and windows above eye level that looked out to the dark garden.

"It's a beautiful room, isn't it?" Anne said to Laura.

Laura merely smiled and looked ahead of her. Anne's heart sank. It was a mistake to bring her. But she couldn't have been left. How horrible it would have been to think of her alone in the kitchen, eating a peanut butter sandwich while they feasted. It would have been impossible, thinking of her so, to enjoy the holiday.

Sarah came racing into the room. "I get to sleep in a canopy bed like the one in *Snow White* when she's dead, and it was Mrs. Watson's when she was *my* age." Sarah emphasized the *my* as if to indicate a linked proprietary state with Jane.

"And we each have a tin of cookies next to our bed in case we wake up hungry," Peter said.

"That was Ben's idea," said Jane. "That's always done in English houses," Jane explained to the children. "Have you ever been in England?"

"Our father's in France," said Peter. "He'll be back on May twenty-second. He's been gone since August thirty-first."

"I want to go to England," Sarah said. "They have the queen there."

"For now, come and have some ice cream. I suppose you've had your dinner."

"Yes," said Peter. "We stopped at McDonald's. I got a cheeseburger, french fries and a Coke. My sister got a hamburger, french fries and a root beer. My mother got . . ."

"That's enough," said Anne. "Keep our nasty secrets."

"Our mother got a *milk shake,*" Peter said, giggling.

"Traitor, you *swore,*" Anne said.

"Tomorrow," said Jane, "you children can help me make pies. Would you like that? Your mother and Mr. Hardy will have work to do. We'll do the cooking."

"Our mother does the cooking," Sarah said.

"Not tomorrow, Sarah," said Jane. "Tomorrow she looks at pictures."

"That's not work," Peter objected.

"It's the most important work your mother can do. She looks at pictures, then she writes about them. She's very good at it."

"We don't know that yet," Anne said.

"Of course we do. We're not stupid," Jane said, leading Ben to the table.

===

She awoke at six. The light, still darkened, only turning silvery, made her feel at first diminished; she seemed small to herself in the white bed with its gray iron frame. The leaves outside the windows were barely visible; she seemed to exist in space. I am in Jane's house, she thought; it is Thanksgiving. Yet I am not expected to make a meal. She swung her legs out of her bed as if she were on an ocean liner, feeling the suspension of the rules that governed and pressed down her life into the shape that made it recognizable to strangers.

The walls of the room were completely white. White curtains, moved by a breeze whose source was mysterious, blew in the thin light. She looked around to see the painting on the wall above her bed. Then she felt ashamed, as if she had awakened forgetting that there was a lover in the bed beside her. It had taken her an hour and a half to get to sleep after seeing the painting for the first time. Jane had shown her to the room, and she had found it on the wall, simply there above the bed in its decorative function.

One of the figures in the painting wore a blue dress, the other, a brown with black stripes. They were walking into leaves that would engulf them; the lift of their heavy feet suggested they were ready happily to disappear.

Their backs were toward the viewer, so their faces were invisible, clearly unimportant. They were going somewhwere, standing for something, for journeys which appeared to be small but which could mean the house unseen again, the town only remembered, the clothes left in the bureau drawers, forever smelling of soap. The women's heads bent toward each other. Their arms encircled each other. The hands (which were not a success, Anne saw; one hand looked rather like a leg of lamb) were about to meet in the middle of the back of the brown figure. Both women's hair was greenish blue to complement the green of the background; their boots were blue-black; their stockings bluish gray. The posture of their backs spelled grief, connection. The figure in brown bent toward the blue one as if she were weeping on her shoulder from sheer weariness. Anne looked again at the hand of the blue figure on the waist of the figure in brown. She saw it then: the figure in blue propelled the other slightly forward. In the curve of her body was impatience for the other's hesitancy—over mourning, memory. The figure in blue wanted to get on: to the woods the color of emeralds. She was not thinking of the town at their backs.

Anne had started when she heard Jane's voice; she had forgotten there was anybody in the room with her.

"It's called *Two Women Walking,*" Jane said. "It's one I would never sell; I can't even bring myself to lend it for the exhibition. I put in your room for the weekend, so you can look at it. We'll talk about it in the morning."

And now she could hear Jane stirring in the kitchen; perhaps that was what had wakened her. She could not dress, she feared, without waking someone, so she risked going downstairs in her bathrobe. If Jane was dressed, it would be awkward; it would indicate that Anne felt more intimate with Jane than Jane did with her. Anne feared friendships between women that began in intimacy and played themselves out in small talk. And she wanted Jane to like her in a way that made her feel both young and crude. For women such as Jane, liking, not liking, she imagined, was of little interest, at most a curiosity, like a bargain to the very rich. When she saw Jane in a red woolen bathrobe, she was prepared to read it as an act of the most perfect hospitality.

"Did you sleep all right?" asked Jane. "I hope my puttering didn't wake you. It's one of the useless blessings of old age to need almost no sleep."

"No, I woke before I heard you. I was thinking of the painting."

"It's me and Caroline," Jane said with pride, with a great, sure joy. But was it? It was as much about Caroline's learning to move her figures off center, about using the Fauve palette but sweetening it, applying what she had learned from the Japanese. Could she say that to Jane? And what was the truth of it? Both were, the memory and the technique. It was possible that Caroline might have seen two other women, complete strangers, in that posture, in that light, and been taken by the accident of shape and color. Yet it was possible that had she not taken that walk with Jane each evening, the idea would not have come to her at all.

Jane was an intelligent woman, but Caroline's paintings were the work of someone she loved; their meaning to her was singular, refracted. Perhaps the paintings were more truly hers because of that, perhaps she had been right to keep them to herself. But Anne couldn't help thinking that more people should have seen them. Yet museums were often stupid, prejudiced; without collectors most painters would have starved or died unnoticed.

She thought of all the different ways a painting—one of Caroline's paintings—could exist: as an object, decorative in its function, pleasing, not pleasing to the eye of the innocent stranger. The same painting was to Anne completely different; she could guess its history, it spun out from itself, like a spider, lines growing forward, backward. To Jane the paintings were themselves and Caroline; they didn't spin out lines to other paintings, other painters; they spun, like a disk of sunlight, from the life of a beloved woman. And there were the collectors, for whom paintings were a different kind of object, an investment or a curiosity, a sign of something: power, taste, discernment. A painting was almost never itself. Yet it was her job to look first at each painting as if it were the only painting in the universe, then to trace the lines backward and forward. Only then could she think about the woman holding the brush, taking experience and making this of it, that of it: beauty that would endure, that would say to life, stop here, now; that would hold life, thicken it and make it valuable, enduring, hard.

And what she would say about the paintings—would it influence the men with money, coming to these objects to secure a name, a safe old age, a shelter against ruin? And here was Jane at the stove, her back to Anne, the back which, in the painting, leaned toward another woman as they walked into the wind.

Anne looked out the glass door. A small brown bird came dipping, pecking at the feeder on the porch. Stairs led down to the garden. Only the chrysanthemums were bright there. The brown leaves fell into dry, dull grass; a yellow maple leaf dropped into the birdbath, floated, and then disappeared. Juniper berries hung, opaque and rich among green needles. Jane handed Anne coffee, standing beside the door.

"It's a lovely house," Anne said, "it must give you great comfort."

"Great comfort. I used only to be able to come here in the summer, but now I'm retired, I come here nearly every weekend."

"When did you buy it?"

"In 1950. I was in a bad way when Caroline died, for quite a few years. Most people would call it a depression, but my family never went in for that, so it was said, 'Jane is rather not herself.' I was told this house would be good therapy."

What did Jane want her to say? Was she one of those people who thought politeness consisted of asking the right questions, or of asking no question at all, of saying something about oneself, or keeping oneself completely out of the picture?

"What was the house like when you got it?" Anne asked.

"Rather a wreck. This kitchen was two rooms, a kitchen and a dining room. I had a wall knocked out. Come around and I'll show you."

She walked around her house as her ancestors must have walked around their estates. The living room, narrow and irregularly shaped, had four small windows and one large bay. Jane explained why she had decided on the bay, the window seat, had had the beams exposed. She spoke of doors and insulation, furniture and curtains, with the same familiarity. She had the androgyne's pleasure in her dwelling: decisions of structure and of decoration both had been all hers. Anne thought with shame about her own fears in relation to getting the wiring fixed. But she was married, and she wasn't rich. She could never inhabit a house with the singular freedom and mastery of Jane.

The house was squarish, solid; the furniture, with its bright slipcovers, the lamps with their cream silk shades, the Indian rugs, the absence of photographs, the walls full of books, the shameful lighter patches where Caroline's paintings had lately been taken down, showed a calculated mix. The rooms were both austere and welcoming; one could work there or read for pleasure. One could come into these rooms quite properly and speak of the death of a son, killed in a war or on a motorcycle. One could get drunk here and talk of the betrayals of a business partner or a wife or husband, but it would not be imagined that one could be sick on the rug, or move, unconscious, to the sofa to find one's way home in the morning. It was a house in which Anne felt she need not fear for her children; it was one she hoped they would remember when, in middle age, they thought about the houses of their childhood.

Jane led Anne into the kitchen. "Now, tell me what you really want to know about Caroline. You didn't need me to tell you about Grünewald;

you knew all about it, much more than I. You were merely being polite, or perhaps my letter frightened you."

"Perhaps," said Anne. "You see, I don't know what I have a right to know. I don't want to seem intrusive or to offend you."

"My dear, I have the skin of a rhinoceros. I've been told a thousand times."

"Still, she is yours in a way that she's not mine. And certainly not mine to give to strangers, opened up and cut to pieces."

Jane gave her a slow, comprehending look. She pushed her hair back off her forehead with the heels of her hands and sat, keeping her back beautifully straight, although it was a bench she sat on and she leaned on air. Anne saw that Jane wanted to tell her things but did not want to seem to be giving them away too easily.

"Tell me about Paris. The first time, I mean. How did she talk her father into letting her go?"

Jane laughed. "Plain stubbornness. My God, she was a stubborn woman. She was a person who could really hold out."

Anne fingered the milk pitcher, an old-fashioned yellow with raised pink flowers.

"She was his favorite child," Jane went on. "Henry, the oldest brother, ought to have been the favorite. He did everything his father wanted: went to all his father's schools—Exeter, Amherst—he went into the bank and followed his father there. But his father didn't like him; he despised him for not having enough spirit. What he wanted was a spirit he could break."

"Did he want to break Caroline's?"

"I don't know. I suppose I'm rather unfair to him because I can't forgive him for being so awful when Stephen was born."

Guiltily Anne felt her own excitement. This, of course, was what she wanted to know about: the scandal of the illegitimate child. It lit up Caroline's life with garish and unnatural yet pleasing color. Who was Stephen's father? And then what happened? Soap-opera questions.

"Poor Caroline," said Jane. "She wasn't young, you know, when it happened. She'd lived on her own for six years; she was thirty-six. She felt she was proving something to her father—that she could be on her own and take care of herself. Then she got pregnant, and she felt it was the end of her life. Yet her father was the first person she told."

"How did he respond?"

"All outraged honor. She had betrayed his trust, besmirched the family name. He retired to the library and wept, I believe."

"You don't believe he was really distressed?"

"Yes, partly, of course he was. It was, after all, a scandal. They were an important family and Philadelphia was not Paris. But he took great pleasure in having been right all along, in having his predictions come true."

"I gathered that from the letters. Pleasure in correct judgment kept creeping through the outrage."

"You do see things, don't you," Jane said, giving Anne one of her considered looks.

Anne blushed. "It wasn't hard to see."

"Listen, my dear, I must give you a piece of advice. It's a kind of ingratitude not to accept praise when it's offered. And it does no good to undervalue yourself. People are always ready to do that for you."

"I guess in my family thinking too well of yourself was the cardinal sin. And then I had a sister who was much less successful than I, and my mother was always afraid she'd feel bad or jealous of me."

"Yes, well, all that's in the past, you're a grown woman now, not a child. And so you must simply stop things that are not in your best interest."

Anne felt embarrassed. She had revealed too much, and in a mode Jane did not find congenial. "You must simply stop things that are not in your own best interest." Jane was not a person she would want to be around if she was feeling weak.

"How did Caroline feel about her father, do you think?"

"For years she was furious and wouldn't speak to him, except in the way she had to. You know, of course, the situation with the money and with Stephen."

"No."

"Caroline had no money of her own until her aunt Adelaide died, which was 1907, and even then it wasn't much. Her money came from an allowance her father gave her. She couldn't afford to be cut off from him entirely, because she needed that money if she was going to paint."

"And Stephen?"

"Her father agreed to be responsible for Stephen's support as long as Caroline promised she would bring the child home and not take him out of the country until he was twenty-one. He kept saying it was France that was the cause of all this heartache."

Jane walked to the door and rubbed a spot off the glass with her index finger. "It was a wicked thing he did. It caused terrible suffering."

She sat down at the table. "Caroline hated America. Particularly Philadelphia. She had never been well received here, and she had been unhappy as a young girl. She said the light was all wrong: the sun was too high, the clouds were useless, there was no silver in the leaves. And there was no place, she said, where one could sit and talk and have coffee, because there was no place that would let you sit, no one you wanted to talk to, and no coffee that was drinkable." Jane laughed. "Of course, it was more than that, but she couldn't work there. She tried. She stayed at home till Stephen was two, and she couldn't bear it."

"What did she do?"

"She packed up and went back to France. It was a very productive period for her."

1902–1908. The years she changed her picture plane, her palette. Those were the years she exhibited with the Fauves; those years showed her transformation from an Impressionist to a Modern, from an American to an international painter.

"What happened to Stephen then?"

"He lived at his grandparents' house. He had a governess. And his aunt Maggie looked after him."

"Did Caroline ever see him?"

"She came home in the summers. She bought a house on the Hudson —you know it from the landscapes. It was the only place in America she liked. She said the Rhine couldn't touch the Hudson; it was second only to the Loire. But she didn't like having a small child around her. They were not good times for Stephen."

"Did she ever like having him around her?"

Jane looked uneasy. "Stephen wasn't always easy to be around. He wasn't a happy person, he became morose quite often. And he was worst around his mother. He never believed she loved him."

"Did she?"

Jane set the cups down in the sink impatiently. "Mother love. I haven't the vaguest idea what it means. All these children claiming their mothers didn't love them, and all these mothers saying they'd die for their children. Even women who beat their children say they love them, they can't live without them, they can't live without them, they wouldn't dream of giving them up. What does it mean 'I love my child'?" She turned quickly. "Come in, my dear, don't lurk in the doorway like that."

Anne turned around and saw Laura, hanging back at the entrance to the kitchen. She was smiling at Jane, but Jane wouldn't look at her.

"Have some coffee, my dear," Jane said, handing her a cup.

"I don't drink coffee, thank you," Laura said.

"Well, then, tea," said Jane, pouring the coffee down the sink as if it had been spoiled by Laura's refusal of it.

Anne wanted to protect Laura from Jane: her quick, angry movements, her refusing looks. Jane had decided she didn't like Laura, and she wasn't the kind of person to try to be nice to someone she didn't at first take to. But Laura was no match for her, and Anne didn't want to see Laura hurt.

"Laura likes cocoa in the morning. I'll make it for her. We usually have a cup together."

"Well, I can't see the point of it," said Jane. "It's no stimulation whatever, and it's terribly fattening. You should learn to drink coffee or tea, my dear. It will make life much easier for you in civilized society."

Anne and Laura drank their cocoa silently while Jane moved around the kitchen peeling potatoes, chopping vegetables. Anne looked at Laura; Laura smiled from over the edge of her cup. Anne could see that there would be no more talk about Caroline with Laura there. But she didn't resent Laura's presence; she saw her as a small, colorless bird about to be swooped on by a hawk who made beautiful downward cuts through the morning sunlight. She was delighted when the children came down dressed and ready, they said, for a walk on the beach. Ben had said he would take them for a walk on the beach before breakfast.

"But Ben's not up yet," Anne said. "Let him have his rest."

"Of course I'm up," boomed Ben, coming into the kitchen. "Just give me a cup of tea and we're off. Good morning, my darlings," he said to Jane and Anne. "Good morning, Miss Post," he said to Laura.

"Why don't you all go," said Jane, not looking at anyone as she gave Ben his tea.

"I'll stay and help you," Anne said.

"Of course you won't. I prefer to do things by myself anyway at this stage of the meal."

"All right," said Anne. "I'll go and change."

Anne knew by the set of Jane's back that she was angry. Her back was impatient, like the back of the woman in the painting. Some high door had closed; the gate had, as Anne knew it would, come down. Anne didn't know how it had happened, but she was glad to be walking out the door. The air was salty; they were only two miles from the sea.

═══════

The children knew the ocean in summer, but in all other seasons it ceased to exist for them. To find it still intact when they had been to school was a sign of richness and benevolence, a treasure hoarded, opened up for them now. Anne worried about Laura, about Jane, worried that she didn't have it in her to do justice to the paintings, worried that the dinner would not be a success, that they would go to bed disappointed, the betrayal of a holiday gone wrong coating their tongues like too much sugar. But she didn't worry about her children. They walked far ahead of her. She saw them as she saw the sea: high, brimming, whole. She held the shells they gave her to collect, the stones she knew would grow uninteresting as they dried; she saw the colors rise on their faces. She ran after them, embraced them, felt, through their thick clothes, the quick, light beating of their hearts.

She thought of Caroline with sadness. She had never felt this for her son, and it was luck, bad luck. Or was it some deficiency of spirit, some inexcusable coldness at the center that cast doubt on all the rest of her life? How could she not have loved her two-year-old child? Jane said he wasn't easy to love. But a child didn't have to earn its mother's love by being attractive or enjoyable or easy to be with. You loved them simply because they were. And because they were yours. Caroline was not an unloving woman. But the child was a bad accident born of the body, fathered in secret, by a stranger whose name no one knew. How primitive it was, this love of children: flesh and flesh, bone, blood connection. The spirits of children flickered, darted: one caught glimpses of them only, streaks of light in the thick forest of their animal lives. She was able to love her children's bodies because her own body had not trapped her; she could treasure the glimpses of spirit since she loved their flesh. And since she loved the body of the man who'd fathered them. Could Caroline have loved her son more if she'd loved his father? She'd died keeping his identity a secret: it was impossible to know.

"I'm afraid I did something to offend Jane this morning," Anne said to Ben.

"Oh, that's always happening. It doesn't mean a lot."

"Only, I wish I knew what it was."

"You'll find out in time. She'll approach you in a sackcloth, covered with contrition for her bad temper. That is, if she likes you. If she doesn't, she'll just go on being icy. One puts up with a great deal from Jane."

"Yes," said Anne, thinking of her gesture, her brushing the hair off her forehead with the heel of her hand. She entered the house fearfully; Jane in a long white apron greeted them with a smile of such radiance that Anne dared to embrace her. She was embraced back, Jane kissed her forehead. "I missed you," she wanted to say, placing her cool cheek against Jane's, which was warm and dryish. But that was absurd; she knew Jane only slightly, she had left her only an hour before.

It was a strange thing for Anne, being served by a woman she admired, sometimes feared. Jane made food appear and disappear, she put out plates and washed them; in the kitchen what she did sent up good smells: rich roasting meat, apples bursting in their pastry. It had never happened to her before: Anne was sent away to think, to look, to use her mind, and down below her someone else took on the part of life that fed the body. But that someone else was Jane, beautiful, learned, masterful. No one could have been less like Anne's mother. Even when she was a child Anne could never have left a dinner wholly to her mother. Even her sister and her mother together seemed unsafe to Anne, as if their slow unhappiness might catch fire in the kitchen and bring the house down on their heads.

Jane gave the call for dinner and Anne came down to the table. It was the table she had dreamed of setting but didn't have the money for. It was a table her mother couldn't have set in thousands of years. The silver candlesticks, the china with its pattern of peacocks, the great variety of spoons and forks and knives, the silver bowl with its chrysanthemums, its brown oak and green holly leaves—it was all that Anne felt she had not been born to.

Everyone sat shyly; the formal beauty made them quiet. Then Jane brought out the turkey, human, comic on its platter. Talk began. The bird was praised; it was coveted; choices were made of dark meat or white. Dishes were passed, and people made arrangements on their plate that pleased them. Jane stood, said a blessing, and Anne felt them all grow ornamented with good fortune, like a spray of diamonds on the dark hair of a woman, as they all acknowledged gratitude in the name of Puritans who must have feared, three hundred years before, the brief appearance of their own good luck.

The two days passed quickly, and yet, since winter was filling in the autumn sky, replacing, dully, the blue flame with bleached silver, there was a solidity to every action, as if people were hoarding something, anything, against a future scarcity they couldn't name. Anne spent her mornings with the paintings, looking closely, making notes, taking photographs so she would have slides of them for her collection. In the afternoons, she walked on the beach with the children and afterwards played cards with them by the fireplace while Jane fixed supper. It was so clearly important to Jane that Anne be freed of domestic responsibility that Anne stopped offering her help. She suggested that Laura do the dishes, an offer which Jane accepted as if Anne were lending her her French maid to iron her collars.

Anne didn't think Laura was having a good time. It was hard to tell, for Laura's face maintained the blank matte she habitually presented. And she smiled, as always, when she caught anybody's eye. But there was no place for her. The children had deserted her in favor of Ben and Jane, and Anne had to keep reminding herself to include Laura in the conversation. But there were conversations Anne wanted her excluded from; she didn't like Laura's listening in on their conversations about Caroline. What could Laura make of a life like Caroline's, that high-colored uneven surface full of passionate triumphs and errors? So the glimpses she got of Laura, staring, smiling when she was looked at, made her feel unnerved. She had to remind herself to feel pity, but always irritation had to be smoothed down, pushed back. Pity was an emotion she had formerly despised; not wishing it for herself, she felt reluctant to offer it to others. But now it was the only thing that kept back the careless impatient gesture, and she felt its value.

It was Saturday evening. The children were in bed and the adults sat around the fire with their books. Anne had bought, on one of her shopping trips with the children, a bottle of Courvoisier for Jane. She and Jane and Ben took slow sips from their snifters, putting them down in the light they read by, watching, occasionally, the light in the amber liquid. The three of them became conscious of a chill in the air; they would have to rise, get a sweater or go to bed. There was a moment of indecision and then, as if a clock had been struck, they knew the evening had ended.

"I must tell you about Sundays," Jane said. "I go to church. Depending upon the hour of your departure, I could go early or late. Will you tell me what you wish? Unless, of course, any of you wants to accompany me."

Anne felt thrown off balance. She thought she had some understanding of Jane. But she couldn't comprehend that within that complicated, finely rendered consciousness, there lodged the image of a prayable being. Was it the same person Laura thought of as she stared over the top of her Bible? Once more, Anne felt at the frontier of an alien land, and one she had no inclination to explore. She looked at Laura, then at Jane. So the two of them had something in common. Perhaps it would make Laura less lonely to go to church with someone.

"Would you like to go, Laura?" she asked the girl, who sat away from them, on a straight chair, leaning her Bible on the corner of the library table.

"No, thanks," said Laura, smiling.

"Are you religious, dear?" Jane asked, as if she were asking her if she could read.

"I have a religious life, but I don't go to church."

"I see. What is the nature of your religious life, then?"

Anne was appalled. How could Jane ask such a question; it was like asking Laura what the nature of her sexual life was. But Laura didn't seem afraid.

"It's very different than what you do."

Anne could feel her heart beat deeper in her empty chest. Now it would happen. Jane would say something demolishing, and Laura would be defenseless. And she couldn't protect Laura without crossing Jane; she knew, therefore, that she would leave the girl exposed.

Jane stood up and poked the fire. "Well, Anne, it's up to you. Do you want to make an early start of it, then? It might be better in terms of traffic."

"Yes, that would be best," said Anne.

She could have wept. Jane wanted them to leave. And it was Laura's fault. She had spoiled the weekend; she had poisoned the well.

———

Anne heard a knock at her bedroom door. She wondered if it was one of the children, knocking through an impulse to politeness or angling to spend the night in her bed. She hated having to make that kind of decision: did one go along with the request, innocent in its own right, or refuse it, fearing to set a bad precedent? "Come in," she said, uncertain of the welcome she would give. She was glad to imagine one of the children in the room with her; the sharpness of Jane's dismissal had unbalanced her, and when she felt off balance, the weight of the children could make her feel set to rights. Yet she thought it was a cheat, to use her children for comfort. It was their dependence that soothed her, and their trust; it was their weakness, after all, that gave her strength.

"May I come in," said Jane, sticking her head around the door.

Anne sat up in bed and covered her chest with the sheet. Her surprise at discovering Jane and not her children at the door made her feel naked.

"I brought the brandy up. I hoped we could talk before you left."

"Of course," said Anne, starting to get out of bed.

"No, don't leave the covers. I'll sit here on the bed, if you don't mind."

"Not at all. I was expecting one of the children. What a pleasure to find you instead."

"I'm afraid I've been rather snappish from time to time this weekend. I didn't want to send you off on that note."

"You've been wonderful."

"Not consistently. I'm not by nature a patient person. It would be nice if I could say I used to be, but in fact I'm far better than I was when I was young. I'm not good at being nice to people I don't want around. Particularly in my own house. I find it lacerating—as if I were wearing some itchy material. Or carrying a cross."

Anne laughed. "You don't like Laura."

"She's a bad piece of work."

Anne felt emboldened by the situation's informality, an informality that Jane had chosen. "Oh, Jane, you simply can't say that. The children adore her."

"The children *adore* Ben; they get along all right with Laura, that's all. She has a dreadful arrogance, that girl."

"She seems to me terribly insecure; she doesn't know what to say next or where to put one foot in front of the other. She's homeless, Jane; she has nowhere to go, and she doesn't know where to begin to look."

"Yes, and she's quite arrogant about it. Have you asked her ever? And think of that vacant smile. Absolutely chilling."

Anne sat straighter in the bed. "Jane, I agree she's not ideal. But the ideal hasn't presented itself, and she's far from the worst. She's very responsible with the children, and I can't do my work without live-in help."

"Surely there's someone else."

"Not in Selby in the middle of the year."

"What about those agencies who send au pairs from abroad?"

"What guarantee do I have that anyone else would be better? I could spend my time comforting a Swiss manic-depressive or a Norwegian alcoholic whom I'd have to hide the liquor from. I'd rather stay with the devil I know."

Jane looked up sharply. "I hope you're right. It's the opposite of what I want, to bring up anything to interfere with your work on Caroline. The children are wonderful, and one would like somebody wonderful to care for them."

"The children *are* wonderful, and I'm not worried about them. Besides, if they learn a little patience and kindness from this experience, it's all to the good."

"Listen, dearest Anne, forgive me for talking like this. I see you almost as a member of my family. The vanity, you know, of a childless woman."

Anne put her arms around Jane and embraced her. How pleasant it was to feel Jane's large bones, her firm flesh. She had always been afraid to embrace her mother too robustly. Her mother was so much smaller than she; her bones were light and delicate. Anne felt for years that she had loomed above her mother, that she could hurt her with her sheer physical size. Jane smoothed Anne's hair and kissed her on the forehead.

"Shall I turn off the light?" she said.

"That would be lovely."

"You'll sleep well now?"

"Yes."

She would sleep well; she was very happy. Jane had taken her in.

———

"Mother, we need to speak to you alone," said Peter, the minute they had got home and had hung up their coats.

Peter's urgent bulletins were undependable. His alarm might be entirely unwarranted or the only true sighting in a world of careless navigators. One could never tell if he was being, on any occasion, the boy who cried wolf or the boy with his finger in the dike.

"Tomorrow's Laura's birthday," he said, short of breath, closing the door to Anne's bedroom, "and we really have to make it good." So Jane was wrong, Anne thought, they *were* fond of her.

"Laura's an orphan," Sarah said seriously. "She's never had a birthday party."

"How do you know that?" asked Anne with concern.

"Well, we asked her if it was sad not to have your parents with you on your birthday. And she said she didn't have any parents," Peter said.

"So that means she's an orphan," Sarah said, looking dreamy.

"That means she must have been brought up in an orphanage," Peter said.

"There aren't very many orphanages anymore," Anne said.

"Well, what happens to you if you have no parents?" Sarah asked.

"You go and live with other people who are like your parents. They're called foster parents."

"I don't think that happened to Laura. I think she lived in an orphanage."

"Why do you think that?"

"Well, if she had those foster parents, she'd write to them, or call them. She never calls anyone; she never gets any letters."

"Do you like being with Laura?" Anne asked, daringly, not knowing what she would do if they said they didn't. So much of life with children, she thought, was throwing balls ahead of you and then hoping you could run fast enough to catch them.

"She does a lot of things with us," said Sarah. "She never yells at us."

"Who yells at you?" asked Anne.

"You do," said both the children.

"I don't yell at you."

"You raise your voice," said Peter.

Anne felt jealousy ripple over her. She wanted to say to the children, Don't you miss me? Don't you hate my not being around?

"They don't let you raise your voice in orphanages," Peter said. "They make you talk in a whisper. They shave your head and don't let you eat anything but oatmeal."

Sarah was looking at her brother with rapt fascination. One could never tell what the springs of romance would be for children. To them Laura was mysterious and exciting. The scent of deprivation that hung on her they picked up. Only, in their nostrils it was an exotic perfume: the stuff of their nightmares made to breathe plain air.

"You're going to make her that daisy cake, right?" said Peter.

"Yes, and I'll invite Hélène, and in the afternoon Laura and I will go to lunch."

"Invite Adrian," Sarah said. "Laura likes Adrian."

"Adrian's very busy," Anne said quickly. "I don't think he'll be able to come."

"Anyway, you can ask him, Mommy," Sarah said.

She felt her children steer her into a corner, as if she were a cow being pushed into a stall. She didn't want Adrian near Laura. The combination seemed to her grotesque. But she knew she had no right to that judgment. If it would please Laura to have Adrian, Anne ought to invite him. It was supposed to be her day.

"And buy her a present from you," Sarah said.

Anne hadn't thought of that. What did you buy a girl like Laura?

"I'm giving her the model I just made. Of a yacht. It was very complicated. She'll like that," said Peter.

"I'm giving her the turkey we made out of pine cones at school for Thanksgiving. I saved it," Sarah said.

"They don't give you presents in the orphanage," said Peter. "Mother, if you and Daddy died, where would we go?"

"You'd go with Aunt Beth and Uncle Richard."

"We wouldn't get to pick?"

"Who would you pick?"

They looked at each other. It had obviously been a topic between them.

"Ben," said Peter.

Anne was surprised. "Why Ben?"

"Because then we could live with him in England. You know, in England they have the queen."

The queen. Anne remembered that when she was Peter's age she had kept a scrapbook about the coronation of Queen Elizabeth. Her sister had colored all the pictures with crayon one day, and she had been furious. But their mother wouldn't say anything to Beth; she said Beth hadn't meant it, that Beth had thought she was making the book nicer. Anne had known, still knew, that wasn't true; Beth was trying to ruin something, and she did. Thirty years later the incident could still rankle. Anne looked at her children, wondering what impress would set on the soft wax of their memories to come out years later, a perfect medal struck in brass, treasured, as any old injustice is, simply for enduring.

"Daddy and I aren't going to die," she said and instantly regretted it. She shouldn't say that to them. She should promise to keep them only as safe as she could.

"When is your job going to be over?" Sarah asked.

"June," said Anne.

"Then Daddy will be home and Laura won't be here and everything will be like it was before," Sarah said.

Just like it was before. She saw her past life as a small warm lake in which she had swum contentedly with slow, plain strokes. But now she felt the bottom had always been muddy; leaves and twigs, weeds, gray-green and shapeless, rose to the surface. She watched her daughter counting on her fingers. "Seven more months," Sarah said, with satisfaction.

─────────

Anne phoned Hélène and Adrian in the morning. Adrian sounded as if he was not alone; grumpily he agreed to come. Hélène's voice, on the other hand, indicated she had been awake for hours. Anne felt its timbre was calculated for reproach. She realized she had forgotten entirely about Hélène, and she hated that about life, that people could be blotted out, sliced off, as if by a blade falling, that life could fill itself up like a television screen or a pointillist's canvas with small hectic dots, creating some images, pushing others out. With people she loved, this anguished her; whenever she encountered it, she was distressed. She didn't like Hélène—she was relieved that she didn't have to see much of her; it was one of the benefits of Michael's absence. Nevertheless, it shocked her that Hélène's life had ceased to exist for her so entirely. How are we rooted in the world, she wondered, when for others we can so easily fail to be?

"I have not seen you or the children or Laura for weeks and weeks," Hélène said.

"I'm sorry, Hélène. I've been so caught up . . . "

"I hope Laura at least has some free time for pleasure."

Guiltily, Anne realized that Laura hardly ever left the house without her or the children. But she couldn't imagine anything Laura would want to do. She worried that she had taken advantage of the girl's unhappy nature.

"She's terribly conscientious," said Anne.

"Ah, yes, I know, it is why I was recommending her. But she is young. She must enjoy her life."

Once more, Anne was struck by how much she disliked Hélène. She was tired of not liking people whom she had no justification for disliking. If she disliked Adrian, Barbara, or Ianthe, she would be able to come up with reasons: Adrian was lustful and self-absorbed, Barbara had an acid tongue and a controlling nature, Ianthe was simply impossible—yet she loved them; she liked to be with them. Hélène and Laura presented to her nothing she could turn away from without a sense of failure.

She was determined to make Laura's birthday successful, memorable even. She was pleased with the gift she had bought Laura, a dress she had seen in the window of Lorilard's, a store that had always puzzled her. She imagined that originally it had catered to the tastes of better-heeled, middle-aged faculty wives whose ideal in casual dress derived from a misunderstanding of the English. The items that made up the bulk of the store's inventory still served this clientele, but as the possibilities for faculty-wife dress broadened, the store had tried to comprehend the revolution. It had failed, and the failure had been one of understanding. As an institution, it had depended on a standard that had no quick variations; when it had to cope with rapid changes of style, its timing was embarrassingly off—a season or perhaps two behind, but that small lag was death. Nevertheless, like a patient, attentive husband who has lost his wife to a new lover, the store had its small victories. Occasionally, you found, passing by the window—for no one anyone knew went in there regularly—something one might think of buying. And if you bought, you always felt good about the purchase, as if it were a charitable act.

The green challis dress she wanted for Laura had caught her eye in the store window because of its brilliant colors. It was a shapeless dress, with long sleeves and a plain collar. Like everything in Lorilard's, it was overpriced, but on this occasion, that, too, pleased her. She thought it was perfect for Laura. She bought, as well, a pair of green wool tights and a long royal-blue wool scarf. Laura could wear the tights with the dress, they would be warm and pretty; she could wear her sandals with them indoors. And, for a while, she could wear the wool scarf with her shapeless brown sweater. When Anne asked Laura if she had a winter coat, she had said she didn't need one.

At eleven o'clock, Anne asked Laura to come into the kitchen.

"I want to give you your present," she said.

Slowly, as if she were in a trance, Laura unwrapped the package. She lifted the dress out of its wrappings, held it up, folded it, and put it back into the box.

"It's very nice, Anne, thank you," she said, without expression.

Anne panicked. "If you don't like it, I can take it back."

"No, I wouldn't do that."

"You could wear it with the green tights. It would be nice and warm. I thought you could wear it for the party if you wanted to."

"All right."

"Only if you want to," Anne said.

"Should I try it on now?"

"If you want to, sure, yes, that would be fine."

Alone in the kitchen, Anne felt clumsy and embarrassed. Had she offended Laura? Had she bought her something she hadn't liked? Laura's response was so peculiar that she had no way to understand it. It made her feel hot, apologetic, as if she were about to be sick at the dinner table. It was rare in her experience to so miscalculate, and she didn't know where she had gone wrong.

In a minute, Laura was in the room again. She was wearing the dress, the green tights. But she was also wearing the hiking boots that Anne had bought her. Anne felt the color rise in her face. The boots made the dress look ridiculous. Any grace it might have lent to Laura's body the boots caricatured and made grotesque. Cruelly, deliberately, Anne felt, they mocked the idea of the gift. Laura stood there in the kitchen, staring ahead of her with a perfectly blank face. She looked like a farm wife coming into town to have her teeth pulled.

It was not possible to imagine that Laura was doing this to punish her, to let her know that she knew that Anne fantasized her improvement. She had to watch out for this new tendency, this suspiciousness that kept rising up in her. Was it living without Michael that was doing it to her? Was it the pressure of her work? Was she fulfilling the dire prophecies about women whose work took over their lives?

She was glad she'd decided to take Laura to the Health Food Restaurant rather than to Marcel's before Laura had managed to annoy her. Otherwise she would have suspected herself of choosing the less expensive restaurant as a punishment. But really, it would have been absurd to spend thirty dollars on a lunch for the two of them. It wasn't the sort of thing Laura cared about, she'd made that very clear.

Resentment made Anne feel she had to force the conversation. They talked about the children; Anne could see that Laura understood them very well, for Laura did not fall into the clichés about her children that so many other people did, and Anne was grateful. By the time the lunch came, she was feeling sympathetic.

"When did you lose your parents?" Anne asked, over dessert.

"I didn't. They're still living," Laura said, looking at Anne and smiling, as if her mistake were a minor faux pas.

"I'm terribly sorry, Laura. I thought you'd told the children you had no parents."

"Well, I'm estranged from my parents. So I thought I'd just say it that way to the children. I thought they'd understand it better." She smiled again. "Do you think I should tell them the truth?" she asked, in a way that made Anne feel it made very little difference to her one way or another, it was Anne's responsibility to decide.

"I'm not sure now, Laura," Anne said, her small reserve of goodwill depleted by the strangeness of what Laura had done and her strange response to it. "I'll have to think about it. On the whole, I try not to lie to them."

"I wasn't really lying, Anne," said Laura, smiling. "I was trying to make it easier for them to understand."

Anne felt the pointlessness of pursuing the topic. With every sentence the problem loomed larger. It was best to let it drop.

———

She was agitated and resentful through the afternoon. There were more of Caroline's letters she wanted to read, she was anxious to organize her impressions of the paintings she had seen at Jane's. And instead she stood in her kitchen, tracing petal shapes on the top of a yellow cake. It made her feel ridiculous. She had done this for the children; they had liked it so much that she extended the ritual for Michael's birthday. Like so many things one did for children, it was absurd but pleasing, and the pleasure came from the anticipation of their pleasure, and from the quality of symbol one bestowed on an act foolish in itself but capable of being, one imagined, the vessel of memory.

Making a cake for Laura was a parody of all that. She probably didn't want it, it wouldn't make her happy, and instead of the accessible and simple feelings of affection she would feel had she been doing this for the children, Anne felt her movements grow jerky with irritation and uneven with dislike. She had to admit it; she didn't like Laura. Liking—you couldn't will it: it wasn't a quality like courage or fair-mindedness that you could work for. And things could only get worse. Living with Laura, every day there would be new opportunities for annoyance. Love grew through observation, she thought; the habits of her husband, her children, had grown dear to her; her knowledge of these habits made up the particulars without which all the feelings they aroused in her would hang on air. But with Laura, each repeated act formed a pattern she watched for evidence, hoping to find some justification for the hardening over, the heaviness she felt when Laura walked into the room.

She was afraid she would ruin the cake from ill-feeling, so it took her three times longer to make than it usually did. The children's excitement made her jittery; they kept popping into the kitchen to see how she did. Even their determination not to steal small bits of icing, even their praise of her—to them—incredible craftsmanship, annoyed her. When she heard her name called at the kitchen door and realized it was Ed Corcoran, who'd been working upstairs, she jumped, like an embezzler who late at night hears the boss's key.

"I'm going to be switching the lights off and on in the kitchen, so I thought I'd warn you. I didn't want you to think you were going crazy, or anything."

She smiled at him self-consciously. "Yes, I know what I'm doing looks like the work of a crazy person, but really I'm quite sane."

She explained to him about the shape cakes, and as she spoke she saw him grow entranced.

"You're a really nice person, to do that, all that work, you know, for somebody who just works for you. Almost nobody would do that. People treat the people who work for them like things. You're really thoughtful. I bet she feels alone, away from her family on her birthday and all."

Foolishly, Anne began to blush. Her pleasure at what the man had said was absurd, she told herself. She washed her hands and invited him to have a cup of tea.

"You know, it's something, birthdays," Ed said. "Before my wife was sick, she used to go all out, for our oldest, you know, Ed Junior. But Brian's never even had a home-baked birthday cake. She's just not up to it anymore. I just buy one from the bakery. I feel bad, though. I feel like a kid should have a home-made birthday cake. Maybe I'll try it, next year. I never baked anything, though."

"Oh, it's not hard. I could show you," Anne said.

He'd told her about his wife's sickness. When she'd been pregnant with Brian, she'd developed a brain tumor; they'd been told it would be fatal. But instead it had sentenced her to a life of incompetence, with periods of madness, with the constant presence of headaches and the knowledge that the life she lived would always be out of her control.

"Imagine me baking a cake. I'd have to wear an apron. Imagine me in an apron." He laughed. "Here, let me try yours on for size."

Laughing, she untied her apron and handed it to him. He was such a large man, an apron could only make him look ridiculous. And he played up the ridiculousness, did a little dance around the kitchen, flicking the apron skirt like a cancan girl.

"Well, back to work, I gotta get out of here before your company comes."

He handed her her apron. Slowly she put it on, pleased it had just come from him. She worked happily now, sensing that he watched her, feeling that each thing she did to make the cake look good was winning his regard. She felt herself enlivened by her time with him; he'd turned an act of drudgery into a pleasure. And what was wrong with that? Life was hard enough, she told herself; it was silly to be suspicious of a pleasure so completely innocent.

Adrian was the first to arrive for the party. He walked into the kitchen and embraced Anne as she tried to set out the plates.

"I feel I haven't talked to you in a year," he said. "The other night was worse than nothing. You know how Barbara and I have to be unbearable children in front of you."

She hadn't thought of that, but of course he was right. "Why do you do it?" she asked.

"Oh, because we know you're so much better than we are, and it drives us crazy. It makes us itchy to torment each other so that you can step in and save us from ourselves."

"Well, whatever you thought about me, these days I'm barely decent."

"Anne, your idea of bad behavior is like Peter's idea of great wealth."

She laughed but took his hand so he would know she was serious. "You don't help me by thinking I'm better than I am."

"I don't think you're better than you are. I think you're perfect. What's worrying you that you've done?"

"It's Laura," she said. "I can't make myself like her. I'm grateful to her for her help, I think she's fine with the children, but I can't make myself feel warm toward her."

"So you're having a birthday party for her?"

"It's her birthday."

"It's Hitler's birthday in April. Maybe you could have a few people over."

Anne laughed. "She said she never had a birthday party. And the children wanted it. She's really had such a sad life."

"What happened to her?"

"I don't know exactly, but I just feel it. She seems so unloved, so unmothered. So tremendously unhappy."

"It's not your responsibility to make her happy."

"But she lives in my house. She takes care of my children. And if I *can* make her happy, I should try."

"What makes you think you can?"

Anne shrugged. "I don't know. Vanity, maybe."

"Listen, you're not her mother. You're her employer. Your responsibility is to pay her a fair wage and not to overwork her. You don't have to save her life. Look, you've got to do your work, raise your children, vote in the local elections, and be faithful to your husband. You don't have to take in strays."

"But who will take them in?"

"Someone who needs them. You have more people in your life already than you can handle."

"I hate that," Anne said. "It's like everybody else in Selby. The wife, the husband, the boy, the girl, the house, the lawn, the college. And there's all this life outside, never taken in."

"So take it in, if that's what you want."

"But I don't want *her*. I wish I could get someone else."

"Now, don't start that. She does a good job for you. That's all you have to worry about. The kids are doing fine with her, the house is spotless. She never goes out; she's not freaked out on drugs or screwing her boyfriend in the living room. Just don't expect too much from the relationship and you'll be fine."

"I've already done too much," said Anne. "I don't see how I can change it. Look," she said, pointing to the loaded table.

"All right, so this is her birthday. But after tonight, be a little more reserved. Maybe she'll make more friends and be less dependent on you; that will ease the burden."

"Maybe," said Anne doubtfully.

"What you need is more time with me," said Adrian. "I'll show you what it is to be ungenerous. Come and have lunch with me."

"I'd love it."

"All right, Tuesday."

Peter ran into the kitchen. "Hélène's here," he said, like a master of ceremonies. "And now we can begin."

In her green dress, in the candlelight, Laura looked prettier than Anne had ever seen her. She laughed when she had blown the candles out; she made appreciative comments about Peter's model and Sarah's turkey. She sniffed happily the lavender soap the Greenspans had bought her, and she tucked one of Adrian's flowers behind her ear. She propped against the candlestick the framed photograph Hélène had given her. It was a beach scene, and on the sky was printed, "Don't walk ahead of me, I may not follow; don't walk behind me, I may not lead; just walk beside me and be my friend." Lastly, she wrapped the blue scarf Anne had bought her around her neck. At nine o'clock Howard said he would take the children home to bed.

"I just want to thank you all for the happiest birthday of my life. Most of all, I want to thank Anne. For everything. Everything," she said, kissing Anne's cheek.

Everyone clapped and raised a glass. "To Anne and Laura," they shouted.

SEVEN

Anne loved her very much; Anne loved her more than anyone had ever loved her. At first she had been frightened to wear the dress. It was beautiful. Too beautiful for you, she thought. "You might as well let your sister have all your clothes, you'll never be anything but ugly." Was this a trick to make her uglier? Did Anne want her to say, "This is too pretty for me"? Was she making fun of Laura by giving her the dress?

Picking it up to put it on for the first time, she held it to her. The bright green, like leaves, the bright small dark flowers. And green tights. They will keep you warm, Anne said.

Laura took her pants and sweater off. Her flesh was white and loose. Veins in the back of her legs showed blue. She pulled the green wool tights up on her legs, up past her stomach. Which was white and loose. Standing in front of the mirror, she forgot that the flesh meant nothing, that her round stomach, white legs, blue veins, all meant nothing. She pulled the dress over her head.

It seemed alive to her. It shone. It lit her face, her hair, which people said was pretty. Standing, looking at herself, she was pleased. Anne had bought her a beautiful dress. Not to make fun of her or to test her. To make her happy. Anne loved her. She would put on the shoes Anne had given her to please her. She walked down the stairs happy, fingering her beautiful dress.

Anne wasn't happy. She looked at Laura in the dress and said, "Fine," but she wasn't pleased. Just like her parents. Whatever she did, they weren't pleased.

She had told the children that she had no parents. That was a mistake.

They were talking about her birthday. "Are you sad that you won't see your parents?"

Quickly the words came out before she thought. Like sparks jumping, the words came, like crackling flames. "I have no parents."

It was true. She had no parents. But in Matthew she had read, "Brother will deliver up brother to death, and the father his child, and children will rise against parents and have them put to death." She understood those words. Jesus had said them, meaning blood ties were nothing, meaning leave behind those you were born into. And everyone who has left houses or brothers or sisters or father or mother or children or lands "will be hated by all for my name's sake. But he who endures to the end will be saved."

Still, she should not have said that to the children. She knew the children loved her. And Anne loved her. Now they were her family. She didn't need her parents or her sister. She smiled, thinking they didn't know where she was, could never trace her. Her father probably worried. Did they call the police when they found she was gone? No one could find her. She had nothing to connect her to the world. Nor copper, nor shoes. No numbers—insurance, Social Security, license plates. All those numbers meaning flesh, food and attachments. They could never find her. She was not attached to flesh.

She liked to think how jealous they would be of her. What would her mother say, her sister, if they saw the party that Anne made for her? Made because she wanted to, she didn't have to. And the presents. she knew how much the dress cost. She had seen it in the window of that store. Seventy dollars. They would never pay that much. On sale they might have bought it, waiting, waiting, waiting till they saw no one else wanted it. But Anne saw it and bought it, saw it shining in the window. Full of love for Laura, Anne went in and paid them all that money. At first Laura had been afraid. Of course, it was so beautiful. The green, the flowers. She had never had such a beautiful dress.

And her room. What would her mother say to her room? The house Anne lived in Laura's mother dreamed of, read about in magazines, but never entered.

All the furniture was old and strong. The furniture would never fail here. The legs would not come off the couch, the stuffing would not break through chairs and fall onto the rug and stay there. In her mother's house the surfaces were made to be shiny, but her mother let them get dull, let rings from glasses set like faces, let the slipcovers bunch up, let Kleenex fall behind the cushions, let cigarettes, bobby pins, shoes lie under chairs, and let the can of hair spray sit on the table. Everything in Anne's house was valuable. She polished things until they shone. The feel of cloth was never stiff, it did not smell of paste or oil. The colors did not shout like her mother's colors. Even when her mother tried to keep the colors in the house from shouting, they would not hold still.

Here things were deep. They did not fly up, fly off, strike the eyes with anger. Her room was a hollow, a valley, a light field. The floors were light and wooden. The small rug beside her bed lay quiet at her feet. The curtains lay in folds. In the morning, sun came to her room, settled on her tables, chairs, her dresser, never glaring. Her sister would be jealous of her room.

And what would they think of the party Anne had made for her? They would never be able to meet anyone like the people who sat around that table, singing to her, honoring her, giving her presents. Three professors, two professors' wives. One professor was Adrian. Her mother would never get to meet anyone like Adrian. Maybe if she took a job at the dry cleaner's, she would get to hand him his shirts. But he would never talk to her. He would never give her flowers.

She knew Adrian really liked her. He said she was a good listener. He was the handsomest man she had ever seen, with his thick gray curly hair, his open shirts, his shoulders. When he came to speak to Anne, she said that Anne was busy, Anne was working, she didn't want to disturb her. But really she wanted to be in the room with him without Anne there. With Anne in the room, it would be Anne that he would talk to. If she went on and listened to Adrian, looked into his eyes when he told her things, praised whatever he said, he would someday like her more than he liked Anne.

What would her parents think if she married Adrian? If she drove up with him to the house in his Volkswagen Rabbit, not having told them anything, not having seen them in two years. If she married him in Anne's house with the house all full of flowers from the garden. It was winter now, but in spring the garden would be full of lilacs, Anne said. White and purple with dark green leaves. At her wedding, they would fill the house.

If she married Adrian, she could always live near Anne. Live in Selby in a house like Anne's, near her, right on the street. She would teach the people all about the Spirit. Teach them that their lives were not important. She would be living their lives but not living them. They would love her but she would not love back as much. Because she still would have the Spirit. They would have to stay but she might leave at any time because she knew that attachments mean nothing. And leaving, she would teach them that.

Still, she would have to be careful. Careful that she did not start to need, careful to remember that it all was nothing, all the flowers and the dresses, all the candles and singing and gifts, the cool and flowered flesh of Anne, the warm, heavy flesh of Adrian. She would never love them back. Not in that way, but in the Spirit, freely, unattached. Then she would leave them. And then they would know.

But she would have to be careful. She would go on saying nothing of the Spirit. She would offer to mend Adrian's clothes, to do his laundry. She would wear the things Anne liked. She would think of projects for the children. In her midst there were enemies. First among them the woman Jane.

"Those who are my foes without cause are mighty, and many are those who hate me wrongfully. Those who render me evil for good are my adversaries because I follow after good."

The Scripture always spoke to her, gave always what she needed. That woman Jane could have no reason to wish evil for her. But she did. Wished her to be separated from Anne out of envy. Wished to have Anne to herself. And envied Laura for the Spirit, which she wanted for herself but did not have. Oh, you could tell by looking at her; she was hungry for the Spirit. But the Spirit did not enter that house.

Anne and Jane loved paintings as they should have loved the Spirit. The paintings they talked about and looked at the way Anne looked at the children when they walked ahead of her or slept. When they could not look back at her and ask her why she looked that way. Laura knew what those looks meant. Attachment and desire. But there was nothing to hold on to, nothing to look that way about. They looked at these things—children, paintings, because they were their treasure. But that was error; it would bring them death. Jesus said, "Do not lay up for yourselves treasure on earth, where moth and rust consume and where thieves break in and steal, but lay up for yourselves treasures in heaven, where neither moth nor rust consumes and where thieves do not break in and steal. For where your treasure is, there will your heart be also." Saint James went further. "Your gold and silver have rusted, and their rust will be evidence against you and will eat your flesh like fire." Jane would lead Anne to the fire. She was proud. Proud of her house, her paintings, her hair. Proud of her beauty though now she was old. Anne was not proud, but Jane could lead her to the fire. Anne must learn to give up her attachments. She must learn her children were no more to her than strangers. Loving them as she did, she could not fly up to the Spirit. Fly up from the flames. Anne needed Laura to keep back the flame. To keep her from the woman and her treasure.

Saint James knew about people like Jane. "You have lived on the earth in luxury and pleasure; you have fattened your hearts in a day of slaughter. You have condemned, you have killed the righteous man; he does not resist you."

Jane condemned Laura; she could feel it. But Laura would resist her. And then Jane would see that Laura was abiding in the Spirit and that she, Jane, drowned in flesh. She could see the pictures burning and Anne burning in the flame. But she could save Anne from the flame.

Jane wished to harm her from the envy of the Spirit. When Laura helped her with the dishes on Thanksgiving, Jane asked, "What will you do when your work with Anne is over?" It will never be over, I will be with her always, Laura thought, but said, "I take the next thing that comes along. Something always turns up." "And have you education?" Jane said. "High school, but there's nothing I want to learn in college." "What do you want to do with your life, then?" Jane said. Laura smiled, knowing her work, the work of the Spirit. "I just do the next thing that comes along. I like working with kids, but I don't care much what I do. I travel light, so I just go wherever something turns up." "But what is it you want from life?" Jane asked. Laura could feel the woman's back go tight; she was getting angry. "I don't want things; I don't need things to make me happy." "Surely you want things," the woman said, "friends, love, food, clothing, shelter." Laura smiled, knowing she was the chosen of the Lord. "I don't need a whole lot to get by," she said.

She would have to be wise. Her saving Anne would not be as easy as it would if Jane were not among them. The strong enemy. The chosen of the Lord were harshly treated. "Remember O Lord how the enemy scoffs and an impious people reviles thy name. Do not deliver the soul of thy dove to the wild beast."

She, Laura, was the dove, she knew. She loved and wished to shelter. With her soft wings she would cover Anne. She had no hard thoughts. She prayed for Jane, her enemy. That she would see the Spirit. Now Jane was the beast that would devour. Devour the soul of the dove. Her breath was hot, her eyes glowed red. She wanted to run at Laura with her strong thick body. She would tear, if she could, the dove's flesh with her teeth.

And yet she would not conquer. Laura knew herself wise and powerful; she knew now she would triumph. Now she knew Anne loved her, Laura would save Anne from the flame.

Coming downstairs for lunch, Anne saw Adrian in the kitchen. "What a nice surprise," she said. "Is this our day for lunch?"

"No, Laura's invited me out."

"Oh, fine," Anne said.

There was no justice in what she was feeling. Laura had a perfect right to take whomever she wanted out for lunch. Of course a young woman would think Adrian a prize; why wouldn't she try for his attentions? Really, the fault was with Adrian if it was with anybody: he should have known that he would turn the head of a girl like Laura. He should stop things before they had a chance to get started.

But suppose he didn't want to? Suppose he enjoyed her company? Suppose he found her attractive? She herself had thought that in a lover's eyes Laura could seem voluptuous. And certainly Adrian knew how to look with a lover's eye: she had always been surprised and rather touched by the catholicity of his taste in women—a diner waitress with varicose veins, a librarian in her sixties. And it would be good for Laura to have as a lover someone experienced and patient. She was so unhappy. Maybe it wasn't familial love that she needed, after all, which was why Anne's dealings with her had been so baffled. Perhaps it was a lover that she needed.

But she begrudged Laura Adrian. She hadn't thought herself possessive of him, but here it was now, the truth, she had to see it. She hadn't minded Adrian's women; she had looked at his sexual life with a mixture of amusement and disapproval, but nothing he had ever done had struck her as this had. Perhaps it was that the women she knew him to be involved with seemed always to be one or another kind of prize. They were beautiful, accomplished, sexy, witty, or at least exotic. She could feel herself valued in his valuing of them. If he thought her attractive, and he thought them attractive, there had to be some commonality. The thought of commonality with Laura disturbed her. Simply, she felt that Adrian's being attracted to Laura took away from her own worth.

Laura appeared at the door. She was wearing the dress Anne had bought her. When she walked into the kitchen, Anne recognized the scent of her own perfume, Fleurs de Rocaille. For Christmas, the year before, Michael had given her an ounce of it. Of course, it was possible that Laura had her own. She might, for example, have bought it at the duty-free shop at Heathrow before she got on the plane, choosing it randomly, because of the name, perhaps. She looked up at Laura, trying to smile. Something else was different about her: she was wearing eye shadow. It was green, the same color as Anne's. But the shadow was common, it could be bought in any drugstore; she hadn't necessarily borrowed Anne's. And Anne would never finally know, for she would never be able to ask Laura. Adrian was holding Laura's sweater, and she was smiling over her shoulder at him.

Why did Laura have such power in her life? She had only to smile over her shoulder at Adrian, to wear green eye shadow, and Anne felt her skin harden over like a rind. But she wasn't the only one to feel Laura's power. It had been a great relief to her to overhear an exchange between Laura and Ianthe. Ianthe had come to the house. She wanted to see Anne. Laura said she couldn't, Anne was working. And Ianthe, who could stand up to cardinals in the Vatican Museum, salespeople at Bergdorf's or Mark Cross, nurses of Park Avenue specialists, hadn't been able to get around Laura. Anne had seen Ianthe contemplating simply pushing past Laura. But she checked herself. It was like a rapier trying to get through a bolster; possibly it could be accomplished, but not with a single, simple thrust, and even Ianthe was able to calculate the carnage. So Laura had prevailed.

She was powerful because she was immobile. Nothing broke her surface; it was all smooth heaviness. She was unsusceptible to humor or to charm. Her interest in Adrian, Anne thought, had nothing to do with his wit or sweetness. She must be interested in him because he so clearly looked as if he would have the endurance necessary to perform. She hated the thought of Adrian and Laura making love. She could see Laura going at it with the same single-mindedness, the same fixity of purpose that she had when she moved the refrigerator to clean behind it. It was unbearable, the things that Laura made her feel. She could have gone through her whole life without feeling them. It was Laura's presence with her in the house, it was the life she had to live beside her that made these antipathies so brutish and so real.

She must forget about Laura. She would go back to work. That was the important thing, the essential thing. Because of Laura, she could turn to Caroline's diaries. There was nothing around the house that needed her attention. So she could put up with Laura, because all the qualities that so annoyed her made Laura the perfect servant. Her dullness, her lack of imagination, kept her from being bored; they made her happy at her job. So that Anne could turn to Caroline's journal and read what Caroline, sitting in her house on the Hudson River, had written seventy-five years before.

I cannot love. I cannot paint. I look at people, at the river, and I know what is called for. Yet I can do nothing. American skies do me no good. They suggest nothing to me, only some vast stupid openness concealing unimportance.

If only I could do something simple: an apple or a branch. To draw as if I were a cobbler, making something ordinary, useful: a pair of boots. If once again the look of things could move me. When M. Matisse had influenza and thought he was dying, he said he was glad he had lived because of his birds, his gardens, they had been so beautiful. If only I could feel that once again: that itch so that the press of human things washed over me: a heavy wave I was not in the path of.

The sun on the leaves: a light, acidic green. Once nothing could distract me from it. The existence of Stephen dulls everything, muddles everything. His unhappiness poisons the house. His relationship to others twists them for me. Because she dotes on him, I see my sister, whom I love, as a fool. My father, who could raise in me a grudging pride, I now despise entirely. His attentions to my son turn him into the complete American, Philistine and boor. When he tells Stephen, "Get out into the open. Don't mope around. Do something, be a real boy," I could strike my father to the heart. Yet I too despise my son for his slowness, his misery. My son. I know where he is. He sits outside my door, waiting for me to finish. I can hear his breath through walls a foot thick. His breath steals mine and blinds me. Sitting out there, covered over with unhappiness, waiting only for the word, the touch I cannot give him, he imagines that, behind the door, I work. I hear his governess tell him to stop sitting by the door, to come outside, to play a game, to hear a story. He will not move.

Poor Stephen at the door, four years old, waiting, doing exactly the wrong thing, what would never gain his mother's affection, only her impatience. And poor Caroline, trapped in her room, pressed down, rubbed raw by irritation, guilt, contempt, the fear she could not work. Three months a year she gave to Stephen: months wrung grudgingly from a dried skin. Leaving Paris, her life, she boarded ships, crossed seas. To get to what? Her son, whose flesh made hers grow cold. Yet in the paintings of him, she had rendered his flesh beautiful. Her freest brushwork, pinks and purples, blues spread quickly, lovingly, made up the flesh of the boy's limbs in *Stephen, Sleeping.* When her father scolded Stephen, she was ready to take knives, to strike him to the heart. Yet around the child she could not breathe. Still, she came to him every year, from June to August. Off the boat she swept, by him, above him, covering them both in a miserable cloud of failure and incomprehension, while she tapped her fingers on the windowsills of the house that had been built by Dutch settlers in the 1600's, and smoked, impatiently, a hundred cigarettes a day to spite her father. Then on September first she left, lifting the cloud and leaving Stephen even more defenseless, naked to the devastating blast of manly expectation, which would only make him wither, sicken, fall into his own unlucky nature, his own sinking heart.

Anne looked at the sketchbooks of those summers. She could see that Caroline was learning in those drawings a new line, quick and bold. She could see it in the drawings of the branches, in the thick line marking the horizon, in the spare, sure strokes suggesting doors and windows. Caroline sat in her room desolated, convinced she was marking time at worthless labor. Yet those drawings were critical to what she achieved in her late work. Would it have mattered, to Caroline, to Stephen, if they had known those heavy, lacerating hours would lead to something? Would Caroline have loved her son more if she had known that what she did while he sat outside the door would point the way to her best work? Would Stephen the child have thought to himself, I am lonely, but it is leading to something? Of course not. Nothing could have helped them. There was no connection between art and life. The backward glance was nothing, or a lie. They had to live their lives. They could only be themselves, Caroline in her room, made miserable by the miserable son who sat outside the door breathing unhappily the air she needed.

The house in the morning thrummed with expectation. The morning sunlight, weak and ordinary, took on purpose. For the children, life was shining: they were going to the city. A wave of strangers would engulf them, beautiful, treacherous, and carry them on. They might see a movie being made; they might see a murder. It was nearly Christmas. Stores would be lit up, lights would be strung through the dense air.

Formally, they walked into Jane's building. Her apartment was small and circumspect; it was clear that her domestic life was lived in the country. The walls of all the rooms were white. They had been covered with Caroline's paintings and were nearly bare. Square drab chairs sat on the living room rug like grounded birds. The curtains were a somber green.

"Come in, my dears, come in," said Jane, sweeping the children forward. "I'd like you to meet my friend Betty Loomis."

Jane had told Anne not to bring Laura; she said a woman who did some work for her would be happy to care for the children. It was a pleasure for Anne to be away from Laura for a day; it was a pleasure, even, to feel she was in league with Jane in excluding her. Would Laura spend the day with Adrian? She wouldn't think about it.

"Betty's staying with me for the winter," Jane said. "She's been helping me around the house."

Betty Loomis was sitting in one of the chairs as if she would be happiest disappearing into it. Her poor thin shoulders folded in toward the center of her body like a coat hanger stepped on by heavy feet in boots. Her hair —five colors, none of them distinct—was pulled back in a red elastic band; there were reddish-brownish patches underneath her eyes suggesting she might have been rubbing them in a particularly violent, desperately habitual way. Her eyes were large and light, covered by a thin, pervasive film of misery, endurance, patience, and bad luck. She wore black ski pants and a Ban-Lon sweater in a shade that twenty years before had been called, too hopefully, royal blue. On her feet were ballet slippers, the thin laces at the instep tied in two neat bows.

"Where are you from originally?" asked Anne, bowing her knees and hunching her shoulders, fearful that Jane's physical abundance, all her size and color, might be too much for this girl if she added her own to it.

"Florida," she said. "My people were from Florida at first. I wasn't actually brought up there. I lived in Georgia for a while, then Alabama. I came here in 1978."

"Yes, of course you did," said Jane. "Now, children, you must be very good and do exactly what Betty says, and more, for she's very kind, and I'm afraid you'll find her easy to take advantage of. We'll be back at four, and then we'll go right off, Betty, so you must see to yourself for dinner."

Betty nodded, tapping a cigarette on the arm of the chair.

"You shouldn't smoke. The surgeon general has determined that cigarette smoking can be hazardous to your health," Peter said.

"Don't be a bully, Peter," Jane said. "There's a very good phrase, 'Every man to his own poison.' You may not have found yours yet, but you will."

Peter fell back on the couch, blushing. Anne was afraid he was going to cry. He was, after all, in love with Jane.

Betty Loomis sat down on the couch beside him. "I know you said that because you cared. Thank you, that means a lot to me." She said the word *cared* as if it had three syllables.

Peter's body corkscrewed into the upholstery with pleasure. Like all moralists, Anne thought, he was at heart a sentimentalist. He would probably marry a country and western singer and spend the rest of his life trying to teach her Greek. Anne kissed the children and gave them each a dollar. Walking down the hall, she wondered what peculiar accident had brought Betty Loomis into Jane's life. She was obviously more than an employee. Standing behind Jane, waiting for the elevator, she knew she would never dare to ask about it, and she thought it at least possible that Jane might never say a thing about it. Jane was the kind of person who was always puzzled when people found her arrangements unusual. With the extreme isolation of the genuinely self-possessed, Jane thought herself the norm.

———

Anne had given the people in the gallery the list she had put together of the paintings of Caroline Watson owned by collectors. Today she would meet the gallery people for lunch, to talk about contacting the collectors and perhaps borrowing some of the paintings for the show. She had seen photographs of only a few of them in exhibition catalogues of the twenties and the thirties. So she was counting on Ben—and Jane—to advise her about which of the paintings might be important to pursue.

They were to meet the people from the gallery at a Japanese restaurant. Their choice of restaurant made Anne even more nervous. A business lunch at a Japanese restaurant. It implied, to Anne, a sublime disregard of convention, a fine, imaginative will to distinguish themselves, these people, from lawyers, stockbrokers, publishers, who sweated in other places over large, dark hunks of meat and, like barbarians, grunted their transactions. She had eaten at a Japanese restaurant only once, in Boston, when she had worked at the Gardner. She remembered thinking it was wonderful, the way the things were done: the small, rolled pieces of fish with their alien coloring and textures, the hot green horseradish, the soup one drank from a bowl one lifted up, the green ice cream that tasted as if it had been made of leaves.

Ben and the two young men at the table rose to greet Anne and Jane; the two young women, seated next to each other, smiled slightly to the left of Anne's head. Anne was introduced to them; the men were Charles and Daniel, the women Cressida and Jill. She was glad to sit down quickly. The four people made her feel like some gross creature shipped in to do hard labor. They were all thin and their clothes had sharp angles. The men wore suits cut close to their slight bodies with thin lapels and thin dark ties. Cressida wore a jacket of a brass-colored soft leather with hard wide shoulders. Jill was entirely in black, and her ankle-length boots were a silver version of the leather of Cressida's jacket. Sitting in her gray wool skirt and tweed jacket, Anne felt dowdy and *parvenu*. That she was dressed in a mode at least recognizably similar to Jane's brought her no comfort. Jane was forty years older than she; these people were more nearly her contemporaries.

"Tell me about that divine pasta you got, Daniel," said Charles. "I want to know everything."

"Well, it's this place in the West Village. this absolutely adorable, tiny, absolutely ancient lady makes it in the back every day. I swear she grinds her own wheat."

"Of course, the pasta in America is inedible if you've spent any time in Italy. As is the coffee," said Jill.

"I know a place that has the most amazing blend of coffee. It's their own, but it really tastes European."

"Obviously, there is no such thing as European coffee. Or American. It has to do with the grinding, the blending and the preparation," Jane said, putting on her glasses to look at the menu.

"Yes, of course," said Cressida, "but if you drink what passes in America for coffee you're drinking dishwater."

"That's nonsense," said Jane. "One can easily get good coffee here."

"I can't drink coffee anyway," said Charles. "Half my salary goes to Zabar's to get their decaffeinated. At least I can get Ferrerelle there."

"I don't understand this craze for mineral water," said Jane. "It's fine mixed with something, but people nowadays seem to drink it plain."

"It doesn't have any calories," said Jill, viciously lighting a match, as if the mention of calories made her feel she should have a weapon close at hand.

"But it doesn't taste good," said Jane. "One might as well drink nothing."

"I think it's got a kind of fascinating, ascetic taste," said Daniel.

"People don't enjoy eating and drinking the way they used to. Don't you agree, Ben?" said Jane.

"Absolutely," said Ben. "And they look the worse for it. In my day, women looked like Anne and Jane, with flesh they were proud of and a good color."

"I think Americans eat too much," said Jill.

"Of course they do," said Charles, "but it's all shit. I mean if you look at the way a French or Italian peasant eats . . . "

Jane was looking into the middle distance, clearly bored. Ben turned to Anne and spoke to her about the children's Christmas presents. For the rest of the meal, he ignored the four young people and turned his attention exclusively to Anne. This made her feel worse. She imagined they thought he had selected her to do the catalogue because she was his mistress. From time to time, one of the four would try to get Ben's attention. They wanted his approval or his contact; he was famous, he was influential, he had access to wealth and property. Miserably she ate the several courses of her meal. Not one word had been said about the paintings.

As they rose to leave, Ben said, "I think we all agree that the selection of the paintings in private collections should be left entirely to Mrs. Foster. She is the best qualified of us to judge."

"Of course," said Charles. "Remarkable piece of research you've done. Just remarkable."

"I guess you have a lot of free time in the country where you live. No distraction. Nothing to see, no other shows. No place to go. Just you and your children in that small, sweet town. It must be very peaceful," said Cressida.

Was she trying to understand or deliberately misunderstanding? Anne felt she outweighed the girl by fifty pounds.

"Really great work you've done," said Jill. "First-rate. Going to be a major show."

"Thank you," said Anne. She felt that they despised her.

In the cab on the way to her apartment Jane said, "That's what I call a nasty piece of work, those four affected sillies."

"They didn't say a word about Caroline's work," said Anne, feeling close to tears. She felt they'd slighted Caroline; it was as if they'd slighted one of the children.

"They're afraid to in front of you," said Ben. "They don't know anything, and they're afraid to reveal themselves before an expert."

"I see how you would frighten them," said Anne.

"Not me, dear. You."

"Me?"

"You know more about Caroline Watson than anybody in the world."

Anne looked out the window. Afraid of her? No one in her life had been afraid of her.

"Where are the children?" Ben asked.

"In my apartment," said Jane.

"Who's looking after them?"

"Betty."

"Betty the Basher?"

"Ben," said Jane angrily. "You're much too old to be puerile."

"Giving her a second chance with Peter and Sarah, are you? Well, I suppose Peter's old enough to look out for himself and his sister."

"Of course he is," said Jane haughtily. "When she hurt her children they were *much* smaller."

"Hurt her children?" asked Anne with anxiety.

"She had a few unfortunate incidents at a time when she was mentally unstable. But she's much better now. Anyone can see that."

Alarmed, Anne sat up straighter. "Jane, did you leave my children with a child abuser?"

"You say the phrase, Anne, as if that were all there was to her identity. There is much more to her besides. She's a brave person, with tremendous loyalty."

"Besides, darling, Jane's rehabilitating her. So we must all be part of the experiment."

"Of course, I wouldn't have done this if I weren't quite sure she was trustworthy. I met her last year, when I was volunteering to teach people to read."

"She can't read?" Anne said, as if that made the woman more unrelia- ble.

"Well, she can now. I've taught her. She's had a most dreadful life. She got pregnant at sixteen. Her boyfriend married her, then joined the army, impregnating her twice more, then vanishing without a trace. Her mother was an alcoholic, her father half dead of emphysema. They told her they couldn't help her anymore. Imagine, they simply said they were tired of helping her. She got on a bus with her children—three days she was on a bus with them. When she arrived in New York, she knew no one. She lived in a single room in the West forties and worked as a waitress in a donut shop. The one man she met who was kind to her left her eventually because he couldn't stand being around her children. One day, after she'd picked up the children from a wretched day care center, her four-year-old, in a fit of temper, knocked over a gallon of milk. Before she knew what happened, she'd broken his arm. Well, she was absolutely undone by it. She called the child abuse center, and they set her up with a counselor. Her life's infinitely better now, I'm sure she never beats children anymore. But her children are in foster homes now—if I told her she couldn't take care of your children, it would be a terrible blow to her confidence."

"Jane, you might have asked me first," said Anne.

"Well, my dear, I knew you'd feel just as I do. We're terribly alike; we could be mother and daughter."

All Anne's anger melted at the intimacy Jane implied. It was absurd, of course; she was nothing like Jane; she could live a hundred years and never would be. But it was an honor even to have Jane imagine it. She couldn't say now what she wanted to say: How could you have put my children in danger? Child abuse was understandable; one could easily see why it happened all the time. In the three years when she had been home all day with the children, her own frustration had shocked her, the boredom that led to irritation at the smallest thing. But she thought of the flesh of her children, and the flesh of the woman who had abused her children took on the odor of contamination. You did not hurt your children. You kept them from harm. That was what you did in the world if you were a mother.

She ran up the stairs of Jane's building. The children were sitting happily on the floor with Betty doing a jigsaw puzzle.

"We had a great time," Sarah said.

Anne hugged them, dizzy with relief. Looking at Betty, she thought of Laura with gratitude. She was boring, she was irritating, but she was utterly dependable. However much she intruded on the peace of Anne's inner life or, Anne thought unhappily, upon her own self-love, she never had to worry if her children were unsafe when they were with Laura.

———

The sky was zinc-colored that morning. Anne leaned her cheek against the windowpane; the cold glass reminded her how lucky she was to be indoors, it made her happy to get back to work. She heard Ed Corcoran working downstairs. He'd asked if he could bring his son Brian on days when something went wrong at home and his sister couldn't baby-sit. Anne had been happy to say yes.

She thought of Ed's wife whenever she watched Brian Corcoran sitting on the floor, playing seriously with his toys, out of his father's way, but never allowing himself to move too far from the protective nimbus cast by his father's body. How were children attached to their father's bodies, where they had never lived, she wondered. Michael's attachment to the children had always seemed so different from hers. When they were babies, she physically ached for them if she was away from them. At night before she went to sleep, she had to restrain herself from lifting them out of their cribs, she wanted so much to have them near her, to put her mouth against their cheeks, their hair. She knew their bodies better than Michael did, for she tended them more, and they had lived closer to her body. They had lived in the curves her body made while she nursed them; she had felt their small, primitive fingers tapping, running up her torso. Flesh of my flesh. Did it go for fathers too? She hadn't thought so. Michael's passion for the children was a remove farther from the body. There was a kind of nostalgia about it, as if in holding his children he was holding the child he wished he had been. He never saw himself as once the flesh that housed them; he didn't see it as a miracle that they got through one whole day of their lives alone. This made it easy for him to give their natures a moral credit she always had to strain after.

But it was different for Brian Corcoran. Safety to him was his father. A mother's safety was a bolster this poor child would never know. But was he a poor child? He seemed happy. Anne admired him; it didn't seem inappropriate in his case to use the word "admire" for a three-year-old. He took part in the world of work. He was a serious person. She could never have left her children with as little attention as Ed left Brian when they were his age. He was happy with his father, but happy nowhere else. He played shyly for brief periods with Peter, who loved small children and was talented with them, but always his glance flicked nervously toward his father. She could see the child's eyes lift with alarm when his father left the room, then drop down again in peace when he could see his father near him. She watched them eat their lunch together, heard Ed talking to his son as she talked to her children, but most men did not, familiarly with an element of gossip and confiding.

Ed Corcoran was very tall; six three, she guessed. It was a pleasure for her to stand near him; he made her feel—a thing she rarely felt with men—not oversized. She remembered Barbara's flirtatious giggles over the blue pages of his estimate and realized she was attracted to Ed too. Were all the women he did work for secretly in love with him? Because he was a nice man, and there were so few nice men? Because they were alone in those big houses?

It was strange to her, this feeling of being attracted. She had felt it before, of course. It was a scintillating feeling, but always before, Anne had been stopped by the solid presence of her husband and the physical life of marriage.

Was she in danger, alone in the house with a man she found desirable? No, Ed Corcoran wasn't the man she would betray her husband with. There would always be, in her coupling with Ed, something comic; they were both so large, so shy, so lacking in the ease of quick seduction.

She would have to be taken over by someone, and Ed was much too nice for that. He would allow her hesitation, and in hesitating she would always choose fidelity. And what would they talk about? He was an electrician. Yet they seemed to have a lot to say. They talked about their children.

He asked if he could work some nights from ten to midnight. His children were in bed then and his wife asleep as well. If something went wrong, his older son, who was ten, could telephone him here. He asked her that after she had confessed that she worked till midnight. How could she refuse him? She had no inclination to. It was peaceful, knowing everyone in her house was asleep except the two of them, who stayed up working. Soldiers on watch, nurses in a battle hospital. At midnight she came down and offered him a cup of tea. So it had come to that: every night at midnight she drank tea with a man nothing like her husband. It was a good thing Michael was coming home soon. He would be there in ten days. But she was in no danger from Ed Corcoran. He would never make the first move. Largely, she supposed, for reasons of class. Still, she enjoyed talking to him every evening; she was sorry that that would stop. She would tell him that when her husband came home he would have to do his work during the day, as he did for everyone else.

Certainly, though, today she could ask him and his little boy to join her for lunch. There couldn't possibly be anything wrong with that. But she wouldn't allow herself to go downstairs and greet them yet. She made herself finish transcribing the passage in Caroline's journal she was working on.

June 15, 1920
Arques-la-Bataille

So I am an "older painter." A troop of trousered English girls arrive at the door, expecting lunch and the freest of accesses to my studio, to say nothing of my life. They imagine they are not vain, but they are as vain as courtesans about their trousers. How they horrify me; yet they are the culmination of all my dreams. If only I, at twenty, had been able to bicycle through the countryside with painting chums, visiting the studios of "older painters," what could I not have done! Yet freedom has only coarsened them; they paint like demented children. If they distort a figure, they imagine they have understood Matisse. To them I am elderly, in long skirts, with thick ankles. And how the *demoiselles* can condescend: "Such attention to drapery," "Such a finely modeled ear." Dear God, that Stephen may not marry one of them. But he is much too fine for them. What they want in their hearts is a brute who'll throw them down the stairs and sweat above them in a drunken stupor.

What an odd letter that was. It always pleased Anne to see Caroline display any fondness for Stephen; it made her feel she could relax her vigilance, he was not quite alone. But it made her sad to see Caroline so vindictive about the young women painters. Her response to them meant, of course, that she was beginning to get old. Why did it always happen, the rebellious young turned punitive in middle age? Perhaps, Anne thought, since she'd been conservative in youth, in age she'd be expansive, even radical. But now she was a woman with young children; she couldn't possibly do anything remotely dangerous; anything dangerous she did would be dangerous to them. The whole shape of her life must be constructed to make her children safe. She couldn't even have an affair with her electrician! Almost reluctantly, she went downstairs to invite Ed to lunch.

They were waiting for Michael in the airport. The plane was an hour late, and the children could hardly bear the excitement. She gave up trying to keep them close to her; she told them where their father would be coming out and said they mustn't stray too far from that spot. Peter, who was nothing if not farsighted, had brought a month's allowance with him, simply to squander. This made Sarah cry; she hadn't brought any money, and Anne, pitying her exclusion from so sumptuous and meaningless a feast, gave her a two-dollar advance on her allowance. Then Peter was angry; he stamped his feet, accusing his mother of her perennial sin, injustice, saying if his sister had forgotten the money she should suffer. Suffer was the word he used, and it made Anne shiver. Sternly she said to him, "There's enough suffering in this world." Peter took her statement for an august utterance, and it chastened him into silence. He always liked, she knew, the runic generalization; it suggested to him that adults were opening the curtain, letting him into a truth he always knew was there but that they had kept from him. Sarah walked ahead of her brother, occasionally hopping. Money had bestowed its grace on her; she had no need of conversation.

Anne had asked Laura to stay home. She didn't want her with the family for their first glimpse of Michael.

She knew that no one else was as bothered by Laura as she was. Barbara made fun of her, but Barbara made fun of everyone. Adrian had lunch with her, he took her to the movies. Did he sleep with her? She didn't want to think about it. Jane disliked her, but Anne suspected Jane of snobbery, of class or of religion, she couldn't be sure which. Anne was anxious to learn what Michael's response to Laura would be. She depended upon him for justice. It wasn't because he was a man; she didn't believe men had born in them a greater capacity for justice. It was that Michael valued reason more than she did, and that justice in their lives was as real and valuable, solid and living to him, as it was vague, impalpable, to her. His justice had helped them again and again. His reasonableness, like a simple bridge, had carried them over nights of babies crying, through financial crisis, through the cruelties of friends, the failures of sex. If it were not for his justice, she wouldn't have been able to have this year, to do her work.

He was coming out the door now; he was walking toward her. She had waited so long to see him, she wanted to see him so much, that for a moment she didn't recognize him. She stood still, afraid to move forward, afraid that this man who appeared to be her husband was the mere invention of desire. Then she felt herself pushed forward. The pleasure of touching the body that was, indeed, her husband's sang in her ears as if she had come up too quickly from beneath the sea. The children ran against him, clinging to his legs. She wouldn't move away from him to give them more access. She had to hold him; she kissed him ten times on the face. She kept kissing his shoulder, disbelieving her good fortune. How handsome he was. The facts of his body came back gradually to her. How odd it was that a body so well known, so deeply loved, could allow itself in absence to be even partially forgotten. It was a surprise to her how slight he was, how fine and straight and light his hair was; only his eyes—light blue with gold or silver in them, never, even when he smiled, relinquishing a kind of sadness—were entirely familiar. His beauty was a simple joy to her; she allowed herself to bask in it as if it were any natural phenomenon: sunshine or fragrant air. She was sure the people near him must have been refreshed simply by sitting with him on a plane.

"We're insane," he said, kissing her hair, leaving his hands free to pet the children. "Why did we leave each other for one day? I didn't think it was possible to miss anyone as much as I missed you."

"I've missed you, I've missed you," she kept saying, not knowing now how she had done it, lived without him, lived without his voice, his body. Walking beside him, leaning into him, carrying one bag for him while he carried the other, she understood that these months she had kept her body's life shut down. Now she flowered; some heavy weight lifted, her head was light with effortless goodwill. The children chattered the three hours back to Selby. She was silent. She kept leaning over in the car, kissing the top of his arm, putting her head on his shoulder. Soon he would be gone again. She mustn't think of it. For three weeks she would have him near her. He took her fingers, kissed them, put them carefully on her lap. The children would be asleep soon. Then all that dark night, she would have him to herself.

=====

She was in the bathroom with Michael. He was shaving; she had just come from the shower and was standing to the left of his shoulder, in front of the mirror, taking pins out of her hair. The slightly overheated air, the dampness in the atmosphere, the smell of soap, created a breathy hopefulness in the room, and Anne could look at herself with a simple, physical happiness. Her shoulders still weren't quite dry; she touched them with pleasure. Laying her face against Michael's back, she kissed him over and over. All night they had held each other, and now the day would be theirs. They would go into stores; they would buy things for the children; they would have lunch, sitting across from each other in a restaurant, touching each other's hands. In the evening, they would have people to dinner. She would sit at the opposite end of their dining room table, and he would watch her with a slow, sexual pride as people lifted glasses, forks, sharing their happiness.

The children were shy with their father; she sent them out late in the afternoon, when the too-early darkness made the air exciting, to take a walk while she cooked. The heavy smells of winter cooking hung in the house, everything was charged with a false, seasonal excitement, but under it all was the jet of sexual love once more heating things, making her feel what all those months had been absent. She'd found it easier to be with Laura when Michael was there; he had asked her simple questions, natural questions, that Anne, fearing either an answer she wouldn't want to live in the house with or a wound too near the surface, hadn't asked. So she'd learned the name of Laura's hometown, that she had a sister, a high school education only and no hopes for more. With Michael near, Anne felt less open to access, several sheets protected her from Laura's yearning. Marriage muffled, it protected, it made it much more difficult to be generous because you were always kept back a little from the lives of others, and so from feeling their need. She was able to be in the kitchen with Laura now, to accept her help with dinner, with none of the anxiety she'd felt a week ago. Possibly, she thought, Michael's visit would make their relationship normal; he would teach her how to be with this girl who, he'd reminded her, was unsettling simply because she was so hard to categorize. When

Michael told her Laura was all right, she was able to believe him. Laura even seemed happier with him around. When he came home with the children and changed his clothes, all of them sat in the kitchen, doing something to help with dinner, and Laura sang Christmas carols along with the rest of them as if she actually once, too, had lived in a family, had had a home.

Anne had invited Hélène for dinner on Michael's second night home. She arrived an hour early. She could almost mar the surface of the evening; she could almost make a parody of it, with her clapped hands, her cooing, her saying to Anne: "But what a genius you have for family life. I can't imagine you would want another work. It is for people that your gift is. Why, the change in Laura is extraordinary. She tells me she has never in her life been so happy."

Then she had to pull Michael from the center of them all, talk to him about the college, hear the news of her friends, so that the weight of the room shifted and everyone looked toward them with a deprived, hungry imbalance, longing to be let in. She was giggling, she was coming at Michael's face with a series of playful slaps; she was telling him how everyone in Toulouse was made for him.

"Speaking of which I got a telephone call, a telephone call, my dear, from Charlotte Mistière. Purporting, she has said, to wish me *joyeux Noël,* but one knows how parsimonious she is. The real reason, of course, was to inquire of your health. It is a genuine conquest you have made, my friend, and with the most prestigious hostess in the town. At forty, her dinners have put out of joint all the older noses of the town dowagers. She is famous for them."

"She's been quite kind to me," Michael said.

Something rose up in the air, something sharp, elusive, it swam back and forth between Anne and Michael like a dark fish possessed of rows of clever teeth, not yet visible. Michael was uncomfortable. Anne could see it; she knew him better than anybody in the world. Twice, three times in the seventeen years she'd known him, he had blushed. He was doing it now; he pulled his sweater down over his hips like a schoolboy.

The hard object in the air flew apart, broke into tiny pieces that were hooks, embedded themselves in her skin and disappeared there. Was that it, did Michael have a lover? Charlotte Mistière. Would she have to think of that as the name of the woman she shared her husband with? No one would be surprised to hear it; he was a young man, a handsome man, he was away from home. She must put it out of her mind. It was true or it was not, and she would have no way of knowing. She could never ask him.

For that was what they had agreed upon: if either of them had an affair, the other would not be told. They'd made the decision three years ago when Michael's best friend from college had come to Selby for a week's colloquium and had propositioned Anne. Michael had had an evening class; she'd come home late with Roger after a wine-and-cheese party. She'd had too much to drink. They'd been making fun of people; they were laughing the way they had the last time she'd seen him, in a Cambridge apartment. They were laughing, then they were kissing; it had all happened terribly fast. "Come to bed with me," he said, "I've wanted to go to bed with you for fifteen years."

The thought of it had made life seem brimful and swimming. She could do it; she could love her husband, she could have a lover. She would talk to him about it, no one would get hurt. In her mind she imagined that Roger would come to town once every few months, and they would have a night together. But it wouldn't mean she loved Michael less; it would just mean life was richer.

They drank more wine; they did more kissing. She sent Roger home and said she would speak to Michael when he came in. Dizzy with wine, she told her husband her wonderful news. His reaction shocked her. He brought his hand down, flat on the surface of the table, like the blade of a wide knife. The wineglasses jumped; small wet pools formed beside them. "Do it or don't do it, but don't talk to me about it," he had said. "Don't ask me if it's all right. It's not all right."

And he had walked up the stairs, to their bed. All night he'd slept as if he slept on the edge of a cliff, as if to move one inch closer to her would be like falling into a dangerous ocean.

In the morning she woke, feeling like a murderer. Guilt settled in her spine like molten lead, rose up and spread behind her eyes. It had marked the end of their young marriage, what she had done, having drunk too much, in just one evening. It hadn't been the end of everything; life came in, covered the bare patch of torn-up earth with the architecture of family life, but she'd had to live with the knowledge that she had done damage to the person in the world whom she most loved. That knowledge led to a resolve: she would never be unfaithful to him. And, months later, when they were able, finally, to speak of it, they'd promised each other, if they were unfaithful, they would keep it to themselves.

It had seemed mature then, and sensible. But now she found it dreadful. How could she go through this time she had so longed for if she suspected Michael of having a lover and could never know the truth. Suddenly all she had taken pleasure in stood up and mocked her. What a stupid thing it was to shape a life with things like holidays, bolstering things up with them, spreading things around them. Making of them some sort of sanctuary so that nothing untoward might happen there. Was it for the children? Yes and no. For the idea that life might be scooped up and made dense with the pressure of a festival, a festival she now saw only as oppressive and absurd? She felt ridiculous to have looked forward to it, to have imagined it was a time when life could be held back. She saw the weeks ahead, the meals, the presents, the parties, the clothes, as a sheet of black glass before her eyes, blank and cold, impossible to break through or to get around.

Michael went on talking to Hélène; the children were cutting cookies. Perhaps she had invented everything; the hooks under her skin might have been of her own construction. Surely if Hélène thought Michael was having an affair, she wouldn't have hinted it in the kitchen. Anne watched her, begrudging her her poorly applied eye shadow, her new acrylic sweater in its inorganic shade of red. Was it possible that this person, so universally acknowledged to be good, was making mischief? Or was she, as Michael said, a genuine innocent simply passing on the great regard, the seasonal good wishes of a new, devoted friend?

Anne felt entirely alone in the room, and then it came to her that she was not; she was being watched. Laura was standing at the counter, absently tearing lettuce into a wooden bowl. Laura's eyes were on her. She, too, had seen the thing, the sharp, solid thing, rise up in the air, she had seen it fly apart, she had seen that the hooks had penetrated. From sheer irritation, Anne knocked the vinegar cruet to the floor; the red liquid spread out quickly past the hillock of glass shards. In a second, Laura was beside her with a sponge, kneeling next to her, helping her, smiling with forgiveness, as if one of the children needed comforting for a mistake. She wanted to shout at Laura as if she were a voyeur at the window. She wanted to scream: You have no right; this is not your place; this is my life. Your understanding of it, what you think of as your understanding, is a theft, a lie, you will never know anything about me. But that was out of the question; it was something she would never do or say. She thanked Laura and, feeling she had to protect Michael from something, walked over to him and put her arm around his waist.

―――――

Driving to her parents' house on Christmas Day, she thought of how she liked it now as she never had when it had been her home. Perhaps that was true for everyone, she thought. A necessary discomfort was engendered by those houses, which, like good and liberal parents, understood that at a certain point the children must heap scorn upon them. Having sheltered those young lives, having circled around them, kept out cold, let in light, did those houses close in purposely upon the young so that they could do, joyfully, that incomprehensible thing: leave home and run to the outside world, as if that were the place where they were safe?

They stopped at a diner for lunch. In the window she noticed a sign: CHRISTMAS SPECIAL: TURKEY DINNER $4.95. She knew Laura might easily have been one of the people in a place like that at Christmas. So it was a good thing that Laura was with them. It was one of the ways you made up for good luck, paid back the unpayable debt, by being kind to the unlucky. Nevertheless Anne resented her presence. She had been a witness to Anne's suspicions about Michael, and as long as she saw Laura, Anne couldn't bury her thoughts about her husband.

She knew that her position was ridiculous whether Michael had a lover or not. If he didn't, she was the suspicious wife. If he did, she was still ridiculous, the wronged wife, the other familiar figure of melodrama or comedy.

She remembered her mother's ideas about male sex. You must never, her mother had told her, allow them to take even the first step, because once they are aroused, they can't control themselves. It couldn't be true, and yet the wisdom of the ages gave support to it. But Michael was no more libidinous than she; they matched desire for desire. Sometimes she took the lead, sometimes he. But had she taken a lover, people wouldn't have said of her, "What could you expect?" It wouldn't have been imagined that sexual deprivation was a physical problem that she had to tend to, like an ingrown toenail. People would have judged her—harshly, kindly, depending upon their approval of her lover and their affection for her and for Michael. With women, sex was never judged as a merely physical event.

Perhaps the error lay not in what people thought about women, but in what they thought about men. Perhaps there was no such thing as simple physical sex, or at least no affair that was simply physical. People needed all sorts of things from one another, and sex was, in some ways, the most straightforward way of getting them. Michael, for example, must have been missing home; his easiest entrée into someone's domestic life would have been through a love affair. Charlotte Mistière: a great hostess, aged forty. Of course she could understand the appeal of it—a Frenchwoman, only just older than Michael, with her potpourris in Sèvres dishes and the perfect lunches she would have dreamed up in her seventeenth-century bath—how could he resist it? After all, they'd both known it was partly what he went into French for: that fantasy of a people who knew how to live a daily life with elegance and warmth. It was perfectly easy to understand, when you thought about it; it needn't seem so terrible. But thought had nothing to do with the stab she felt at the center of her body, the primitive ache, as if a crude stone weapon had been driven through her. It was easy to understand his reasons for doing it; she had some of the same reasons herself. She understood how desire made things seem possible. She, too, felt desire. Only, she was faithful. But possibly he was too. Her feelings about Hélène might have pushed her over some self-invented precipice. But at the center of her body was the wound. Whatever the nature of the weapon, whoever's the hand that drove it, it had been driven through. She had been violated. Even if she had done it to herself, it had been done. Surely Michael must know something had happened. Knowing her so well, how could he not have seen she was distressed, that she had moved away from him. Perhaps that was the greatest sorrow to her: he hadn't noticed, or if he had, he'd turned his back. But she had said to him, "Don't tell me." So there was nothing he could do.

Anne's parents came out to greet the car. It saddened Anne to see the children so polite with their grandparents, so held back. She felt the children's shyness as her own reproach: she should bring them here more often. They were only three hours away. But she had always felt that her parents didn't take particularly to being grandparents. They weren't very good at it, not exciting and indulgent as Ben was, or Jane. She wondered if they had liked being parents. It occurred to her that one couldn't simply say someone was a good parent: one had to be a good parent to *someone.* So her father had been a wonderful father to her, but with Beth he had always bungled. And her mother did far better with Beth than with her. What would Sarah and Peter think as they grew older? She didn't see her failures as they would.

When they took their coats off, Anne's mother said defensively, "Things will be quite a bit later than we had hoped. Beth and Richard are snowed in, and they were bringing the turkey."

"They have access to the only pure turkeys in the world," Anne's father said. "You know, turkeys from really good families. Turkeys that don't fool around."

"Don't mock Beth's concerns, Les. She certainly has a point about all the dreadful things we put in our bodies."

"If they don't get here soon, we're not going to put anything in our bodies," said Anne's father. "How long does it take to cook a turkey?"

"It's not a very big one. And a fresh-killed bird is much faster than a frozen one."

"You're hedging, Susan," said Les Elliott.

"Well, Les, it shouldn't take more than five hours or so. We'll have a nice late dinner. It will be European."

"We'd be glad to help with anything," said Peter. "Our mother lets us dry the lettuce." The way he said "our mother" to her own mother made Anne sad.

"Well, why don't you children help your grandmother, and I'll take this opportunity to invite my elder daughter on a walk. Michael, you can catch up with the last ten issues of the *New Republic.*"

"That's terrific restraint, Les," said Anne's mother sharply. "You actually let Anne be in the house for five minutes before taking her away."

Anne was glad that Beth wasn't there. She could take pleasure in her father's pleasure in her without worrying about what it was doing to her sister.

"What would you like to do, dear?" Anne's mother said to Laura.

"I have needlepoint to do," said Laura, smiling.

"Well, then," said Anne's father, "we're all squared away. Come, fair and tender maiden, I want to show you my latest folly."

Les Elliott had built a greenhouse. He had a place for vegetables and ferns, but his passion was dwarf irises. It was her father who had taught Anne to garden. She remembered with poignant pleasure the look of his large hands covered with earth, the wet knees of his gardening pants after he weeded. He opened the greenhouse door, and she gave herself over to the sourish, humid air. It was a place, she thought, where no moral act was possible: one could be neither good nor bad in a greenhouse. She didn't have to worry about being fair to Michael, kind to Laura. She was simply happy in the warm air with her father, touching soil and leaves, following as he praised and muttered and despaired.

"You must bring Beth and Richard when they come. They'll be impressed with the solar operation," she said.

"Yes, but they'll want to talk about it, and they'll know so much about it and tell me everything that I've done that's wrong. I'm bound to feel like a failure within ten minutes. Come, my dear, let me show you to my irises."

It was a joke they'd had for years, the stock-in-trade of their mock courtship. "I want to show you to my roses," said an eighteenth-century gallant to a young beauty, implying the treat would be theirs. Her father said it every time he brought her to his flowers, and she laughed each time.

With pride he showed her the new varieties, purple, veined in lavender, the pale yellow with its definite golden spine, the violet with its center of evening sky, the dreamy white with the hint of pink under the bowl.

"Beautiful, Daddy. You must be so proud of what you've done."

"Are you all right? You and Michael?"

"Fine," she said. More than anything, she wanted to put her head on her father's spongy shoulder to say, "I'm afraid my husband's been unfaithful to me," to weep for an hour, then to have him stalk into the house and accuse her husband in a flourish of paternal eloquence. But he must never know; he was the last person she could talk to. Long ago, she had stopped telling him when she hurt herself. As a child, his grief for her had made her worry and feel guilty about her own pain. He would never forgive Michael. And she didn't even know if there was anything to forgive. As it was, his and Michael's relationship was distant, amicable: two tall men who respected each other as men of principle and hard work. But it was a frail alliance. She sat looking at her father, wanting his protection, protecting him—from the truth of her own nature or of the events, she couldn't quite be sure which.

"We're fine," she said. "It's hard being separated."

"Worth it?"

"Daddy, this is the most wonderful thing, this work. I hadn't realized how much I missed it."

"Don't slip back now. Keep it up."

"I will if I can."

"You must, darling. You've got a first-rate mind. Don't try to make a lifework of your children. They're no one's magnum opus. It would be wonderful if your mother and I could take credit for you. But it seems to me you've always been your own invention."

"I wonder if Beth and Richard are here. You really must bring them out here, Daddy."

"Yes, I must," he said. "I'm doing better with her now, I think."

"You mustn't favor me so in front of her. You must work at it."

"I'll try," he said, sighing, "but you're my favorite person in the world. I don't see nearly enough of you."

"Come visit *me* sometime."

"Maybe I will."

But he wouldn't, she knew. He was never comfortable in her house; he didn't like her cooking for him. She thought that probably he didn't like the idea of her living with another man.

When they walked into the living room, Peter, Sarah and their cousins Liam and Sam were sitting on the couch with their grandmother looking at pictures of their mothers as children. Sam and Liam were eleven and twelve; they seemed enormously adult to Anne, compared to her two children. Beth was carrying her baby, Ariel, in a front pack sling. Anne could hear the baby sucking as she came close to her.

She had always been afraid to touch Beth's children too fondly, afraid that if they responded to her too warmly their mother would see evidence of a new generation of betrayals.

"I believe someone was just about to say, 'Wasn't Anne a beautiful child and wasn't Beth sturdy-looking.' "

Anne was about to demur that it was Beth who was the lovely child when she saw that Beth and her mother were laughing. She saw that that was what had happened: her mother and sister had absorbed the bitterness they felt toward her, built it into a safe, durable structure that excluded her and made her foolish, while they sat inside, women of the world trading wisecracks. She was hurt for a moment, then relieved. Her sister was no longer quite alone.

"Hello, Daddy," Beth said, standing on her toes to kiss her father.

"I was hoping you and Richard might take a look at the greenhouse with me. I'd like your advice on the vegetables."

"Give it a rest, old man," said Beth. "Just because I caught you with your hand in the cookie jar, you don't have to do a ballet of liberal guilt."

"I'd love to see your father in tights," Susan Elliott said, "the premier danseur in the new production of *The High-Minded Lawyer,* or *You Can Trust Me Even Though I'm a WASP.*"

Everyone laughed, and Anne pretended to, so as not to appear conspicuous. People thought it was all right to laugh at her father. He was a nice man; he was so successful.

"You'll all be sorry when I install a barre and a full-length mirror in the living room. And lots of pretty ballerinas."

Don't, Daddy, Anne wanted to say. You haven't the knack, and it makes it worse.

Sarah said, "I know the five positions."

"Will you do them for us?" Anne asked.

With tremendous seriousness, Sarah did the five ballet positions she had learned in school. Her little-girl belly stuck out in a most unballerina-like way, but her arms were in perfect alignment.

Everyone clapped for her, and Beth's baby began crying.

"I don't know what's wrong with her today," said Beth. "I guess she's picking up on my uptightness. It's incredible, the symbiosis."

"I envy you, nursing another one. I was brokenhearted when I weaned Sarah," said Anne.

"You could do it if you really wanted to, Anne. It doesn't take brains, you know," said Beth.

"I think it takes more patience and generosity than I have left at this point," Anne said.

"Well, I hear you're very grand now with your lady painter," Beth said.

"She was a wonderful painter, a very courageous woman. I think her life would really interest you, Beth."

"It probably would, if you weren't the world's expert," Beth said.

Beth was in therapy; she was being counseled to be "up front in her aggressions." She had told Anne that it was very important, "for my life" she had said, that Anne put up with her aggressiveness and not try to defend herself. For a couple of years she said to Anne, "That isn't much considering what I've had to put up with from you for thirty-two years." Anne had agreed; Beth could insult her publicly, she would be silent. But she found the process dispiriting and exhausting. She didn't believe it would ever end; besides, there was nothing new in all of it, it had been years since she had said a word when Beth attacked her, and Beth had attacked her ever since she'd learned to talk.

"I had almost caught up with you," said Beth. "Then you pulled this out of the hat."

"It was pulled out of the hat for me," said Anne apologetically.

"I almost impressed Daddy with the farm and our antinuclear activity. He almost thought I was a person with a mind. Almost. But now I'm back at the bottom of the class."

"Beth, dear, if the planet survives, it will be because of the energy and responsibility of people like you and Richard," Lester Elliott said, putting his hand on her shoulder.

Anne felt tears start at the back of her eyes. Quickly, she was able to stop them. She could bear her mother's nudging her out into the cold, but she couldn't stand her father's leaving her there while he made his way to the fire. In the middle of her parents' living room she stood, a large ungainly child, friendless and wordless in the company. She knew that Michael knew what she was feeling and would help her if she walked across the room to him. But she had forfeited her right to his help, or he had forfeited his right to give it to her. One or the other, depending upon whether he'd in fact been unfaithful, or she'd imagined it.

It was late when they left; they wouldn't be home till two in the morning. Yet Anne liked the feeling of them all there in the car, warm and tired and not talking. It was the first time all day she felt family comfort. No, she thought, that wasn't true. There had been the time with her father in the greenhouse, there had been the children on the floor with their presents. Michael had been kind and helpful, but there was something between them. That it might be of her own invention made it no less real.

So now, with the children asleep in the back of the car, with speech impossible for a while, she allowed herself, out of sheer hunger, to feel some closeness to her husband. She was grateful for the way he had behaved to Beth. He had been silent when Beth accused him of taking money from a CIA-based operation. It was something Michael had researched scrupulously; it was simply untrue. She saw the effort that it took him to look down at his plate, to say it was hard to figure out who the villains were, and then to have Beth reply, "Not if you have nothing to gain from the villains."

She was sorry that Laura had been left out of things, but Laura hadn't done much to change the situation. The children spent very little time with her, Anne's mother had tried to talk to her but had quickly given up, and Anne's own attempt to have Beth and Laura talk about handicrafts —Beth wove—was a failure. Beth kept trying to make a point about the alienation of modern man from craft, from ordinary objects. She wanted Laura to agree with her on the superiority of natural dyes and the excellence of the craftsmanship of "so-called primitive peoples." There was no entry possible into this conversation for Laura, and Beth lost interest in her when she realized that Laura was working on a design of Minnie Mouse for Sarah's winter jacket.

As they got closer to home, Anne began increasingly to dread the moment that would have to come. Laura had asked if she could see Anne alone for just a few minutes. Anne knew that some complaint must be forthcoming, whether it would be about wages or conditions she was unsure. Or perhaps Laura wanted Anne to confide in her; that would be worst of all. But now she would have to be alone with her. How could she deny her? It was a simple, straightforward request: a few minutes alone.

Anne and Michael carried the children, already in their pajamas, into bed, and Michael went to bed himself. Laura sat in the kitchen, waiting for Anne.

"Hi," she said, as Anne came into the room. "Is now a good time?"

Anne smiled nervously. "It's fine."

Laura reached into the deep pocket of her dress. "I got you this present, and I wanted to give it to you while we were alone." She handed Anne a small box wrapped in scarlet tissue paper tied with white wool twine.

Anne opened the box. Inside it was an amethyst necklace, one large stone in a floral golden setting, hung on a delicate chain. She took it out of the box. The stone picked up the weak light of the kitchen and held it: lucid, chaste. It was beautiful. It was exactly the sort of piece Anne would have looked at in the window of one of the antique shops on Fayerweather Street. She would have looked at it lovingly; she would have lingered on the street in front of it, then walked away, deciding she couldn't buy it. A little cloud of self-pity would have descended on her, which she would have had to shrug off. She would have said to herself that it was an indulgence she didn't need, the children needed something, or the house. Still, she would have gone back, looking, every time she stopped for something on that street, until someone had bought it and it had disappeared forever. And she would have mourned.

Anne felt the necklace warm and thicken on her palm. She didn't want it, she didn't want it because Laura had given it to her. She began to wonder if she could give it away: to her mother, perhaps, or Beth. But looking at the girl, she knew it was impossible. Laura was watching her like a teacher who has waited till the class has been dismissed to give the smallest child, the slowest child, a test.

"It's beautiful, Laura," said Anne, "but you must take it back. You shouldn't have spent so much money."

"I wanted to. I wanted to give you a present you'd never forget. So you'd think of me whenever you wore it, and remember."

Kissing Laura, thanking her, Anne felt the words close around her. The girl wanted remembrance, and Anne had hoped that after she left the house, Laura would be forgotten. She saw now that this would never happen. Laura would always be with her, reminding her forever of the failure of her heart. The jewel would be a witness: she would never be able to think that Laura had been impervious to the life of the house, that Laura had not understood her. Looking at the necklace in her hand, Anne knew that Laura had broken into her life. And she could no more welcome her than, standing naked, she could welcome the voyeur's face at the window, silent, seeing, intimately holding in his mind's eye all that she would never give.

S he and Anne were just alike: she knew it now. Their families were
just the same, their parents didn't love them. She was the only one who
understood Anne. Other people thought they loved her, said they loved
her, but they came to her for what she gave them. They came to tell her
things or to be near her, thinking from her looks that she was always rested,
always glad to see them. But Laura knew when Anne was tired, fearful,
lonely, when she was angry and wanted to be by herself, when she wanted
her children and did not want them. She knew what Anne's husband
didn't know: that she had moved away from him. That she had, while he
was away, looked at another man as she had not looked at him. She had
felt it in the air as she lay sleeping in the room above them, Anne and that
man, the electrician, sitting so late in the kitchen, drinking tea. She could
feel Anne's body and the man's desiring to be near each other. She had
prayed above them that the two might not embrace. And they had not
embraced. She knew that. She had prayed that the man would go away,
and he had gone away. He would come back, but she would keep Anne
from him. She must keep Anne from him or Anne would be lost. Swallowed up, desiring the body of another person. And she must keep Anne
from the woman Jane. Or else she would be lost to the proud world. She
had found, in Ecclesiastes, the words God sent her for her understanding:
"And I found more bitter than death the woman whose heart is snares and
nets, and whose hands are fetters; he who pleases God escapes her, but the
sinner is taken by her."

    She would not allow Anne to be taken in. Jane, the proud woman, would
fall before her feet. She had prayed for guidance and had opened to

Ezekiel. "Her proud might shall come to an end; and she shall be covered by a cloud." So the woman would disappear and Anne would never see her. Anne would know, through the will of the Lord, that only Laura loved her. She would see that even her children did not love her. That Laura loved her with the pure love, stronger than the love of children, or the love of men's desires, or the love of father, mother, or the proud love of the mind. She would see, and it would not be long, that only Laura loved her with the Spirit, before which all other love must be consumed and die.

Now that she knew Anne loved her, now that she knew that they were just alike, she could start. Now she could teach her, give her messages and guidance, pull her from the love of others, the temptation of false love. The hour was upon them. Now she would touch Anne with the burning hand of love: the flesh of Anne would burn and open. And the Spirit would fill her, driving out the error of her life. Oh, she was ready now, Laura could see, to know that her life was an error, that she had put her treasure where the moth ate and the thieves stole. But no more. Laura would help Anne to leave behind all that she thought she loved.

And then the children, too, would follow. She did not mean that Anne should not be with her children. "Suffer the little children to come unto me." Jesus had said it. She, Laura, would help Anne with the children. Anne would care for them, and Laura would instruct them. There was no need to keep the children from their mother. Only they must learn in time, as Anne would learn, that that love, too, was false and a delusion. That children must leave mother and father. That only the love of the Spirit was abiding. That all other love was death.

She imagined how their life would be. First Anne would leave her husband. Laura did not like Michael, the husband. For Christmas, he gave her two books: *Fear and Trembling* and *Waiting for God.* He tried to tell her about them. But she didn't care. Books would lead no one to the Spirit. In the Scripture she found all she needed. The rest led astray. He talked to her in the voice he used with Peter, the voice that rose and fell in false curves. She saw the shape of it, the shape that said, "See, there is nothing that you know." She would pretend to read his books because that would please Anne.

She would let Anne read books if she wanted to when they lived alone together. When she had left her husband. How had Anne been able to lie with him? She must have done what Laura did. Had closed her eyes and let the Spirit leave her. Had covered herself over with white sleep. A cloak, a cloud. Then opened her eyes and saw the dangerous, heaving body. And heard him crying out. Sleeping in the room beside them, Laura had heard his cry, the first night he was home, as he lay with his wife. She had not heard Anne cry out. Because it could not bring her pleasure. Pinned unmoving underneath.

Often she thought of what their life would be like. Hers and Anne's. They would go away from everyone they knew. They would live together in a small house by a lake. Anne would cook and clean the house and tend the garden. Laura would sew and read the Scripture. In the evenings, late, they would drink tea together. Laura would speak of the Spirit. Anne would brush Laura's hair for her and kiss her thankfully for having given her her life. When the children went away, they would see no one. They would die at the same moment. Holding her hand, Anne would let Laura lead her to the throne of God.

She had feared the husband could raise up his hooves and crush her underneath. Could lift his wife onto his back and carry her away. But Laura knew now that his power was nothing compared to hers. Was not even as strong as the power of the other man. For he had had another woman, and Anne knew. But that was the hand of the Lord. And Anne would know soon that the love of men was the root of death.

Because she had loved Anne, Laura had lain with Adrian. He had not wanted to at first. The Scripture said you should not lie with men. But had not the good woman Naomi counseled Ruth to lie upon the floor where Boaz slept so that the work of the Lord could come to pass? So she had been wise and cunning, knowing that only if she knew the love of men could she keep Anne from it. She had thought once that she might make Adrian marry her so she could be near Anne. But now she saw it was not necessary. Now she saw how easy it would be to show Anne no one loved her, that what she thought was love was like fresh grass that before her eyes would wither into nothing. Into dry stalks, into air.

Although she had lain with men, Laura was still innocent. Her body had been there but not her spirit. She remembered nothing of it. She had closed her eyes and caused her spirit to depart. She had come to him again and again, and he had taken her into his bed out of pity. It was through pity she had got to him at first. She had said to him, "No one's ever said that I was beautiful. Or even pretty." It was so easy to make them do what you wanted. She pressed the button of his pity; like a cheap top of the children's, he had moved his hands, his arms.

She asked him to turn the light out, not out of shyness, as he thought, but so he could not see her laughing. He made her touch him. "Sometimes I need a little help at first." Then she didn't know what they did. Only her body lay there, but her spirit traveled. Afterwards, her spirit entered her body, and she saw him lying next to her, worn out, trying to catch his breath. Love, they called it, what they did. She thought of that as they lay together, their flesh damp like dough left out. She began to laugh because that was what they could call love. He asked what she was laughing at. I'm happy, she said. That was all he needed to hear. Then he could roll over and sleep. He lay on his back, his mouth open, snoring, making loud disgusting noises like the animal he was.

She knew that it was Anne he wanted in his bed. She knew that it was Anne he thought of as he pinned her underneath. Once he told her how lucky she was to be living in the house with Anne. He said it thinking she would think he meant she was lucky to have the job. But she knew he meant she was lucky to walk on the same ground, eat the same food, to see her first thing in the morning, to sleep as she slept, hearing, through the wall, Anne's breath.

"Was Anne ever your lover?" She asked him that as he cooked an omelet for her. She had found, in the drawer where he kept string and tape, a picture of Anne with the children. They were sitting on her lap, smiling, nearly babies, clumsy on her knee. She sat holding her babies, and her face was golden, the face of light. Seeing the picture, Laura worried. How would she be able to convince Anne that her children, too, were grass that would wither? "Anne Foster my lover?" Adrian said and laughed. "I thought about it once, but it was crazy."

So she knew that it was Anne he thought of as he lay above her.

"I would never take Anne for my lover," he said. "Not just because of Michael, who is my friend, but because I'd always be afraid that she'd go to bed with me because she thought it was her fault that I desired her. That she'd have to make it up to me."

"Don't you think she likes sex?" Laura asked him. She hated him so much that she could hardly speak. At the end of the world, the Lord would wither him with one blast. He was a creature drunk on lust, hardly above an animal. She couldn't even try to help him. It was not to help him that she lay with him; it was for Anne.

"I'm sure she's very ardent when she's with Michael. But she *likes* sex, she doesn't *need* it."

"Not like me," she said, giggling. It was so easy to know what they wanted you to say.

He knew nothing about Anne. Laura knew that Anne desired the man who drank tea with her every night, his gut sticking over his belt like a pig. And she knew that Anne knew that her husband had another woman.

Christmas had revealed the truth to her. Anne with her family. Alone among the ones who claimed to love her. In the future, Laura knew, Anne would look back at that Christmas as the time when Laura gave her the necklace. She would hear Anne saying, "That was when I knew *you* were the one who loved me. Only *you.*"

Poor Anne. Since she did not yet know the love of the Spirit, she was hurt by her parents showing her they didn't love her. That they loved only her sister. Laura couldn't remember anymore what it felt like, the pain of thinking she was alone because her parents loved only her sister. Now when she tried to remember, she was covered by the thin white sleep. The peace of the Spirit that came when it was needed. Nothing hurt her now. She felt no anger, no bitterness. Only love. The pure love of the Spirit, which shone like the sun. That was how she loved Anne. That was how Anne loved her. In the Spirit, there was no suffering.

Now Anne must suffer. She must stand in her parents' living room alone, knowing they didn't love her. Anne's parents were exactly like Laura's. Anne's sister was exactly like Debbie. Laura had seen in one minute that Anne's mother had never loved her.

"It's hard work, taking care of two children," Anne's mother had said to Laura. She was small like Laura's mother, and like Laura, Anne stood above her mother in a way Laura could tell Anne's mother hated. Laura's mother had said to her, "Don't hang on me. You make me sick, hanging on me." She knew Anne's mother had said that to her. And it had hurt Anne as it had hurt Laura, before the Spirit kept her from all hurt.

"I love taking care of the children. They're wonderful." She said that because she knew that was what Anne's mother wanted her to say.

"I suppose I never had the talent for it," Anne's mother said. "I would get very bored. Neither of my daughters takes after me in that. They're both more domestic than I ever was. I guess every generation of daughters has to reinvent family life."

Laura didn't know what she meant. She smiled, because the mother wanted her to smile.

"Anne was lucky to get you," said the mother. "But then, Anne's always been lucky. Not like poor Beth." "Poor Beth" meant the mother loved Beth only.

"What will you do when you're finished with this job?" the mother asked.

They all asked that, not knowing. I will never be finished. I will be with your daughter through eternity.

"Something will turn up," she said.

"I admire people of your generation who aren't burdened with anxieties about the future. Perhaps it's your faith. Anne says you're interested in religion. My daughter Beth is the religious one in our family. Some mix of Buddhism and Transcendentalism with a drop of pantheism, from what I understand. I don't think Anne's thought about it much, one way or the other. They were both brought up quite irreligiously. I went to convent school for twelve years and had all I could take. Perhaps that was rash."

Anne will abide in the Spirit. She will be taken up, consumed in a garment of shining flames.

"I don't know what she tells the children about God," the mother said.

"She tells them God is love," said Laura, smiling.

"True enough and vague enough, I guess, not to give them any trouble later."

They are safe with me. Together we will all be carried up. I will lift up Anne and her children. You will never hurt them; you will never touch them. Stay with your other daughter, whom you love.

The sister said, "I suppose my sister's quite the taskmaster with her Mrs. Dalloway fantasy that you have to bring to life. Only, now she thinks she's Mrs. Dalloway and Virginia Woolf rolled into one. Very handy, with you to pick up the pieces."

Laura didn't know what they meant, what the words said. Except the words were saying, "I have always hated my sister." I will save you from this hate, she said to Anne in her heart. I will lead you to the Spirit, where there is no hate or sorrow.

And the father did not love her either. Did not say to the sister, the mother, "Do not hurt my child." Stood by, gaping, laughing, while they made a fool of him. Took the other daughter's side, said it was she who was important. Said to Anne (the murmur underneath the words), "I will always desert you. I will always leave you alone."

I will save you, Anne. Only in the Lord is safety, Laura was saying in her heart as Anne stood in the center of her parents' living room alone. When her father said, "If this planet survives, it's because of the energy and responsibility of people like you." Meaning, I do not love Anne, my daughter. See, I leave her alone in the center of the room. See, I cause her tears to flow. Should she fall to the floor from the weight of her sorrow I would do nothing for her. Should they all surround her, trying with their hands to kill her, I would stand and watch them.

Anne could hear her father saying that, Laura knew she could. Could hear the murmur underneath the words. Why couldn't she hear the words of Laura's heart to her heart: I, only I, can lead you into safety. She could not hear those words that day because her husband was there, her children.

Because she looked out at the white sun in the clouds. The white sun in the clouds was not her safety. Or the strength of her husband's arms. Or the sweetness of her children's bodies. That was the error that Anne lived by that the Lord would teach her in the proper time. The day was coming when Anne would know herself alone, unsheltered, and would turn to Laura, who would lead her to the Lord.

Sarah's Christmas dance recital had been canceled because of snow; it was rescheduled for January sixth. The cancellation had caused in her that dark, late-morning storm of despair that children can't know is merely disappointment. Early on in motherhood, Anne had learned the truth of children's moods: postponement, as an idea, meant nothing to them; the future stretched ahead like death. Empiricists to the bone, faith was to them unimaginable. What was not present wasn't possible.

On that day three weeks before, Anne had watched her daughter suffer, knowing the suffering would lift, but that while it hovered, there was nothing she could do. She offered her diversions, feeling even as she did that she insulted Sarah's grief. Sarah sat at the kitchen table crying. Peter, who couldn't bear to see her unhappy even when he had worked to make her so, kept popping in and out of the room with toys, books, card tricks, jokes. His desperation only burdened Sarah further; she had her own unhappiness to deal with, she could not bear his sense of failure. Wearily, she put her head in her mother's lap, a shipwrecked survivor holding for a moment to a soggy plank. Anne felt her breathe deeply. "Oh, well," she said, "at least Daddy will be able to see it now."

The weeks passed, and Anne had forgotten about the recital until January second, when she met one of the other mothers at a party. Sarah was in a dance class called pre-ballet, for girls aged five to seven. She had wanted to join it because her best friend, Margaret, was in it. Ambivalently, Anne had agreed. The ballet school daunted her. It was run by a woman, Terri Blake, who at forty-five had a better figure than anyone Anne knew at seventeen. She walked around her studio in leotards. To receive checks she put around her a silk wrap skirt. She wore her hair pulled tight on the top of her head so that her eyes, ringed heavily with liner, looked a bit Chinese. A whole cadre of mothers paid her homage with a sycophantic devotion born of their sense of the inadequacy of their own slow bodies. Gratefully, these women sewed costumes, painted posters, passed out leaflets, printed tickets, raised money through bake sales and raffles, so that Terri Blake could save their daughters from the fate of their mothers' lives. Anne was glad that she had the excuse of her work not to participate, even though it was well known that the best parts were given to the daughters of mothers who "cooperated."

Anne could see that Terri didn't like to teach younger children, but pre-ballet was her most profitable class. She had had ambitions as a ballet dancer. She had had a short and vaguely unsuccessful career in New York. She drove her talented older students mercilessly, determined that some of them would make it into a company. How could she enjoy the clumsy, boneless bodies of the five-year-olds, their simple portrayals of angels and snowflakes, when what she wanted was to put her older dancers through her adaptations of Jerome Robbins' later works? Still, she worked hard with the little girls on "Angels and Snowflakes" to "Dance of the Sugar Plum Fairy." And the children adored her, for some reason Anne couldn't understand. She had learned that it was quite impossible to predict the adults that her children would be drawn to.

Anne loved children's performances if her children weren't performing, but when Peter or Sarah was involved, she was in agony. As the curtain went up on Sarah's number and she heard the first notes of "The Sugar Plum Fairy," she gripped Michael's hand in terror. Every time she touched him now, she wondered if the other woman touched him in that way. He smiled at her, patting her other hand. "Sarah will be fine," he said. "Don't worry."

Six little girls dressed as snowflakes knelt in the middle of the stage, their noses to their knees. They were supposed to be sleeping. The angels came onstage. Sarah was the smallest of them, and the last. Her wings were much too big for her, and she looked not magical but comic. Her body was implacably earthbound; her halo sat on her head like a helmet. When she came to the middle of the stage to touch her snowflake with her magic wand, sprinkling her with spangles, she tripped and fell. Overbalanced by her wings, she couldn't get up. Everyone onstage giggled, and the audience began to laugh. The little girls froze into their positions as the music ticked away. Suddenly Terri Blake lunged onto the stage and picked Sarah up roughly by the arm. The audience applauded. The music had stopped, but the dance was only half over. Taking her bow, Sarah was shaking with sobs. The great applause only made her cry more.

Let the theater blow up, let us all be buried alive in tons of rubble, Anne prayed, crying in her seat. The audience went on laughing and clapping. Sarah couldn't get hold of herself. The more she sobbed, the more the audience clapped. Finally, the curtain was pulled roughly down.

Anne got up to go backstage.

"Stay here a minute," Michael said. "Don't let Sarah see you crying. I'll go. You come later."

He got out of his seat and disappeared into the darkness. On the stage was a young boy in a skeleton costume dancing to Saint-Saëns. Anne couldn't stop crying. She was glad that Peter, who had come later than they, was sitting with the Greenspans. Her child had been exposed. People had laughed at her. It was Sarah's first experience in humiliation, and Anne felt the sting in her own body. But she must go to Sarah; it was Sarah who was important. She got out of her seat and walked backstage.

Sarah was on her father's lap; he was wiping her eyes with his handkerchief. She had taken off her wings but not her halo. Michael smoothed her hair. They were both silent. Sarah still cried, but the shame was gone. She had her head on her father's shoulder and they sat on in silence.

"Let's go home," said Michael. Anne put on Sarah's coat. The three of them walked out into the cold, bright afternoon, like Union soldiers coming home from Shiloh.

━━━━━━

They were driving to Jane's. The trees, covered with icicles, shone unnaturally in the brilliant sun. The snow, which had melted, then re-hardened, glistened on the surface, the freezing air enlivened the plain slab of hard blue sky and even the most undistinguished shrub was interesting. Anne loved winter with its forced speed of the blood, since she saw herself as naturally indolent. At the center of her being she perceived a sleepiness, a torpor, a passivity, that in a climate always warm she knew would take her over, once and for all. She thought it was this passivity that had brought her to the decision to give up the hard thing she'd been cherishing, suspicion of her husband and the isolation it had forced her into. Simply, she couldn't bear it anymore. She felt, when she breathed in or walked too quickly, a sense of wounding. But had she inflicted the wound herself, or had it been inflicted by her husband? She would never know. And what she had decided, seeing Michael with Sarah on the day of the recital, was that it was better that way. If she asked him, something real with solidity and mass would grow up between them. Better a vapor, which allowed at least the possibility that one of them could keep his honor. It was the way she wanted it to be; perhaps it was all she had courage for. She had done one courageous thing, had lived without him, had stayed at home to live a separate life while he went away. Why had she imagined that nothing would be risked and nothing lost in the arrangement? It was what her generation always did, expected everything and was always shocked, like children, when something had to be given up.

There was no model for her to consult. Of course she knew that there were marriages where infidelity was practiced and concealed, but what was missing there was intimacy: they were couples contracted to each other for some reason having to do with the outside world. And the marriages where everything was dragged out, discussed, where neither partner was allowed a private life, where any unshared thought was seen as a betrayal, lacked, in Anne's mind, the dignity and the respect that she thought marriage called for and ought to bring forth. To know a person, to need him yet to leave him occasionally alone: this is what, she felt, they'd both believed in as the ideal for their marriage. It was what had made them able to agree to keep infidelities to themselves. So perhaps that was how Michael had acted. He was more consistent than she, and more stalwart. Perhaps he kept silence about what he had done to honor the ideal of their marriage. Perhaps he suffered now, knowing she had removed herself, but knowing that if he spoke he could only do damage to their idea of what they were. Sitting beside him, she felt infinitely sorry for both of them. Their position was so fragile and so tentative. Their absence from each other required that they live in an economy of scarcity, and scarcity took its toll. There they were, she and Michael, married, parents, living apart from each other, at the end of the twentieth century. Their marriage had no historical or social and certainly no religious significance. If it broke up, it was only a private misfortune, and not a rare one. It wouldn't even be the worst thing; any bad thing that happened to the children would be much, much worse.

She thought of Caroline and even Jane and how different life was for them. The shape of things had meaning; they expected things to last. What would Caroline have done had she suspected infidelity? Perhaps it wouldn't have bothered her, perhaps she thought it was simply the nature of things, of men. Or would she have indulged in some operatic accusing scene, which left after it the great blank peace of reconciliation?

Anne knew nothing of Caroline's sexual history; she never spoke about sex or even romantic love in her journals. Was it because she thought it unimportant, or too important to commit to writing? She'd never mentioned anyone who might have been Stephen's father. Neither Jane nor Ben had a clue. For all anyone knew, Caroline might have been ravished one night in an alley; or might have secretly been carrying on, for years, a liaison with her dearest friend. She kept her secret to the end, and her keeping it meant that she thought it was either of no importance or of the greatest. But whatever she thought, she'd acted, as she so often had, clearly, consistently, and with great force. Would she have despised Anne for being equivocal? Would Jane? But then, neither of them was really married. Jane was wedded, really, not to her husband but to his mother.

She tried to predict Jane's response to Michael, but she couldn't fix on one that would please her. She wondered if most wives wanted the people they admired to believe that their husbands weren't good enough for them, the implication being that no one was. She supposed she didn't actually want that. What she did want was for Jane to like her best. What a child I've turned into, she thought. But Jane's regard for her was like a brilliant shield in which she saw herself enlarged and noble. She didn't want to see the image of herself diminishing to a well-drawn miniature of the perfect couple, decorative and minor.

Nevertheless she was part of a couple. There were things she wanted to say only to Michael; things she could say only to him. She'd imagined a rich, figured cloth she would weave for him while they were together again; she could tell him about Caroline, about Jane. She could let him know what had happened to her life since Caroline had entered it. She could ask him things about the artistic climate of Paris in the early teens. She could explain to him the odd set of feelings she had about Caroline as a mother; how on some days she grieved for Stephen and her heart for Caroline became a heart of stone, she felt herself the accuser, bristling with justice. But on some days, when she'd looked at one of the paintings or read a particularly engaging letter, she forgot about Caroline's inadequacies as a mother. The image of the suffering Stephen faded in her mind, as it had so easily done in Caroline's. What does that mean about me as a mother, as a scholar, she wanted to ask. And Michael was the one person she could ask, himself a scholar and the father of her children. But now, having felt all that she did toward him, she was shy. She didn't know how to begin a conversation with him. She couldn't pick up the thread. It occurred to her, though, that they had to talk about Laura. That was a practical issue; it affected, immediately, all their lives. Whatever the state of their relationship, they inhabited a family. And she needed his help.

Laura's Christmas present had shown her that she would have to work hard to keep distant from her, yet to maintain a smooth relationship. She saw that her kindness to Laura—if it was that; more properly, she thought, it should be named cowardice—had been misinterpreted. It had happened to her all her life. She had been kind to people when they had wanted her to love them, so they felt betrayed. But it was worse with Laura. What she had felt for people, what they mistook for love, could have been anything from mild affection to disregard. But every day that Laura lived beside her in the house, she disliked her more. Some days, even the simplest civilities were grueling to her. Yet every time she turned away from Laura, she felt Laura's yearning, like a furnace left on in a summer house. She knew that Laura craved love. But the best Anne could do was to keep herself from being cruel.

How could you keep yourself from wanting to do damage to the spy, the watcher at the window? For his knowledge could only be theft. She had to stop thinking that way. She needed Michael's help.

"Tell me what you think of Laura," she said.

"I think she's kind of pathetic. Lonely, empty in some dreadful way. But that emptiness makes her good with the kids. She has a terrific amount of patience. People whose lives are really full aren't the best with children. They don't have that endless time that children need."

"What a terrible thought. It can't be true that children should be brought up by old people or idiots. They'd all grow up dreadful bores or greedy for attention."

"I know. But I'm trying to make you feel better about living with someone who gives you the creeps."

"Is it that evident?"

"To me it is."

"What about to her?"

"Of course not. She's in love with you."

"Oh, Michael, don't say that. That really gives me the creeps."

"Don't worry about it. I don't think she lies awake dreaming of your sweet flesh. I'm sure it's on a much higher plane."

"That's almost worse. Besides, I think she's sleeping with Adrian. Should I get rid of her?"

"Who would you replace her with? And what would you do while you were finding someone? It wasn't easy to get her."

"The truth is I need her. I can't get this work done without her. And she *is* good with the kids. They seem fine, don't they?"

"Never better. They're much more independent of you. Which is great by me. How about you?"

"I don't notice it, so it must be all right."

"In any case it's only another five months. Then you'll have me to contend with."

"That will be awfully nice," she said, wishing she could have said it purely.

She moved toward him. Give me a sign, she cried out to him silently, let me know that you haven't been with anybody else. But his eye was on the rearview mirror; they were about to be overtaken by a truck.

"Have you met any nice people working at the gallery?" he asked.

"No, they're all horrible. They think I'm Ben's mistress and that's why I'm doing the catalogue."

"It's only because you're beautiful," he said proudly. "Men suspect a woman if she's beautiful."

"And hate her if she's not."

"Actually, men prefer their colleagues plain. It's part of Hélène's great success."

It was the first time Michael had said anything even mildly negative about Hélène. Was it his gift to his wife? Was he acknowledging that Hélène had done mischief? Was he, with great tact, telling her he knew she had suffered, and that he was sorry? Even the imagination of his act brought her closer to him. And it had pleased her to hear him call someone she disliked plain. It was so complicated, it was almost comic—all that life between the sexes, all that must be left unsaid. She looked out the window. They had crossed a river. Icy patches broke and moved across the water like slow gray boats.

―――――

Jane stood with Ben in the doorway blinking, for the sun on the snow was dazzling, dropping rich disks like jewels onto the flat whiteness of the yard. No one, it seemed, had walked there, not an animal or a bird; it was a stretch of surface and of light. Anne envied Caroline and people who could understand, in an instant, the implications of that small space, who could make relations come to be where she saw none, and could do it without ever searching after language.

Coolly, Jane surveyed Michael. It was as Anne's husband she surveyed him first. Anne saw Jane's eye flick from her to Michael, back and forth, like a bird choosing branches. She cast on them her searching intelligent look, the look that always surprised Anne when she met it, for it was the look of a dark-eyed person, yet Jane's eyes were in fact a light gray-brown. Looking at those eyes directly, you could imagine them easily weeping. But looked at by them, you had the impression of being fixed by a sharp, precise instrument. Having looked at Michael as Anne's husband, Jane, Anne could see, encountered him simply as an attractive man. She must always have known herself to be a beauty, must always have known—it would have marked the end of childhood for her—that the glance she directed toward a man would be returned with pleasure. Anne watched Michael smiling back at Jane with no fear in his eyes. She saw the gallantry, which must have something of relief in it, bestowed on a beautiful old woman by a young man. The relief because they knew nothing was expected of them as the hale, prize animals they were, that their power would not be put to the test. She pitied the situation of men; no wonder they were so often vengeful.

"My dear boy, what a fine sight you are," said Ben, embracing Michael. "This is Jane, whom you have doubtless heard of."

Jane gave her hand to Michael and welcomed him to her house.

"I feel like a bit of an interloper here, as if I were the only one who didn't speak the language," Michael said.

"How did you come by such becoming modesty?" said Jane, cocking her head flirtatiously. "Handsome young men don't usually see the need of modesty. There's no profit in it for them. It must be that living with Anne has brought out your finer instincts. Let me show you my house." She took Michael's arm, leading him through the door in a way that told the others clearly that she did not want them to follow.

"How was Christmas, darling?" Ben asked, pouring her a glass of wine.

"I'm a fool about Christmas. I get caught up in it every time. Isn't it funny how some ages were good at some holidays, like Christmas in the Middle Ages. The Renaissance was better at Easter. The nineteenth century had marvelous Fourth of Julys."

"What are we good at?"

"I don't know. Nothing, really. Did you have Christmas with Jane?"

"Oh, yes. The two of us and Betty the Basher and her children. Very edifying."

"What was she like with her children?"

"Afraid to cross them. They'll obviously grow up tyrants. She'll never be able to correct them, she's so appalled at what she's done."

"How do you go on, knowing you've done something unforgivable?"

"Oh, darling, I don't know. I've always been put off by the workings of human beings. That's why I went in for paintings. All that marvelous surface."

"Were you in touch with your family on Christmas?"

"Yes, certainly. They all sent cards. Of course, my children have been middle-aged for years: they've been on their own for ages."

Anne could never comprehend Ben's detachment from his family. It saddened her, frightened her, perhaps most of all disoriented her that a man so richly, fully human, such a splendid friend, could be entirely devoid of family feeling. When Ben spoke of his family, she always wondered if one day her children would speak of their family like that. She had thought it would be Peter, but as the children aged, it became clear that Sarah was in far less need of her family than her brother was. Sarah never presented her mother with a soul open and bleeding; always there was some reserve. Some self-protection, some self-nourishment. If anything happened, it would be Peter who would remember and mourn.

"In working on the diaries," she said, "I've found a reference to an article Caroline wrote for a magazine that Stephen briefly published."

"My dear, I'm utterly astonished. How unlike her to write something for public consumption about her painting. I wonder why she did it."

"Well, it was Stephen's magazine."

"Ah, yes, Caroline always loved mixing generosity with some project that smacked of self-reliance."

"Come and have lunch," said Jane, bursting into the room. Her ten minutes with Michael had made her ten years younger. Laughing, she poured soup, cut bread, served salad, drank her wine. How nice it all is, Anne thought, the four of us together. Perhaps we should all live together. The children would love it, and the older people wouldn't have to be afraid of a future of boredom and loneliness. Quickly she ate a piece of bread. Whenever she drank too much, she contemplated asking people to move into her house.

"I see you have a lot of Simone Weil," said Michael to Jane. "I've been trying to write about her in the tradition of French classicism. Her essay on the *Iliad,* particularly."

"How splendid that is," said Jane. " 'Most of the world has gone by far from hot baths.' "

"Perfectly ghastly," said Ben, "like every word out of that neurotic's mouth. Michael, be a dear boy and don't go on about Mademoiselle Weil. It's bound to make Jane and me come to blows. All that hatred of the flesh. And any moment Jane will declare she must sell all her goods, give them to the poor and work in a blacking factory."

"That's Dickens, darling, not me," said Jane, prepared to ignore him. "It was Simone Weil who brought me to a religious life. Well, she and George Herbert."

"How so?" asked Michael.

Anne was embarrassed. She thought that religious people shouldn't talk about such things in public; it was like a libertine bragging in front of virgins. But Michael, she knew, had no such qualms. To him a religious disposition was only one more example of odd human traits quite randomly bestowed, like buckteeth or perfect pitch. Anne felt it was something powerful and incomprehensible. It made people behave extraordinarily; it made them monsters of persecution, angels of self-sacrifice. How could it be talked about at lunch?

"Well, you see," said Jane, "I was overcome with the sense that there was no forgiveness for me. That in not loving my husband I had killed him. That I couldn't make it up to him, I could only live doomed."

"Jane, I beg you. When you talk like this I begin to get the most dreadful headaches. Stephen always had weak lungs. He was always depressed. He drank too much before you ever met him. Do let's stop. At Oxford there's a rule: No serious conversation at table. Very sensible, I always thought."

"All right, darling," Jane said, taking Ben's hand. "Let's talk about something perfectly trivial. Let me tell you how the bread you're eating now is baked. I shall open to you the secrets of my oven. Perhaps I'll write a cookbook. What d'you say, Anne? Let's collaborate. We'll call it *A Cookbook for Literate Women.*"

Anne smiled. She wished Ben hadn't stopped Jane as she was beginning to move away from the topic of religion to the topic of her marriage. Why was Ben like that? And why had Jane given in to him so easily? Was it because they were lovers? Was it because she feared that in crossing Ben, in revealing the secrets of her heart, she would be less attractive to Michael? Anne was sure that it was one of those female silences, one of those feints and dodges called good manners that had everything to do with sex.

=====

Michael left on January seventeenth. The children behaved badly. His leaving again frightened them. His having gone away and then come back, rather than suggesting his eventual return, only stressed in their minds the precariousness, the unpredictability, of adult life. In the days before her father's leaving, Sarah spilled her milk at every meal and then whimpered and trembled as if she were about to be whipped. Peter grew fanatical. He went over his collections of coins, leaves, rocks, toy dinosaurs, convinced that someone had been tampering with them. He accused his mother several times of getting his things out of order when she cleaned his room. Only Laura carried on as she always had, wiping up Sarah's messes, answering Peter's accusations calmly, as if they were reasonable. The children reserved their keenest anger for their mother, knowing she wasn't leaving.

When Peter's tears stopped in the car on the way home from the airport, and he noticed that his mother wasn't crying, he furiously accused her of hardness of heart. "You don't even care that he's alone in that airplane. He's putting his life in the hands of *strangers.*"

Where had Peter learned so early the rhetoric of pulp fiction? She didn't find *True Confessions* under his bed; he didn't spend his afternoons watching *The Guiding Light.* And yet he had always seen life painted in the tones of melodrama: railway accidents, false promises and sudden final partings were the landscapes of his dreams. "John Barryless," his father called him; she saw him as Henry Irving in *The Bells.* But his fears, however overexpressed, were real. He couldn't sleep the night his father left. Anne understood, she felt something like it. His walking away from them at the airport meant the end of something: the dull, potent life of holiday was over, the long afternoons of food and talk, the mornings with the children, the late nights lingering over a drink.

And it meant, perhaps, that she was sending him back to his lover. She wanted to run after him as he entered the airport gate to ask him just as he was leaving. But that would be unfair; he wouldn't have time to explain, to defend himself, or to accuse her of injustice. It was certainly possible that she'd made everything up. And as it was, they'd had a good holiday. If she spoke, she'd ruin everything in a minute.

Now he was gone she could get back to work. In the New York Public Library, she tracked down the issue of Stephen's magazine that Caroline's article was in. The magazine was called *The Expatriate,* and it was meant to be an outlet for those writers and painters—not only American—who had left home to live abroad. There were distinguished contributors—Ford Madox Ford, Gerald Brennan, Cecilia Beaux—but the magazine had had only two issues. The theme of the first was "Can We Ever Leave Home?" Each of the contributors was supposed to take a position. The universal answer was no; each of these people, English, Russian, Spanish, American, felt himself formed and stamped by the native land he found unlivable. Caroline's essay was entitled "Memory and Inspiration."

I believe that everyone learns everything important to him by the age of six. This is especially true of the artist, and since I think it the height of modern vulgarity—old-fashioned as I am—to pick at one's past as if it were a fascinating sore the public longed to have exposed, I will speak only of my work.

Memory is the great taste maker: what we judge in later life to be excellent is only the refinement of some scene or image pressed into the molten wax of early life. The child has no word for beauty; he early accepts a miracle and has no sense of being "marked for life by it." Having no word, he carries with him only the deep impress, which when touched in later life, makes the heart cry out, and the adult voice finds the word "beautiful."

The artist is always painting the same five or six scenes cut into his heart so deeply he no longer feels the wound. For myself, three events, all taking place before my fifth year, have charted my artistic course.

The first was an accident which happened in my father's house when I was four. Some careless person had left the cistern uncovered and I, heedless as always, stepped unknowing into that great square of darkness. Someone entering the room saw fluttering petticoats in the black abyss and put down the long hooked stick used for drawing up rainwater by bucketfuls. My memory of the incident has nothing in it of fear; it contains only enchantment at the square of light I saw overhead and the black and gold of the disturbed waters. I remember, too, a strong sensation of the group I had just left: my aunts and cousins, seated on the grass, reading aloud and working at embroidery. I saw a wide leghorn hat, flowing skirt of white or pale colors, and one very smooth dark head.

The last two memories are of my grandmother. The first is of her person. I asked to be allowed the privilege of observing the end of my grandmother's toilet, the point at which she braided her fine, abundant hair and pinned it underneath her cap. She was a Quaker lady in her late sixties when I was a child; she never wore anything but white and gray and black. All her clothes were beautifully made; what she lacked in color, she made up for in needlework; her linens were perfect, and highly wrought. It was shocking in so meek a person, whose hallmark was a now-incomprehensible modesty, that her hair had never grayed. At seventy it was a remarkable chestnut. Oh, she was vain of it, although she could not have admitted it. I would sit at her feet and watch her brush her wonderful hair, then pat it to a satin smoothness. Then she would add just her cap and pin it to her hair with small gold pins, which shone for a moment against the fine white lace, then disappeared. I have always loved to paint women at their toilet, but they must be American. The Frenchwoman before the mirror exudes pastel or smoky colors: the American woman flashes out; her stuffs, her bottles catch the light, as if to challenge all the Puritans who settled that cold country. Now I paint my daughter-in-law in front of the mirror. She is the flowering of all that is beautiful in American womanhood. She brushes her hair, the same shade as my grandmother's (only Americans have it). It pleases me, of course, that on the Rue Jacob I re-create the scenes I loved of my otherwise detested Philadelphia.

In that city, which admits only dull monochrome into its atmosphere, my grandmother's garden was a righteous thumbed nose of color. And she cultivated weeds—cornflower, milkweed, tiger lily—along with the fat, full-bodied flowers she preferred. Her prize was a blood-red peony around which bees buzzed, quite transfixed. The greens in her grass were American—without the smallest touch of blue. I asked M. Matisse when I worked with him if he had clear memories of gardens as a child. *Bien sûr*, he said, he, too, had had a grandmother. Away with fancy theories of the Fauve palette!

Anne turned the page of the magazine, looking for an ending, some sense that Caroline would bring her essay back to its topic. How like Caroline it was: exuberant, quick, passionate, arrogant. How she must have irritated the editor. But the editor was her son.

========

She sat in the living room of Jane's apartment in New York at four o'clock, drinking coffee with her. Jane had told Anne that Stephen had destroyed all the copies of the magazine in his possession, but she gave Anne access to Stephen's papers when Anne asked if perhaps some correspondence might have been retained. Jane handed her the files and left the apartment, suggesting that Anne work in her study.

It was pleasant there; Anne liked working in places where people she admired had worked. Their imprint was on all their books and papers, on their desks and pens. Working in Jane's study was like borrowing the clothes of a successful, glamorous, beloved older sister, it inspired confidence and ease. She had spent the afternoon going over *The Expatriate*'s correspondence. It was thrilling to come upon famous signatures: Edith Wharton, Man Ray, George Balanchine. It was heartening and sobering to see they signed their names, wrote letters. That's why people collect autographs, she thought; it's proof that their idols inhabit the world, that the miracles they love are not their own invention.

"Tell me about *The Expatriate*," Anne said to Jane.

"It's distressing to remember those times," she said. "Poor, dear Stephen. Such a good idea, like most of his ideas, and it came to nothing, as all of them did. It was Caroline who spoiled it, probably with the most excellent of maternal intentions. You see, she knew everybody. She was fascinating and brilliant and argumentative, and Stephen was so very retiring. So people wrote for the magazine as a favor to Caroline. You can see that many of them addressed their letters to her. And then some people like Gertrude Stein wouldn't support the magazine because they hated Caroline."

"Why did Stein hate Caroline?"

"They had a fight over Jane Austen. Jane Austen was terribly important to Caroline, and Gertrude said she was the greatest bore of the last two centuries. They went on arguing, and Caroline became agitated. She told Gertrude she couldn't understand Jane Austen because she wasn't a lady. Gertrude threw her out."

Anne laughed. "A lady." That was a concept that had vaporized. "Act like a lady," she had been told as a child. But she wouldn't dream of saying it to Sarah—it would sound ludicrous. Yet she could see it had meant something and, vestigially, meant something still. Jane was a lady, and Anne was not. It was something about walking through the world assuming things—which no one of her generation, she thought, could now do. Everyone wore jeans and did housework. But to call someone a lady or to assume someone would be insulted—someone like Gertrude Stein, of all people—by being called "not a lady" would never happen again.

"Caroline was humiliated that that had slipped out, and Gertrude was, of course, shrewd enough to see she had uncovered something rather nasty —and she pounced upon it. Caroline made a great thing of not being class-conscious. She smoked the cheapest cigarettes and dressed like a beggar. Nonetheless, it was there in her, all that she came from, and she couldn't weed it out entirely."

"How exciting it must have been for you. Paris in the twenties. Everybody dreams of it," said Anne.

"Actually, I was studying at the Sorbonne, and I felt much more comfortable among the medievalists—who were like monks. All that talk about art bored me to tears. I'm not much interested in painting, you know. Caroline's work interests me, but that's because she did it. But all those others gassing on about volume and the picture plane—I couldn't have been more bored. And then they put all the pretty girls together, so I was always having to sit next to someone's mistress who bathed once a month and couldn't read. I kept disappearing with my books. Of course some of the people who came round were great fun. There was one young man, from Ohio, named Jake Golden. Some kind of journalist. He made Caroline laugh, all of us, really. He went home to New York and started a girlie magazine. Then he went far right. Supported Franco with a vengeance. Had a dramatic conversion to Catholicism at the feet one supposes of the Generalissimo. Caroline broke with him over that."

"Over the politics or the religion?"

"Oh, both, really. She thought religion was for fools and cowards. I often wonder what she'd say to me now of my religious life."

Anne hesitated for a moment. She and Jane were alone. Jane was telling her things that could be considered intimate. She thought she had a right to ask about something in her friend she didn't understand.

"How did it happen, that you became religious?"

Jane looked straight ahead of her. "I had done something unforgivable. I knew that after Caroline died. That both of us, together, had destroyed Stephen."

Her tone was flat and reportorial. "I had done something unforgivable," she said, as if she were saying, "My hair is gray, my eyes are brown." Anne met Jane's gaze; she felt Jane wanted that.

"I told you, I think, that I fell apart after Caroline's death. It was the loss of her, of course, that did it, but then I understood that I had taken up with Stephen because I wanted Caroline in my life. I wanted a formal tie with her, since I couldn't have a blood one, and between the two of us we crushed that poor boy into the ground. We killed him as surely as if we'd poisoned him. The air we breathed was poison to him."

"I'm sure that's not true," Anne said. "You give him no credit for having control of his own life. He was an adult when he met you, after all."

"But you wouldn't run a race against a cripple and then blame him for losing. Or say he simply wasn't a good enough runner. Anyway, Stephen's dead now. I shall never know the truth of Stephen's will, how strong or weak it was. It doesn't mean it was a creditable thing I did: to marry a man I didn't love so I could have his mother for my mother. It's curious, Caroline was a perfectly murderous mother to Stephen, but to me she was a mother made in heaven. Whereas I felt no more for my own mother than I felt for a rather distant cousin."

"I can't believe that," Anne said.

"No, you're a great believer in the power of blood. A real primitive you are, aren't you? Perhaps it's because I never had children. But I am convinced, you see, that some people who are dreadful parents would be divine parents to someone else, perhaps someone they haven't met. But I'm meandering. To answer your question, I turned to faith because it showed the possibility of forgiveness for the unforgivable. But we were talking about *The Expatriate* and how Caroline spoiled it for Stephen. She would keep coming to the office and commenting on things. So that, as I said, the people who were her friends addressed their comments to her, and the people she didn't like who'd agreed to write for Stephen—well, she made such fun of whatever they contributed, she would hoot with derision or spit out vitriol. Stephen was quite interested in the Surrealists, and Caroline thought they were beneath contempt. In the end, he just lost energy and gave it up."

The apartment door opened, and Anne turned to see Betty in the room.

"Come in, come in," Jane said to her, getting out of her chair. "Sit here. You must be tired to death."

"I got a promotion," Betty said, smiling shyly. "Now I'm cashier."

"How marvelous," said Jane. "This calls for a celebration. Let's have sherry."

Anne raised her glass. Gertrude Stein, Jane Austen, and Betty promoted to cashier. She wondered if one day her encounters with Jane would no longer seem to her like going over Niagara in a barrel.

———

At ten-thirty at night the doorbell rang. Anne was in the study typing a letter to a woman in Dallas who owned three of Caroline's late paintings. She was frightened for a moment as she wouldn't have been if Michael had been there, as she wouldn't have been before he came for Christmas. Who was ringing the bell this late? It could be a maniac, a robber, someone whose family had just been wiped out in front of her house. A woman alone, she thought, always imagines disaster at the tone of a bell after dark.

She pulled the curtains back and saw Ed Corcoran on the doorstep. Her first thought was that she should change her clothes. What a shame that he would see her for the first time in a month wearing a gray sweater from college full of mended holes. She took her hair out of its clip and let it fall; she hid the clip in her jeans pocket, said hello and gave him her hand. "Come in, come in. It's terribly cold out, isn't it? Aren't you cold? You must need something warm to drink. Shall I make you some tea? Come right in, we'll have some tea." She could hear her own voice babbling like the Mad Hatter's.

"I tried to phone you. I left a couple of message with your baby-sitter. I guess you've been busy."

"I never got the messages or I would have called you right back. My husband left a week ago. I mean, I didn't see any sense in your working while he was here. We'd agreed to that, you remember."

"It's taken me so long to do this job, he must think you hired a real goofball."

"He didn't say anything about it. I didn't say anything about you to him. About the wiring, I mean. I felt it should be my affair. I mean," she floundered, "I thought I should be responsible."

"Well, I saw the light on in your study and I knew you were still up, so I thought I'd just stop in and talk to you about finishing the job."

"Oh, then, you'll be finished soon," Anne said with disappointment.

"Well, if I go on doing it in dribs and drabs like I have, it'll take a lot longer than it should."

"That's good," Anne said. "I mean, it's fine with me if you want to come late at night as you did before. Can you have tea now?"

"Sure, if I'm not disturbing you."

"Oh, no, I just finished typing a silly letter. I have to go to Dallas next week. Isn't that awful?"

"Gee, I'd love to go. See what everybody's talking about. That's where the money is these days, you know, the Sunbelt."

"Whenever I hear 'the Sunbelt' I imagine all those businessmen wearing belts made up of gold suns. Or some kind of god like Orion wearing the sun for a belt."

"Orion, that's the first constellation I showed my kids. Before the Big Dipper even. That's what I would've loved to've been. An astronomer. What would you've liked to have been?"

"I'm doing what I want to do. I just hope I'll be able to go on doing it."

"Bad times," he said. "My wife wanted to be an artist. She used to paint before she got sick. But she still likes to look at art books. Andrew Wyeth is the one she loved. She loves to look at this Andrew Wyeth book she bought downtown. Do you like Andrew Wyeth?"

"Some things," she lied.

"My wife's got this thing she really wants to do. You know that painting of his, *Christina's World?* Of the crippled girl."

"Yes."

"Well, she wants to find that hill, the place where he painted it, and she wants me to take her down there and then take her picture posing like that girl Christina."

"Oh," Anne said. Rather desperately, she began pouring tea.

"I think it's a bad idea. I mean, the guy painted the picture once. That's enough. I don't see why my wife wants to do it. But we'll probably go this summer."

You see, she said to herself, he really is a person whose instincts are fine. He understands about art, about the primacy of the image. He just hasn't had the chance to get an education. Perhaps he could go to night school, take courses part time at the college. He clearly has a good mind; it would be a shame if he didn't get to cultivate it.

"How is your wife?" she asked guiltily.

"She was real bad around Christmas, upset. So we had to be kind of quiet, you know. But she's good right now. I told her about you. She'd really like to meet you. I told her you had all these art books, and she said she'd really like to come over and look at them sometime. I told her maybe you could lend her some."

"Of course," said Anne. "She's welcome anytime."

"I told her that," Ed said, smiling rather brilliantly. "I told her you were that kind of person."

"Well, I'll let you go now," he said, putting on his hat and jacket. At the door, he kissed her on the cheek. "It's great to see you," he said.

"Great to see *you*," she said, squeezing his hand.

As she closed the door she heard Laura coming into the living room. She turned to her sharply.

"Ed said he left several messages. You never gave them to me."

"They must have slipped my mind," Laura said.

"If any messages come, will you please make sure I get them," Anne said, without the edge she would have liked.

"Of course, Anne," Laura said, looking into Anne's eyes.

She could see that Laura was suspicious. It was dreadful, really, how people couldn't imagine that a man and a woman would be simply friends. Perhaps that was what had happened to Michael, perhaps his relations with Charlotte Mistière were no less innocent than hers and Ed's.

===

She and Barbara made a date to see a documentary about women in the labor movement of the thirties. The faces of old women appeared in the darkness. Plain faces, working faces. Caroline would not have looked like that, she thought. The women spoke of the work they had done, terrible work, arduous and dangerous: they worked in slaughterhouses where people regularly lost limbs and fingers, they worked in laundries twelve hours a day. They made her think of Ed, who worked hard and was gallant. She turned her mind back to the movie. "None of the people really involved in the movement had children," one of the women was saying. "They'd been too busy and, besides, it was too dangerous."

As they talked about leaflets and picketing, jumping on chairs in rooms where the workers did not stop their sewing machines as they listened, for fear of attracting the attention of the bosses, Anne thought of these women who in their old age could look back with pride on youthful acts of courage. Public acts that brought a public danger. She would never have that. What would she have to look back on when she was old? Furniture, a house, grandchildren whom she never saw? Some work, if she was lucky. But nothing she had had to risk much for. Like most women, she would not have had the experience of facing down an enemy. Most women faced their enemies in darkness, certain they would lose. But the women in this movie stood on chairs, on platforms, they raised their fists at the raised fists of bullies, they shouted down the voices that said they would starve, would die in jail, would never work again. They had been afraid for their lives but had stood fighting. They had not had children.

Afterwards she and Barbara went for a drink.

"What do you think having children does to your moral life?" she asked her.

"What moral life?" Barbara said. "I'm the Neville Chamberlain of the moral life. My moral life consists of appeasing the gods. 'I love little Pussy, his coat is so warm, and if I don't hurt him, he'll do me no harm.' That's my moral life since I've had kids."

"Was everybody always like that? Mothers, I mean."

"How would we know? Nobody ever asked them."

"I look at these women of Caroline's generation, and they seem so courageous compared to us. All of us huddling by our little hearths."

"Well, they were also very naïve."

"It breaks your heart to think about what faith people had in the Russian Revolution. Caroline's friends in the twenties, they thought they'd found heaven on earth."

"They still had the luxury of believing in such a thing. You know, I used to think a lot about that woman, Kathy Boudin. The one who was a Weatherwoman, who robbed the armored car and killed the driver. She had a kid. I could never figure it out. I admired her, though, to believe in some outside thing enough to put her kid at risk. But then sometimes I just felt like slamming her for being irresponsible."

"It's what I always feel about Caroline. Sometimes I want to slam her for being a bad mother, then sometimes I think it didn't matter, she was a great painter, so what was the difference."

"Nobody gives a shit if Monet was a bad father."

"I know. It isn't fair."

"Maybe I'll have a moral life when I get older. When my kids are gone. But by then I'll be too tired. Or scared for myself, instead of them. Maybe it's just myself I'm scared for anyway and I use them as an excuse."

"It must be possible to have children and be decent."

"No," said Barbara. "When you're a mother, you think with your claws."

She left the house with everybody in it still asleep. It was adventurous and yet luxurious for her to do this, to leave behind a sleeping house. She was alone and purposeful in the unlit morning: she would fly to Washington to see the paintings of Caroline's that were in the Eastman Collection. The Eastmans owned a dozen small Bonnards, six Vuillards, a large Gauguin, as well as works of their American contemporaries: Dove, Marin, O'Keeffe. Eastman had lived abroad as a young man; his money had come to him, flowed to him, from one of those solid unnameable sources of American capital that has, like some beneficient embodied deity, no beginning and no end. At fifty he married his mistress of twenty years. They moved back to his home in Washington, and for the next thirty-five years devoted themselves to each other and to their collection.

Jane had described Ted Eastman to her. A dreamy look had come over Jane, a look that told Anne that democracy would never touch Jane's deepest heart, as she said, "Ah, he was a gentleman. Caroline adored him. He was terribly smart, of course, and they were terribly flirtatious with one another. You can tell that by their letters. I love this one," Jane had said, reading one Ted Eastman had sent Anne. When he corresponded with Anne, he'd sent her copies of all the letters he'd had from Caroline.

Dear Dr. Princeton:
   So you liked my show, not that your taste is entirely trustworthy. Imagine seeing anything in Mr. Klee. For me, a show is only an agony. One sneaks restlessly from room to room, looking furtively to the right and the left, with the bad conscience of a criminal. And finally, the shock! One meets up, face-to-face, with one's own offspring—and immediately runs away, if only to avoid being discovered and pursued. At this show, which gave *you*, you say, such pleasure, I began by looking at the pictures on the first wall very calmly. Then I saw the one of the little Hungarian girl with the wild roses . . . and I ran away. Quite out of breath—the image, do agree, is risible—I panted into a café and ate three pastries. Then I took up with life. So when are you leaving Grace for me? I've spoken to her; she's a generous girl, she says she'll give me you for ten years, or at least an equal share. Anyway, she's much too good for you. I've a feeling no one would say that about me in relation to anyone. Except, perhaps, for Herbert Hoover. When are you coming to supper? I may even allow you a glimpse of the glorious Jane. High-minded, aren't I?

Anne had a letter from Ted Eastman dated July thirtieth; now he was dead. He had developed leukemia and died, after only three weeks in the hospital.

She felt queer visiting his widow, who was said to be grieving deeply. "I don't envy you seeing Grace," Jane had said. "I should think this is the end for her. She'll probably go dotty." And now, Anne thought, she had to walk into the room of a stranger, bearing a letter in the hand of the beloved dead. She knew how she felt seeing Michael's handwriting when he was away from her; it made his body come to life. Even more than his clothes, it could make her miss his absent body with a sharp, surprising pang. And what would this letter make this wife feel, this woman who would never again see the man she had lived beside for nearly sixty years?

She was shown into the library of the large house. When the door closed, she could hear the heels of the Jamaican servant on the green marble floors outside. The door of the library opened silently, and a small old woman appeared dressed in a shapeless tweed skirt and thin olive-green sweater. At first Anne thought she must be a servant, but then she realized no servant would be tolerated if she dressed so badly. No servant could come to work in brown felt slippers ripped in twenty places; no servant's hair—thin, uncombed, unwashed—could speak so clearly her distress. The sorrow of a paid retainer would have had to be far more concealed; no one who worked for wages would have been allowed so boldly to embody grief.

"I'm Grace Eastman," the woman said. "You must be Mrs. Foster. Would you like to look at the paintings? Yes, of course you would, that's why you've come. All the way from Massachusetts. But you'd like a cup of tea, wouldn't you? Of course you would. My husband always gave people who came to look at the paintings something to drink. But then you never met my husband."

"No," said Anne, "although I had a letter from him."

"Yes, I know you did. We did everything together. Everything."

"It must be a great grief to you," Anne said. She kept getting glimpses of the pink cotton straps of Mrs. Eastman's bra and slip through the cigarette burns that were dotted across her sweater like buckshot.

"Are you married, Mrs. Foster? Of course you are, you're a Mrs. But are you still married? So many people aren't nowadays."

"Yes, I'm still married. My husband's a professor at Selby College."

"I know people who went to Selby. All of them are dead. My husband was a Princeton man. I went to Oberlin. I was a social worker. In a settlement house. That's where I met my husband. He was helping me raise money. Of course I gave it all up to marry him. We lived abroad."

"Jane Watson has told me about you. She revered your husband."

"Everyone did. There was no one like him."

"What an exciting life you had. You've known many of the marvelous people of the century."

"Yes, but they're all dead now. There are no more marvelous people."

Anne laughed. "I sometimes agree with you."

Grace Eastman looked at her oddly, as if she had spoken nonsense. "My husband was a great man. But he died a terrible death. An ignominious death. I saw everything."

She began to wring her hands. "He had leukemia, at least that's what they said. He stopped making red blood cells. The oxygen stopped going to his brain, so he lost his mind. I was there when it happened. He looked at me terribly. Then he said, 'I have no more ideas.' That was when he lost control. He began swearing and thrashing about. He had to be put under restraints. He befouled his bed. Then he shouted, 'There is no justice.' "

The woman began crying. Anne didn't think Grace Eastman remembered she was there.

"What do you think he meant by that 'There is no justice'? Do you think he meant it in the universal sense? Or do you think he was referring to his own case?"

"I don't know, Mrs. Eastman. I didn't know your husband."

"No, of course you didn't," she said. Clearly she'd lost interest in Anne. "You can have any of the pictures you want. My secretary will make the arrangements."

She walked out the back door of the library as the servant entered with a teapot, plates, cups, saucers and a dish of cookies on a silver tray.

On the plane, Anne's mind lurched between the paintings of Caroline's that could be included in the show now and thoughts of Ted Eastman, who had chosen and owned them, dying as he did, strapped to his bed, crying out against a cruel fate. Suppose that it was true, that all one valued —love, perception, virtue—was a trick of the blood? There was no supposing about it. It was the case. She remembered the woman she had met once at a party whose story she'd found horrible. The woman had had a ski accident; she had hit her head on a tree. After she recovered, she lost her senses of smell and taste. But she also lost what she called the reflex of affection. "I would see my husband and my children," she said, "and I would say to myself, 'Here are my husband and my children, they are people I love. But I feel nothing for them.' " This went on for a year, until the woman's sense of smell came back and then her taste. Only after those returned could she feel anything for her family.

But then she thought about the paintings Mrs. Eastman had said she could have: the two early ones, scenes of the Freeman family—the blue-green grass, the red daylilies, the reluctant sister in her out-of-season black hat, the mother coaxing the baby to eat while the cat, his fur bluish in the luxury of the grass, slept outside the family gravity, beneath a hammock. In the other painting the mother sewed, one girl read to the family while the younger one sat on the window seat, the thin white curtain blowing near her hair, the light casting a barred, square shadow on the floor.

After eighty years the paintings were the same—untroubled and suggesting life was good, mothers and their children, the light on a yellow bowl. And the late one that had excited her, that suggested that life was valuable, was solid. It was of a woman entering the bath. She was middle-aged, her belly sagged and in one hand she held, in pity or in weariness, one of her drooping breasts. The body had a vigor and a toughness Caroline could not have rendered as a young woman. It was a real addition to the show, and she wouldn't have had it otherwise, for it was the kind of painting of Caroline's that Jane didn't like. It was not a landscape; it was not of her.

But it was all over, all that life that Caroline had set down, all those children and their mothers, all those women entering their baths. Yet the painting went on saying what it had always said. Was it true that some people found comfort in the permanence of art? She couldn't begin to believe it. It was something some people said because it went on being said and they wanted to be the people who went on saying it. She thought of Michael and the children. Would it one day be possible that some blood would stop, some messages wouldn't get to her brain, and she would look at them and not remember; would stand next to them and feel herself entirely alone?

When she got home, the children were bathing. She ate a salad and some lentil soup that she had made before she left. She poured herself a glass of wine and sat at the kitchen table. She was fond of her kitchen with the wooden cabinets painted in blue enamel, the butcher-block counters, the pots that hung from hooks, the plates she had collected resting on their shelf. She was looking forward to reading to the children in their beds. Nothing was nicer than being close to them as they lay giving over to the pull of sleep. She thought it could almost make her forget the terror she had felt all the way home. But the terror would be there as she held them, read to them. And they must never know.

Walking down the hall to Peter's bedroom, she stopped at the door of her own. The light was on, and she meant to turn it off. Opening the door, she saw Laura unpacking the suitcase she had left on the bed. Quickly, deftly, Laura went through Anne's clothes, sorting them into piles: white and colored, clean and dirty. She put her hands into all the inner pockets of the suitcase and, with a sharp, certain gesture, turned the case upside down and shook it. A gold earring fell onto the bed.

Anne stood in the doorway horrified, as if she were watching someone commit a private sexual act. She felt she had no right to be there, in her bedroom, watching someone unpack her bag. She wanted to go away, to say nothing, to pretend she hadn't seen it. Then, slowly, outrage rose. Laura was going through her things. She shouldn't have been doing that. It was one of those thresholds of civilization everyone agreed about.

"What are you doing, Laura?" she asked.

Laura raised her eyes from her task and smiled at Anne as if she'd said something foolish. "I'm unpacking your bag," she said.

"I'd rather you didn't do that."

"I knew you were tired and I was going to do a wash while you were reading to the kids."

"I'd rather you didn't go through my things."

"But I always do the laundry. It's one of the things I always do."

"I know that and I'm grateful. But I'd rather you didn't go into my bags or my drawers."

Laura walked out of the room. Anne closed the door for a moment, unbalanced by a sense of defeat. Shocked by the depths of her own anger, she had once again been too mild. But what should she have done? She couldn't fire someone for doing what was helpful. What Laura did didn't hurt anyone. It only gave offense. She had asked that it not be repeated. That ought to be it. But she felt she had made a mistake. Dealing directly with Laura had made Laura more daring. It had begun with her expressing her annoyance at Laura's having forgotten to give her messages. As if it were the signal she had all the time been waiting for, Laura had, since then, assumed more and more. She had, as well, lost her shyness with Anne. Anne felt in her behavior the night that Ed had come, as well as tonight, a new note of defiance. She carried with her to the children's room a sense of violation that made her unable to concentrate on the book she read.

"I've wanted to ask you about Laura," she said to the children. She was conscious of wishing to punish. But she had to know what they felt. If they were unhappy, she would have to fire Laura. "Has she been acting different lately?"

"No," said the children.

"Has she been acting nervous or unhappy."

"What do you mean 'unhappy'?" Sarah asked.

"You know, as if she's not glad to be here."

"No," said both children.

"She cleans my room up a lot more," Sarah said. "All the time. Sometimes she doesn't put things back the right way."

"I'll say something about it to her," Anne said.

"No, don't, Mom," Peter said. "It'll make her feel bad."

"All right," said Anne. "But if she does anything that you don't like, that makes you feel uncomfortable, you must tell me."

She felt the children's attention leave her. They were looking toward the door. She joined their glances. Laura was standing just outside the children's room. She looked in at all of them, smiled, and walked down the corridor.

Anne and the children gave one another panicked, shamed looks.

"Do you think she heard us?" whispered Sarah.

"No," Anne whispered back, unconvincingly. "And besides we weren't saying anything bad."

"Yes, we were," said Peter. "Talking about people behind their backs is always bad."

"Well," said Anne, "she shouldn't have been eavesdropping."

"She wasn't, Mother. The door was open," Peter said.

She didn't want to discuss with Peter the fine points that distinguished *vrai* from *faux* eavesdropping. He could too easily use it against her. And she wanted to leave the children. She felt desperate to apologize to Laura. But for what? She wanted, then, to assure Laura that she thought she was doing a good job, that she didn't mistrust her. She knocked on Laura's door.

"I was just going to run down to Friendly's for some ice cream. What kind would you like?"

"I don't care for any, thank you."

"Okay," said Anne. "But if you want some, please feel free to take some later. It'll be in the freezer."

"Thank you."

Anne got into the car. Now she would have to buy ice cream that she didn't want. How did she always manage to make herself appear in the wrong with Laura, even when she knew it was she who'd been offended? The girl had a kind of genius for offense, she thought. Or was it just that she herself was hypersensitive. She had read about women resenting other women who successfully took care of their children. Perhaps what had happened tonight was a result of meeting Mrs. Eastman; perhaps that had unsettled her. But that wasn't it. Her response had not been odd. People weren't allowed to go into your suitcase without asking; they weren't allowed to lurk in doorways listening. Her car skidded on the icy road. If she got into an accident on this fool's errand, it would be no more than what she deserved.

===

She was walking in her backyard, searching for green shoots. It was the first of March, any day the crocuses would be appearing. Last spring, seeing her crocuses, she had conceived a plan: she would plant a bank of them in a circle around the oak that stood on the small rise at the far end of the garden. But in the fall at the nursery, she'd stood before the trays of bulbs for over an hour, unable to decide on which she wanted. She loved the vivid yellows and dark purples, but then she loved the cream-colored blossoms, and the white with violet stripes, the pale yellow folding out of the gold stamen at the center like a flame. In the end, she bought four dozen bulbs all mixed. She hadn't the courage for a unified field; she couldn't live with leaving so much out.

There had been an early-morning rain. It made the lawn a patched affair of snow and mud and grass. The sun shed gray light weak as water. It was a healing weather; the sense of failure she had awakened with was beginning to fall away. She had awakened believing what she was trying to do for Caroline was impossible. She wasn't good enough; Caroline deserved better. She botched everything in her life. She'd been wrong in her handling of the business of Michael, clumsy in her dealings with Laura. And her mind was not first-rate.

Ed was waiting for her in the kitchen.

"I was wondering if I could bring my wife by for lunch today. She was in a real good mood this morning. And she asked me to ask you. She hardly ever wants to do anything, so I thought I'd ask you, even though it's awful short notice. If you can't do it, believe me I'll understand."

"No, of course, it's fine," she said, feeling panicky. "I'll just go down to the deli and get cold cuts and things."

"That'd be great. It'd be easy for her to eat. You know, soup or things like that, they can be a problem for her. It upsets people, you know, the way she eats. Most of our friends can't handle her. She upsets people, her looks, and sometimes she says things that are a little off the wall. Even her family doesn't want to see her now. Bunch of drunks," he said, in the first unkind tone Anne had ever heard him use. "They should be proud she did so well for herself. She even started college before she got sick."

From her bedroom she watched Ed and Brian getting out of the car. Ed had never come in a car before. Always he arrived in his white van and pulled into the driveway. But the day must have seemed special to him. He parked in front of the house. When he got out she saw he was wearing a shirt and tie and a corduroy jacket. How handsome he looks, she thought proudly. He waved when he saw her at the window. She could see that he was glad to see her, that her face at the window gave him particular pleasure. Little Brian ran up the steps to her, dressed in flannel slacks and a blue blazer, and jumped into her arms when she opened the door.

Ed walked around the car to open the door for his wife. The sight of her was shocking. If Anne hadn't known, she would have thought that Rose was a retarded girl of, perhaps, twenty. She had the bloated look brain-damaged people seem to have, the skin that always seems susceptible to rashes or to boils or small diseases that ought to be able to be kept back. Her legs were swollen and she was wearing flat suede oxfords. Her coat was too small for her; it wouldn't button, so she kept holding it closed, furtively, shamedly, looking around her to avoid uneven ground. Ed held her elbow. With every step he told her how well she was doing.

"You must be Anne," she said when she was three steps from the top of the stairs. "I'm Rose, but you know that. But who else could I be looking like this?"

"You look fine," Anne said. "I'm glad you've come."

"Well, you can say I look fine, what else can you say? Of course you didn't know me before. I was considered very attractive. When we first got married, people said they didn't know how Ed Corcoran snagged such an attractive girl."

"I still don't know. It must have been my brains," Ed said, laughing.

"No, Ed, I used to be smarter than you. It was sex appeal. My husband and I had a very passionate sexual relationship. I suppose you wonder if we still have intercourse in my condition. Everybody wonders that. I'm here to tell you that we do. That part of my brain still functions. I can still perform my wifely duties, don't you worry."

"Sit down, Rose. Let Anne take your coat," said Ed. He didn't seem embarrassed.

Anne was happy to go into the other room, where Brian followed her.

"Can I have a pop?" he said.

"We're about to have lunch, sweetie. But you can have one for dessert."

"Okay. Can I play in Peter's room?"

"Peter's in school. But you know how to be careful."

"I know there's stuff I'm not allowed to touch. So I never touch it," he said self-righteously.

"That's good," Anne said. She kissed him on the forehead. He was such a nice child, such a good child. What a wonderful father Ed was to have kept him happy in the tragedy he had to live out.

"Don't you be any trouble or you'll get it from me," Rose said to her son.

"He's never any trouble," Anne said. "He's a lovely little boy."

"That's because we don't let him get away with anything," said Rose. "You can't let them get away with anything nowadays. With the drugs and all. I think my husband lets him get away with too much. He can be very fresh."

"I keep being amazed at how well behaved he is for his age. My children would never have been that good about not touching Ed's tools and things," said Anne.

"Well, there are a lot of spoiled kids around," Rose said.

"Rose is very interested in art," Ed said pleasantly.

"Perhaps you'd like to look at some of my books. Or borrow them," Anne said.

"I have this Andrew Wyeth book I love. And *Christina's World*, that's my favorite painting. Ed told me he told you about my idea. To go down there on that hill where he did that painting. It's still there, you know. I thought I could get into that pose, like Christina. Then Ed could take my picture. It would be appropriate, because I'm crippled, too. Ed doesn't think it's a good idea. Do you, Anne?"

"I think it would be lovely," Anne said, trying to look steadily at Rose. She continued to wear her sunglasses in the house, so it was impossible to see her eyes.

"You see, Ed, she thinks it would be lovely. You're the only one who thinks it wouldn't be a good idea."

"Maybe, then, if Anne thinks it's a good idea, we'll go in the summer. When the weather gets nice."

Rose snorted. "Seeing is believing."

"We'll go, maybe," he said. "Maybe we'll take Anne and all the kids and make an outing of it."

"Of course, in the summer, my husband will be home," Anne said quietly.

"It must be very hard on you, being separated from your husband. Physically, I mean. Of course, I don't know if you and your husband have a very sexually passionate relationship."

"I miss him very much," Anne said. "Would you like to look at this book on Renoir while I'm fixing lunch?"

"Can I help?" Ed asked.

"You can open the wine."

Ed followed her into the kitchen and closed the door. "She's not embarrassing you, is she?" he asked.

"Oh, no," Anne lied. "I think she's doing very well."

"She is. When you consider what she's gone through. She had to learn to walk all over again; she couldn't even dress herself. Still, she upsets most people; there aren't many places we can go without me worrying she'll get someone upset. But I knew you'd understand."

"Of course, Ed. Everything's just fine."

"I knew it would be. I knew this was a place where we could all relax and have a good time. Not worry." He gave Anne a hug that was over as soon as it began.

———

Laura came into the kitchen sullenly when Anne called her for lunch. She greeted Ed with the air of a headmistress ready to dismiss, at the slightest sign of infraction of the rules, the scholarship pupil reported to be of great promise. Anne tucked a napkin under Brian's chin and kissed the top of his head. She pushed his chair into the table. She liked Brian for himself, liked him as much as any child she'd known, but he received, deflected, the tenderness she felt for the person of his father. That he was Ed's child softened the boy's lines, blurred him beautifully, as if he were a child in a picture or a story she had loved while she was still a child.

"What a nice boy you are, Brian," she said. "I'm always so glad when you come to visit."

He rolled his eyes to the top of his head so that his irises disappeared.

"I almost died having him," said Rose. "I was fine before I got pregnant with him."

"I made my mommy very sick," he said to Anne. He spoke seriously, but he didn't seem disturbed.

"No, Brian, that's not right. Something in Mommy's body made her sick. Like when you get a sore throat or a cold," said Ed.

"You know, Anne, I'll never be all right," said Rose confidingly.

"You're fine, Rose," Anne said, taking her hand.

"No, I'm not. I know what it's like to be like you. Pretty and happy and on top of things. I remember that." She began to cry.

Ed gave her a handkerchief from his hip pocket. "Look at how much better you are than last year, Rose. We were afraid you'd never walk again."

"It would be better if I died. That's what you think. That's what everybody thinks." She began to sob audibly—choking, gasping sobs that whipped the air like a storm.

Laura put her hand flat on the table, as if she had only to move her hand to make the storm stop. "If the Lord wanted you to be dead, you'd be dead in the blink of an eye," she said, looking stonily at Rose.

Anne felt shocked and frightened. It was a terrible thing to say; she was sorry for Ed, for Rose, that Laura had said it. But she felt frightened because some curtain had been opened, some thick veil removed. It was the first time she had ever heard Laura mention the word "God." If Hélène hadn't told her, if she hadn't seen Laura reading her Bible every night, she might never have known that Laura was religious. It was a secret she guarded, like royal birth. Now it was open, now Anne must look, for she had given it to Anne, like a spy who purposely leaves crude clues to his identity.

Rose turned her head to Laura. She had stopped crying, a final, complete stop, as if she had no sense that she had just shed tears. "That's what the priest says. He says I'm alive for a reason. You're lucky to have a boy and a girl," she said, turning pleasantly to Anne. "I was hoping little Brian would be a girl. I love the clothes. They're so much fun to dress up. Like little dolls."

Anne was so relieved that Laura hadn't offended Rose that she began to feel light-headed. "Unless you have a little girl like Sarah," she said, "who has to be tied down to have a dress put on her. My mother sends her beautiful dresses with smocking. They just hang in the closet. Sarah says they're creepy. She likes jeans."

Ed laughed. "Sarah's always involved in some enterprise. She's afraid dresses will slow her down."

Anne looked lovingly at him. He understood her children. He appreciated them, not as genre pieces but as complicated people, just as she did. So few men did that.

"Eddie, let's go home now. Lunch is finished and I want to take my nap."

"Will you stay for coffee?" Anne asked, the pot in her hand.

"I want to go now," said Rose.

Ed picked Brian up and walked Rose to the living room, where he helped her with her coat. In seconds they were out the door.

"I'll be back next week," he said to Anne over his shoulder. "I have a rush job I can get done in a few days."

Anne waved good-bye. Don't leave my house. Come back quickly, she wanted to say. She walked into the kitchen. Laura had already cleared the table and was doing the dishes. The set of her back was grim.

"I've had an idea, Anne," she said, keeping her eyes on the sink. "I'd like to give the house a good spring cleaning. Top to bottom. The basement. The attic. Turn the mattresses, wash the curtains, clean out the closets, straighten all the drawers, shampoo the rugs and furniture."

"Oh, you don't have to do that," said Anne.

"But I want to. I enjoy it. It's the time of year."

"I was thinking that since the nice weather was coming you might want a few days off," Anne said.

Some shelf dropped over Laura's eyes, as if a shutter had been closed on a summer pavilion where the dancers still danced, the music went on, but to the outside there was a presentation of only darkness and a silence so severe it could be meant only as reproach.

"I thought it would be a good thing to clean the house," she said, looking straight at Anne.

Anne felt as if the girl held a gun to her head. It was ridiculous, what she was feeling. Why should she refuse to have her house cleaned? There was no sense being absurd about it. If Laura wanted to clean the house, why not?

"All right, Laura," she said. "That's very nice of you."

The next five days were beautiful, ideal for Laura's purposes. Cool and fresh, the wind flew as if from the sea. On the clotheslines, the perfectly hung sheets snapped, the curtains billowed like sails, the house all day was redolent of polish and soap. Laura seemed, for the first time since Anne had known her, happy for a long, extended period. The vacant smile was gone; she wore, all day, the calm straightforward face of one in love with her vocation. She barely spoke, she left things on the table with crisp notes. Anne left the house early in the morning and did her work in the library. There was no quiet anywhere; doors banged, rugs were beaten, water gushed from faucets and was poured down drains, drawers slammed, windows were shot up like rockets and shot down like the gavel of a firm and certain judge.

Laura's hand touched every object in the house. From the health food store she bought dried lavender, and at night she made the sewing machine whirr for hours of short spurts as she made sachets for every clothing drawer, for each shelf of the linen closet. She took out the wedding presents that were never used—the fondue set, the cocktail shaker—

washed and dried and polished them and put them in some new, efficient place: in the cellar, in the steamer trunk Michael had from college. In the attic she opened the cartons of the children's outgrown clothes. Anne had given away most of them, but she had saved some because she loved them, because they marked some season, some event of happiness. They kept the past in a shiny husk, like the shell of a nut. And now the husk was opened, now Anne had to say, "I want to keep this dress, this shirt, this pair of boots." She had to justify to Laura—who looked judgingly at her, as if she were refraining from reminding her of the poor who needed clothing— her need to hold on to these objects to keep the past from flying away. So the past was no longer the dark contained thing it had been: now it was cracked; the inside, duller, chambered, never whole, was picked at and consumed. Anne put things back that Laura touched and questioned, but they were not the same. Even as she successfully rescued something, she felt that she might as well have given it away.

The house was cleaner now than it had ever been. How could she turn the girl out for this? Barbara told her every day how she envied her. The children weren't disturbed. Peter was annoyed to find that something he had left out was put in some new place, but he had always been like that. Any change had always seemed to him an affectation. Sarah was swept up in the tremendous wave of energy: she dusted and polished with Laura, she ran up and down stairs, she interrupted her mother's work to say, "Laura wants to know if we really need this, or if we can throw it out."

Anne found it difficult to work. She couldn't banish Laura's peaceful, triumphant face, exhausted at the day's end from righteous labor, to concentrate on Caroline's paintings; she could not still the noise of tearing, casting down and casting out, the machines that roared and sucked, the objects placed down heavily, the bottles clanked together. And she was coming to the end of the letters and the journals. The last years of Caroline's life were unhappy. She stopped to weep when she read Caroline's letter to her dealer in New York:

> You write and ask for something new. But you see, dear Frederick, there is nothing new, and will not be. It is all over. My eyes are gone; the cataract operation was botched, and I see well only in memory. And so, what now? People come and pay me homage, as if I were a statue. And my darling Jane is imprisoned by my state; she is my only joy, and knows it, so she does not leave me. I say I think she should, but if she did I would simply die. It is interesting, really, the people who become valuable when one's senses give out. The foolish wife of a foolish

landscape painter comes and sits, sews while she talks nonsense, brings
her puppy. And I am grateful! I do not like this new emotion, gratitude,
but it is better than the nullity that is my common lot. We dine out
every night; and search for gardens. To taste, to smell seem miracles. But
seeing was my life! My life is a useless old woman's, worse than useless.
For I steal life from Jane.

How she loved Jane, reading that letter, Jane, never patient, nursing an
invalid, searching out gardens, restaurants. She wanted to see Jane. She
longed for Jane's wholeness and her sanity. Life now seemed to Anne made
up of impossible situations: Michael, Ed, Laura; she felt, in trying to make
sense of it all, as if she were trying to braid branches of thorns. But Jane
had courage, she had that adorable detachment Ben had spoken of—"like
an admiral walking the deck of a ship." She had encountered dreadful
things, in life and in herself, and had come through. Life brimmed in her.
She never responded to it, as Anne felt herself doing now, with the
conviction simply of her own fatigue that clung like the memory of illness
and left her with the invalid's incompetence. She wanted to see Jane; she
wanted to be out of her house. So she contacted Ben and told him to set
up an appointment with Jane and the gallery owners. It was earlier than
she would have liked, but she had to be involved in something. She had
to be away from her house.

On the bus down she felt sick and short of breath. I am an unjust person,
she kept having to come back to herself to say. I am a person who hates.
She knew that she could have gone through her whole life not having to
say these things about herself if she hadn't known Laura. And now Laura
had touched every object in the house. It would never be free of her
impress.

She thought of Ben and Caroline, how they inhabited a world of sense
rather than of morals. "Is it beautiful, is it pleasurable, is it interesting?"
These were the questions that came to them, not "Is it good, is it important, is it true?" She knew how Caroline would walk into a room, into a
town. In Spain once, she had stayed in one small village for six weeks
because she said the girls had faces the color of aloes. She wrote about
meals as if they were operas, about a piece of cloth as if it were a book.
Ben did the same thing: he spent evenings with dreadful empty people
because they dressed well, served wine that was superb, had beautiful
furniture. She didn't understand this, it was an instinct she did not possess.
Beauty couldn't move her to action: when her heart filled and she shed
skin after skin, she didn't assume the experience was connected to the rest

of life. She might choose to vacation in a small town because of its view of the mountains, but she couldn't settle in if the natives seemed unhappy with her presence.

She thought of Ed Corcoran, whose life had so little in it of beauty or of pleasure. The worst thing in the world had happened to him, a cruel random fate, a nemesis. There would be no relief from it, and there could be no explanation. He was never free of it; like the Furies, it buzzed always near his head, and it was never silent. He was like the victim of tragedy, but unlike the spare heroes of the Greeks, Ed had to live on day to day, looking after things: the house, the children, medicines and doctors. He had always to worry about money; Rose's illness had put them eighty thousand dollars into debt, he told her once. He couldn't rest for a minute; he had to work to keep up with his payments, his children needed him, his wife at any time could thrash out at him like the wounded creature that she was, saying he didn't love her, he didn't care for the family, that one day when he wasn't there she'd kill herself and kill the children too. Each day the path he'd cleared the day before grew up around him. And he hacked and cut the vines and branches without anger, without rancor, as if he had all the time in the world, as if it was all not less than what he had expected. Pressing her face against the green glass of the bus window, she thought what an extraordinary person he was. She'd never known anyone like him; he was one of the most admirable people she'd ever known.

===

Ben said he would meet her at the bus terminal. It was unnecessary, but his courtliness pleased both of them; she wouldn't dream of throwing on it the cold water of democracy or common sense. It was March, and the melting snow ran brilliantly down the long streets. People looked over their shoulders as if they would throw their winter coats into a litter basket if no one was looking.

"Let me tell you about Harriet Brevard," said Ben. "A woman of parts, as we used to say. Frightfully attractive, very sexy, though not pretty. Not at all like you. I've known her, of course, since she was three. We were all together in Paris. Her father made a fortune buying Klees and Légers for five dollars apiece; he filled his attic with them. Very solid, very jolly. Now, my darling, you must be at your singularly most impressive for this lunch. Harriet's extraordinarily pleased with what you've done. She's thinking of taking you on on a permanent basis. Her father used to do all the research for the exhibits, but he's a bit past it now. So you mustn't get girlish and modest when someone says you've done good work."

"It would have been better if you hadn't told me. Now I'll be afraid of everything I say."

"Nonsense, you'll know that everyone thinks you're extraordinary. It'll buck you up no end."

She couldn't begin to make Ben understand; if someone told him he was extraordinary, he accepted it as a compliment that was his due, it was, to him, no more than recognition. But to her, it was a treasure she must be suspicious of. It could so easily be spurious, it could so easily be lost.

They passed a famous shoe store on the corner of Fifth Avenue and Fifty-seventh Street. A sign was in the window: 2/3 OFF. Anne stopped and looked. Her eye fell on a pair of green leather boots, soft and low-heeled like riding boots, except that the tops could fold down. Two-thirds off. It was like being at the beach on a fine day; it might never happen again. But probably they wouldn't have them in her size. Still, they were two-thirds off, and Harriet Brevard might want to hire her.

"Ben, can we stop here a moment?"

"Of course, my darling, we have piles of time."

He opened the door for her. There were no men like Ben in the world now; if there were, she would have to dislike them.

The shop was as big as a ballroom. Fashionable women walked around as if it were their kitchen. They tried on shoes they couldn't possibly walk comfortably in, but then, Anne thought, they probably never had to walk very far. The salespeople were blessedly ordinary, shabby even. They looked tired, grumbly, overworked. A woman of about sixty, her hair the color of face powder, walked over to Anne.

"You want something?" she asked in a Middle European accent. Her expression was so pained, it was clear she was hoping Anne didn't want anything, had wandered in by mistake. It occurred to Anne that the woman looked as if her feet hurt all the time. Surely that was bad for business.

Anne pointed to the boots in the window and told the woman her size. The woman disappeared into the back room with a shake of her head that conveyed that she thought the project was doomed from the start. A few minutes later she returned, carrying a box.

"You're lucky," she said. "Not many people wear size eleven."

The boots slid onto her feet, her legs, like a silk sleeve. She looked at herself in the mirror. She was so pleased with what she saw that she began to blush.

"They do suit you wonderfully," said Ben.

"How much are they?" she asked the woman.

"Now a hundred twenty-five. At the beginning of the season they were three seventy-five."

Nearly four hundred dollars. She didn't spend that much on clothing in two years. Now they were a hundred twenty-five. Still, they were a great extravagance, boots you wouldn't feel right wearing in the snow. She looked down at her feet. Her heart lifted. What would Michael say? He would want her to have them, but she would see his eyes go worried about the money and she would back down. But it was different now: she had more money. And if Harriet Brevard hired her, she would have even more. What a nice thing money was. It said, you can have this, and this, and this, this you can put against your skin, that in your mouth, and on your feet boots that make you swoon with pleasure. This book is yours, it said, that record. You have all the time in the world, it whispered. Don't rush, don't be worried. She hated to say it, she hadn't believed it, ever in her life, but at this moment she knew it to be true: money made a difference.

"I'll take them," she said to the woman whose name, she saw pinned on her jacket, was Solange.

What exalted past had she dropped down from, to be kneeling here, her hair the color of face powder, writing a bill out on her lap?

———

Harriet Brevard answered the gallery door when they rang the buzzer. She was a tall woman of fifty with short black Japanese hair. Her hands were distractingly large, and as if knowing that and deciding to acknowledge it by drawing more attention to them, she wore a large square emerald the size of a pat of butter.

She shook Anne's hand and looked her frankly up and down. Anne was glad she was wearing her new boots; she felt they gave her something more to offer.

"You've done a remarkable job," she said. "You're to be profoundly congratulated. I've done a lot of exhibitions, hired a lot of people, and you've done the best job I've ever seen."

"Thank you, I've enjoyed it," Anne said, forcing herself not to look at the floor.

"Jane said we're to meet her at the restaurant," said Harriet. "You've got a good press agent there, you know."

"Jane's very kind."

"She's as tough as a sailor and nobody's fool. She terrified me for twenty years."

Anne laughed. "What happened after twenty years?"

"I had a baby. Jane Watson is absolutely dotty about children. Spends a fortune on little sweaters. Well, I couldn't quite be terrified after that."

"My son's in love with her. It's the first grand passion of his life."

"How old is he?"

"Nine."

"My dear, wait till he's twenty. My son is living with one of his high school teachers. Earth science, whatever that is. I'm chilled to imagine."

Anne laughed again. "How many children do you have?"

"Two boys. Older than they have any right to be. One's sailing down the Amazon, finding himself. It drives me mad. What drives me maddest is that they're out of the house. I miss them dreadfully."

"You've gone on liking them for twenty years?"

"Of course. They're wonderful people. Who takes care of yours while you work?"

Anne groaned. "It's a long and dreadful story."

"You must tell me all about it at lunch. I'm sure I can top it. Cressida," she called over her shoulder.

One of the young women Anne had lunched with appeared at the door of the back office. She seemed to have shrunk in Harriet's presence, she was almost shy.

"We'll be back at two-thirty. Take messages. Dreadful girl," Harriet said. "They're all dreadful. Anorexic and ungrammatical. That's why I want you to come work for me. I always know if I'm going to work well with someone within twenty seconds of meeting them. Don't you?"

"No," said Anne. "I've come to believe I'm a very bad judge of character."

"She's too kind by half," said Ben.

"Ben, you must stop saying that. You've no idea what goes on in my mind."

"It's like the way you go on about her being pretty," said Harriet. "No one wants to be told they're kind and pretty anymore."

"Whyever not?" asked Ben.

"Because it makes them seem powerless. As if they ought to be dozing by the fire, wearing a pink ribbon around their necks. People want to be more tigerish nowadays."

"Harriet's absolutely right," said Anne.

"Of course this is all guesswork," said Harriet. "No one's ever accused me of being kind. Or pretty. My words are 'striking,' and 'dynamic.' I think I must come across like a stevedore."

"Women are never satisfied with their looks," said Ben.

"Jane is," said Harriet. "She knows she's beautiful. But that's because she's had Ben for forty years, and he's told her so often."

"That's not why," said Ben proudly. "It's because her beauty is so undeniable. She's the finest woman of her time."

Jane was waiting outside the restaurant.

"How are you, Harriet?" she said. "Have you told Anne you're going to hire her?"

"Not yet, but I'm about to."

"And, of course, Anne, you'll say yes."

"I'll have to hear first, Jane."

"Nonsense, it's perfect for you."

She was right, Anne learned, when Harriet made her offer. She would work in the office three days a week: she would research the exhibits and do the catalogues. Her first job would be to do a complete inventory of the gallery's holdings. The pay would be small. Ten thousand dollars a year. But she would be free to do more work free-lance if she desired.

"So you'll take it, of course," said Jane, reading the menu in a slow bored way.

"Of course," said Anne.

"Bravo," Ben said. "Let's order wine."

They toasted Anne and Harriet. It was luck, Anne thought, once more good luck had brushed her with its tender and enlivening wing. She knew that she had done good work, but many others did and were not so conveniently rewarded.

"I must tell you about my worst *au pair* and then I want to hear your story," said Harriet. "She was a sculptress from Bennington, in love with a young Algerian man who had come here for a year. She ran up phone bills of hundreds of dollars, which I could never get her to pay. I didn't know what to do; I didn't feel I could withhold her salary. She just kept saying 'I can't pay for that, I don't have the money.' But she kept on making the calls. She said she couldn't help it, whatever that meant. The children hated her. Every time I walked in the door, everyone was screaming and crying. But there was nothing I could do. I had to finish a show. I sat them down at the kitchen table and told them they would simply have to cope for six more weeks and there was nothing else to say."

"And did they?" asked Anne.

"Of course. They always do."

"My situation's so much less bad than that," Anne said. She told them about Laura's lurking presence, her eavesdropping, her fanatical cleanliness. To her astonishment, as she told the stories everyone laughed. When she described Laura's refolding all the paper bags into precisely identical shapes, the three people at the table thought it was hilarious. Anne felt as if she had just been told she could put down the sack of stones she carried around her neck. If she could see Laura's behavior as ludicrous, perhaps she could be free of her. It was only another two months; if she could just laugh at Laura. She felt as if her friends had introduced her to a new invention, the typewriter or the vacuum cleaner. It was wonderful what they had done for her.

━━━━━━━

Her mood was high. She decided to phone Ianthe and arrange to go with her to the place where Ianthe got facials and pedicures and where she had her legs waxed. "Just do it once, darling. Just for once cut the brown rice and sleeping-bag motif and indulge yourself. My treat," Ianthe had said at Christmas.

"What a heavenly idea," she said when Anne phoned her. "I'll meet you in an hour. But don't expect anything glamorous. These people are all business. Very medical, really. I'm sure they did abortions in Budapest in the thirties, in whatever little back rooms they had then. Anyway, darling, it's all very brutal, but you end up feeling divine."

To Anne's astonishment, Ianthe burst into tears when she told her about the job Harriet had offered her. "I don't think you know what working with you is like," she said. "Oh, I know, I'm a selfish slut and no doubt I take advantage of you, but, you see, you're the most perfectly splendid companion. You keep everyone at bay, including my demons, and all the while sailing above things like some beautiful ship, no, like some Van der Goes angel—you know how one sometimes mistakes the look for stupidity, but really it's this terrific vision. And underneath it all, my dear, dear friend, is a first-rate mind. It's a terrible loss for me. And then you'll end up liking Harriet better than me, I know it. I've always been madly jealous of her—that emerald, for one thing. Now, promise me upon your children's lives that you'll never like her better than me."

"I promise."

"Well, you don't mean it, you're just humoring me. But it's all right. By the way, did I tell you I'm fucking Adrian again?"

"After you burned all his clothes?"

"You see, that was my opening gambit. I invited him to Balmain and bought him a whole new wardrobe."

"You two are so lucky. You just go to bed when you want, and burn each other's clothes up when you want, and the universe goes on."

"Now, what is that wistful tone I detect? And why are you suddenly at Gilda's? If I didn't know better, I'd say the natives were getting restless."

"Oh, Ianthe, don't be ridiculous," Anne said. "Who would I possibly get involved with?"

"Well, when I'm in the mood, darling, I just pick whoever's nearest."

She rang the buzzer of a door, marked GILDA COSMETOLOGIST, that looked like any of the other offices on the corridor of what was, after all, an office building. A downtrodden-looking girl wearing a blue kerchief around her head and a nurse's uniform answered the door silently, her eyes on the floor. She gestured Ianthe to a room off the main one. It was dark and the size of a large walk-in closet. Silently she turned on the light and indicated that Anne and Ianthe should pick up a sheet.

"You strip here, love, and wrap yourself up in this. Just like the gynecologist."

Inside the main room, fluorescent lights buzzed cruelly and only half lit the area. In the back, a window was opened, and sunlamps shone on the faces of supine women, who looked as though they might be dead. No one spoke. Fortunately, Ianthe knew what to do. She lay down on what looked like a doctor's examining table, and told Anne to do the same. It was covered with white paper. On the paper were clots of wax the size of half-dollars. "First the legs," Ianthe said to a woman in her fifties who mysteriously appeared. Her eyebrows were heavily penciled, her eye shadow was electric blue. Through a series of grunts, she indicated that Anne should turn over on her back. Several times the room went utterly silent, then suddenly another woman would appear, massage the face of one of the corpses, and speak to her fellow worker in some Middle European tongue.

The woman who was in charge of Anne and Ianthe dipped into a white enamel pot with a wooden spoon. She scooped out a spoonful of taffy-colored hot wax and slathered their legs with it.

"Now, Gilda, this is my very best friend in the world, so try not to be quite so savage. It's her first time."

"What you do before me—shave?" the woman asked Anne.

"Well, yes," Anne said, feeling pitifully the inadequacy of her reply.

The woman merely grunted. She waited for the wax to harden, then pulled it off in long strips, looking dreamily into the middle distance.

When she finished Anne's legs, she grunted in the direction of the sun-lamp area.

"Close your eyes now, relax, don't make more wrinkles," said the young woman who had let them in. She covered Anne's face with steaming cloths, then dug at it with a small sharp instrument. When she had finished with these, she massaged Anne's face with lotion, humming a slow unmusical tune that sounded like an incantation. "Heavenly, Irena," Ianthe kept saying to the woman who was doing identical things to her. But Anne was too frightened to respond. She kept thinking of a movie with Boris Karloff and Bela Lugosi. Karloff comes to Lugosi, a plastic surgeon, and tells him he's ugly, to give him a new face. Lugosi makes him hideous, then blackmails him into committing crimes to earn a proper operation.

"Darling, you look radiant," said Ianthe, when they were in the changing room. "Now, don't you feel ready for whatever it is you have in mind?"

"I don't have anything in mind, Ianthe."

"Listen, my love, I'm longing to know the details. But I know you'll never be a chum and tell. My only advice is, don't go all girlish and confess. It would destroy Michael."

"Thanks a lot, Ianthe. That's very helpful."

"Well, to tell you the truth, Anne, the thought of your being unfaithful makes me sick. I'm sure you don't know what you're doing. You mustn't do it. I'm quite serious. You have the only decent marriage in America. It's worth a little self-control."

"Ianthe, for five years, you've been carrying on about the unquenchable demands of the female libido, how you're driven as no man on earth has been."

"Yes, but that's me, darling, that's not *you*."

"Anyway, nothing's going to happen."

"Mm, perhaps, but remember, you can't touch pitch and not be defiled. Meanwhile, I must fly. I'm going to meet Leonard Armitage for a weekend at the Ritz in Boston."

"What about Adrian?" Anne asked.

"Well, what about him, darling?" said Ianthe, fastening her bra.

———

She was reading to the children when Ed came and sat down among them on Peter's bed, taking his shoes off, putting his arm around Sarah. The room smelled like all children's rooms, a mixture of clay dust and wax, a neutral and unfleshly smell that always made Anne sad. They were meant to be grown out of, these small rooms, and Anne felt their generosity, like that of a wife about to be abandoned who makes up a packet of sandwiches for her husband's mistress. Ed laughed as the children laughed at Mr. Toad and his car crashes.

Anne let her arm brush against his on the bedstead. She wished she could prolong this scene forever. It was like being in her father's greenhouse, where the air was rich and warm and moist, where the loamy smell and the dampness came together in an atmosphere so purely, innocently sensual that no act could have a moral tone. It was so natural for her to be there with Ed, with the children. She kept being aware that in a minute they would have to get up, to separate the children, to put them in their separate beds, turn off the lights and walk away somewhere, somewhere cold and dry and solitary where everything would take on a new shape.

They walked downstairs into the kitchen. It came to Anne suddenly, as if she had stepped into the path of a wave and felt herself overturned, over and over in a foreign medium, that she and Ed must be lovers now. She would do it. It was the right thing to do, she was sure; she would invite him to her bed, she would tell him she loved him. It was true, she did love him, not in the way she thought she would her first adulterous lover, not desperately. Her love for him was not a burden or a threat. It blended into her life easily, she was immensely comfortable with him. She told him things; he told her things. They talked about the children. That was why she hadn't until now recognized it as love. But it was love, and it was, overwhelmingly now, desire. Her limbs felt incompetent on their own; they needed to be with his. She wanted his body with her body. She wanted all that went with that, all the sweetness they had had, and all that wasn't kind or comfortable or patient or benign, all that was hungry, driving, driven, strained.

Now she would do it. She'd never done anything like it before. When she met Michael she was twenty; they finally went to bed after a month's discussion, after nights and nights of kisses and caresses and the furtive incomplete knowledge of each other's body learned from hesitation that embossed the wrong things, they would find out later, with the stamp of genuine *frisson*. But she wasn't twenty now, there was no possibility of discussion, no time for gradual buildup. He had to know right from the first that sex was what she wanted. How would she tell him? She couldn't use words; words were for the brash or for the very young. She would simply have to take him in her arms.

She closed the kitchen door and leaned against it for a moment as if it were a springboard. She looked at Ed, trying to make her desire clear. She walked toward him slowly. She put her arms around his neck.

"Anne, are you all right," he said, holding her as if he were afraid she would fall.

"Yes," she said quietly, putting her head on his shoulder.

"Come here, sit down," he said.

"I don't want to sit down."

"Are you feeling dizzy? Here, sit down. Now put your head between your knees."

She put her head between her knees. Then she realized that that was exactly the wrong thing to be doing. She lifted her head. "Ed," she said, "I'm not sick. I just want you to hold me."

"Hold you? Like hold you up?"

"No, I want you to embrace me."

Almost rudely he let go of her and walked to the other side of the room. "I don't understand what you're saying."

"I want us to be lovers," she said, looking at the floor.

He began to pace heavily in a circle. He kept clasping his hands, unclasping them; he took off his watch and put it in his pocket. "I just don't believe you mean that. I just don't think you know what you're saying. You're not that kind of person."

She ought to give up: she knew it. But it was too late, they would have to have it out. She felt slightly sick, but some stubbornness pushed her forward.

"What kind of person do you mean?"

"Like all those women I work for. Married women with nice families. Trying to talk me into going to bed. I thought you were different." He looked up at her with a childish look of pure disappointment, as if he had seen his favorite teacher drunk.

Nothing he could have said would have made her feel more humiliated. All those women in all those houses. All those undifferentiated women. She had joined the ranks of hungry women throwing their bodies at a man, their loose breasts flapping, their behinds white, fat, in the stage light. The predatory woman was always a comic figure. Venus and Adonis. Fellini's whores. Now she was in that company.

"I thought you were fond of me," she said weakly.

"Of course I'm fond of you. I love you like a sister. I thought we would be friends for life."

She began to cry. That was the worst. They would never be able to see each other again.

"Anne, I don't understand. You're a married woman."

"My husband has a lover in France," she said, and realized with shame that to have her way, she'd turned doubt into fact.

"Okay, that's bad, but two wrongs don't make a right."

She looked up at him. She still wanted him. "Why would it be bad, what we were doing? Who would we be hurting? They'd never have to know."

"Anne, we're married people. We made promises."

"But my husband broke his promise. And your wife, well, she's not a real wife to you anymore. She can't be."

"That's not her fault. She tried. A terrible thing happened to her. She's lost everything. I would never do something like this to her on top of it. I thought you understood."

He turned his back to her and leaned on the counter. "If you're going to be out of the house for the next few days I can finish the wiring by Friday."

"All right," she said. "I'll stay away."

He nodded his head and walked out the door. As the door closed she could hear Laura sweeping the dining room floor.

"What are you doing out there, Laura?" she said sharply.

"Sweeping the floor."

"I know that. But why at this hour?"

"Because I rented a floor waxer for a day. And I've spent the day waxing all the wood floors in the house. This is the last one. The machine has got to be back at nine in the morning."

"Surely you're not going to do it tonight. It's nearly ten o'clock. You can rent the machine for another day."

"I want to do it now."

Hate carried Anne up the steps. Suddenly she blamed Laura for everything. This thing she had allowed herself to feel for Ed was a result of the intolerable pressure of living with Laura. She had turned to Ed for solace and friendship, then misunderstood it as sexual desire. She had never done anything like that in her life before Laura was in it. And now Laura knew everything; she must have heard everything standing outside the door. She stopped herself. She couldn't blame Laura. She despised that tendency in people, that abdication of responsibility in favor of some totemic theory of the power of proximity: "He was next to me, he pressed against me, I had to act." It was her own responsibility; the shame was hers.

She hadn't felt this kind of shame in her life before. Embarrassment, of course, guilt, mortification, but nothing like this realization that she had done a serious wrong that was damaging, and foolish to boot. There was the built-in debasement of a woman desiring a man who didn't desire her. But what was worse, she had violated a friendship. It had been important to her to believe that men and women could be friends, could inhabit a pleasant well-lit room where sex was kept out, and she had betrayed that belief. She had also gone against all she believed of marriage. She had exposed her husband to a stranger's censure, perhaps without grounds. She had denied what had been important to her: the idea of marriage. She'd said that if the circumstances are extenuating, then the vows don't hold. And she had lost a good friend.

She didn't have many good friends. There was no one she could call up at this moment, no one she could go to, because there was no one whose friendship she found substantial enough, rich enough to warrant the exposure of her husband's possible offense, and of her own. She couldn't go to Jane. Jane didn't know Michael well enough. She couldn't tell Barbara because Barbara had desired Ed Corcoran too. Ianthe had demonstrated that she was out of the question. And she couldn't tell Ben or Adrian because they were men. The experience of having been turned down in a sexual offer aroused an ancient female *pudeur,* she didn't want to reveal herself a sexual failure to men who she hoped still found her attractive.

She couldn't tell anyone. She abode in marriage; it was the house she lived in, and outside it there was no one who ought to have access to its flaws. If it was cold and hard and comfortless, as it was now, that was simply the way things were, the condition of life on the estate.

She couldn't read; she couldn't lie in bed. She tried to take a bath, but the hot water made her restless. She kept walking around her room, picking up a hairbrush, a bottle of perfume. She longed for some ritual place where she could be cleansed. But she was who she was: a woman of the twentieth century, rational, responsible for herself, for her own acts and for her marriage, which she had just come from damaging. It didn't matter that she was, technically, physically, chaste. She'd given up her chastity; she would never have it again.

—————

Weeks before, Jane had agreed to come to Selby for a few days to help Anne with the parts of Caroline's diaries she found illegible. But she didn't want to see Jane now; she felt she wasn't good enough to see her. Her encounter with Ed made her feel defiled; to be in contact with someone like Jane, whom she so admired, who might falsely admire her, seemed to her an offense against any ideal of fineness.

"You're tired, you look tired to death," Jane said, stepping out of the bus. She never waited to begin talking till she had stepped from one place to another: she talked over her shoulder on stairs, as elevator doors were opening; she would have felt quite comfortable, Anne thought, delivering speeches from moving trains.

"I've been working hard," Anne said.

"Hard work doesn't give you that look. Hard work is exhilarating. It's some kind of strain. You don't mind my saying so, I hope, but you look as if you've aged since I last saw you. At your time of life, of course, it's nothing to be horrified by."

"I haven't been sleeping well. I guess that's it."

She didn't want to talk to Jane about the incident with Ed. She couldn't mention her problems with Laura because Jane already disliked her. Like a climber slowly making his way up an icy slope, what she wanted most, was determined to get, was equilibrium. She wanted to finish her work and to avoid having it out with Laura. It was March twenty-third. The catalogue notes were due on May thirtieth. And eight days before that, Michael would be home. If she was careful, quiet, if she didn't make fast moves, everything would work. But she mustn't speak to anyone about it: if the climber voiced his fear, the danger of the fall loomed large.

"If I were home I'd make you a *tisane, une infusion.* Infusion. It always sounds so effective. So hydraulic. As if the best minds of the Industrial Revolution were behind it, so you're bound to be all right. And yet it's so wonderfully simple, not mechanical at all."

"My sister makes her own herb teas."

"Oh, my dear, those things right-minded people serve one now. Made of stewed Kleenex and ammonia. And the messages on the sides of the boxes. Nietzsche and George Eliot. It's enough to drive one to Nescafé."

"I hope things will be quiet in the house. I told Laura to take the children out and keep them busy for the afternoon. There's a lot I need your help with. The later diaries are in a very shaky hand."

She brought Jane into the study. Not having worked there for a week, Anne felt herself a stranger to it, a betrayer of the room. She smelled the beeswax polish Laura had used on the furniture. Her desk, Michael's desk, shone with a dull rich glow. She rearranged some papers on it, quite unnecessarily. She took new pencils from the drawer and sharpened them; she adjusted the flexible neck of the desk lamp.

"Here's a passage from 1938 that I can't make a thing of."

She handed Jane one of the notebooks. There were fifty-six of them, identical blue-covered books with inside pages mottled like a plover's egg. Caroline used a new one for each year, she began a new one even if the old year's was only a quarter full. A firm in Philadelphia made them specially for her. She began keeping a diary in 1884, when she was twenty, and continued until the year of her death fifty-four years later. Anne had been through all the books. A few days ago she had come to this entry, the last, made two weeks before Caroline's death, and had not been able to read it.

"Caroline loved notebooks, particularly these," said Jane. "She loved good pens and fine paper. She used to say that an artist has as much obligation to address an envelope beautifully as she does to render justice to her most beloved model. She was vain of her handwriting, and contemptuous of her male peers who didn't care about this kind of detail."

Anne smiled. She loved the notebooks too, the yellowish pages and the ink gone brown, the sense of physical intimacy that reading the careless handwriting, seeing the words crossed out and written over, the hasty marginalia, gave. Caroline's was a beautiful hand, a formal hand, an artifact now. No one wrote beautifully anymore, unless their writing was deliberately, self-consciously anachronistic. Then they sent away for calligraphic pens and special inks. But they didn't write that way for the butcher; if you found their laundry lists, the hand would be inevitably of the twentieth century, functional, forthcoming, plain.

"I remember that day. October 18, 1939," said Jane. "The doctor had just left her when she wrote this. She was very weak all the time by then. She knew she was dying. The doctor, a friend of her cousin's, such a nice man, we all adored him, had told her when she asked him that she had at most a month. She wept. I was surprised, for she had known for some time that she was dying. When I told her I was surprised, she said, 'It's that I feel I've just been given an invitation to a wonderful party I know I'll have to miss.' She asked me to bring her the book. Look at the poor writing, how weak it is." Jane patted the page as if it were a small, sick animal. "Of course you couldn't read it. I can barely make it out. I'll read it aloud, if I may."

"I have not been a good woman. Near death, I say this, knowing there is nothing I can do about it now. I have been a bad daughter. Indifferent to my mother, I did not mourn her death. My father died my enemy. I left my son to wither. I knew what he needed: warmth and care, and moist rich soil. And I left him in a stony place, a leafless place. He died still a boy. Rootless, unrooted. My friends are dead. I was a good friend to them if it didn't cost me much. In old age I learned love. I have loved Jane. I have loved her above all people. Yet I swept her up, I kept her to me when I should have let her go. If she would follow me, I should have, like Naomi, led her to a husband. Instead I encouraged her affair with Ben, and kept her to me. What heaven can there be for someone who has lived as I have lived? The heaven of the kind, the just, will close itself to me, in kindness and in justice. I have loved beauty. I have loved above all the light on the water, a yellow pear in a blue bowl, a winter sky shot through with silver. Yet perhaps to earn an eternity of beauty one has had to live a life of goodness. So perhaps I will sit, weeping and shuddering, in eternal darkness. I am right to fear."

Tears were running down Jane's cheeks as she finished reading. Anne, too, wept.

"How I hate the word 'goodness.' What an obstacle it is to the moral life," said Jane.

"Do you find goodness and morality incompatible?" Anne asked.

"Of course not. But the term 'goodness' has been so perverted, so corrupted, it now covers only two or three virtues when there are hundreds."

"Was Caroline a good woman?"

"She was marvelous. What she said about herself was right. She was often unkind, impatient and unjust. She was terrifically self-absorbed. But she was loyal, honest and courageous. She was a great painter. She had only to open a door to make life come into a room. In her presence despair was impossible, depression the invention of the Russians or the English or someone in some country far from where you were."

"But what about Stephen?"

"She was not a good mother. But she was a splendid human being. What an immense egoist she was. Imagining my love affair with Ben was her doing. We fell into bed before she'd time to catch her breath."

"And you've been lovers all these years?"

"Does that shock you?"

"No, it delights me."

"Of course, he was terribly in love with you."

"With me?"

"Oh, yes, my dear. I've known about you for years. Since that summer in London when you were twenty. He asked me if I thought it would be frightfully immoral of him to marry you. I asked him if he wanted more children. He said no. I told him in that case it would be frightfully immoral."

"Jane, I'm astonished. What would you have done if we had married? Would you have gone on being his lover?"

"No, of course not. Because if he'd married you it would have been a real marriage, and I'd never have interfered with that. So, naturally, it was in my interest to stop the match. Are you outraged?"

"Of course not. You were perfectly right, and I'd probably have married him. I'd have been miserable deprived of children. It's my ruling passion, maternity."

"I see that. But I've never felt it, although I love children passionately. It's like a potato left out of the stew."

"I've always been amazed at how detached Ben is from his family. Have you ever met them?"

"No, he's kept us carefully separated for fifty years."

"What about his wife?"

"Not a glimpse, not a word on the telephone. He never speaks of her. Of course I have my ideas. But Ben is loyal. Never a word against her. Or for her either, for that matter."

"I don't understand that kind of marriage. What can it possibly mean?"

"Ben is one of those men who need to be married because they need to live in a certain kind of house. But he has no genius for family life, that kind of man never does. His affective life is always outside it—as if he felt it unseemly to have strong emotions in the same place that he eats and sleeps and has his clothing."

The telephone rang, and Anne jumped. It was Lydia Garrison, the wife of the emeritus professor of economics, who lived in the house behind. "I hope I'm not interrupting something important."

"No, of course not," Anne said, thinking it was impossible to tell the truth to someone who declared she hoped she was not interrupting.

"I don't want to sound like an old busybody, and doubtless I don't know how people bring up their children these days, but I'm watching your children at this very minute. They're playing on the ice on my pond. Not that I mind, they're always welcome, they know that, I've told them that, but it's just that I'm not sure the ice is firm enough to hold them. I didn't go rushing down because they have an adult with them, their baby-sitter, I believe, and perhaps I'm wrong, perhaps the ice is firm enough, only I'm not quite sure."

"Thank you, Lydia. Thank you very much."

Anne hung up the phone and ran out of the house. The Garrisons' pond was at the bottom of a steep slope five hundred yards from the Fosters' house. She could get to it two ways: by running three blocks on pavement or by scrambling down the hill. The hill might be icy, but it would save time. She saw her children fallen through the ice, saw their eyes close on dark water, their mouths frozen, their limbs helpless to move. Running down the hill, she slipped twice, got up hurriedly, and cut the palm of her hand on a sharp stone. The pond came into view. The children were running on the ice; she could hear their laughter. The surface of the pond was slushy; she could see the prints their boots left on the quickly melting snow. As she rushed forward she imagined every minute she would see them going under. She would be punished for her lifetime of good fortune. She had always known she would have to pay for it one day, but it was too cruel, what might happen any moment before her eyes. Any moment she might see her children disappear. And she would dive in after them, perhaps losing them forever, perhaps rising to the surface wet and frozen, having left her children underneath. But she would not come up; she'd stay there too, stay with them always. It could not happen. She would get there; she would save them. She offered anything in place of the disaster that she might at any moment see: her own life, Michael's life. She would be willing to live years a hopeless invalid, entirely impoverished, alone, or mad, if only her children could remain in her vision for a minute longer, if only for one more minute the surface would hold.

She was at the shore of the pond. She knew she mustn't cry out to the children or alarm them. They must walk slowly, steadily, the hundred feet to where she stood. She called their names. Peter looked toward her guiltily.

"Are we in trouble for getting our clothes wet?"

"No, of course not, sweetest. You're not in any trouble at all. Just walk very slowly to me, very slowly. Make Sarah walk slowly, but don't take her hand."

The intrusion of the ordinary was like a blow; here were her children, they were talking about misbehaving, about catching cold. They wouldn't die before her eyes, their lives would go on and hers would; the horror had lifted, life had been breathed back. Her heart was beating terribly with the strain, which was like the last desperate burst of a runner's heart, to keep her voice from screaming out.

The children walked toward her, slowly, as she had told them. They reached the shore.

"I was afraid we'd be in trouble," said Peter. "We're soaking wet. Our feet, our jeans, everything. But it's not Sarah's fault. It's mine. I told her it was okay, even though I knew it really wasn't. I knew we shouldn't get wet on a day like this when we might catch cold."

"No, darling. It doesn't matter that you got wet. What matters is that you are all right. You were in danger. You might have fallen through the ice."

She suddenly remembered Laura. Rage rose up in her: a loud clatter of dark wings. The wings flew, blocked the light. They twisted, they became involved in a tremendous whirring circle. She heard nothing, could see nothing but a circle of confused wings, whirring horribly, and the sharp beak somewhere about to strike.

"Did Laura say it was all right for you to go out on that ice? Where is she?"

Peter pointed. "She's sitting behind that rock reading. We asked her if it was okay, and she just smiled and nodded. I don't think she was really paying attention. She was moving her lips while she was reading. I didn't think grown-ups did that. Some of the kids in our class, in the C reading group, move their lips when they read, but they always get in trouble."

"You stay here. Don't move," she said to the children. She felt she must move away from them. She had become the wings, the beak; she could feel her body whirring, she could feel her limbs grow long and thin and pointed, ready to swoop, ready to strike. Her movement across the snow felt like a heavy flight. It took her only seconds to get to the rock where Laura sat.

Laura looked up and smiled. "Hello, Anne," she said, closing her Bible.

"Laura, what are you doing here?" said Anne, keeping her fists clenched so she wouldn't strike her.

"I'm reading."

"Didn't you see what the children were doing? Didn't you see that they were on the pond and that the ice might not have held them? What were you doing here, letting them do something like that? What could you possibly have been thinking?" Her voice was a knife; she heard it and was pleased.

"They're all right, aren't they?" asked Laura, still smiling.

"Yes, Laura, at the moment they're all right. But if someone who saw them hadn't phoned me, they could both be dead."

Laura looked up at Anne, shielding her eyes from the sunlight. She smiled at Anne for several seconds. Anne waited for her to speak, but she said nothing.

The desire to put her hands around Laura's throat, to take one of the large rocks on the shore and smash her skull, to break the ice and hold her head under the water till she felt her life give out was as strong as any passion Anne had ever known. As strong as her love for her children, for her husband, stronger than the things that made the center of her life was her desire to inflict damage on the smiling face of this girl who might have let her children die.

"I'm sorry, Laura, but you'll have to leave. I don't think I can trust you with the children. I'll take them away for the evening. We'll be home at nine. I want you gone by then, with all your things. Don't leave anything behind you; I don't want you to come into the house again."

Laura took her hands away from her eyes. She was still smiling. "All right, Anne, if that's what you want."

"There'll be a check for you on the counter. Two weeks' salary," she said, her back toward the girl.

"Thank you, Anne," she heard Laura say.

"Wait here for ten minutes, Laura. Then start for the house. By the time you get there, we'll be gone. I don't want the children to see you."

She told the children to walk the three blocks of sidewalk; she would walk up the hill alone. Her steps were heavy, certain, long. She didn't slip once, although the climb was steep and the ground icy. Her legs ached at the top of the hill. She was glad of that: the physical pain made her seem herself to herself, someone she recognized, still human. She was frightened by what she had felt. Like a figure of allegory she had become one quality, one vice. She had become entirely anger. She had felt herself close to killing. She might have killed. She thought of murderers; she knew now what, when he raised his hand, the murderer felt.

When she got to the house the children were waiting for her, holding Jane's hand, looking up at Anne in fear and confusion and sorrow. She must comfort them; she must show them she was the person she had always been, the person that they knew. She smiled at them and said as gently as she could, "Change out of your wet things, my darlings. We're going to go out."

She had failed. Anne did not love her. Anne's heart had turned to stone. But why had Laura lost heart when God was with her? She was the favorite, the chosen of the Lord. And now her heart was once again within her. For the work of the Lord must be done through her, in violence, in desolation, for Anne's heart had turned to stone within her and must be plucked out. "I will take out of your flesh the heart of stone and give you a heart of flesh," Ezekiel said, the words of fire. The fire of love, love like a wind of violence, rushing, love the wind of fire. Oh, Anne, how beautiful is the face of the Lord. I will bring you His face, His face shall be before you in my hands.

She had lost heart because she had thought the flesh was going to prevail, it would swallow up the spirit of the one she tried to save. Was she no match against the Prince of Darkness and his heavy cohort, flesh? She knew the heart of Anne. With eyes of love she pierced and saw a heart choked up with lust and anger. Anne had coveted the husband of another. She lay all night on her bed of thorns, lust was her bed, her rest, her solitude. The face of God must sweep it out, must leave behind a bare room stripped and sweet. Swept with the broom of fire. But Laura had lost heart. Because the heart of Anne had turned to stone, turned from her, turned against her. The hard heart became a sword to drive into the flesh of Laura, the Lord's messenger, the chosen of the Lord. Who loved Anne as no one else could ever love her. Whose hands would bring the white face of the Lord, the shining face, the beautiful before the mountains.

She had been careful, prudent, had not made mistakes as before. For the work of God she had practiced deceit. She read the word of God in private, or if she read in public, read casually; as others read the books they read, she read the Word of God. So there was nothing to alarm, to frighten, to reveal. She had been careful, and she kept the secret in her heart. She had said nothing when she saw that Anne desired the flesh of the man not her husband. Secretly in her room she had written the words she wanted to say, the warnings of the Lord, of blood, of fire. Hosea's words. The Lord had made the prophet plead with the adulteress:

That she put away her harlotry from her face,
and her adultery from between her breasts;
lest I strip her naked
and make her as in the day she was born
and make her like a wilderness,
and set her like a parched land,
and slay her with thirst.
Upon her children also I will have no pity. . . .

When she first read that, when the Lord led her to read it, she wanted to run in to Anne, to wake her from her sleep, for it was night and dark. Only Laura was awake; the Lord had spoken in that night to Laura, spoke the warning and the truth. She wanted to wake Anne and say the words the Lord had shown her. Do you want this, is this what you want, she imagined herself saying, pulling Anne's blankets from her, shining the light in her eyes, giving her God's message in the cold night. This is what awaits you if you follow in the path you want to walk. If you put your flesh beside the flesh of this man who is not your husband, but another's. Is this what you want, a wilderness, a dry land and your children cursed? Turn away, listen to me. I can keep you from this. I will lead you from the desert to the cooling spring. Your garments will be white as snow. Your face will shine like the sun. Your heart will soar above you. Turn, turn from your sin to me. I will lead you from the path of thorns into the path of righteousness. I am the messenger of the Lord. I will show you his face in my hands.

But she sat silent and was prudent. She said nothing to Anne, although at night she burned with fear for her, with fear for the sin she planned. She closed her eyes and tried to sleep. But she could see them, man and woman, beast and beast, locked in each other's bodies. She knew what it was like, for she had done it. She knew what was meant by flesh and why the prophets sickened when they spoke of it and why the wrath of God came down because of it. Of course the wrath of God came down because of it. How could it not? She could see the bodies lock and tear and afterwards the eyes with nothing in them but the blackness which is sin, is death. So she prayed, with the sight of them behind her eyes that this sight would not come into the world, into fulfillment. And her prayers had worked. The man had gone away. The darkness left the house. She waited for the Spirit. But the Spirit did not come. The darkness of the flesh had moved away, but the light of the Spirit did not replace it. Only stone and hardness. Only the heart turned to stone.

But why had she lost heart? The hand of the Lord was in everything. The path she followed had been wrong, the path of prudence and of counsel. She had been frightened; she had feared that she had failed. That was why she had the thought of cleaning everything. Because the house had been defiled.

Just as her mother's house had been. She thought now of her mother's house. The house of her birth, the tubes, the red jars, caked black sticks of makeup, the brushes left around, left out, black on the towels, on the sheets, the stains of lipstick left on cups, on glasses, on the cigarettes that multiplied like dead things in gray ashes that flowed onto the tables, on the rugs, the floor. The cigarettes thrown in the toilet, floating with the red scar up, scar of the mother's mouth, the black ring on the tub, scar of the mother's filth. Her mother was a filthy woman. She had always known it. She had known it as a child. As a child she had to see the bloody napkins pinned in their harness dropped on the bathroom floor, the bedroom floor. Red blood, brown blood, blood on soft sticks, cotton stubs in garbage cans because the septic system would not take them. Cover them up, cover yourself, hide it from me. As a child she cried in the bed she kept clean herself. Why do you let me see, why must you keep showing me? I am small, I am your child, and there are things you should hide from me. Lovely mother, mother beautiful in clothes, smelling of perfume, of shampoo, keep me from this body life, oh keep it from me. Show me only your light dashing arms, your quick feet in their pointed shoes, the turn of your skirt as you dance somewhere. Keep me from the body life of curses, groans, the blows you deal me. Keep from me your naked body, the black triangle of hair. Hide from me the man who comes in the mornings when you think I sleep, the man I have to find, the door I have to open, and the curses you then have to rain on me for finding what I have to find. I am your daughter; I am a child. Keep things from me.

I will keep the house clean for you, Mother. I will follow you and hide the things you ought to hide, will wash away the foul smells and the food gone bad, will clear away the evidence. Oh, beautiful, quick mother, mother like a shining bird, I will do this for you, do everything, if you will say that you will love me.

Why could they never see, the mothers, that their houses were their sanctuaries? For the children to be safe in, to be happy. So they must be pure as snow; nothing must be permitted of corruption. For the children. It must all be beautiful for them. If defilement entered, then the Lord would curse. Curse everyone, the mothers and the children. The Lord had told Ezekiel: "Wherefore, as I live, . . . because you have defiled my sanctuary with all your detestable things and with all your abominations, therefore I will cut you down; my eye will not spare, and I will have no pity."

They did not know, they had forgotten because the Lord had kept His wrath disguised, had covered up His face, had kept His dark voice silent. Only a few saw. The rest were as if dead. It said in Revelations: "I know your works; you have the name of being alive, and you are dead." The Lord gave warnings in those days, but even then the people did not hear. They did not know; they thought the Lord was far away and could not see them, could not hear them. But He was coming; He was coming. And they were unready. Anne, her children, were unready. They saw nothing, heard nothing. Only Laura knew. The Lord would come at night, a thief. And they would not be ready. The Lord's curse would come on them. They would perish, they would burn alive, they would be swallowed in the cloud of night, they would be blotted out forever from the book of life. All this would happen if she could not make them hear. And yet sometimes the Lord had mercy. Sometimes He kept his chosen ones to shine a light before them. "Yet you have still a few names . . . , people who have not soiled their garments; and they shall walk with me in white, for they are worthy. He who conquers shall be in white garments, and I will not blot his name out of the book of life."

She saw the garments, shining, stiff with majesty. She saw how she would walk in them, her head high in the light of God's own countenance. For she would conquer. But the others would not conquer if they did not listen to the chosen of the Lord. They must listen. She had been afraid that she would fail to conquer. She had been afraid that the darkness was too strong for her. That Anne's heart had hardened against her as her mother's heart had hardened against her. Her mother would have her name forever blotted from the book of life. Since the Spirit came to her, she knew that. But she was afraid for Anne.

She had seen Anne turn against her. She had seen her body stiffen; heard her voice go hard. Your voice is a knife of stone, she wanted to say to Anne, put it away, turn it from me. Anne was saying all the time: "Don't look, don't listen, don't be near me." When she said, "Thank you," she meant, If only you were not here. It was her mother's voice, the knife of stone. Every word her mother said was really saying, If only you were not here. The knife of stone had fallen on her heart until the Lord had sent his word, and she learned that she was the Chosen One. Now her mother's voice could never hurt her. But when she heard Anne's voice, the new voice that was always saying, If only you were not here, she felt again the knife of stone. The Lord took his shield from her and exposed her heart. But she had not given in. She had prayed. She had worked to cleanse the house of its defilement. And the Lord had spoken to her now. He had told her the answer. The answer was of blood.

She could do it now. The final thing, the violent thing. No more must she be wise as serpents and as innocent as doves. Now she was the Angel of the Lord. The word of God came in a blazing light, in fire and sword. The Word of Love. She had cleansed the house with water; she would cleanse it now in blood.

First she would write the letter. She would take the paper from her notebook, where she wrote the special messages of God.

Dear Anne:
I am doing this because I love you. The Lord will come as a thief, and you must now repent of your defilement. You hardened your heart to me; now I must speak to you in blood. I am always with you. No one will ever love you as I love you. I will never leave you; you will never be alone. I am the chosen of the Lord. You never knew this for your heart was hard and it was hidden. But now the time has come and it must not be hidden. I am the chosen of the Lord, and I have loved you as the Lord has loved you. I will show you his face in my hands.

She would read Isaiah's words. She would write them down for Anne.

Can a woman forget her sucking child,
    that she should have no compassion on the child
        of her womb?
Even these may forget, yet I will not forget you.
Behold, I have graven you on the palms of my hands.

She would take the razor. She would cut her hands just at the wrists. The cut would be in the name of Anne. She would lie down in water and be thinking of her glory. Of her snow-white garments and the radiance of her face. Shining before the mountains of the Lord. She would shed every drop of blood she had for Anne, so Anne would see how much she loved her.

Their mood was high as they drove home from the movies. Jane had done it; she had made them feel courageous, dashing, bold. They hadn't mentioned Laura, but as soon as they were seated in the diner Jane had said, "There's only one thing for it. I must be asked to move in and care for these dreadful creatures till the project is complete."

The children jumped up and down in the red booth, knocking over water glasses, salt and pepper shakers, in their joy. Together, Anne and Jane mopped up the mess with napkins, laughing, handing the sodden paper to the waitress who had sullenly come to take their order. It was such an enchanting idea, so unlikely, so extravagant. It easily replaced the somber news of Laura's leaving, which the children had listened to in silence, stony-faced. Anne exchanged the bruise of guilt, remorse and anger, the unhealed fear of her children's danger, for the dry, well-formed white bone of justice. She *had* been just; her anger *had* been justified. She had been extreme, but the situation had been extreme. For once in her life she had been clear and forthright. She had seen what needed to be done and done it. Justice: what a small part it had played in her life. Like most women, she feared it. Justice to her had conjured up the implacable God of Moses, depriving his servant of the promised land because of a rock struck twice. She had believed like Hamlet: "Use every man after his desert, and who should scape whipping?" But Hamlet wasn't a very good model. He had certainly muddled things. It was better, much better, to act as she had acted with Laura, as she had acted for the first time in her life. The girl had been negligent. She had placed the children in grave danger. They could no longer be left in her charge. She was troubled, that was obvious; Anne supposed that really it had been so from the beginning.

But when Laura's troubles became a danger to the children, she had to
be got rid of. It was as simple as that. Anne knew Laura would be upset,
was, perhaps at that very moment, in pain. But she had endangered the
children. Whatever moral consideration Anne owed to the rest of human-
kind was dwarfed by her first duty: to keep her children safe. People who
didn't have children could take in people like Laura. She could go to
Hélène. That was the perfect place for her to go. She could imagine Laura
and Hélène telling each other what a monster she was. She could imagine
them sitting on Hélène's couch, Laura whispering her suspicions about
Anne and Ed. Saying that she had kept them apart only through constant
vigilance. And then Hélène would feel she had to tell Michael. Well, let
her. And if he said anything to her, she could deny it in good conscience.
She was innocent. Nothing had happened at all.

The thought of Ed left her once again exposed and bruised. But she
would bury it. For tonight, she wanted to feel triumphant, a great judge
carried on the shoulders of a reverent crowd.

On the way home, Jane and the children sang "Over There." Jane told
them about the First World War, which America had entered when she
was nine years old. She told them about her brother who had driven an
ambulance in France. How splendid it would be for them to be with Jane,
Anne thought. How wonderfully everything was working out.

When they turned the corner, Anne could see that all the lights on the
second floor were lit.

"Damn it," she said, in an undertone to Jane, "either she's not gone yet
or she's left the lights on just to be annoying. That would be typical of that
girl. Annoying to the end."

"Do you want me to go ahead and speak to her if she's there?" asked
Jane.

"Of course not," said Anne. "I'm not afraid to confront her."

The children ran into the house first; they were incapable of not racing
each other to the kitchen table. Anne walked behind them. They stopped
racing when they got into the living room.

The living room floor was covered by a pool of water a quarter-inch deep.
Water was splashing down the stairwell. Between the newel posts a steady
stream spilled to the wall below, down the spines of the books on the
shelves above the piano. Water splashed on the piano. From a spot in the
ceiling underneath the bathroom a globe of water hung, dripping a puddle
onto the rug.

"Oh, boy," said Peter. "Someone must have left the bathtub running
for a really long time. I'd better check it out."

Only when he was halfway up the stairs did Anne notice that the water was not clear. A light raspberry stain had spread over the walls, settled at the bottom of the dripping globe of water on the ceiling. She tried to understand what had happened. What was this thing that seeped and dripped and colored all the walls? Not water, or not just water. Water with something passed through it.

Instantly, she knew. The word lodged in her brain, a small dark pebble, then softened and exploded in her mind. Blood. Blood had passed through the water. She knew Peter was looking at blood.

He stood unmoving at the bathroom door. From the set of his back, she knew that he was terrified. Quickly she ran to him. She stood beside him in the doorway. For a second, two seconds, she stood still beside him, unable to grasp or to believe what she saw: a dead girl lying in a tub of red water, one hand, the left, grazing the white tile floor.

Every organ in Anne's body enlivened, tightened and then hardened and grew cold. At the same time she was riven, a torrent split her, top to bottom, with a violent slice. Blood, death. The words, almost absurd in their simplicity, drove through her body like a blow. This is the end of our life, she heard a voice inside her skull say. Life as we will know it will be different. We are looking at the dead.

But it was not the nameless dead they looked on. It was Laura, whom they knew, whom she had hated, whom she had sent away. And who had killed herself most horribly. The horror took her over. A scream bloomed in her throat, then choked her like the taste of blood. I cannot go on, I cannot go on, she heard inside her skull. Someone must help me now. I cannot do a thing.

But there was no one; it was she who had to act. Laura had spilled her blood there in the house. In the house that she had imagined she would keep her children safe in. She knew she must put aside the horror now, the grief, the terror, whatever she felt that would transfix her so she could not act. For now she must protect her children. She felt Peter looking up at her; she felt alive beside her his desire for her, as his mother, to speak or to move. He needed her to do something, to round things off or tie them off, to stop them shading into the rest of his life. She walked to the tub and turned off the water. Then she walked back to Peter's side. Beside him once again, she made herself look as he had looked.

There was Laura. She was dead, but death had not made her unrecognizable. The pale flesh against the heavy hair, the white limbs: it was the body of someone Anne had known. Laura's eyes still looked; their gaze stretched upward at the ceiling. She seemed to smile. It was hypnotic, the similitude between the living body and the dead. Anne felt herself entranced. How young Laura looked, even in death. What had made her do this dreadful thing, to make herself, so young, into one of the dead? All her relations with Laura swam before her eyes. Did she do this, Anne had to ask herself, because I sent her away? What did I do to her, what was I in her mind? Peter took her hand. Sharply, she willed herself to move. She could not think about Laura any longer. She must take her son away. The image must not burn into his mind a second longer. She put her arms around him and led him down the stairs.

"We'll have to tell Jane and Sarah now," she said, holding his hand as they walked down. "But we must make sure that Sarah doesn't see, so I'll ask you to stay with her at the Greenspans until I have things taken care of."

"No, Sarah mustn't see."

"It's important. I'll depend on you for that."

Walking down the stairs, she felt the pressure of having to put into words what she had seen. To take from the event its carapace of silence seemed to brutalize it yet again. But she had no choice. For what she must do, above all, she told herself, was remove the physical evidence. As far as she could, she must render it impossible that anyone should see again what she and Peter had seen. She took Sarah into her arms. How did you bring the news of horror to a child? "Laura is dead," she said, holding Sarah to her.

Sarah began to cry. It was such a relief that someone had a natural reaction that Anne felt them all turn a corner. She held her daughter's solid body, lively in its grief. She looked over at Peter. He was away from them, sitting on the couch, his hands folded in his lap, his eyes dry and brilliant.

Never had she felt her position as a mother so impossible and so false. She had no idea what the right thing to do for him was. He had taken himself away from them. Should she let him be alone? He had seen a terrible thing. More than that, he had been the first to see it. Of all of them, he was closest to the event; of all of them, he must feel the least innocent. Yet he was still a child. He was the same child who had sat at the diner half an hour ago and blown, for the amusement of the company, bubbles in his milk. He would never be quite her child again, for seeing what he had seen, his childhood was no longer intact, and he would never again need her in the simple way he once had. She began to embrace him and felt him stiffen away from her. She would let him do that; she would let him be by himself. His moving away from her made her see how everybody waited for her action. And suddenly, action seemed the only chance. She saw herself as a machine, bicameral: one part could function and the other, where the cold gears seized, could be closed off. She could act; she did not have to feel or think. She could be like a clock that went on keeping time although it could no longer sound the hours. She must not feel or think. The problem had its physical dimensions; now those would save her.

"Mommy wants us to go to the Greenspans until she takes care of things," said Peter to his sister.

"When will you come and get us?" asked Sarah, beginning to cry again.

"I don't know, darling. You may have to spend the night. But I'll come and tuck you in."

"I'll go with them, Anne, and explain what happened. Then I'll be back and help you. We must get started on all this before it does any more damage," said Jane.

Damage. How much damage had been done already? They would never lose it from their lives. But physical life had the first place now. Upstairs a body lay. Oddly, this body, dead, had needs. And they were not dissimilar to what the living body had required. It was wet, it was cold, it was naked. It could not stay in a tub of water.

She must prepare the body of the dead. She must touch the flesh that she had shrunk from while it lived. The police were coming. Jane had called them. They would be there soon. And Laura's body must be clothed before they saw it. What Laura had done was private, and the face she wore was the private face of death. Anne felt the body was painful in its exposure; she must protect it from the gaze of strange men, of men who came from the outside. She felt that Laura's body, having met death in her house, became her child. So she must protect it from the violations of the outside world as she protected her own children.

She put her hand into the tub. Pulling the plug, she allowed the water to run out, slowly first, then quickly, with a heavy final gush. She waited until all the water was gone and only a thin greasy coating of blood remained before she tried to lift the body out.

The weight was terrible, for it offered no resistance. Torpid, languid, the limbs flopped passively. The body could do nothing to compose itself, to dignify itself, to save itself from the fate of the grotesque. Anne had to drag it from the tub in slow stages, putting it down on the floor from time to time. The flesh was icy cold against her flesh, her clothes were wet from its wetness, and she couldn't lift it from the floor. Horrified at the spectacle of the only course physically possible to her, she dragged Laura through the quarter-inch of water in the upstairs hall. The trailing feet made a playful swishing noise, a seaside noise, a holiday noise, a noise children might make for the simple pleasure of the act. She got the body to the door of Laura's room and stopped, exhausted, letting it lie flat on the floor for a moment. Her arms ached; her legs thrummed with fatigue. But she must prepare Laura for the police.

She placed the body in the center of the bed in a posture that might be like sleeping. Then she looked among Laura's clothes. There were so few: a pair of jeans, some T-shirts, underwear, socks, a sweater. Alone in the closet was the dress that Anne had given her. None of Laura's clothes seemed right. She went into her own room and got her bathrobe. Coming back into Laura's, she thought, as if it were a problem in physics, how she would begin to dress the body. She sat down on the bed and spread the bathrobe out. She lifted Laura's head and upper back and held them against the front of her own body. As a posture, this was not unfamiliar to her; it was not unlike dressing a sleeping child. She pulled the arms through the sleeves and let the body down to rest once more against the pillows. Straightening the robe underneath Laura, about to put the sides together and tie them, she looked at the girl's body. There were the breasts, the sex. There was the waist, the white thighs, the surprisingly delicate ankles. She remembered that Adrian had been Laura's lover. The thought shocked her: the juxtaposition of death and sex seemed wrong, as if the sexual activity one knew the dead to have been involved in had failed in its promise to bestow eternal life.

She closed Laura's eyes, arranged her hands at her sides. The police were downstairs; she heard Jane talking to them. Now she must go and tell them what she knew. Which was nothing. That a girl who had been alive was dead by her own hand. That she didn't know why she had done it. Except that she might have been disturbed by an incident earlier in the day in which she had been told that her services were no longer needed. She would not say to them, although she knew it was the truth, "She was driven to death by the hatred I bore her. She died because I could have killed her."

She heard herself saying these things in her own mind, calmly, at a remove, as if she were being sentenced in a dream court. Calmly, she walked down the stairs, through water that splashed with every step she took, toward the police who were sitting on her couch.

They asked questions; she answered them as simply as she could, determined to talk about what had happened as little as possible. When she brought them upstairs and took them into the room where Laura was, they told her she shouldn't have moved the body.

"We would have liked the coroner to see her as she was, ma'am," the policeman said. "The cause of death has yet to be established."

"But she cut her wrists in the bathtub," said Jane impatiently. She'd followed Anne and the policemen up the stairs; she was trying to protect Anne from them.

"We're not in any position to determine the cause of death. We're just here to investigate the circumstances of the crime."

"The crime?" said Jane.

"Legally speaking, it's a crime, ma'am."

"I don't understand what you need to investigate. It seems quite straightforward to me," said Jane.

"Well, there could have been foul play. Someone could have drugged the victim, for example, and then cut her wrists and put her in the tub like that to make it look like suicide."

"How absurd," said Jane.

"We're not inferring anything, ma'am. It's our job to investigate all areas of the incident."

Jane spoke to the policemen as if they'd wandered impertinently onto her estate. She expected them to listen to her; she expected them to leave. But Anne thought they were right: there had been a crime. They would never know the name of it, and they would never name her as the criminal. But she had done it. She had closed her heart to Laura. She had driven her to death.

The policemen looked cursorily at Laura's body, then seemed no longer interested. They turned their attention to the rest of the room.

"Here's the note," said the blond policeman, reading it quickly and passing it to his partner, who passed it to Anne.

"I thought you said you weren't close to the deceased, that you hardly knew her," said Officer Planck.

"That's true," said Anne, staring in horror at the words Laura had written.

"There's no telling what some people keep bottled up inside, is there?" said Officer Duffy.

"No," said Anne. "No telling."

"Thanks, ma'am, we'll just look around up here by ourselves. We'll call you if we need you."

Anne went downstairs and handed the note to Jane.

"My God," said Jane when she had read it. "But, Anne, you mustn't take it as meaning anything, not for a moment. It's a work of absolute derangement."

"We can't talk about it now," Anne said. "We can't even think about it. What we must do now is clean things up."

========

She knew that if she could just start, just make the first step, perform the first gesture, it would not be so impossible. She must make her mind a shape that could surround the things, a fence that could divide the labor from the rest of life. She must arrange things into parts, above all she must disturb the plane, break the surface, deconstruct the sheer impression that kept coming to her, so that she could see, beneath the smooth, complete appearance, divisions and parts. For that was what defeated her. Every movement made the problem worse; it literally stirred the waters. Every step was an incentive to damage. And the damage was so various and so particular in its effects. The rugs would merely stain, the floor would stain and warp, the books would stain and swell so they could never close again, not properly, so that they would never again be pleasant to the hand. Plaster would fall from the ceiling; the linoleum would come up. Unless she acted. Unless she did something right now. She went into the living room and began moving the furniture, the rugs. She must take up the drenched rugs. They must be rolled up, taken outside, laid flat on the grass. But how would she do that alone? The rugs were heavy in themselves and much heavier wet. She needed the help of someone strong. Jane was seventy-five; she couldn't ask her. She would have to try herself.

As she moved the couch back so that it rested against the north wall, Barbara walked in the front door. She was carrying several plastic buckets filled with towels and rags.

"I thought you might need a hand."

"I was going to take up the rug."

"I'll help you."

Silently, the two women rolled up the carpet. A few inches at a time they pushed and pulled it till they got it out the back door. Barbara turned the porch light on. They unrolled the rug on the black lawn.

"I wonder what this will do to the crocuses," Anne said.

"I always hated crocuses," said Barbara. "Too sprightly. Too goddamn much of a can-do attitude."

Anne smiled. I do love you, Barbara. I do think you're a splendid friend, a superb person, she wanted to say. But she felt a danger in allowing any discourse outside the world of objects.

"I gathered up all the old towels I could find. I thought we'd spread them around on the floors. Why don't you go say good-night to the children while I do that."

"All right," said Anne.

"By the way, I've met Jane, and I'm in love. She's going around the neighborhood cadging towels. I asked her to do it, because it seemed clear that people would simply give them to her without question. And she wouldn't feel the need to explain. Whereas I'd be invited in for cozy chats that would end in serious quarrels."

Anne put her hand over her eyes as if the light had suddenly become too bright. "I'm going to the children. You know I can't thank you enough."

"I've called Adrian. He'll be here in a minute."

The children were sharing beds with the Greenspan children. Anne had always liked the Greenspan children's rooms. Barbara's theory was that children need some free zone, a legal red-light district she called it, where they could be as messy as they liked. Their rooms were like the warm, cluttered nests of hibernating rodents. She understood why her children loved to be there.

"May I just talk to Peter and Sarah alone for a moment?" she said to the Greenspan children.

Quickly, they ran away.

"Are you two okay?" she asked.

"Yes," said Sarah, who did not put down her book.

"Did the police come?" asked Peter.

"Yes."

"Are they still there?"

"Yes."

"Is Laura still there?"

"Yes, sweetheart, but not for long."

Peter came closer to his mother and put his head on her breast.

"You can't really say she's still there, you know," said Sarah. "She's dead. It's just her body." Having said that, she went back to her book.

"Where do you think she is now?" asked Anne.

Sarah shrugged. "Who cares?"

The shock of her words hit Anne with the cruelty of a surprise blow. What did it mean, this callousness? It was, as people would say, a way of coping. Yet it was a very unappealing way. This was her child, six years old, to whom this monstrous thing had happened. Peter began to cry.

"I just don't see what the big deal is. You didn't even like her, Mommy. You were the one who wanted her to go away," Sarah said.

"I know," said Anne, "but I'm very sorry she's dead."

"Why? You didn't even like her."

"But it's a terrible thing, darling, for anyone to die when they're so young. Especially the way Laura did."

Peter looked at his sister tearfully. "You didn't see her. It was horrible."

Sarah looked at her brother and made a clicking, exasperated noise with her tongue. "Oh, Peter, you always act like you're the big cheese."

"Let's not talk about it now," said Anne. "Just try to sleep. We'll talk about it in the morning. Don't stay up too late with Daniel and Josh."

"Barbara said we don't have to go to school in the morning. Daniel and Josh do, but we don't," said Sarah.

"Sarah," Peter said with outrage. "That's not true. You made it up."

"I think you should go to school," Anne said.

"Forget it," Sarah said.

"What do you mean by that?" asked Anne.

"Just forget it. Who wanted to hang around here anyway? I might as well go to stupid school."

"Just try to sleep, my darlings," she said, turning Peter's pillow. When she tried to smooth Sarah's hair from her forehead, Sarah flicked her head away, not violently, a small resentful gesture of disgust.

In despair, she closed the door of the children's room. What was this doing to them? What should she do to help them? Even this she couldn't think about. Not now. She had to go back to the house.

There were towels spread over the living room floor, up the stairs and in the upstairs hallway. Adrian and Ianthe were there, squeezing sponge mops into buckets, emptying buckets into the toilets, into the tub.

"Thank you for coming," she said, moving away from Adrian's embrace.

"Just tell me what you want done."

"What you're doing. I'll leave the upstairs hall to you. If you can give me those wet towels, I'll put them in the washer."

They worked all night. At one, the police had finished their work and taken Laura's body with them, wrapped in a black plastic bag. The absence of the body, the first signs of dawn, made the house seem light. Anne felt as if it might float up, fly off and away any minute, like a toy house in a child's dream of a hurricane. But there was something about them all in there, accomplishing an immense labor, that kept the house held down. She didn't think of Laura. She thought of one job at a time. She bent and straightened her body. She wrung out wet cloths, emptied water into the kitchen sink. The sun rose silver gray at first and then the sky took color, its blues deepened, cleared. It became a beautiful day.

At eight o'clock the doorbell rang. Adrian, who was nearest, answered it.

"I was wondering if there was anything I could do to help," she heard Ed Corcoran say. Adrian brought him into the kitchen.

"I heard what happened," he said to Anne. "My wife has a police-band radio. She told me about it. I was wondering if I could help." He spoke looking down at the floor.

He is embarrassed, Anne thought, welcoming embarrassment into the room, the old woman whose arrival one has dreaded, whose *louche* story saves the party from the hatred of the most important guests. It signaled, once again, the hold of the ordinary, the press of the trivial: a third-rate and quotidian emotion.

"Thank you," she said to Ed, not looking at him. "But I think my friends and I are managing."

He turned his attention from her and looked around the room, a competent professional about to give an estimate.

"You don't have a pump in the cellar," he said. "I'd better check down there."

"The cellar," she said ashamedly, "I hadn't thought of it."

He disappeared down the cellar stairs.

"I think the water's gone from the floors. We've taken the rugs up, the books are off the shelves. Shall we put them outside to dry? It looks like it will be a nice day," Barbara said.

"Thank God it was just the one bookcase," Anne said. "We could put them on the lawn on blankets. How many of them are ruined?"

"Not many," said Barbara. "But they'll probably always smell queer."

Memento mori, Anne thought. Not the clean, well-formed skull, but the smell of mold, the feel of pages crumbling.

———

For the first time, she felt able to stop long enough to place a call to Michael. The overseas operator put her through in seconds. She heard her husband's voice say *"Allô."* The foreignness of the word, the familiarity of the tone, made her feel like a swimmer who sees, far off, the lifeboat coming toward him but cannot stop his movements for a moment to rejoice. So she couldn't weep to him; she couldn't say much. Barely, she told him the facts.

"Don't talk. I understand. I'll be home as soon as I can," he said. "Just hold on. I'll be there. Hold on to the children."

Then the voice was gone and she felt more alone than ever. "Just hold on," he had said. Yes, she must do that. When he came home, everything would seem more possible, for her and for the children. They could see that all of life was not affected by what had happened. That life went on, somewhere, that planes took off and landed; that you could dial a telephone and, from five thousand miles away, someone you loved could come to you.

She heard a step behind her.

"There's an awful lot of water in that basement," said Ed. Anne had forgotten he was in the house.

"I have a friend down at the oil-burner place," he said. "He'll probably let me borrow one of those big suction vacuums they have, you know that takes care of oil spills and things like that."

"That would be wonderful if you could get that," Anne said, looking out the window.

"The only thing is, I'll have to dig a hole in the backyard to empty all the water in. It'll sure mess up your lawn for the summer."

"That's all right. Do what you have to do."

"I'll just give that guy a call."

Anne nodded.

"You know, Brian talks about you all the time. He really misses you. He keeps asking if we're going to come over here again, if we're still friends."

Anne smiled neutrally. She thought they were not.

"I told him of course we were still friends and we'd get together when your husband got back in the summer."

"That would be nice," she said.

She turned from him to rinse her cup. They wouldn't see each other again, because she didn't want to see him. His rejection of her had replaced desire with shame; both were faces of the coin of sex, but you could look at one face only at one time. And without desire he was not someone she needed. He needed her, she saw that now, to be his charade wife, someone doing, in another house, all the things that were not done in his. He understood her well enough, perhaps it was that he understood women— that, after all, was his power—to understand that he had to court her sexually for the charade to have substance. If you had told him that his courtship was seduction, he would have been shocked. For that was not, truly, what he meant. He had to be formally loyal to his wife; without that, all his devotion would be empty and a sham, unlivable, unable to be carried out. But he needed from her that lively attentiveness that came only with sex. And she had given him that. Now, seeing that she had been wrong, there was nothing she could give him. They could not be friends. Without desire, all their differences were bared: where the surface had been charming, the interior was rugged, pocked, run-down. She pitied the situation, pitied Ed's life, pitied herself for her obvious mistake, pitied the institution of friendship, which was so fragile. But she pitied them distantly. Compared to the real event in whose aftermath they now all lived, their incident was trivial and shallow, possible to do away with, to forget. What had happened last night was not forgettable. She looked at Ed as he spoke on the telephone. She had no wish to touch him.

"The guy says it's okay," he said. "I'll be back in ten minutes."

"I may be upstairs."

"You get some sleep. I'll try to be as quiet as I can."

She knew she was tired, but she couldn't bear the idea of sleep. She saw herself lying in bed, her fists closed beside her, her eyes wide, looking at the ceiling like someone just let out of a straitjacket. What she wanted was a bath. But she would have to bathe there, where it had happened. They had to take possession of their house. It was their house; it did not belong to Laura's death. They would have to use things as they once did, normally and naturally. And if someone had to enter first the place of death, it should, she knew, be herself. Laura's hand had touched everything, but they couldn't think of that. The house was theirs.

She got a towel from the dryer. You must do this, you must do this thing, she said to herself with each step. It is a simple thing to do; you've done the hard things. Just this one thing. You must do it now.

The bathroom sparkled. Someone had polished every surface. There was not a hint of blood. She turned the shower on. The water came down clear; the silver needles ran. She stepped into the tub. Just do this thing. Think of the water. Smell the shampoo. But her terror didn't leave. A death had happened here. It would never be their house again. The memory, the shock, would spread through the air of the house like the sound of a struck gong, struck again as the last undertone began to be absorbed.

She dressed quickly and dried her hair. She could hear Ed running the machine in the cellar. Then she heard it stop, and from the window she could see him digging a hole in the backyard.

Burying the remains, she thought. Blood and water. Lively elements; the spirit was there much more than in the heavy bones and flesh. And so her spirit would be with them, wherever her body went. She had thought nothing about what would happen to the body. What did one do? Whom did one go to? Who should say what was to be the final disposition? It should not be her decision. Then she realized what had to be done. She had to contact Laura's parents; she had asked the police to leave it to her.

They were estranged from their daughter, she knew that, but surely they must be told what had happened. However estranged they were, it was their right to know, and the funeral decisions were theirs. But where would she find them? She went into Laura's room to look for clues. She had never seen Laura carry a pocketbook. But she must have had a wallet. She opened the bureau drawers, feeling the violation.

On the flyleaf of a notebook in the middle drawer, in Laura's round, childish handwriting, was her name and an address. Thirteenth Street, Meridian, New York.

She looked at the map and found Meridian. It was in the western part of the state. She would drive there. She would go now while her friends slept, before anyone could tell her not to go, could say that the family might not be there, might have moved or died, or might not want to see her. She called the AAA. It was two hundred and sixty miles from Selby to Meridian. She could drive it in five hours. She must go now. She would leave a note. It was the only thing to do.

———

The day was fresh and light. The roads, washed clear by a morning rain that had fallen southwest of Albany, shone like the ocean. She imagined children at the ocean; it was that kind of morning. Her shoulders and her neck ached with fatigue, but her eyes were lively. She felt she could drive forever.

At one o'clock, she decided to stop at a diner for lunch. A neon sign, turned off now in the sunlight, advertised the Tomahawk diner with red letters and a picture of an Indian brandishing his weapon. She ordered poached eggs. Her father had told her when she was a child to order only eggs in places she was unsure of. You always knew an egg was fresh, he said; if it weren't, they wouldn't be able to fool you. She thought how odd it was, the things that parents said that stuck, that grew into the myth in which love flourished at the center, a delicate plant, nourished by the humus of affectionate detail. And now she would have to tell parents who had not seen their daughter since she had left their house years ago that the daughter was dead. That she had killed herself. Anne had brought Laura's note with her, although she would have preferred not to, because she thought the parents had a right to it. She brought as well the notebook she had found. It was obviously a repository for biblical quotations that had struck Laura. In the margins, Laura had sometimes written people's names, and drawn thick, childish arrows pointing to the quote. In the front of the book, the name was mostly "Mom"; in the back, it was her own name she kept seeing, except for two entries, concerned with lust, that had Adrian's name beside them.

The waitress brought Anne's eggs. She was young, younger than Laura, Anne thought. Anger bristled around her like live wires. Were most young women angry now, she wondered? Were they right to be? She hadn't been angry at nineteen. But she had not had cause.

Reaching for a napkin, her eye fell on the jukebox. She didn't know any of the songs. Her eyes ran down the column. "Why Have You Left the One You Left Me For?" "Ain't No Such Thing as a Good Chain Gang," "All I Ever Need Is You," "Spring Fever." Of course the waitress was angry; of course everyone in the diner was. This is what they believed in, what they had been promised. But that was not what had made Laura angry. She had believed in God.

Her note said that she had killed herself to bring Anne to God. But how could Anne ever love a God who let a young girl bleed, who let her die thinking she should give her life to bring someone else to Him? It was not God; it was evil. But the God Laura believed in watched it happen. If this was His work, then His face was the face of evil. She looked out at the road. The only sane thing was to say that God was not within the Universe. Or it was God who held the razor to Laura's wrist.

It was two-thirty when she reached Meridian. Off the main street, the houses gave the impression of concavity, as if the ground might swallow them up or they might fall into one another. They were expecting the worst. They seemed to have too many windows, too much porch; they bore the shame of providing more room than the shrinking families they held could use; they flinched under the monthly curses that the oil bills produced. Even the old trees on the road did not look proud. The spring was late here, the buds on the trees were folded tight still, yellow-brown. Patches of gray snow and ice took root in isolated inches on the lawns beside odd objects that the melt left bare. Everywhere, Anne felt, the loveless effluvia of domestic life were exposed. Dolls' heads, dogs' dishes, wire hangers, buckets, bent snow shovels, plastic detergent bottles, cans with their labels still legible adhered to the soil or mud as if they had grown from it. At the end of one lawn was a bathroom sink like a pulled tooth. Cars that would never run again sat horizontally across driveways. It was as if some weakening disease had hit the town, as if the people in the houses wasted, cradling like dolls their useless limbs. It was only the end of winter, but it could have been the aftermath of a flood. It was the bleak testimony of a place down on its luck, of bad times, no jobs and no money.

As she drove up the road the qualities she thought she had just understood changed quickly. The scene became unfamiliar to her: each house, it seemed, was not merely a dwelling but a small private business. Energy bristled like static; unprofessional signs that would entice no one were on every third lawn advertising reupholstery, aluminum siding, pet grooming, TV repair. Then the signs stopped, and the houses grew smaller, newer. They had nothing to pretend about; their offers, made after the war, were clear. They promised to be convenient, and they had been. No one had a right to complain about false promises, and no one did.

The house that went with the address in Laura's book was a yellow ranch. There was a small yard, a cement path, a single step leading up to an aluminum storm door. When she rang the bell, a man who could have been any age between forty and sixty answered. He was thin, he had a neck too long for his body, and as if he thought it would help, he wore a gold chain around his neck. His glasses, she saw, were thick like Laura's, but his body was nothing like hers. His plaid pants exaggerated his short torso, its relation to his long, thin legs. He looked like a bird drawn for comic effect on the front of a birthday card. He didn't look unkind. When she asked if he was Mr. Post he smiled, and smiled again when she said that she had come because she had news of Laura.

"You've seen her, then?" he asked.

"May I come in?"

"Of course, I'm sorry." Anne could see that his teeth were newly false and that he was uneasy about it. He kept wanting to put his hand in front of his mouth.

"Who is it, Larry," asked a voice behind him.

"A friend of Laura's."

A woman appeared. "What do *you* want?" she said without expression, as if she expected Anne to cheat her.

Anne tried to decide if she thought the woman was good-looking. Like her husband's, her age was difficult to fix. She was a small woman, with a trim, well-cared-for body, a body that had been won away from every natural process. Obviously she had some ideal of beauty clear in her own mind, but Anne had trouble placing it. Her hair was a flat gold color, cut into a style called a wedge, a style inspired by an ice skater, which had been slightly out of fashion for five years. Her fingernails were long and polished reddish black; her toenails were the same color. She was wearing high-heeled wooden sandals with no backs; a strip of leather across the front was fastened with visible studs. What were these two people trying to look like? They were obviously in costume; they were trying to play some part. Anne looked at their faces closely and realized that they were probably no more than five years older than she. And then she understood: they were trying to have an adolescence. Their actual adolescence had been given over to marriage, parenthood, the acquiring of this house. They felt it had been stolen from them, and now they wanted it back.

"Laura worked for me," Anne said, sitting on a chair no one had offered her. "She took care of my children."

"Where did you come from?" asked Mrs. Post.

"Selby, Massachusetts."

"You with one of those religious groups?"

"No."

"How'd you meet up with her, then?"

For a moment, Anne couldn't remember. "A friend of mine met her on the plane."

"So you hired her to take care of your kids?" The woman snorted. "I wouldn't hire her to clean my toilets. Of course, she'd be real good at that. She's a real tidy thing. Drove me crazy. You can see that's not my forte."

Anne looked around the room. Magazines, filled ashtrays, curlers, makeup, dirty plates lay around. It was the kind of mess a teenager would have made and lived in.

Her position was impossible. She had left it too long, she should have told them the minute she came into the house. She felt like a fool and a fraud. She should have stopped the woman before she said insulting things about her daughter. It would make her feel awful now.

"I don't know quite how to say this," she said, standing to speak. "But something terrible has happened. Your daughter's dead. She's taken her own life."

"You mean she killed herself?" said Mr. Post.

"Shut up, Larry," said his wife. "Don't say anything. What do you want from us?" she asked Anne. "What are you doing here?"

"Well, first I wanted you to know, of course. And then I didn't know what you would want done with the body."

"Look, lady, I don't know who you are and where you come from. As far as I'm concerned, my daughter's been dead for years. So you do whatever you want with her now. She's of age. She's your problem."

Anne looked at the husband, hoping he would urge his wife to some new action, some word of modification. But he stared silently down at his cowboy boots.

"She leave a note?" said the mother. "I suppose she blamed everything on me, as usual."

Anne handed her the folded letter. The woman read it and handed it back to Anne.

"Mrs. Post," said Anne, "you must tell me what you want me to do."

"I want you to get in your fancy foreign car and get out of here. I don't care what you do with her. Just don't tell me about it. She's over twenty-one. She's not my responsibility anymore."

Anne looked around the room. There were photographs everywhere of another child, a dark child, in a ballet costume, a cheerleader's outfit, a prom dress. There was not a single picture of Laura.

"She was never any good to me. Never. Not from the minute she was born. Not from the minute she got started. You know how old I was when she was born? Seventeen. It was the end of my life."

Anne picked up her bag and started to leave.

"She never meant anything to me, not from the minute I saw her. She was always ugly. She was never happy. She tried to make me miserable. She always hated me, whatever bullshit she said she always hated me. She always looked at me that way, like she hated me, since she was a kid. Watching me, making me feel like a piece of shit for breathing. You know she tried to kill me once? Put her hands around my throat and tried to choke me. I'm a good mother. I have a wonderful daughter, Debbie. She's everything anybody could want. But Laura was no good from the beginning. So now she's dead and you expect me to tear out my hair? Forget it."

The woman went into the kitchen and slammed the door.

"I'll walk you to your car," said Mr. Post.

He held the front door for her and followed close behind her down the walk.

"She was named for me, you know," he said. "You know, Laurence, Laura. She was always so unhappy. But my wife was wrong, she was a cute little kid. But never happy. Mad all the time. Her and her mother never got along. They were always at each other. Then she got religious, and I thought that was good for her. She calmed down a lot. I thought she was happier. I guess not."

Anne leaned against the car door. She didn't want to look at the man.

"Don't pay attention to my wife," he said. "She doesn't mean what she says. She doesn't feel like that, not really. She's been real upset by Laura for a long time. And not hearing from her's made her real upset. She gets like that when she's upset. You have to understand how upset she is. A thing like this."

"I understand," said Anne.

"I'm sorry you had to go to all this trouble. I'd like to pay for any of the expenses." He handed her a card. "Moriello and Post, Certified Public Accountants," it said. "That's my office number in the corner. Call me there, not here, okay? I don't want my wife to get upset. But I don't want you to have to pay for anything. That's my job."

———————

The day was still as beautiful, as fresh, the air as washed, the sky as thin a blue as it had been that morning. But now she drove in terror. For what she had seen was more disturbing than the sight of a dead girl. She had seen the face of hatred, not contorted, not grotesque, but smooth and distant, like a face on television. That woman had said she had hated her daughter since the moment she was born. Anne thought of holding her babies, of her cheeks against their cheeks, their mouths on her breast. The woman was a monster. Motherhood was a place where hate could not enter. That was what you said, holding your baby: No one will hurt you, I will keep you from the terrible world. But that woman had brought hate with her, put a knife between her breasts, pierced her child's flesh and poured in poison. How could Laura not have been what she was? She had been hurt and damaged. If she limped because her mother had broken her leg, no one would have blamed her. How could she have loved? But it was worse than that. She could not love, and no one could love her.

She was a twenty-two-year-old girl whom no one mourned, a dead child for whose death the first emotion was annoyance, then relief. She was out of the world now, and no grief followed her. Her mother said, "I don't care." Her father said, "I'll pay the bills." And I, Anne thought, feel only, Why did you do this in my house, in front of my children? Why did you do this to me?

Even now she didn't love her. Even now there was no moment, no small endearing memory, to spark the flame of love. Never had she looked at the girl with pleasure. She had tried to be kind, to be just, in the end simply to be decent. But she had hated being near Laura; she had hated her presence in the house. When their bodies accidentally touched, something closed down and hardened over in her; she had nearly flinched. Now, how would she begin to mourn her?

You could not mourn categorically. You could not say: she's young, she's dead; the young should not be dead. You had to mourn the face, the voice, the posture, the loved gesture. Or what you felt was not the real thing but regret, that useless leftover emotion, the heart's morning-after, and its trash.

Still, she felt Laura needed her. She couldn't bear to think of the girl alone among the dead. So cold, so unaccompanied. She would not leave her to the dead. She *would* mourn her. She would fill her heart with grief. She would say, Poor child, life was cruel to you. At least she could do that.

═══════

When she walked into her kitchen, she found a note on the table in Jane's handwriting. Please call your mother if you're home before ten, it said. She looked at her watch. It was nine-fifteen. She didn't hear Jane; she supposed she was sleeping. She would call her mother now.

It wasn't something she wanted to do. Her mother was no good at comforting, at being a support. Yet she felt that, as a mother herself, she had to make the formal gesture. She didn't think she'd gone to her mother with a grief for twenty years. Grief was something to be kept from parents, she'd thought. In her father's case, her pain caused him so much pain that she ended up comforting him. And yet, she thought, these memories are old; they may be obsolete. She had not gone to them with griefs because in twenty years she had not had many. Some arm had always sheltered her, some wing provided shade. Now the arm was gone; the sun beat down on her bare head. But why not? Her grief was overdue.

"Michael phoned from France," Anne's mother said. "He thought that we should know. You must be very upset."

Anne could hear the anxiety in her mother's voice. She didn't know what to say to her daughter, and in her dreams, mothers and daughters swam an easy channel of buoyant water back and forth into each other's lives. But it had never been that way with them; their congress had been partial, balked, confused. They loved each other. There was that pull of flesh, of childhood. But they had never talked. Anne saw her mother always behind a screen, running back and forth, vague, apologetic or else febrile in her joys. And Anne frightened her mother, she always had, by her looks, her good fortune, her ability to please the father, her mother's husband, who was a stranger to her still.

"I won't come to you, if you don't mind. It's midterm time and I'm awfully busy. Besides, I'm sure you don't need me. You've always had so many friends."

"Everyone's been wonderful," Anne said, realizing how disappointed she was. She wanted her mother to come.

"And I won't tell Daddy. He's awfully busy, too, and he'll drop everything and come to you. And you know how anything wrong with you upsets him. The only reason he likes life at all is because he thinks it's on your side."

So her mother would never forgive her, and perhaps she was right. Her father preferred her, he always had. She hadn't meant to do it, but it had happened: she had won her father away from her mother. He had told Anne over and over, "You are my favorite person in the world." She had taken so much from her mother, it was only fair that her mother should keep her husband back now, when her daughter really wanted him, at the one moment when not having him would hurt.

"No, don't tell Daddy. We'll come for a visit in a week or two. We'll tell him then."

"How are the children?"

"It's complicated. I don't know."

"All right, dear. Call if you need us."

I won't, she thought. That is the one thing I won't do. I will not call to you, I will not call *because* I need you. Laura called, and no one came. And so I will not call.

She leaned her head against a window. It was infantile to cry like this, at thirty-eight, because she wanted her parents and they wouldn't come. There was no hand to hold, you learned that when you grew up. Perhaps she was an adult now. Perhaps that was what made the difference between adults and children. Adults knew they were alone; their solitude was final, and there was no rescue. Children's terror, children's sorrow, was all based on disappointment; adults took their grief from certainty and loss.

She walked into the living room. She was surprised to see Jane reading by a dim light. Jane raised her hand to Anne in greeting. There was something monumental in her gesture, in her posture, in her sitting in the semidarkness; and it made Anne angry. Something in the way Jane looked reminded her of the rage she felt, for Jane, too, worshipped what Laura in worshipping had died of.

Anne approached her directly; there were things she wanted Jane to hear.

"She looked to God for love," Anne said. "And she got death. I thought that when you asked for bread you weren't given stones."

Jane was silent.

"I suppose it's easier for you. You believe in God."

"No, it's much harder for me. As I believe in a loving God, it is much more difficult to understand."

"How can you love a God that lets this happen?"

"I don't. This is the God I fear. The dark cruel face I cannot understand that looks on while His children suffer."

"She did this because she wanted to bring me to God."

"No, she did it because she was desperate, and angry. And quite proud. And of course, she got what she wanted. You will never forget her."

Anne looked at Jane, whose face was sorrowful and yet composed. The planes of her face were beautiful. At her center was a supple and tense cord that kept her back beautifully straight, that let her hold her arms now, resting lightly on the chair.

"What is sadder than anything," said Jane, "is that she missed the whole point of the Gospels. She read them over and over, and she never got the point."

"The point?"

"That she was greatly beloved."

Anne didn't know what to say.

"Of course it is never enough, the love of God. It is always insufficient for the human heart. It can't keep us from despair as well as the most ordinary kindness from a stranger. The love of God means nothing to a heart that is starved of human love."

Jane's words made Anne sleepy. Love, she thought, feeling sleep come over her. I have always been beloved. I have never been alone.

"Michael is upstairs, asleep," Jane said.

Anne stared at her a second, then left. She passed the children's room and heard them breathing.

Michael sat up when she opened the door. The sight of him made her know how important it was that he was there. There were things that she could tell him only, must tell him, as the father of their children. What she had learned was dreadful in itself and dreadful in what it had opened up about life, the life they had brought two others into, the life of which they had said to two weak vulnerable creatures: This is yours, you must live. In giving them life they had opened them up to terrible things. And they had done it together. Michael opened his arms to her; for the first time she could weep. And he knew what it was she wept for, for he said, "Weep for all of us."

And that was why she was weeping. For Laura, for herself, her parents and her children. For Laura's parents who could not love, for her own heart that had closed down and hardened over at the cry for love. She wept and wept. People were so weak, and life would raise its whip and bring it down again and again on the bare tender flesh of the most vulnerable. Love was what they needed, and most often it was not there. It was abundant, love, but it could not be called. It was won by chance; it was a monstrous game of luck. Fate was too honorable a name for it. You were born, and you were laid open to the world. And the world raised its whip against the child, or sheltered it with its soft wing, and waited, always waited, to bring down the whip.

"Her parents didn't love her," Anne said, raising up her head. "They didn't want anything to do with her. They didn't want her body. The mother said she wouldn't have hired her to clean her toilets. The father said he'd pay for everything."

"Poor child."

"They didn't love her. They never did. No one did. I didn't love her either. I didn't even like her. In the end, I hated her just as her mother did."

"She wasn't likable."

"But it wasn't her fault. No one had ever loved her."

"No, it wasn't her fault. But its not being her fault didn't make her more likable. She was starved."

She was starved, and she had died of it. And Anne let her husband's love feed her. Let the shade of its wing shelter her, cover her over. But no wing had ever covered Laura. The harsh light had exhausted her until she could only go mad. And then the whip had fallen. And Anne knew that she had helped the whip descend.

When Anne told Jane that she thought there should be some kind of funeral, Jane said she would see to it. She had learned, through Adrian, that Frank Pointer in the Classics Department had staying with him a priest, a former classmate who had been a missionary in the Philippines. "Probably a whiskey problem," Jane said. "He has that bruised look, as if he's afraid he's going to be rusticated to the West of Ireland. Still, he's a type I like," Jane said, "shy, melancholy, convinced that he's a failure. Much better than the gung-ho breed." He had agreed to say some prayers for Laura.

Jane spoke to Harold Cusher, the undertaker, and arranged for Laura's body to be cremated. "Was there any place that Laura liked particularly? Mr. Cusher wants to know," Jane asked.

She couldn't say. She would never be able to say if anything had made Laura happy. She had seemed happy the day they all went on a picnic in the woods near Emerald Creek, when they had planned her birthday party. For the birthday that was not her birthday, but a made-up day, Anne had discovered, finding Laura's driver's license. She had lied about her birthday to get a party. Anne was glad she had. She had done something for her that she could be fairly sure Laura had liked.

It was a cold morning in late March. The mild week's weather just before had been betrayed; the sky was crystal-blue and wintry. No clouds gathered, and the ground was hard. Three cars had come to the place where Anne and Laura and the children had had their picnic. Fourteen people were there: Anne and Jane and Ben, who had come up to be with Jane, the Greenspans, Adrian, Ianthe, the Garrisons, whom Anne had invited at the last minute, Hélène, Frank Pointer and his friend the priest. And Michael and the children.

The poor boy, Anne thought, looking at the priest, but he was not a boy. His underjaw was slung like a bulldog's; his face was covered with a purplish rash, which could have been caused by anguish. She had never seen anybody look so unhappy; he wore his unhappiness like a suit passed down from an older brother.

"It was good of you to come," Anne said to him, realizing she sounded fatuous, an official hostess.

"Not at all, the poor soul. She needs our prayers," he said. She almost laughed; he was so nearly the stage Irish priest. But who could laugh at him, he was so kind, and so unhappy?

He gathered them into a circle. The children stood next to Anne, formal, straight-backed in their good clothes, with Michael on the other side. Peter looked at his shoes; Sarah looked up at the sky.

"We'll just begin, then," said the priest.

He prayed for Laura's rest, that light perpetual should shine upon her. He read two psalms: "Out of the depths have I cried unto thee, O Lord," and the One Hundred and Twenty-first Psalm, which Jane had suggested. "We read it at Caroline's funeral," she said.

Anne thought of Caroline as the priest read. What could be more different than her death and Laura's. So different, they were hardly the same category of event. In the end, Jane had told her, Caroline died peacefully. The terror, the despair, she had expressed in her last journal entry had disappeared. She died painlessly, holding Jane's hand. And she'd left, in her will, elaborate plans for her own funeral. It was to be a party; she'd planned the menu, selected the music. There was to be dancing. And everyone, Jane said, had danced. She'd died an old woman; her life had been a success; her work had been admired; she had been beloved.

Had Caroline not lived, Laura would not be dead, Anne told herself. Each time now that she thought of her work on Caroline, she would have to wonder if Laura had been its sacrifice. Her death would touch even that. Had she not met me, she might not have died, Anne thought, listening to the priest. Had I not ignored her distress trying to finish my work. The

work I did for Caroline, she thought, listening to the psalm that had been
read for her as well.

> I will lift up mine eyes unto the hills, from whence cometh my help?
> My help cometh from the Lord, which made heaven and earth.
> He will not suffer thy foot to be moved: he that keepeth thee will not
>   slumber.
> Behold, he that keepeth Israel shall neither slumber nor sleep.
> The Lord himself is thy keeper: the Lord is thy shade upon thy right hand.
> The sun shall not smite thee by day, nor the moon by night.
> The Lord shall preserve thee from all evil: he shall preserve thy soul.
> The Lord shall preserve thy going out and they coming in from this time
>   forth, and even for evermore.

It was so beautiful, and it was such a lie. From what had Laura been
preserved? Hatred, madness, death had all struck her undefended. Yet she
was glad the priest had read those words. Perhaps it was true for Laura
now. Perhaps now Laura was protected. Perhaps now someone preserved
her going out, her coming in. Or perhaps not.

As if obeying the psalm's first line, Anne looked at the mountains. The
morning sun shone clear and shadowless. From whence cometh my help?
She had never noticed it before, but the way the priest read it made it clear
that the words were a question. From whence cometh my help? She looked
at her children. They were waiting for her to say something. She wondered
if she should ask everyone home for something to eat. But she decided
against it. You came together after a funeral only to talk about the dead.
And no one had anything they wanted to say about Laura. None of them
mourned her; they were not really mourners of the dead, they were here
out of politeness to a friend, to Anne. Nobody was bereaved. So they
should not sit together eating, talking. They should separate and go on
with their lives.

The priest asked to speak to her alone. "These are the ashes," he said,
handing her a parcel done up in newspaper. "The funeral director said you
were to have them."

"Yes, that's right," she said, smiling at him with pity. Never had she
seen anyone look so unhappy. "Thank you, Father, you've been very kind."

She had told Michael what she knew she must do. She signaled to him,
and he took the children away.

She walked into the woods. She walked in an envelope of greenish light;
the sun slanted between the branches, coins of shadow lay upon the forest

floor. What she was doing was itself a crime. The funeral director had told her it was against the law to scatter the ashes of the dead. But what I don't know, he said shrugging, won't hurt anybody. So rarely had she done an illegal thing that she couldn't stop herself looking over her shoulder to make sure no one followed.

She came to the spot near the brook where she had sat with Laura and the children. She undid the parcel. Inside the newspaper wrapping was what looked like a silver coffee can. She opened the lid. She had promised herself that she would look. Ash and bone. Nothing that could come to life. The spirit could breathe and breathe over it, but there would be no quickening.

This was what was left of the girl who died because she could not love her. With a quiet motion she emptied the can onto the ground. A mound of ash with tiny bone splinters lay in a hillock on the earth. Quickly, the wind took them.

I did not love you, she said, not to the ashes that the wind took but to the girl, whose going out and coming in she had been told was blessed now. But I brought your ashes here because here at least I knew I wished you well. That was something. There was something in me at that moment at least that was not of death. I did not love you. But I mourn you. I will always mourn you. I can give you that.

She waited till the wind had taken the last of the ashes. A few bone splinters still remained upon the ground. Anne brushed them into the creek, carefully, with the side of her hand. Then she walked back to her husband and her children, waiting for her in the car.

Peter had been having bad dreams every night in the month since Laura's death. They happened shortly before dawn. Anne would hear him scream, and then he would appear next to her bed, shaken, ghostly, in the gray, translucent light. At first, after Michael had gone back to France, she had let him get into the bed with her, but then there was a fight with Sarah in the mornings. Sarah claimed that Peter was being rewarded for not sleeping through the night while she was being cheated and cut off. There was something to what she said. Anne didn't want to reward her son for being troubled. And she knew it wasn't good: a mother and a son to share a bed, however briefly, in the early morning. It had to stop. Yet she could not leave him comfortless. He looked so alone in his thin pajamas, so frail, like a bird whose ardent heart seems nearly visible. Without saying anything to Peter, she moved the rocking chair from the living room and placed it by her bedroom window. It looked over the white lilac bush, over the lilies of the valley.

How much, she wondered, was her son having bad dreams for her? She didn't mind the interruption of her sleep, she suffered for her son's distress, for all that he had suffered, but she was happy there with her boy in her arms, rocking as if they were suspended in the insubstantial light. The light kept the white lilac leaves in a deep shadow, only gradually did they reveal themselves. Solid, bluish, somber, they held up the white flowers which absorbed light for an hour before they took on brightness. Below, the lilies of the valley opened up like paper stars unfolding from their cone of darkness. White and green and blue-gray tones abounded: before her eyes a landscape for the wounded eye, the invalid's view, the palette of consolation. A cool sobriety was in the air those hours of the morning, a sweetness, a regret, a stillness, as if life happened under water. It was the only time that she could think of what had happened.

She covered her son with a blanket. He was sweaty after his night terrors, and his hair was damp, as if he had been in a fight or a fever; his hair smelled acrid, overripe, like stored grain; she put her lips to it and got a yeasty taste. They never spoke about the dreams; he didn't remember them, he said, only that he was frightened, too afraid to be alone. She held him to her, both of them knowing there was something a bit ridiculous in the posture. He was too big to be held so; his legs dangled and his arms had no place comfortable to go. In this chair she had nursed him, but he was in no way her baby anymore. His long legs hummed with an animal life in his sleep. Soon he would leave her.

Something terrible had happened. He had seen a dreadful thing. A dead girl lying in her own blood. What would it do to him? To Sarah, who had not seen it, who had in that month grown sullen and impatient, at six cynical and full of scorn? Soon what had happened would disappear into their lives; it would no longer be the thing they thought about when silence struck, when no act or job pressed upon them. Michael would come home for good. Life would go on. Soon he would no longer be marked as different from them, spared from the event that shaped them, the escaped member, the traveler away when the plague struck or the enemy invaded. They would feel sometimes that he was different from them, unmarked, unwounded. But the children would grow up different from her, too, would grow up knowing life was terrible and they were never safe.

They would grow up like the children of the poor. Not for them the images in stories of small animals and houses decorated with light colors, of adventures where the dangers would be vanquished and the bleeding hero make his way back home. The children of the poor knew something —you could see it in their faces, on the city streets, in grainy pictures in the papers, in news footage of the dusty dead towns. And they were waiting, the children of the poor, it was the thing that they were good at, waiting, and they would not be surprised. Yet this early news of sorrow did not always bring them wisdom. It could bring despair, the heart's death, the empty hopelessness of the young killer who knows anything might happen and so anything is possible to do. Children should not know violence, she thought. When they did, they stopped being children. Childhood was a middle-class invention, a luxury the poor knew better than to try to hold too long. But she had had a childhood: a false spring, an everlasting summer. And Michael, too, for all that he had suffered, knew it, they had had it in mind for their children, they had shaped their lives to give it to the two that they had brought into the world. Now the children had lost their patrimony. Lost the blessing of their parents' house: the confidence, the safety they could wear into the world like a gold ring, a sign.

What would they wear now into the world? What would replace what they had lost? Would kindness replace safety, like a richer cloak, or would they wear the bloody skins of the impossible-to-think-of poor, or would they go half-naked, like the freezing Lear, with no fate for them but an animal's bad luck?

If it were true that sorrow brought with it the guarantee of virtue, that would be the kind of economy anyone could live under. Only the superficial would rebel; the rest would live in peace, in comprehension. But there was no guarantee. Some grew in the face of sorrow, and some were undone. Some opened and enlarged, and some were ground to dust. Some became, only in sorrow, truly human; some were turned to animals who bit and snarled and lay in wait, who killed the weaker, in contempt, for nourishment and from a natural obedience to force.

She kissed her son's damp head. She knew nothing about him, nothing of what he would become. Yet no one knew him better. He was hers, for now at least it was to her he brought his terrors and the dreams he could not people yet or name. She would die for him in an instant; it would not even be hard. And yet she could not say of either of her children: this is what they feel, this is what they will remember. It was the strongest love she knew, this mother love, knit up of blood, but it knew nothing, and it could keep nothing back.

And what could you say of it that was true? She used to think it was, of all loves, the most innocent, but now she knew she had been wrong. There were mothers who loved their children in a way that cut the children's breath and stopped their hearts; there were mothers who, in a passion of love, took their children and pressed them to their bosoms and in the next moment threw the children screaming from them, covered them with blows. There were mothers for whom the sight of their children meant nothing: no love stirred, no part of the heart lifted. There were mothers who hated their children from the moment of their births, who hated the first touch of flesh on flesh and went on hating. There were mothers who loved their children but could not love them, for they bent to kiss the children's flesh and felt the flesh stop up their mouths and make them fear for their next breath. And children throve or starved, and no one knew why, or what killed or saved.

And there was the other part of mother love: it was not all of life. And that was wonderful; it was a tremendous mercy. For there was so little you could do for them, even if you spent every moment with them, gave them every waking thought, there wasn't much that you could do. You gave them life, you loved them, then you opened them out to the world. You could never protect them; so you left them to themselves. That was the mercy, that you could turn from them to something else, something they couldn't touch or be a part of. You could turn, sometimes, from the sight of them, making their way in the world, so dangerous, so treacherous; you could put down the burden of that mother love, could swim up from it, passing the exhilarating sights, the colorful quick fish, the shining rocks and bubbles. And pass, too, the clumps of weeds. There was all that in the world that was apart from them: intractable, too, and difficult, eluding what you wanted to say of it, impossible to compass or get right. This morning she could turn to the work of a woman forty-five years dead. Possibly what she said would matter very little; possibly she would get things wrong. Yet she would take her mind, sharpen it, make it single; she would take the facts that she had learned, the words that there were for them. Join them together. She would make decisions on the dates of paintings. She would write, "It should be noted," and "The style demands." Hard words, formed words, white stones that she could hold and separate. And then, refreshed, she could dive back down to the dense underworld, to her children, and say, "This is life. What shall we make of it? For it is terrible, and shining, and our hearts are sore. Something dreadful has happened to us; more will happen: terrible, beautiful, there is no way of telling. And anything might lie and then uncoil and strike, in silence, in the darkness."

Peter began to stir. He got to his feet; he was ready to go back to his own bed. There was a light wind. Clouds moved in the sky that had begun to take on color. She brought her chair up closer to the window and looked out.